HONOR'S SHADOW

HONOR'S SHADOW

Voula Grand

KARNAC

First published in 2011 by
Karnac Books Ltd
118 Finchley Road
London NW3 5HT

British Library Cataloguing in Publication Data

A C.I.P. for this book is available from the British Library

ISBN-13: 978-1-78049-000-7

Typeset by Vikatan Publishing Solutions (P) Ltd., Chennai, India

Printed in Great Britain

www.karnacbooks.com

For Thibault and Melanthe Grand
with mother love

What has marked you is still marking you.
There is a place in us where wounds never heal,
and where loves never end.

Michael Ventura
Meeting the Shadow

ACKNOWLEDGEMENTS

Many people have helped me over the years of writing this novel, and I want to express my heartfelt thanks to:

Jacqui Lofthouse, my writing coach and mentor, a great source of support and inspiration.

The Karnac team: Oliver Rathbone who showed faith in me, and Constance Govindin, Kate Pearce, James Darley, Lucy Shirley, and Jo Jacobius for their unstinting efforts in support of *Honor's Shadow*.

Christelle Raczak for the cover art.

My writing buddies, Rowena Dunn and Lorraine Bateman who have reviewed sections on a frequent and regular basis, often over dinner and a glass of wine or two, keeping me on track with helpful feedback and suggestions.

My reviewers of early drafts for taking the time to provide thoughtful and constructive comments: Melanthe Grand, Paul Greenfield, Dorothea and Chrysanthy Tsoflias, Marie Greenfield, Heather Cox, Bob and Doris Overton, Maggie Wilkinson, Nathalie Heyden, Dawn Johnson, Elizabeth Cudd (and members of her book club), Valerie Spence, Nicola Potts, Yvonne Marsden, Lindsey Harding, Carole Brown, Tamsyn Zeitsman, Emma Judge, Sandy Cotter, Sally Potter, Alice Kingdon, John Mitchinson, and Penny Holroyde.

My family, for providing the constant background support and emotional safety net. They are my children and stepchildren: Thibault, Melanthe, Philippa, Jennifer, and Alex. My siblings: Dorothea, Chrysanthy, Tino, and Pat Tsoflias. My father and step mother: Anthony and Claudia Tsoflias.

To my late mother, Carole Tsoflias: whilst she hasn't lived to see this book, during my younger years she encouraged me to read and write: without her, this book would not have been written. So thanks Mum.

And for the day by day, moment by moment support, to my beloved husband Paul Greenfield: thank you for all the happiness.

CHAPTER ONE

Something wasn't right.

Honor knew it before she'd even opened her eyes, as she drifted, dreamy, up to the surface of herself, waking to it, like a psychic nagging toothache. Turning restlessly, she tried to locate it, stretching, trying to shift—what? Yes, today, that's it, this shadow date. Shuffling across to Eliot, she tucked her body against the warm length of his, sliding her arm around his waist. He stirred and murmured. *Could I tell him?* She asked herself the same question every year. *Relieve myself of this secret?* The same answer came: no, she couldn't. That was the price of being married to a man raised in the strict Catholic tradition, even if he did pick and choose his commandments to suit his own convenience.

With a heavy sigh, she eased herself quietly out of bed.

At breakfast, listening to the chatter of her three children, and Thea's eight-year-old excitement about today's school dance show, she reminded herself why she did it: to protect them—and herself.

As she drove to work, through leafy North London suburbs, the trees blossoming in the spring sun, sadness wound itself around Honor like a shawl. She shivered. *If I could only do for myself what I do for my clients. They tell me their secret selves and then they're free.* No wonder she could provide relief, she knew just what it felt like to carry that burden. *I envy my own patients.*

1

Awaiting her first client of the day, Honor glanced at her watch, picked up a notebook from her desk, and went to the easy chair at the far end of the room. Her new client would arrive any minute, and she needed to remind herself of the background of this new case: Tisi Clements, aged thirty-four, referred by her GP, suffering from a relatively common case of anxiety and depression, with no discernible unusual features.

Tisi arrived a few minutes late, out of breath, and effusively apologetic, quite out of proportion to the transgression. Barbara showed her in and asked what they both wanted to drink; Honor noticed how exceptionally deferential and grateful Tisi was, as though it was unusual to be offered a perfectly ordinary standard of hospitality. And she addressed Honor as Doctor Sinclair.

"Tisi, please do call me Honor ..."

This again drew the most profuse apologies. Honor wanted to put her at ease. "Why don't I take a few minutes to explain a little about what I do, and what I could offer you, if you felt I was the right person to help you?"

Tisi interrupted immediately, in a breathless, high-pitched voice. "Oh Doctor, I know you're the right person, I couldn't be more sure of it. I actually know someone who came to you; she said you were a miracle worker, completely brilliant. So I know you could make me feel better, and that would be so great, it's all been dreadfully difficult, and I badly need some help ..."

Honor raised a hand to halt her, and smiled gently. Inwardly, she was slowing and deepening her own breathing, hoping that she could soothe Tisi with her calmness, and protect herself from being infected with the depths of Tisi's anxiety, always a challenge at the first meeting. The very act of admitting to oneself that things are now bad enough to see a therapist, and can no longer be solved by a long chat with a good friend over a glass of wine, can drive stress levels sky high. Honor was finding it unusually difficult to create the atmosphere of gentle calm that would lead to the trust needed for a soothing and constructive discussion.

"Let me talk for a while, Tisi. You sit back, make yourself comfortable; relax. Let me tell you a little about how we might work together."

Tisi drew breath to speak again, so Honor smiled and raised an eyebrow at her. Tisi exhaled, gave a little laugh, and then sat back, though Honor noticed she sat with her back poker straight, and fidgeted, playing with her hair and examining her fingernails.

As Honor spoke, she took stock of Tisi's physical appearance. She could learn a lot from her first impression of a client's presentation, demeanour, and behaviour. Tisi was an attractive woman, groomed to the glossy standard of a fashion model. Her shiny brown hair, past her shoulders, was expertly cut in a straight style, with some light streaks at the front. She was tall and slim, though quite curvy: a wide belt on a blue-grey dress accentuated her small waist; though the pull of the dress across her thighs suggested a disproportionate heaviness. Subtle jewellery in gold and diamonds glinted at her hands, ears, and neck. Her high-heeled shoes of soft grey leather and suede were an expensive, designer brand. If they hadn't been meeting professionally, Honor would have asked her where she'd bought them.

Tisi's make up was subtle and immaculate: smudgy dark eye-shadow accentuated her luminous blue eyes. She had flawless skin, high cheekbones, and a delicate jaw line: the kind of face that you wanted to go on looking at.

As Honor talked, deliberately, in low, hypnotic tones, she felt Tisi relax a little, though her energy never completely lost its jagged, brittle quality. Her immaculate exterior, alongside her frenetic energy and her incessant apologies, were a little disturbing: her outer poise and polish so at odds with her interior world. Such a disconnect between inner and outer reality could be expected in therapy clients, but the mismatch was more jarring than Honor would expect from a client with such a straightforward clinical profile.

Psychotic patients, such as Honor encountered in her psychiatric practice at the hospital, were, in contrast, much more integrated: chaos and confusion reigned both inside and out, perfectly matched. For them, recovery was more obvious: they started turning up for sessions wearing the same colour socks, or in regular trousers instead of pyjamas. Diagnosis was simpler: everything was more clearly and definitely wrong, so there was less need to seek out the more subtle clues.

"I must emphasize, Tisi, it's difficult for us to know how our work will proceed. I'm sure I can be helpful, but I don't want to mislead you and promise outcomes that may not be possible."

Tisi sighed, her shoulders dropped and her head sagged. A tear dripped onto her hand.

"But that's not to say I can't help you." Honor felt her own throat constrict, in sympathy. Tears, usually so necessary to the healing process, were often her undoing; it had taken her many years of training and hard work to learn the best ways to evoke and direct them in clients, without feeling overwhelmed by her own old wounds.

Honor gestured to the box of tissues on the table, and Tisi took one, dabbing her eyes and raising her head. Her voice dropped to a whisper. "Please help me. I don't know what to do. I don't know what's happening to me; I can't control my thoughts."

"Why don't you tell me a little of what's bothering you? So that I can understand something of what's on your mind, and get an idea of how I might help you? Take your time."

Tisi took a deep breath and launched into a long explanation, with many detours and sub-plots. It took all Honor's concentration to piece together the basics of her story. Essentially, she was devoted to her son and daughter, aged four and six respectively; she worked full time, and found the demands of her career combined with motherhood particularly stressful. Her husband, to whom she had been (happily, she thought, until last week) married for ten years, was having an affair with a woman at work. He considered himself to be in love with this woman, who happened to be a distant friend of Tisi's, and he was considering leaving his family in order to make a new life with her—though he was not entirely sure. He criticized Tisi for her lack of attention to him: he felt neglected since the children were born, and this, he said, made him vulnerable to the attentions of another woman. In short, in his opinion, his behaviour and the resulting circumstances were all Tisi's fault.

Tisi was unable to tell this story without several bouts of tears; and tirades of anger against her husband, Don.

"And what would you like to have happen between you and Don now?" Honor asked.

More tears. "I want it to go back to how it was before I knew. I cannot bear knowing that this has gone on for over a year. I keep thinking of times when we were together and she was there ... or good times we had together, and knowing he was thinking of her."

"That's very painful for you ..."

"How could he? How could you do that to someone you love? I could never do that, never, I could never hurt him like this." She leaned forward, her head on her knees, gripped by despair.

Honor waited until the deepest of her sobs had subsided. She swallowed the lump in her own throat. *If she was my friend, or my daughter (especially if she was my daughter) I'd tell her to go home and pack her husband's bag and throw him out. Take the pain now, don't live with the anguish. And God knows, I should know. I've tried in two marriages.* But she wasn't her friend or her daughter, she was her client. So she must listen closely, question sometimes, and interpret occasionally. But she must never, never offer guidance or advice.

"I can see how badly hurt you are; and that's something we'll explore, over time, if we decide to work together."

Tisi sat up, dabbing her smudged eyes, and gazed at Honor with a haunting depth of sadness.

"What do you want going forward?" Honor spoke gently, looking directly into Tisi's eyes. "What do you want to happen next? That's what I can help you work towards."

Tisi's entire body tensed, her eyes flashed, and her jaw clenched; her face transformed into a savage mask. "I would like him to die."

Honor sat back in her chair and regarded Tisi calmly. Inwardly, she deepened her breathing. Some years ago, she had learned how to manage her energy, so that she could rapidly control and soothe her own emotions, while she was at work at least. She had never regretted the years it took to practise and perfect this technique.

"You would like him to die ..."

Tisi broke into fresh sobs. "You see? I can't think straight; and I can't control my thoughts. I'm ashamed to say it, but I must, so you can help me, so you can stop me doing some of the things I think of doing. I need someone to stop me. I need *you* to stop me."

Honor gave a slight nod, steadied herself, and thought carefully about her next sentence. "Tell me the thoughts in your head."

"The other night, something terrible happened, that frightened me so much. I'd put the children to bed, they were asleep; Don was already in bed. I'd asked him to sleep in the spare room once I found out about Jackie ..."

(*Jackie!* Honor's heart jolted at a horrible, ten-year-old memory of her ex- best friend.)

"... but he refused. He said that until we decided what to do, he'd sleep in his own bed ... and since I didn't want the children asking awkward questions or being disturbed by what was happening, I felt forced to continue sleeping in our bed myself. My daughter often comes into our bed at night. Don says that's yet another problem, as if there's some long list of problems, most of which I'm ignorant of, but all of which are my fault. So I had a hot bath to calm myself down; but the bathroom's such a mess—we're having a wall knocked down, there's

5

builder's dust and tools everywhere—so I didn't stay in there long. I sat on the toilet, and as I sat there I noticed, next to my foot, a large hammer, next to the builder's tool bag."

Honor was listening with growing concern. By and large, she believed that most things are better said out loud, but she also thought that, at the extremes, some things are best left unsaid. There are some things a person simply doesn't want to hear herself say: it's too shocking. So she thought about stopping Tisi at this point.

But Tisi continued: "I picked it up, it was heavy in my hand. I was overwhelmed by the desire to walk into the bedroom and smash Don's head in. I could imagine it, vividly, the hammer hitting him, hard, several times, and the blood, everywhere, all over the pillow, ruby red. And the satisfaction of seeing his face change."

Honor knew she needed to stop her now. "And what stopped you doing that?"

"If only I could say it was compassion, or humanity; but what stopped me was thinking how it was impossible to do that and not get caught. I could imagine myself being arrested. I wouldn't have minded that, it would have been worth it, but then the children, what would have happened to the children?"

"So it was your sanity that stopped you. That was your sanity, your understanding of consequences."

Tisi held Honor's eyes with hers. Honor could sense Tisi beseeching her for something, if she could only guess what.

She must be terrified.

Heartbroken, betrayed, and terrified of herself.

And furiously vengeful.

* * *

Is she a danger? To herself or to others?

The question had come, unbidden, into Honor's mind, as she'd listened to Tisi's stream of enraged invective against her faithless husband. Honor doubted that she was a danger to herself, her fierce protection of her two young children would see to that. *But I wouldn't want to be in her husband's shoes right now, not for anything.*

If Honor could only forget the expression on her face, she would feel easier. Surely she'd been speaking metaphorically, when she said: "I want him to die"?

If she was a danger to her husband, there was only one course of action: Honor must section her for his safety; and take a woman

6

away from her children. As a mother herself, it was hard to imagine a worse fate.

This was a dilemma she had always hoped to avoid. Where her best, often anguished, judgement could never really be tested: who knew what would happen in an alternative set of circumstances? She simply hoped that, overall, in the greater scheme of things, she was doing more good than harm.

Her session notes would provide clues: she knew she was likely to over-react, on today of all days. The woman had disturbed her: vague recollections and sickening feelings were signalling to her, as though a ghostly serpent, uncoiling, awakened ghastly old memories.

To calm herself, she settled into her armchair feeling it absorb and hold her, making her safe, as though the chair was imbued with all the knowledge, experience, and wisdom of her long career as a psychiatrist. She leaned back and looked upwards, spotting, in one corner, a small and perfect silvery cobweb, its inhabitant moved-in newly today, she suspected, as the daily office cleaner knew how Honor hated cobwebs. They can only appear in neglected places, she felt, places abandoned and unloved. She didn't want any of her people or places to have cobwebs. Or herself.

The room, her working home for so many years, was spacious, and softly lit. From her seat, she could look to the other end of the room, her office area, her antique walnut desk and leather chair. Her laptop computer was the only item on the desk: she didn't like clients to see it littered with post, files, pieces of paper, books lying opened at some reference page. She scooped all of that into the desk drawer before a client arrived.

Opposite her was the comfortable sofa for clients, with a soft pillow at one end for those who preferred to lie down, and a woollen blanket folded at the other end. Many clients had swaddled themselves in that, as they spilled out their tears of griefs long past, yet still so live. Insights and realizations can be shivering.

Honor scanned her notes: she wanted to recall as many details as possible of this therapy session. She needed a walk to clear her head. The day was fresh and bright, and the park across the road from her office was looking its best, with well-mowed green lawns, deep herbaceous borders, and beds of purple and magenta petunias. She breathed in the fragrance of fresh cut grass as she walked along the neat pathways.

She passed the children's playground, the young mothers grouped together, one eye on their toddlers on swings, the other on each other, catching up on their news. Scraps of their conversations wafted by her. What age for potty training? Back to work or not? The world changed, but some things didn't: the pressing and crucial concerns of young mothers, who loved their children but wanted some fulfilling work to do as well.

She walked on a little further, leaving behind the noise of the toddlers' shrieks and the women's laughter, to arrive at a small wooden bench, under a willow tree, empty apart from an abandoned copy of *The Sun* newspaper at one end. Sitting down, looking around, she absorbed the sight and sounds around her, and recalled the end of her session with Tisi.

"Shall we meet again next week, Tisi? What d'you think?"

"Oh yes please, Doctor, I know you can help me. D'you think I'm crazy?"

"You're terribly upset, that's clear; and you have reason to be. But it's important, especially for your children, that you're able to keep calm and clear-headed. You may have difficult decisions ahead, and I'd like to help you work them out."

"Yes, yes, of course, Doctor, thank you so much."

"But there's a condition, if we're to work together effectively, something I must insist upon."

"Of course, anything you say, just tell me, I'll do it."

"You must do no harm to yourself, or to anyone else; do you understand?"

Tisi looked down. "No, of course I won't. Though I guess I can have my fantasies. ..." She gave a short laugh.

Honor would have felt more confident if Tisi had met her eyes when she spoke.

I'm pretty sure she'll be fine. It was quite a step from wishing someone dead to actually murdering them after all. Who hadn't, at some point, wished that someone would simply disappear? Meaning dead, of course, what else? And yet, on an almost daily basis, the newspapers reported terrible acts of violence and revenge in families, among people who were meant to love each other.

No, she didn't need to worry unduly about Tisi. Not about her killing her husband. About her finding some kind of peace, well, that was another story: the pain of her betrayal by her husband would take a long time to subside, as Honor knew only too well. She was aware that aspects of Tisi's story were bringing back some distressing memories, not least the way Tisi's husband, Don, was using Tisi's behaviour as an

8

excuse for his own. As though it wasn't bad enough having an unfaithful husband: being blamed was a second betrayal. And how unfortunate that Don's mistress was named Jackie. Honor had met a Jackie of her own, aged five, on their first day of school. They had looked at each other, with a childish moment of instant recognition, reached out their hands, and that was it. Friends for life. Though it hadn't quite worked out like that. Friends until ten years ago anyway.

Honor looked up, at the sunlight filtering through the long green fronds of the willow, and felt the sun's warmth on her face. She closed her eyes and sighed deeply.

As she stood to leave, she noticed the newspaper at the end of the bench and a photo caught her eye: a girl's face, looking vaguely familiar. (And the date, reminding her again of today, of Thomas. She pressed her hand against her heart, feeling it contract around its deepest wound.)

She sat down again and leafed through the paper to find the story. There was a double-page spread about the girl, Bella, with a big picture of her, dressed in a tiny dress, and a close up of her face. Something about her reminded Honor of ... whom? Bella was one of that breed of rather pretty, very available, not particularly talented glamour girls who seemed to fill the tabloid press and reality TV programmes. What had she actually done? She had stolen the boyfriend of another girl, and, since the boyfriend in question was a famous pop singer, this was, apparently, headline news.

Who did she look like? Reading with increasing curiosity, Honor discovered that Bella came from Cardiff, a few miles from the town where she herself had lived until she was in her late twenties. She stopped, gasped, and spoke aloud, "Oh! Madalena!" Dropping the newspaper to her lap, she leaned back, breathless. *So, Bella was Madalena's daughter. No wonder she looked familiar.*

Madalena. Another ghost from the past, on a day of ghosts. More than a coincidence, surely? Jackie .... Madalena ... two reminders.

The article described Madalena as a stunning Beyoncé lookalike, living a life of luxury with Jack, her long-term partner (*so they never married then ...*) and Bella, their only daughter. So she had finally got what she wanted, a wealthy husband, or partner anyway. It was true, she was very beautiful. Since she was about sixteen. Before that, she'd just been some gawky kid: Honor had no idea, at that point, how dangerous she would become. She had set her cap at Thomas with relentless determination, obviously thinking he would be the one to give her the life she wanted.

I almost lost him to her completely.

Honor stared at Bella's face, and held the picture out in front of her, to get some distance on it, examining her face. What was it about her? With her straight black shiny hair, and light eyes, she showed little evidence of her mother's ethnic origins. She squinted, trying to look through the picture as though it was a complicated magic eye diagram, looking for its deeper, more meaningful structure. Her heart jumped as she saw who Bella was: the striking resemblance, that extraordinary bone structure. Bella looked just like Thomas's mother.

The paper crumpled in her lap. She couldn't be. Could she? She lifted the paper again, looked at the picture, and then searched the text: how old was this girl? Twenty-one. So that would be? Her brain calculated rapidly, pulling back memories, and placing them in sequence. When was it, the year that Madalena tortured her? The year that Thomas was torn, undecided.

Honor squeezed her eyes shut, holding back tears, and leaned forward, folding her arms across her chest. She swallowed, hard and painfully, stifling the sob that bubbled in her throat. Pressing the heel of her hand against her breastbone, she rocked herself a little, then sat up and wiped her eyes.

She held up the paper and stared into the eyes of Thomas's daughter.

Yes, it could be. It could have happened.

CHAPTER TWO

Walking back to her office, for her final client session of the day, Honor felt dizzy. Twice, she had to stop, and steady herself; finally she sat down and leaned forwards, dropping her head down to counter the feeling that she might faint. Sitting herself back up again, the world around her seemed to dim and recede, as her inner sickening overwhelmed her sense of reality.

Her head felt full: Thomas, his family, the haunting face of Madalena; all of them jostling for her attention, a clamour of demands.

She looked in on Barbara, whose office was a shrine of cleanliness and order: her large glass desk held only the desktop computer and the office printer. Not a single piece of paper could be seen anywhere, not even a coloured post-it note; and not a pen or pencil in sight. Barbara worked almost entirely without paper, and had recently tried to convince Honor that she should use a mini laptop to take session notes: "We could get rid of your collection of tatty notebooks then, Honor."

Tatty notebooks …. As though she was going to sit in a session staring, unblinking, at a screen; rather than looking at her client and jotting down the occasional note.

Barbara turned away from her screen, towards Honor, and smiled. "I'll send Gordon through as soon as he arrives shall I?"

Everything about Barbara was round, like a child's drawing: round face, round eyes, round body, dark round curls on her round head. She never wore a scrap of make-up. Honor had been amazed one evening, when she and Eliot had bumped into Barbara and her husband in a restaurant, and Barbara was actually wearing mascara and lipstick. Only a little, subtle smudges, but even so, *Barbara?* Honor had never seen Barbara in even the vaguest sexual light: she was something of a mother figure.

Within minutes of Gordon's arrival, Honor felt restored to her professional self, as her own troubles receded in the presence of her client, a man she had worked with for over a year. With quite some success, too, she thought, as he settled down opposite her, smiling broadly, a picture of health and happiness.

"Hi, Honor."

Honor inclined her head. "Gordon …"

It turned out Gordon had good news. He had decided to marry his long-suffering girlfriend of the last twelve years.

Honor beamed. "That's marvellous, Gordon. Tell me what happened?"

Gordon explained, at length, and in depth, his moment of realization, of revelation, after the last time they'd met, when their exploration of his commitment phobia had broken through to a new level of understanding, and had stimulated an intense dream.

"All I can say, the only way I can describe it, is, I woke up; not just from sleep, from the dream, but from who I used to be, with all that fear. It just disappeared from one day to the next."

Yes, overnight, after a year of intense reflection. There were few things that spontaneously disappeared. Nothing, actually. Everything needed a push, whether it was a slight nudge or a great big heave ho! with your full weight behind it.

Gordon left, glowing with energy and pride. Another satisfied customer. Soon, she would broach with him the topic of bringing his therapy to a close, her best indicator of success. She felt lucky to have work she enjoyed so much, and that was so appreciated by her clientele.

Watching him leave, Tisi intruded again into Honor's mind. *I shouldn't doubt myself, of course I can help Tisi; I am never defeated. I will do my best for her, as I always do.*

It was a relief to get her working day over. Collecting her bag and coat, she went into Barbara's office.

"Could you check something out for me please?" Honor handed Barbara the page from *The Sun*. "Could you contact the paper, and see if you can get me prints of these photos?"

Barbara inspected the page. "Who is she?"

Honor stifled a sigh. This was the downside of having such a long-standing assistant. You couldn't help becoming friends, but then they felt they could ask you questions, challenge you even, instead of simply doing as they were told.

"I think she's related to someone I know, but the pictures are a little grainy, I need better copies."

Did that sound a bit thin? Possibly. However, as Barbara couldn't see (presumably) the maelstrom of emotions that accompanied this request, she simply nodded.

Barbara had been running Honor's life efficiently for the last ten years. Eliot said she was Honor's shadow, an expression he meant in a poetic, metaphorical way, not, as Honor understood it, in a psychological way: your shadow personality, the repository of all you reject in yourself, the characteristics that were disliked and discouraged in you by the people who raised you. She had tried to explain it to Eliot:

> "When you think of all I learned at my mother's knee: be a good little girl; don't be mean; don't hurt others; turn the other cheek. So all my aggression got tamped down tight, and buried deep in my shadow self, never to be seen or heard again. Until you're older and it starts to haunt you, if you're unlucky. Or lucky, depending how you see these things."

Barbara couldn't be her shadow, as in many ways Honor would love to be like her: in control; making things run smoothly; orchestrating her efficient working life. The whole edifice would implode around her if Barbara left. Not immediately, but a gradual decay before a final crumbled collapse.

Honor didn't envy all Barbara's characteristics though. Barbara had little tolerance for uncertainty or vagueness, needing clarity and predictability in all things; and she was a woman of no imagination whatsoever; a perfect balance for Honor. For example, her children's names: Janet and David. When Honor's children were small, some people were actually quite rude, even derisory about their unusual names: "Celestine? That's a funny name." or "Eden? Thea? Wherever did you get their names from?" Honor would never dream of saying to parents

13

like Barbara: "Have you no imagination at all? Wouldn't you like to give them a name as heavenly as they are?"

"Bye, Barbara. See you in the morning."

"Are you OK? You look pale."

"I'm a bit tired, it's felt like a long day."

"Well, Thea's show will soon take your mind off it. I hope it goes well."

Honor set off for her daughter's school, the late afternoon sunshine inspiring her to fold down the roof of her Mini. Eliot had tried to persuade her that their second car should be a sporty little number, but Honor had set her heart on the car she'd always wanted. Despite her dream of red, she had fallen in love with a metallic purple model. The car was small, self-contained, and impervious to other people's opinion. Just as she wished she was, in fact. Perhaps that was what people did, they chose the car that was most like their ideal self. Like Eliot, wanting a car that was all about speed, colour, and making an impression.

The school was twenty minutes away, a pleasant drive through tree-lined country lanes. Sequins of sunlight glimmered through the dense tunnel of trees and Honor felt her spirits rise. Taking a series of deliberate deep breaths, she turned her attention to the crowd in her mind and imagined each one receding, leaving her. Tisi, Thomas, Bella, each of them left her. Jackie lingered still: it proved harder to shake off someone who had been part of Honor's life for so long. She still missed her.

She turned her mind towards her daughter's impending dance show, hoping she was not at risk of becoming one of those sad stage-door mothers, living out her own dreams through her child. Whenever they went to buy Thea's dance clothes, Honor was ecstatically happy, especially looking at the tutus. Eliot joked: "Why don't you buy one for yourself, Honor?"

Honor had yearned for dance lessons as a child, but had been quite unable to make her parents realize how desperately she wanted them. She pleaded, cajoled, cried, offered to give up all pocket money and do all household chores, but they were unmoved. They were poor, they said, and could not afford for all three of their daughters to have lessons.

"But the others don't even *want* them. I've asked them. They don't even *care*. Why can't you see how much I want them?"

That wasn't the point, they said; they must be fair to all of them, even if that meant that none of them got anything.

Turning into the school drive, Honor headed for the car park. The Howell Jenkins College, an architectural classic, was set in rolling parkland. The main buildings, glowing in the late afternoon sun, formed a square around the famous quadrangle, as green and smooth as a billiard table. She could see several neatly dressed pupils on the criss-cross path. By some strange chemistry, communicated magically between all the children, the "Don't walk on the grass" rule was never disobeyed, except once each year. On their final day at school, the upper sixth form all ran shrieking across the quad, an unspoken rite of passage into the adult world, watched indulgently by the younger pupils and the teachers.

Thank God our kids are having such happy and successful school days. Not that her own were that bad, but they certainly didn't seem to have the cheerful, sunlit quality that this school was able to provide. Early on, at Celestine's parents' evening, one of the teachers said to her, "It's not natural you know, for children to be as happy at school as they are here."

She pictured her old school, austere and forbidding, a tall, brooding red brick workhouse building, its walls seemingly contaminated by the centuries of misery and poverty it had contained before it became a girls' grammar school, providing its pupils with a good, formal, education. It wasn't a place to have fun: everything was strictly controlled.

Remembering the Plain Janes, and how she and Jackie had treated them, Honor felt the hot prickling on her face, the sensation that would herald the spectacular blushing, triggered by the remotest hint of embarrassment, that was the bane of her life. The Plain Janes were close friends in her year, brought together by the same name and their total lack of good looks. Plain was a compliment to them: they were both dismally unattractive, one tall, skinny, and translucently pale, the other short and fat. They were both brilliantly clever, vying for first and second place in all the exams at the end of terms. Honor had tried her best not to care, but constantly coming third in everything wore her down after a few years. Skinny Plain Jane was the only person Honor had ever met who could blush redder than she could: "The Plain Janes are lezzers!" was guaranteed to make her poor, acned face flame crimson.

Where were they now? Maybe they lived together, a pair of blue-stocking academics, sharing a suburban semi. All these years later,

15

and she was still being mean to them. *What on earth is the matter with me? For all I know, they have successful careers in government or commerce. Couldn't I at least allow them that? Perhaps I should find them and ask for their forgiveness, and be redeemed.*

She hated to be reminded of the nastier side of her nature.

After parking her car, Honor walked around to the quad, glancing back to admire the Mini from a distance, as you would a painting, standing back to appreciate the full impact of its purple glory. She smiled to herself at the sheer satisfaction of getting something she had wanted in life, even if, as in the case of the car, it had taken nearly forty years from the first longings of her five-year-old self.

The foyer was abuzz with parents milling around and chatting, waiting to be ushered in to the auditorium. Honor looked around to see who she knew, and headed over to a group of mothers of girls in Theadora's year, where she was greeted warmly.

"Hi, Honor. Good to see you. Where's Eliot today?" Amanda, mother of Thea's best friend Charlotte, smiled broadly and greeted Honor with a kiss. Amanda was the type of woman who loved her children a little too much, and her husband not quite enough. Her eyes lit up for her little ones, but dimmed and hardened when she turned, reluctantly, to her husband.

"Hi, Amanda. He's picking up Eden and Celestine. It's my turn to watch the concert."

"Tell him I missed him."

Honor's heart tightened. She looked at Amanda, raised an eyebrow and said, "You missed him? Surely you only saw him yesterday?"

Eliot did the school run daily and was popular with the mothers. *What does she mean? What is she saying?*

Amanda gave a tinkling laugh and brushed aside Honor's comment with an airy wave of her manicured hand. "I'm looking forward to seeing the girls dancing. I went and helped with their hair and make-up: they look amazing."

Envy stabbed Honor just below her heart. This was what she missed when she was working: she couldn't volunteer to help out at the school events. She tried to smile back, feeling the thin tightness of her lips, and the falseness of her face. "They must look so sweet."

"I convinced Thea to have her hair up in a ballet dancer's bun, like Charlotte; they look delightful in their matching tutus."

Honor gave an even meaner smile, before her attention was mercifully caught by the call to make their way into the auditorium. *I hate*

16

Amanda. In two sentences she had succeeded in claiming ownership of her husband and her daughter. *I expect it was just a turn of phrase, about Eliot, the sort of thing you say as a reflex.* Eliot attracted women without even trying, he couldn't help himself. So he said.

The lights dimmed. The heavy red velvet drape edged in gold braid drew back. The music started and a line of tiny six-year-olds in white Arabian Nights costumes skipped across the stage, synchronizing only occasionally as they danced in a line. They looked completely captivating, and the room melted with collective adoration of the little girls. A few fathers stood up to video the moment, and mothers exchanged soft glances with their friends.

Honor sat through several such performances, until Theadora's turn. She and Charlotte were dancing together, the two little girls identical in their sparkling white net dresses and white satin ballet slippers laced up their skinny legs. Honor could hardly see through the haze of tears as they danced on stage, looking earnest, concentrating to get their steps exactly in time.

Surreptitiously (she hoped) she pulled a tissue from her sleeve and dabbed at her eyes. Her children found her shows of emotion at any of their performances deeply embarrassing, so she smiled broadly towards the stage, just in case Thea was able to catch sight of her across the lights. Their dance finished, and they curtsied to the audience's rapturous applause, their faces breaking into beaming, toothy smiles of relief and pleasure.

After the show, Honor hurried around to the back of the theatre to find Theadora. They hugged extravagantly, amid showers of kisses, and "I love you," "You were brilliant." Honor held her close, breathing her in, feeling her adored child's tiny body still quivering with the excitement of her triumph.

Amanda passed beside them, turning to Honor to suggest getting Charlotte and Thea together for a play date soon. "I'll make the arrangements with Eliot."

I could slap her. I really could. She turned her attention back to Thea, resolving not to let Amanda spoil her time with her daughter.

They set off home, Thea chattering happily about her day.

Me and my little girl, just the two of us. Heaven.

Honor thought of Tisi and her two children, and remembered something she'd said about them. "I'd kill for them, and I'd die for them."

Surely, something every parent feels, and says?

She glanced across at Thea, whose eyes were closing in happy exhaustion.

How could any mother bear to be separated from her children?

But when all your goodness is in your mothering, where does all your badness go?

They arrived home, too quickly it seemed to Honor, and Thea ran in as her mother parked.

She sat, gathering herself, trying to be calm, especially trying to forget Amanda's comment …. Surely she'd never have said that to her if she and Eliot were involved in some way? *Stop it; don't poison yourself; don't let her poison your evening with Eliot.* She sighed, knowing that all she was doing was pushing her suspicions down, deeper …. She dropped her head on to the steering wheel. *Thank God for my work, my career … somewhere I can forget my own troubles and help others work theirs out.*

By the time Honor got into the house, she'd lost Thea, who was sitting on Eliot's lap. "I wish you'd seen it Daddy, we didn't make a single mistake, not a single one, Miss James said it was a perfect performance!"

Eliot smiled at Honor, over Thea's head. "Go and get changed, darling. I'll give Thea her tea, she needs an early night, our little dancer must be exhausted."

The bedroom was cool, the light dim; the white voile curtains closed against the late evening sun, fluttering slightly from a light breeze at the open window. Honor looked out at the garden. The lilac bushes were in blossom, a fragrant border enclosing the orderly garden, their heavy scent reaching her faintly.

It was a relief to step out of her sensible black work skirt and beige blouse: clothes designed to make her look as little like a real flesh and blood person as possible. Everything was about her clients and patients, not about her. She tried to be invisible, concealed by her own clothes.

She pulled on her jeans, and surveyed her shelves of sweaters and tops with mild smugness: she had recently tidied them into neat, colour-coded piles. They would stay like this for about a week, after which they would slowly degenerate into a chaotic spaghetti. Then she would blitz it again and get them all into military precision, as they were now. Two piles of darks: black, navy, brown, charcoal; two of neutrals: white, cream, beige, camel; and two of delicate pastels: pink, blue, and lilac. Next to these, Eliot's stack of exuberantly coloured T-shirts yelled: look at me! Nothing pale or neutral for him: his side of the cupboard was always an immaculately tidy rainbow of primary colours, each one a striking contrast to his black hair and dark skin. Eliot's best friend, Will, had a long-standing joke that vaguely offended Honor: "Talk about the Virgin and the Gypsy."

She pulled on a pale pink cashmere sweater, revealing herself: a mother, a wife, a woman.

Celestine burst into the room, shattering the peace, her face a dark scowl of indignation. "Did Dad tell you what happened today? The disaster I had? Did he tell you?"

"What darling, what happened? He didn't mention anything."

"That's so typical! He doesn't even care! He's not even sorry!"

Honor took her daughter's hand and led her to the small sofa in the bay window. She could feel the agitation of her girl woman, her fight against the childlike impulse to sob on her mother's shoulder about whatever fresh challenge the world had thrown at her.

"Everything is ruined! Everything!" Celestine was inclined to drama. When she was a toddler, her parents were convinced she'd end up on the stage. Now, she simply had a talent for making everything in her life worse, just by the language she used. What on earth would she say if there was a real disaster? She'd run out of superlatives.

Honor put her arm around Celestine's narrow shoulders, and looked into her eyes, a mirror of her own: milky green, with an oriental tilt. Cat's eyes.

"What happened?"

Celestine was on a mission to become more self-sufficient, in readiness for becoming a full-time boarder at school the following year. Her biggest concern was her washing, so she'd been doing this herself for the last few weeks. The catastrophe of the day was that she'd put all her white underwear and socks in the washing machine and run it on a hot wash. Unfortunately, Eliot had earlier that day dripped egg on his T-shirt, and he'd taken it off in the kitchen and thrown it in the washing machine.

"And it was his *emerald green* one, Mum! Like, not even a red or blue one! Who wants pale green bras and pants? And socks? And d'you know what he did when I told him?"

Honor pressed her hand to her mouth to quell a laugh as she imagined Celestine's high decibel shriek when she opened the washing machine door.

"What?"

"*He laughed.* Almost laughed his head off in fact."

"Oh dear …. Men eh? No idea …. What else did he say?" Honor felt her relax a little.

"He did say he'd pay for me to buy all new."

"There. See? Every cloud …. All new undies. How good is that?"

Celestine stiffened again, not ready to be mollified yet. "Mum, you have to go shopping for me tomorrow. I can't go to school in green *socks*. Can you imagine what that'll be like? *Have you any idea*?"

"Hmm, I see. I'll pop into Marks tomorrow. And on Saturday you and me'll go shopping and kit you out."

Honor watched Celestine's face as the sunshine returned to her world.

As she left the room, she turned at the door. "And don't get me the socks with the ribbing, Mum, just completely plain, alright? And plain knickers, just the white boy shorts ones, size 8–10, OK?"

Honor nodded and smiled brightly. *Nice to have my orders, I must say. As if I haven't got enough to do.*

Thea was settling down for bed, so Honor went in for their good-night snuggle. She lay down next to her little girl and wrapped her arms around her. Sometimes she fell asleep like this and Eliot had to come to wake her. She nuzzled Thea's silky hair. She longed, sometimes, for another baby. A well-known politician, her age, had recently declared herself pregnant: the result she said of a welcome accident. Honor had felt deeply envious. Another couple of years, and her little girl would be almost a teenager.

Theadora, truly her gift from God. The third child they never planned, their you've-had-an-affair-but-we'll-get-over-it baby. And how they loved her. Honor held her tighter. A child especially cherished, because they almost didn't have her.

When she thought of Jackie, she hated her for her and Eliot's joint betrayal; but without her, she would never have had Theadora, so she felt grateful for that. Wasn't that the hardest thing? When you loved and hated someone at the same time?

Eliot was in the kitchen, singing to himself and cooking. A couple of evenings a week, they made sure they had dinner together, just the two of them. It was one of the many ways in which they looked after the marriage they'd almost lost.

Eliot handed Honor a glass of cold white wine. "Here darling. Let me tell you a funny story about Celestine."

"She's told me. Your comedy, her tragedy. I tried not to laugh." She took a sip of the wine, and closed her eyes, feeling her muscles soften, releasing the day's tension.

20

"How was your day?"

"Hmm …. OK, a bit full on. I had a new patient."

"What was upsetting her?"

Honor didn't talk too much to Eliot about her work. He didn't really understand why people dwelled so much on their problems: he himself lived a life of cheery denial and Pollyanna optimism. In their early years together, when Honor was still trying to work him out (as if he was a puzzle, like a Rubik's Cube), she worried that he would, one day, be hit by a deep depression as all of the sadnesses in his life caught up with him, refusing to be suppressed any longer. She had told him this once and he was completely unabashed. "Don't you know me at all?" he'd said. "I play out all my sadness on my sax; why d'you think it's called the Blues?"

So Honor hesitated. Should she tell Eliot what was on her mind? It would alter the mood between them, cause a slight tension, and turn their minds back: reminding both of them instead of just her. She would have liked to tell him about Bella, but the subject of Thomas was taboo, as Eliot harboured a belief that he had won Honor on the rebound. Although he had never actually said that Thomas shouldn't be spoken of, his tense smile, lack of enthusiasm, and rapid change of subject if his name came up made his feelings crystal clear. So she returned his question.

"How was your day?"

"Good, actually …. And I need your advice." Eliot was currently collaborating with his friend and colleague Will on a composition they had been commissioned to write for a West End show, and they'd been working on a tragic score.

"We ended up in an argument about sadness. How many varieties there are: I said there's really only one, but definitely no more than five. Will said there are at least twenty, and he'd put money on it. So we've got a twenty-pound bet, and we want your opinion. Will said that if anyone knew, you would. Melancholy, I conceded, yes that's a form of sadness. Even misery, depression, moroseness and dejection. But, honestly, weepy? Tearful? Lachrymose? What d'you think, Honor?"

Honor was laying the table, and laughing. "Hmm, well, they sound more like what you might *do* if you were sad: behaviours not feelings. Did he get to twenty?"

"Only if I allow regret and remorse. We agreed we'd stand by your opinion. And I'm sure you agree with me that they don't count." Eliot placed a steaming dish of lasagne on the table with a triumphant flourish and looked at Honor expectantly.

Remorse and regret. I have felt them all day. Do they count as sadness?

"Well," she chose her words carefully. "They're similar aren't they? But I think remorse and regret can be causes of sadness, not the sadness itself."

"There! I knew it! The winner!" Eliot performed a victory dance, pulling Honor to her feet and twirling her around the kitchen.

Honor didn't mention Amanda's comment at school. She didn't want to turn herself into the person she became when she was suspicious of Eliot; that person who sneaked around checking the post every day, perusing the credit card and bank statements, calling to query unusual items, trying to get hold of his mobile phone and check his messages. She hated herself when she was like this, and then she hated him for making her hate herself. She was watching him now. *Could he? Would he? Surely not again?*

"What, Honor?" Eliot, staring at her, broke into her reverie. "Why are you looking at me like that?"

Honor shook her head and smiled at him. "Nothing, Eliot, nothing. By the way, I saw Amanda. She wants to arrange a play date for the girls."

She was going to ignore it. Eliot wasn't the only one who could deal in blind denial.

It was an unspoken agreement between them that these dinners a deux would end in slow sensual lovemaking. On these nights, no swift, functional coupling to send them both off into peaceful sleep, but a more deliberate act of love. After dinner, Honor would prepare their bedroom, burning scented oils, rose and lavender, and playing soft music. Sometimes they would begin with a massage. Honor would choose erotic lingerie: white stockings and suspenders were Eliot's favourite, but she would sometimes wear all red, or black. Any colour worked.

"I'll clear up, Honor, you go on up."

"OK, but I just need half an hour in my study, El, I need to check something out for work tomorrow."

Eliot's face fell.

"No, really, I just need half an hour, then I'll be with you. Tell you what, I'll go and run you a nice hot bath, and you can have a soak, till I join you."

Honor went and set the bath running, then went up to the attic, to her private study.

She was looking for her old photo albums: her pre-Eliot, pre-children careful catalogue of her life in pictures, in neatly labelled books.

Here she was, aged twenty-two, a young bride, overflowing with hope and happiness.

And there was Thomas, by her side, her handsome new husband.

And on her other side her bridesmaid, Jackie. Involuntarily she reached out and stroked her face. "I miss you," she whispered. "I can't forgive, and I can't forget. I wish I could tell you my troubles. But I can't because you are one of my troubles."

She flicked over a page of the album, looking for the pictures with Thomas's parents, searching for his mother. Finding her, she stared at her face, then back to Thomas's. There was definitely something. Yes, here was a picture of Thomas, his mother, and his older sister Caroline. She found she could see a real resemblance, if she looked at the women, rather than at Thomas. Once she got the original pictures back from the newspaper, she would be able to compare them.

Yes, it's there. I am right.

Such disturbing events, on this shadow date, and its reminders: Thomas and Madalena; Jackie and Eliot.

Something had been set in motion in her.

She paused, listened; she could hear, or feel, a low brooding rumble, tectonic, releasing a hiss of vapour that dispersed, reverberating, across her body, heart, and mind.

She closed the book and went to join her husband.

CHAPTER THREE

Honor set off for work, a little earlier than usual, on the day of her second meeting with Tisi. As she turned into the road of her offices, she was struck by how attractive her building looked in the morning sunlight. The Georgian terrace was one of a crescent of private residences, apart from the three at her end, which housed a doctor's surgery, a dental surgery, and a holistic health centre, where Honor had half the ground floor.

She was so early today that even Barbara, who always arrived on the dot of 8.30, was not there. Her influence was evident: the brass plaque to the right of the door had been polished to a brilliant shine by their cleaner, who was micro managed within an inch of her life by Barbara.

Dr Honor Sinclair MD; BSc; Dip Psych.

Psychotherapist

Consultant Psychiatrist

Letting herself in, Honor passed by the door of Ann, the Gestalt therapist who had the other half of the ground floor. She could hear the murmur of voices.

She and Ann had moved into the offices on the same day, ten years ago. They'd met in the hall and Honor had taken one look at Ann's hair, hanging straight to her waist (*What exactly is the right age to stop having long hair?*) and her Indian print cotton skirt and sighed inwardly. Ann, smiling broadly, had held out her hand and shook Honor's firmly, saying, "How great! A new office and another therapist across the hall. We can brew some spells together."

Honor had smiled tightly and said, "Pleased to meet you," then retired quickly to her own office.

Muffled sounds overhead told her that the massage practice, like Ann, was busy with the morning shift: the early efforts of stressed office workers to get through the day. The whole of the first floor of the building was occupied by a group of four masseuses who, between them, offered every type of massage. Honor sometimes referred clients to them, in accordance with her belief that words had their limits: most neuroses have their physical parallels, so it was amazing what could be shifted by a good massage. Rolfing and Heller particularly could provoke a depth of tears that could take months of therapy to achieve. She'd had a course of Rolfing herself, and had found it agony, physically working at the deepest level of musculature, in an attempt to release deeply held defences. After three sessions, she'd stopped. It turned out she had defences that she needed; that she didn't want breached. Who knew what might happen? That was the danger of working in depth, whether through the body or the mind: you simply didn't know what might be unearthed. You hoped it'd be good, energizing, a re-birth, a release. But if it wasn't … . Well, the history of psychiatry and psychotherapy told some terrible tales.

Honor let herself in through the inner door to her office, a room that in days gone by would have been the front drawing room and the back dining room. Now, the two rooms had been knocked through to form her tranquil office and consulting room. She had chosen the colour scheme carefully, with both herself and her clients in mind.

Cream voiles screened the windows at either end. The floor was carpeted in a deep pile air force blue carpet. Each room still had its Georgian fireplace: at one end, an antique firescreen embroidered with purple flowers stood in the grate; and a large silver-framed mirror was mounted above the mantelpiece. At the seating end, an extravagant glass vase of cream lilies stood in the fireplace, their pungent perfume filling the room. On the mantelpiece above was a modern arrangement of candles in silver and purple.

There were no pictures, apart from several framed certificates of Honor's professional credentials. She hoped that these gave her clients the confidence they gave her.

At the end of each working day Barbara tidied Honor's desk, putting everything away except the laptop computer. She then placed Honor's daily schedule, printed on an A4 sheet, next to the computer, in perfect alignment. It felt like heresy to disturb this fine example of Barbara's borderline obsessive compulsion, but Honor did it every day nevertheless. She and Barbara accepted this as the way of the world: Barbara tidied; Honor untidied.

Honor scanned the sheet: five clients today, all of them people she had been seeing for some time, apart from Tisi, who she was seeing before lunch; she felt her stomach lurch at the thought.

In search of coffee, she left her room and unlocked Barbara's office, a small room at the back, probably the kitchen when the building had been a home. She switched on the coffee machine and sat down in the black leather chair that was kept there to seat clients who arrived early. They rarely did, after the first couple of appointments. By what curious osmosis did they come to know that it was frowned upon to turn up ahead of their allotted hour? Even late was more forgivable … . How did they all succeed in arriving thirty seconds before their appointment time? Though five minutes waiting under the eagle eye of Barbara would be quite enough to ensure future punctuality: Barbara had that maternal ability, which Honor deeply envied, to show her disapproval simply by a dimming of the light in her eyes and a slight, disappointed fade of her broad smile.

Honor worked here three days a week, seeing private psychotherapy clients. She worked at a National Health psychiatric hospital on the other two days. She didn't know which work she preferred. In her psychiatric practice her patients were often in desperate need. In contrast, her therapy clients were holding their lives together, but they were going through a difficult time and needed some support: full recovery was entirely likely.

There was no guarantee of that for her psychiatric patients, who fell into two categories: people who had functioned quite well, held jobs, and had relationships, but at some point had a mental breakdown; or those on the margins of society, who had never really functioned well. For the latter group, their chronic mental illness was what defined them, and they were in and out of mental health institutions for most of their lives.

On days like today, when she was in her consulting office seeing therapy clients, she definitely felt a little lighter of heart. Though today, thoughts of Tisi were weighing heavily on her.

Taking her coffee into her room, she heard the door go. Within minutes Barbara came in, handing Honor the notebook for her first client. "Here you are, quite a quiet day today."

27

"Thanks. Yes, maybe I'll try and get off a bit earlier."

"Anything special you need from me today, Honor? I'm planning to talk to Dr Williams's secretary about the way she's managing her referrals to you. She's not orderly or thoughtful about your time at all; I'm going to suggest she follows the process I use."

Honor felt a fleeting moment of sympathy for Dr Williams's secretary, along with a familiar sense of gratitude to Barbara for taking such good care of her. "No, nothing, that's fine. Though if there's any opportunity to get me a little extra time before Tisi's session this morning, that'd help. I just haven't been able to stop thinking about her."

Barbara looked at Honor, her head on one side. "Hmm .... That's not like you, is that something you need to be talking to Bill about?"

Barbara was right; she should discuss this with Bill, her professional supervisor, and get his help. Years ago, when she was first practising, she'd found it hard to leave her clients behind once their session was over, and ended up walking around with the weight of people's misery on her shoulders. Her supervisor helped her become more proficient: the deep breathing, the visualizations, and the setting and holding of emotional boundaries, so it was rarely a problem for her now.

"When am I seeing him again?"

Barbara had Honor's diary at her fingertips. "Two weeks' time. Do you want me to schedule an earlier time?"

"I'll decide after I've seen Tisi today." Why had she said that? Tisi had disturbed her terribly, her and Madalena between them. She needed a dedicated session with Bill to try and process whatever it was that was surfacing in her. But she was nervous of what could be dredged up. Some things were best left alone.

Some things that happened to you were agony forever.

Tisi didn't turn up for her appointment.
No word as to why.

* * *

Eliot was cooking dinner for the family when Honor got home.

"Guess what, Mum?" Eden said, the minute she walked into the kitchen. "I'm going to be captain of the football team. Mr Edwards said he'll try me out at the match this weekend, and if I do well, I'll be it for the season."

"Brilliant. What d'you actually have to do as captain then?"

Honor tried to keep track of the technical football discussion that ensued between Eden and Eliot, but an anxious knot in her stomach was distracting her.

It was unknown, in her experience, for a therapy client not to turn up for a session, without advance explanation, as they quickly came to depend on their weekly session for some peace of mind.

Psychiatric patients were another matter: they frequently didn't turn up. Sometimes they told you, sometimes they didn't. Some didn't really want to come at all: they were told to attend, and they didn't have to pay.

Therapy clients, on the other hand, were known for their high level of motivation: they elected to come and they paid with their own hard-earned money.

Tisi was behaving like a psychiatric patient.

Either that, or something dreadful had happened.

Once dinner was over, the kids cleared up, and Eliot and Honor took a bottle of wine into the garden.

"I'm so worried, Eliot. D'you remember me mentioning my new client? She didn't turn up to her session today."

"Why not?"

"I don't know, we didn't hear from her."

"That's unusual isn't it?"

"Unheard of."

"Are you going to call her?"

"If we hear nothing by mid morning tomorrow, Barbara will call her."

"What could have happened?"

"The question is, what could have happened that stopped her from calling to cancel? I was worried about her the first time I set eyes on her. Worried sick in fact: even then I wondered if I should be seeing her at the clinic, not the office."

"And what did you decide about her?"

"That there was no risk, or only the slightest."

Honor's mind turned to the concluding moments of her session with Tisi. "Oh no. I've just remembered what I said when we made the second appointment."

"What?" Eliot poured each of them a glass of white wine.

"I made a condition. I said I'd work with her as long as she promised not to harm herself or anyone else." Honor put her hand over her mouth.

What had she done?
What has Tisi done?

Honor went to her study, where stacks of old photo albums sat on her desk. She started scanning some of the pictures onto her computer. All her recent photos were on there, in well-ordered albums, all neatly labelled. Barbara would be proud of her (and amazed): this was one of the few aspects of her life where she was consistently methodical and orderly. Here was her past, in chronological order. Here were all the people she had loved, and still loved; here were her family and her friends, having good times; here were her beloved children.

Here were all her memories, so that she would never forget.

It didn't take too long to scan in all the photos she had of Thomas. They'd met when she was nineteen, he seven years older; and they'd married when she was aged twenty-three. Five years of pictures; yet, aside from their stack of wedding photos, there were only a dozen or so pictures. It was amazing seeing them on a big screen: Thomas was good-looking: silky black hair, and the bluest blue eyes. She zoomed to close-up: it was like looking into his eyes again.

I can't wait to get those pictures of Bella.

She gazed at the image of her first husband.

I wonder what you would have looked like now, Thomas? How would you have felt to know you'd left behind a daughter?

Honor called in at the office on her way to the hospital next morning, just in case there was anything in the post from Tisi. A vain hope.

A busy morning in her clinic provided more than enough challenges to leave no space for thoughts of Tisi. Lunchtime came around quickly, and she checked her phone for messages: nothing. She called Barbara: nothing. Honor suggested she leave a message for Tisi, giving her Honor's mobile number to call. Barbara pointed out, sharply, that they absolutely never did this, for very good reasons that Honor was perfectly aware of, and there was no reason to break this rule now.

Honor couldn't eat any lunch.

She tried to concentrate on her afternoon clinic, and a new referral. A young mother, her wrists bandaged from an attempted suicide, and deep dark rings below her reddened eyes, had been abandoned by her husband. He had taken their two children, including a three-month-old baby daughter. Her depression was so profound that she barely spoke, and Honor had to resist the urge to wrap her in her arms and rock her like a baby. Sometimes her professional training seemed totally inadequate.

Unable to sleep that night, she went to her study, and checked out the news headlines on the internet: *Any domestic murders or suicides in the last couple of days? How foolish of me. These things are so common that they barely make the news.* She went back to bed, and lay there breathing deeply in her efforts to relax. She fell into a fitful slumber, waking an hour later with a startled shriek, having had a quite sickening nightmare. Eliot woke up and held her, soothing her. She didn't tell him about the nightmare: she didn't want to hear her words said aloud.

The next morning, at the office, a breathless and garbled message had been left on the ansaphone at seven o'clock the previous evening.

"Oh my God! I'm so sorry, Dr Sinclair! Sorry, I mean Honor! I'm so sorry, how can you ever forgive me? I just completely forgot our appointment! I can't believe it, I'm so sorry! I was in an all-day meeting, I only just got your message. I didn't write it down, it wasn't in my diary! I'm so, so sorry. I'll call in the morning to re-schedule. I'm sorry again."

Honor felt as she had as a young mother, losing sight of a small child for a few minutes: torn between scolding them or hugging them.

So she forgot. Really? The things we remember, the things we forget: selective memory. We don't forget what's truly important to us; and we always remember what hurt us, however hard we try to forget.

It was impossible to bury it deep enough, in Honor's experience.

Barbara spoke to Tisi and arranged an appointment the next day.

"I got those photos." Barbara handed Honor a large brown envelope.

"That was quick."

"You can't order them. I asked. They sent me online to print them from there. So I did."

Honor raised her eyebrows and smiled. "What would I do without you?"

Pulling the pictures out of the envelope she examined them. They'd be better on the computer screen; she'd scan them in tonight.

"Who is she?" Barbara was standing, arms folded, watching Honor.

"Oh … ." Honor flapped a hand vaguely in the air … "The daughter of someone I used to know."

"Why the interest?" Barbara could be like a dog with a bone.

"No special reason. Now, how are we going to manage Tisi tomorrow? I have no idea what sort of response I can expect from her. You know, I have some serious worries."

"Shall we check that the panic button's working?"

On the inside of the arm of Honor's easy chair was a small button, barely visible, which could alert Barbara to the need for her to come into Honor's office. So they checked the button, which successfully distracted Barbara from the photos.

There was no need really; Honor knew that it was not her that was in danger from Tisi.

CHAPTER FOUR

I have no idea what I can reasonably expect from Tisi.

Until Honor had a deeper understanding of Tisi's character dynamics it would be difficult to predict how she might react to comments and observations.

Honor had an extraordinary memory, not for facts and figures, but for a total experience. She thought of it as her magic memory, invaluable in her chosen profession. After a short meditation, she could conjure up a client in all their dimensions: how they looked, sounded, and felt, along with her own reactions and responses. In Tisi's case, she'd been unable to clear her from her mind, so this magic was unnecessary.

Tisi arrived a little early, and Honor heard her profuse apologies to Barbara, who handled it professionally, maintaining a cool distance.

At the allotted time, when Honor went to collect her, Tisi greeted her with stammering apologies. *If I could just get this woman to stop saying sorry, I'll have given her some serious help: her fear of failure is crippling.*

They settled into the consulting room and Honor looked at Tisi expectantly.

Tears welled up in her eyes. She looked down, and mumbled something.

"I can't hear you Tisi."

She raised her head slightly. "I'm sorry I didn't turn up for the session."

"Why don't you tell me why?"

Silence. Honor looked at Tisi's bowed head. She'd done something different to her hair; there were wavy tendrils on the top layer, looking a little Bohemian. She was dressed all in black; slim black trousers, well-cut over her heavy thighs, sleek snakeskin boots, a black V-necked sweater, cashmere by the looks of it; and modern silver jewellery, set with glowing topaz: earrings, a large pendant around her neck, and a chunky bangle.

A tear splashed down on to her hand. Honor broke the silence.

"Did you really forget?"

A shake of her head.

"Tell me."

She took a deep breath and looked Honor straight in the eye, making Honor realize how often Tisi avoided direct eye contact. "I was scared."

"What were you scared of?"

"Of telling you what's in my mind."

"You told me last time."

"I don't want to hear myself say things like that again." Tisi was shaking her head.

"You don't have to say anything you don't want," Honor said.

"You won't make me?"

"Tisi, I'm not here to make you say or do anything. I'm here to listen to you, and to help you work out what you want, and how to get it. Let's start there .... What is it you want?"

"If only I knew the answer to that. Don says he wants to stay, he's ended his affair, he wants us to make a go of it."

"And how d'you feel about that?"

"I know it's right for the children. It's best for them. I love them; I want what's right for them. I don't want them to be hurt."

"Tisi, I hope during our session today that I can hear a little of your history, and background, but right now I'm curious to know whether your own parents were divorced?"

Tisi leaned forward, thrusting her head towards Honor, who hadn't noticed before what a long slim neck she had. She spat: "No they weren't. But they should have been. That would have done us a favour."

Honor felt her own energy contract. *Such vitriol. I should follow it, I know I should. But I just can't go there with her.* Against her better professional judgement, she tried to distract her: she needed to keep Tisi calm during this session, for her own sake, if not for Tisi's.

"There's obviously a lot to talk about there, but we'll discuss that later. Tell me about your feelings for Don, how you feel about his desire to stay with the family?"

Tisi took a breath and leaned back, tilting her head back slightly against the back of the sofa, and looking upwards at the ceiling. There was a long silence. Then she looked at Honor, calmer, speaking in a low voice. "He hasn't suffered enough yet, I want him to suffer."

"Do you love him?"

"That's got nothing to do with it. He's hurt me terribly, and he must suffer; he must be punished. Then we can talk about what happens next."

Honor, mindful of Tisi's fears of expressing her destructive fantasies, didn't want to provoke her. "I'm hearing progress, and that's encouraging. You had much worse imaginings last time we spoke. Now, you've a perfectly natural desire to even the score with Don, to hurt him as he has hurt you."

Bill would practically have a heart attack if he heard me make this prescriptive and inauthentic intervention. Talk about leading the witness. She knew that her alarm at the feelings Tisi awakened in her was compromising her, driving her to say anything to control Tisi, and herself. For some women, the rage against an unfaithful husband is bottomless, as she herself knew.

It didn't work anyway, judging from what Tisi said next. "I thought of poisoning him."

Honor hoped Tisi didn't notice that she nearly jumped out of her skin. Just a figure of speech? Or did Tisi know that poison's one of the few ways to kill someone and not be found out, if you're smart? She tried her best to hide her alarm with a cough and a change in posture.

"Yes, poisoning him. It seems only fair, to poison him as he has poisoned me. He has poisoned me." She sat up, thrusting her head forward, with a disconcerting undulation of her long neck. She hissed the "s" in poison.

"Sit back, Tisi, try to relax. Take a deep breath … that's it … and again …. That's right, keep breathing slowly and deeply."

Watching her calm down, relax a little, Honor said: "What I would normally do, at an early session like this, is start taking a history of your younger years, and your family. Is that something you feel ready to start now?"

Tisi nodded slowly.

"I'll tell you an interesting place to start, and that's with some of your early memories. We can get a sense of how far back your emotional memory goes, and think about how those experiences may have affected you. So let's start with that shall we?"

Tisi gave a nod.

"Take a moment then, to think back to when you were aged six, if you can, and tell me what you remember from that time."

Apart from those rare people who had cleverly avoided registering any emotional memories whatsoever, clients enjoyed this activity. Honor had only once worked with someone who couldn't engage with it: he'd come for help as his wife was threatening to leave him because of his complete lack of emotionality. Honor thought he was seriously repressed initially; but it was worse than that: he felt nothing, he never had. The only reason he was distressed about his wife's threat was that he had a practical concern about how he would manage domestically on his own.

Tisi relaxed, smiled, and looked a little playful; her eyes lit up. "Okay. I've got one."

It was a bit like a parlour game, marvellous for building rapport and intimacy. Professionally, Honor could learn a huge amount about a character from these recollections.

She nodded to Tisi to go ahead.

"It was when I was at school, the first year I was there. I was a quiet child so nobody took much notice of me really, except when teachers asked my name, when they would ask me lots of questions. The teacher told us to make a picture. So I drew a chubby bumblebee, with wide yellow and black stripes on its body and a smiley face. Then I surrounded the bee with green grass, and a mass of daffodils, some smaller bees in the flowers at the back of the picture, and a bright yellow sun in one corner, with yellow rays fanning out across the garden. My teacher asked me: 'Where did you get the idea?' and held it up for all the class to see and admire. I took it home to show my Mum and she stared at it for ages with a funny look on her face; and when my Dad came home, she showed it to him, and they kept looking at me and the picture, and at each other. They thought I was clever and they were happy. I felt all warm inside. I still draw that picture sometimes. The next morning my Mum had put my picture on the wall and something was different: the way my Mum and Dad looked at me, as if they could really see, right inside me. Their eyes were smiling. It made a nice change from the fighting."

Tisi was smiling broadly at the memory.

"What do you think of when you think of bees?"

"The sweetness of honey."

Honor was startled: she'd expected her to comment on their sharp sting.

"And did you continue to draw pictures as you grew older?"

36

"I went to art college, I was considered gifted. I still like to paint as a hobby."

"And what do you like to paint?"

"Gardens, in watercolour."

Gardens. Good clue. The symbol of her inner life. "Real gardens? People's gardens?"

"Gardens from my dreams. My ambition is to paint a garden so perfect that I can call it the Garden of Eden."

Another clue. Adam and Eve? Man and woman in harmony? "Paradise. You want to imagine and paint Paradise."

Tisi's smile was radiant. "Yes, that's exactly what I want to do."

"Shall we try another one? An earlier memory, if you have one?"

"OK …. Umm. Let's think … yes, I know … my sisters and me, I'm the youngest of three girls. We all shared a big bedroom, like a brightly coloured dormitory, each of us having our own corner, with a bed, a wardrobe, and a chest of drawers. One of us had to get out of bed and switch the light off, and run back to bed in the dark, and then we'd frighten each other. I'd beg my sisters not to, I was so scared, and they'd promise, but the minute I switched it off, they'd call out: *Snakes and ghosts! Witches and spiders!* I practically took flight in my fear and hurry to get back to the safety of my bed."

"And what was the overriding emotion of that experience, Tisi?"

"Well … fear … but also their meanness to me made me feel bad, as though they didn't really love me."

"What are their names and ages?" Honor picked up her pen and began sketching out a family tree.

"Seph is six years older than me, and Ari is four years older."

So she's the baby of the family …

"Such unusual names: where are they from?"

"Greek myths: Persephone, Ariadne and me, Tisiphone."

Honor put down her pen and stared at Tisi. "Tisiphone?"

"My mother was an academic, a classics lecturer, specializing in Greek mythology. I ended up with three names: Tisiphone Alecto Megaera, three sister goddesses."

"And your sisters? Did they get three too?"

"No, they got just the one. My parents couldn't decide out of the three they liked for me and I was to be their last child, so they gave me the lot. They said I could choose when I was older. But I was always called Tisi, I never get called anything else."

Honor jotted down some notes, then looked back at Tisi. "One more memory?"

Tisi gazed into the distance, past Honor, her face flushing. "It's not a good one … it's a bit vague. Me, Seph, and Ari were at home, my Mum was there. Dad came in the house, with two little boys, that we were introduced to, I can't remember their names. I just remember me and my sisters standing in a line, and these two little boys standing opposite us. Then my Mum crying loudly, wailing. And my Dad shouting at her."

"And the overall feeling?"

Tisi made the familiar gesture: her head thrust forward, that strange movement of her long neck, the narrowed eyes. Honor wouldn't have been surprised if a forked tongue had darted from her mouth.

"Hatred. Sheer fucking hatred of my father. And it's never left me. I still loathe him. I *detest* him. *He killed my mother*."

Honor felt a tightening deep inside her body. *What is the purpose of hatred? How do we use it to defend ourselves? From what? Love?* She took a deep breath, attempting to regain some inner calm.

"How did he do that?"

Tisi's eyes glittered. "Slowly. Painfully. Over many years of sheer mental cruelty. A long, slow, agonizing death."

OK. So we're not talking actual criminal murder here. That's a relief.

"It sounds as though there's a complicated story with your parents. Let's set that aside for the moment, and focus on your present situation."

Tisi tossed her head, and the wavy tendrils of her new hairstyle snaked, Medusa-like around her head. "OK."

She's got a long history of damaged relationships with men that must be unpacked slowly, and carefully. I'd better divert her from that now.

"Tell me a little about Jackie, Tisi."

Honor steeled herself. How she wished Eliot's old lover was not called Jackie. She breathed deeply and commenced a mental mantra.

This Jackie is nothing to do with you Honor.

She repeated this to herself several times.

Jackie was an acquaintance of Tisi's (*not her best friend*). She worked with Don, and they had some friends in common.

"What are your feelings towards her?"

Tisi was coldly rational. "I want her to pay for what she has done; I want her to suffer."

This Tisi doesn't frighten me. "In what way?"

"I want to drive her mad. I want to haunt her. I want her to wake up every day filled with dread, scared that she might see me or hear from me."

Honor's heart lifted. *Yes. How brilliant.* Shocked, she gave herself a mental shake, and repeated her mantra three times to herself.

"Have you spoken to her or seen her since you found out about her affair with Don?"

"No. I want to, but Don has asked me not to. I'd like to tell her husband about their affair, for her to feel the risk to her children, the risk that I'm feeling. I want her to suffer more."

Yes. To tell the husband. Perfect. Balanced, a neat, fair symmetry. Let's all know what's going on here. Let's not pretend any more. How about we share the suffering around a bit?

Honor's mantra was evidently useless, but she repeated it to herself again anyway, in an effort to assert her professionalism, and quell her personal feelings. *What's happening to me?*

"You need to think carefully and deliberately, Tisi, about any action you take towards Jackie."

"That's what Don says."

"And that's what stops you?"

"No. Why should I listen to him? What stops me is my fears for the kids. My fear of Don leaving, them losing their Dad."

"I see. Tisi, I want to suggest something else, a technique that will help you keep control of what you do, that will stop you taking action you might regret."

Ann, Honor's Gestalt friend across the hall, had trained her in this process some years previously, once they had become friends. Despite Honor's initial coolness (these Gestalt types were all a bit mystical for her taste) Ann had persisted in talking to her. She had helped Honor when she was dealing with her grief at Eliot's infidelity, and had shown her the technique then. Ann suggested, gently, that Honor might also want to use it for older betrayals, and she did consider it. To her surprise, she discovered that she didn't want to let go of earlier wounds. "So," Ann had said, "you want to go on tormenting yourself do you?"

"This is called the unmailed letter, Tisi. Emphasis on the unmailed .... So don't write this in your email programme, you don't want to be tempted to press the send button. In your letter to Jackie, you write down everything you would like to say to her. What you think of her, and of what she's done. How she's made you feel. What you wish you could say or do to her. What could happen to make you feel better. Everything, unedited. Leave it for a couple of days, then read it again, and edit it according to your thoughts and feelings now. Repeat this process three or four times. You'll find that each edit will alter your thoughts and feelings. Eventually, you'll have a detailed and precise expression of your feelings for Jackie."

Tisi was sitting forward, bright eyed, enlivened. "Fantastic. And then I send it to her, right?"

"No, no, this is not to be sent, ever. Its purpose is for you to clarify your feelings."

"So I go to all that trouble, take all that time, then I don't even tell her? What's the point of that?"

"It can transform and neutralize your feelings. I'd like to see if it's a helpful process for you. Your feelings are running powerfully, in several directions, at this difficult time of your life. I'd like to help you find ways of soothing yourself, and finding ways to keep control. Will you try this, between now and our next meeting?"

"OK." Big sigh.

"And you mustn't send it, that's the whole point. An unmailed letter. Not to be sent. You do understand that? I need you to agree, to promise me that you won't send this letter; can you do that?"

Long pause. "OK." Even bigger sigh.

Honor did not normally feel the need to be so explicit, so insistent.

Tisi left, in body anyway.

Spiritually, Honor carried Tisi home with her that night, and she stayed, stuck in her emotional system, as she cooked a spaghetti bolognese. Her anxiety about Tisi distracted her from her enjoyment of dinner with her family. Later, when Honor went up to her study, Tisi was still on her mind as she scanned her new photos of Bella onto the computer. She made a montage: Bella, Thomas, and Thomas's mother. She would bet everything she owned that there was a blood relation there: the jaw line, the brow perhaps, the set of the eyes. Anyone could see this resemblance, she was sure of it.

Her conversation with Tisi was prompting her. What letter would she like to write? Not to Jackie, it wasn't her that was gnawing at her. It was Madalena. She'd like to say something to her. And it would be short, sweet, and to the point. Idly, she opened her word programme and jotted down a few sentences, then sat back to decide which was the most satisfying. *Where does she live exactly?* She typed into Google: Madalena Morris; and hit the search key; then another search, Jack Norman.

That night, she dreamed a sleepy-eyed snake stirred, deep inside her, signalling, calling her to action.

CHAPTER FIVE

Tell Jack who Bella's father is.

Madalena stared at the six words, in a child's handwriting, on the single sheet of lined paper. She looked around the room, as though to check she was alone. Then she looked at the page again. Carefully, she turned the sheet of paper face down in front of her, on the table, and picked up her coffee cup, took a long sip, then replaced the cup on its saucer.

She picked up the small brown envelope that the note had arrived in, turned it over and inspected the childlike writing: Miss M Morris. Hadn't she seen a similar envelope in Jack's post on the hall table, ten minutes ago, when he'd left for work? She was sure of it: she'd seen him off, handing him his small pile of post. So how come it was in her post now? Were there two letters?

Turning the note over, she read it again. Did she imagine it would have changed while she wasn't looking at it?

Folding the letter back into the envelope, she folded all of it, once, twice, into the palm of her hand. She was going to ignore it; just pretend she'd never received it.

Making her way to the west wing, she shivered slightly and hugged herself. The temperature of the house was maintained for Jack's comfort, so Madalena was permanently chilly. When they'd first moved here, a few years ago, she'd bought herself several cashmere stoles. Jack had frowned and said she looked like an old woman in a shawl, so she gave them to the housekeeper. She would rather suffer any discomfort than look old.

Her thoughts turned to Bella, and the simmering conflict between her and her father. Bella wanted to live full time at their London apartment, near her new friends and her burgeoning career as a model. The whole thing had come to a climax three days ago, with Bella's appearance in the press.

She remembered the look on Jack's face as he'd looked at the pictures; his tense "What the *hell*?" and his angry glare, at her, not at Bella. The intensity of his stare could make Madalena feel that he was looking right through her.

"You'd better talk to her, get some control over her," he had growled.

"She's a woman now. We could trust her to stay in London, don't you think?" She felt the familiar knot of tension in her tummy, as she tried to hold his gaze: a point of principle for her, not to show her anxiety.

"It's not a question of trusting *her*. It's everyone else I don't trust. We have to protect her; anyone could take advantage of her. She's too beautiful for her own good, like you were."

Were. "But I came to no harm …"

"Yes, well, you met me, that's why. God knows where you'd be otherwise. I don't want Bella ending up a single mother or married to the wrong man."

Madalena stifled the impulse to point out that she herself was an unmarried mother. "She's focussed on her career at the moment. I can understand that. After all, I was working when I met you."

Jack had laughed. "*Working?* D'you mean training those kids? I'd hardly call that work."

"What would you call it then? I spent hours drilling them for their competitions."

"I'd call it a hobby. You certainly weren't paid an amount that anyone would consider a living wage. I'm not changing my mind, Bella's not staying alone in London and that's the end of it. She needs to finish with that boy too. Talk some sense into her."

Madalena had pressed her lips together and nodded.

So far, she hadn't succeeded in convincing Bella of the benefits of keeping her father happy.

Entering her dressing room, Madalena looked around at the wide cream wardrobe doors along one long wall, and the closets along the other. The only blot on the streamlined room was her dressing table area, where her hairdryer and several different hair straighteners lay in a tangle of electric flex, alongside a vast range of products all claiming to aid her incessant quest for poker straight hair. She could get it mostly straight, but the slight frizz around her hairline, that last bastion, proved impervious to even the most powerful chemicals in her collection. As a teenager, she had tried shaving it away, an experiment that proved disastrous: it just grew back, even curlier, something she hadn't imagined possible.

She pulled on a pair of track pants and a T-shirt, and glanced in the mirror. Pausing, she looked again, turning to see her side view. There was nothing about her figure that she disliked: she was tall, slim, and toned; the cream of her clothes a striking contrast to her caramel skin. Something about her breasts had caught her eye. Was it her imagination, or did they look a little lower, as though they had sagged slightly? She stripped off from the waist up and looked carefully at her naked breasts. They were three years old, a present from Jack for her fortieth birthday. One of the few things she had enjoyed about her pregnancy was the experience of having breasts. Despite Jack's preference for a larger size, she'd gone for a 32DD. "It'll look classier, Jack," she'd said, and he'd relented.

Looking in the mirror, she turned this way and that, inspecting herself from every angle. Were they drooping? The sense of threat that had gripped her since opening the letter intensified. She was getting older, she was unmarried. Her security felt precarious. She leaned into the mirror, examining the skin around her eyes. Was it time yet? She smoothed out her brow, trying to massage away the frown that had settled on her face since breakfast.

Making her way downstairs to the basement gym, next to the swimming pool, she resolved to have a half hour run to calm herself, and then she'd talk to Bella again.

Revived by a run and a hot shower, Madalena went to Bella's suite, an entire apartment especially for her. Madalena could not walk into the warmth of Bella's suite without a quick memory of the cold emptiness of the small room she had occupied as a child. It was a daily reminder of her gratitude to Jack: that her daughter could live in such comfort.

Against one wall of the sitting room was a small glass desk, upon which Bella kept her laptop, the centre of her social life. Madalena had

43

once asked Bella to show her how to use the computer, a request that was a source of great amusement to Bella and Jack who had exchanged eye rolling looks and hoots of mirth: as if you'd understand it!

Bella took the laptop everywhere with her, so Madalena had no chance of taking a look on her own. How hard could it be? Everyone had a computer, even her personal trainer.

Bella was sitting at her desk, still in her pyjamas, tapping away at her laptop. Madalena settled on the couch along one wall. She could see the computer screen; Bella was chatting to friends on Facebook.

"There's no point starting a war with Daddy, you know it's not the way to get what you want from him."

Bella swung around in her chair, to face her mother and pulled a face. "I'm fed up of pandering to him. I'm twenty-one and a grown woman. I should be able to do what the fuck I want."

"Language, Bella. You should thank your lucky stars, daily, that you've such a generous and protective father. I know I do."

"He's not *your* father." Bella muttered.

"Oh, you know exactly what I mean. He looks after both of us as though we're princesses. Why aren't you grateful?"

"Because I don't need protection any more. And he's only generous to make me do what he wants. Like you do, all the time."

"Yes, I do, that's right. Because that's what makes a good marriage. I please him and he pleases me."

"Marriage? It didn't work, though, did it, Mum?"

Madalena resisted the urge to shake her daughter. She gave a tight smile. "Tell me about Euan. What has he said about the photos? What has his girlfriend said? Has she dumped him?"

Bella wailed. "What am I going to do, Mum? He says he can't leave her because of the baby. But he wants me, too. Why doesn't she dump him? What girl would put up with that?"

"A pregnant one, I should think. Does he want to have a baby?"

"She's five months now, there's no choice. We're going to keep seeing each other in secret. She made him de-friend me on Facebook, but he got another mobile phone so we can speak."

"He really likes you then."

"I love him, Mum, he's really brilliant …"

"I want you to think about your attitude to Daddy. He's not happy with you at all at the moment."

"Once I start earning enough money from modelling he can go and take a running jump."

"I'm not sure you understand just how much money you'd need to live in the luxury you're used to. So if I was you I'd think very carefully indeed before you upset Daddy any more."

"I've got a rich boyfriend now, so maybe I won't have to do what he says quite so much."

Madalena leaned forward, put her hands on Bella's shoulders and faced her squarely. "I'm sure that Euan is nice .... But all he is is the winner of a talent contest. There's no guarantee whatsoever that he's going to be rich or famous for any length of time. If you're looking for a wealthy boyfriend, you'd be better off finding a footballer. They are *seriously* rich."

"People are saying Euan's going to be seriously famous."

"Hmm, we'll see ... maybe so. But he's not necessarily a good bet. If I was you, I'd go for a successful businessman, ideally a good bit older than you, and appreciative of a sexy and devoted young wife."

"Mum, you're fucking pathetic. Like you did, you mean."

"*Language.* If your father heard you .... Well, it certainly hasn't done me any harm. Or you either come to that."

"Mum, he won't even let you have a *computer.*"

When Jack arrived home that evening, Madalena greeted him, as always, with a passionate kiss. Smiling, she looked into his eyes. Was it her imagination, or did he pull back slightly from her? He was looking back at her, with ... what? Something was different in his look wasn't it? Maybe not.

She wasn't going to think about it.

Their new housekeeper, Jinny, a nervous Filipino woman, served dinner.

"Where's Bella this evening?" Jack asked.

"She's gone over to Tamsin's, and she's staying there overnight." Madalena smiled at him.

"No mail for her this morning I hope?"

Since Bella's appearance in the newspaper, she'd received two angry letters from strangers, berating her for stealing another girl's boyfriend.

"No, nothing. Hopefully we've seen the last of that. There are some strange people out there aren't there?" Madalena said.

Jack looked at her across the table, examining her face. "There are, yes." He continued to stare at her, and she looked away.

Jinny came in, took their plates and placed a steaming apple crumble on the table, with a jug of custard.

"Pass me your bowl." Madalena spooned a large portion of dessert in his dish, and poured the hot custard over the top. "There. Your favourite."

In the days when her mother still used to come and stay, she'd said to Madalena, "Why can't he serve himself? He's not crippled is he?" "No," Madalena had replied in surprise, "but he likes me to wait on him. Why not? After all he does for me?" Her mother had grimaced, one eyebrow raised, and said: "I suppose it's a small price to pay."

"Thanks babe." Jack tucked into his dessert.

"How was your day? Is our Dubai trip all arranged? I'm really looking forward to it." To Madalena's relief, Jack turned his attention to the details of their forthcoming trip, business for him, pleasure for her, before going to his study, where he stayed, unusually, long past bedtime.

At breakfast the next morning, Jack was tetchy.

"Where's Bella? What is this? Is she on some kind of strike?"

He would tell anyone who listened that he liked to see his woman and his daughter looking pretty at the breakfast table to start his day off well. He used to say "my two girls" or "my two princesses", until Madalena turned forty, when he'd started calling her his woman, rather than his girl. "Wife" would make her age irrelevant, as Madalena had pointed out. Jack had laughed and given her a playful smack on the bottom.

"Girl, woman, wife … just words Madalena, don't get in a sweat about it."

She'd swallowed a scream, and spent most of the day reminding herself: it's a small price to pay.

"She stayed over at Tamsin's last night, I did tell you."

"Did you talk to her? Get her head straight?"

"I tried. She's still upset with you."

"*She* is upset with *me*? After her behaviour?"

"She really does need to be in London. She's going today, for an audition."

"She doesn't need a job and she needs to stay away from that boy."

"If she agrees not to see Euan, can she at least go for the audition? We can't take everything away from her; she needs either a boyfriend or a job. Personally, I don't know what's wrong with the boyfriend."

"(a) The boyfriend belongs to another young lady; (b) that other young lady is expecting his baby; (c) even without all that, he is not treating our daughter with respect."

It was worse than Madalena thought; once Jack started talking in bullet pointed lists, he was unlikely to change his mind. She waited. She knew he was trying to think of a (d).

"And, (d) she hasn't got a job as such .... Simply a series of auditions and a few odd assignments."

"This audition could be important. It's for a new hair-straightening product, probably a long campaign, with lots of repeats. The exposure could be the making of her. Her agency thinks she has a great chance of getting it."

"Why?"

"They're going for the black hair market: every black girl in the country is trying to get their hair ironed straight."

She could see the muscle in Jack's jaw twitching, his teeth clenched. "What's that got to do with Bella? She's not black."

"She's got that slight kink in her hair ... not as much as mine, but she can get hers looking silky straight, that's the look they want."

"I'm saying this for the last time. She's not going. She needs to do as I say, she doesn't need a job, and she shouldn't be making an exhibition of herself with the pop star."

"But ..."

"Not another word, Madalena, not another word about it, do you hear?"

Madalena turned her still green eyes on him. Holding his gaze, she went to the door, closed it, and locked it. She pulled her dress over her head, undid her bra and released her breasts.

Madalena swayed towards Jack, hooking one thumb into the side of her white lace briefs and pulling them down a little. She stood in front of him, just out of his reach, naked apart from her panties and her high-heeled sandals. Then she leaned towards him, her breasts close to his face. As he leaned to take one into his mouth, she pulled back, and cupped her breasts in her hands.

Then she kneeled down in front of him and unzipped his trousers.

She knew exactly how to get what she wanted from Jack.

Later, when Jinny came in, bringing more toast, Madalena and Jack were sitting in their customary places. The only discernible difference to ten minutes earlier was that Jack was smiling.

"Shall I get Joe to take Bella to London?" Madalena asked.

"Good plan, I don't like her driving all that way on her own. I can manage without him today; make sure he brings her home this evening though."

47

Madalena went to the front door with Jack. Giving her a last warm hug, off he went, whistling to himself, a man satisfied in all his appetites, contented and happy. Or so Madalena hoped. When she saw how happy she made him she wondered why he didn't make her as happy, simply by marrying her. He said it was because (a) married women always let themselves go physically, and (b) all his married friends complained of a lack of sex (with their wives anyway), (c) his mother would probably have a heart attack.

Madalena stood at the door watching him, waiting to give a last wave, before she closed the front door, and leaned against it. He was all right wasn't he? Everything was still the same, surely? Nothing had changed: her safe and comfortable life was as secure today as it was yesterday.

CHAPTER SIX

Madalena was lost in Dubai airport. She didn't know what to do, or where to go next. Jack had brought her here, checked her luggage in, got her boarding pass, and seen her through the departure gates. Now she was alone.

She always travelled with Jack, who took care of everything, so she wasn't in the habit of paying attention. She was returning home, because Bella was in trouble again. Jack couldn't leave: he was in the middle of his business deal.

Madalena hadn't enjoyed the last few days. Had she imagined it, or was there something slightly different about Jack? She had caught him staring at her once in a way she didn't recognize, as though he was reading something in her face. Most uncomfortable. She hadn't been sleeping well, often lying awake, listening to Jack's contented breathing, staring into the dark night, wondering who could have sent that letter?

An encounter with one of Jack's clients had led to a familiar argument. "How nice to meet your lovely wife," he'd said, and Jack had laughed and said "She's not my wife; I can't get her to marry me."

"Why not though, Jack? Why not?" She hated to hear the slight pleading in her voice, when she spoke to him about it later. She still dreamed that one day they would go off on one of these luxurious trips and Jack would surprise her with a wedding. She didn't travel anywhere without a simple cream or white dress, just in case.

"We've been happy all these years, Madalena. Let's not spoil it."

"I'm getting older, Jack, I'd like some security. What if you died?"

Jack, watching her, spoke slowly. "We dealt with this years ago. You're well looked-after in my will, you know that."

"I've been good to you, all these years, faithful and devoted. I've borne you a lovely daughter."

Jack's jaw tensed. Madalena could see his teeth gritting. "Hmm … yes …. But then I guess you sowed your wild oats before we met, didn't you? You certainly had plenty of choice."

"I always chose you. Maybe you think I'm not good enough for you, like your mother."

Jack's face was hard. "This is nothing to do with what my mother thinks. Let's stop this conversation right now."

Madalena knew exactly what she could do to end this argument. But for once, she simply didn't feel like it. She walked out of the room.

Now, lost and uncertain, confused by the echoing noises of the airport, Madalena tried to get her bearings, oblivious to the fact that everyone was staring at her. When she first met Jack, he pointed out: "See how everyone is staring at you? People can't quite believe your beauty. And you're all mine."

Occasionally, someone would approach her. "Are you someone famous? Can I have your autograph?"

She had cultivated an air of aloof detachment to discourage people and, for those who persisted, a disdainful stare.

Seeing a large board, she went and stared at it, hoping it might offer up some meaning. Where was the club lounge? Jack had been emphatic. "Don't go to the first class lounge, will you? It was short notice, I could only get club. Look for the club lounge, OK?"

But she couldn't see any signs to help her. Looking around, she inadvertently caught the eye of the man standing beside her, and blurted out: "I'm looking for the club lounge. D'you know where it is?"

"Show me your boarding pass?" He spoke with an American accent. Obediently, she handed it to him.

"Same flight as me; follow me, I'm going the same way."

Relieved, Madalena walked along beside him, trotting, as he strode ahead, silent. He was dressed all in black and his dark hair was slightly greying. Madalena knew he was gay. She could tell this in an instant,

50

from the total lack of interest in his eyes, the look that she was so used to seeing in the face of every straight man that looked at her, however briefly.

They arrived at the club lounge, and she made her way to the ladies' cloakroom. Back in the lounge, refreshed, she found a comfortable chair, collected a drink and settled down to wait, checking to see where the American was, so she could follow him when her flight was called. She picked up a magazine from the pile on the table next to her: the latest copy of *Grazia,* the one causing all the trouble.

"TEMPTRESSES!" screamed the headline on the front.

Bella's picture, along with half a dozen other minor celebrities, illustrated the story, a long article, with a commentary from a psychologist. Madalena hadn't yet read it in full. Her attempts to read reminded her of her school days: "Madalena Morris, are you stupid, lazy, or both?" By the time she was fourteen, some clever sticks had discovered dyslexia and Madalena was labelled: not stupid, or lazy, just dyslexic. Is that some sort of illness?, her mother had asked. By the time Bella was also found to be dyslexic, the world had changed: an expensive school, dedicated support, and numerous friends in the same boat left her unscathed.

She would have another go at reading it on the plane; she'd got the gist, but she needed to go over it again; she hadn't quite grasped what Jack was making all the fuss about. She'd do some yoga breathing to relax and go through it again.

Yesterday, when Jack had seen the article, he rang his assistant, barking out instructions to get Madalena on a plane home as soon as possible.

He glowered at Madalena. "I told you Bella wasn't to go to London to see him. For God's sake get a grip on the girl."

Madalena restrained herself from pointing out: she's not me; she can do what she likes. "I don't know how we can stop her. She's an adult."

"It's easy. I'll stop her allowance. We can't have her all over the press like this; my mother'll have a fit. Have you seen what they're saying about her?"

"She's old enough to know her own mind, surely? The publicity can't hurt her career, anyway."

Jack had tutted. "Career? A few pictures in a hair advertisement. Hardly a career."

"It's a start. Maybe she won't need to work anyway. Euan seems crazy about her."

"She could have anyone. Why did she pick a boy that's already got a girlfriend? And a pregnant one at that?"

"That's not her problem, that's up to Euan. And you can't help who you fall in love with, as you and I know."

A loudspeaker crackled into life, interrupting her reverie. Her flight was being called. She picked up her bag and coat and followed the American at a distance.

Boarding the plane, she met the stewardesses with her habitual remoteness. Early in their relationship, Jack had accused her of flirting with every man she met, so she had perfected the art of looking at people without making eye contact, by looking in the general direction of their neck or their hair.

She was directed to her seat and sat down, relieved to have got to the right place, virtually alone, under her own steam. Leaning her head back, she closed her eyes, and took several deep breaths. The routines of the aircraft were underway: seatbelts, hot towels, drinks, and newspapers.

An exasperated tutting close by disturbed her. The American was attempting to settle himself in the seat to her right and facing her: the opposite flatbed seat. The folding privacy screen between them was open.

The American turned, scowling, saw her and gave a curt nod, then took hold of the privacy screen between them and tried to raise it. With an irritable huffing he pulled on it hard, but it wouldn't move. Without looking at Madalena he accosted a passing stewardess who tried to close the screen, failed, and called one of her colleagues, who also failed.

"It's broken, clearly," the American pointed out. "Can you move me to another seat please?"

Madalena sat back in her seat and closed her eyes, irritated by his blatant rudeness. She wanted the screen closed too, but he spoke as though she wasn't even there; she felt tense, and annoyed by his unpleasantness.

"I'm very sorry, sir, there are no spare seats, the plane's completely full."

"Oh for God's sake, this is ridiculous. I expect to be able to sleep in privacy. The price I've paid for this ticket, it's unbelievable."

The stewardess, all diplomacy, suggested he settle himself down, she'd bring him a drink. "Remember sir, once you fold the bed down you can't see the other passengers anyway."

What a horrible job, having to soothe the annoyance of such a rude man. Then she realized that she spent much of her time doing exactly that for Jack. And no pay packet. Not an obvious one anyway.

Sitting up, ignoring the American who was still sorting out his bed space, she picked up the dinner menu. The stewardess, passing close to Madalena, gave her a sympathetic glance, mouthed the word "Sorry" with a roll of her eyes to the American, and offered her a glass of wine. On impulse, she accepted: maybe it would help. Taking a tentative sip, she pursed her lips and shuddered. As a child, she had seen her mother drunk almost daily. As a teenager, she had got drunk once, on cheap cider. It had made her cry, publicly, for a long time; then she was violently sick, again publicly. She had felt ill for several days after. Although she hated the physical illness, what disturbed her most was the shame she felt at showing her feelings: she had let everyone see who she really was and what she really felt. She had sworn that she would never touch alcohol again, and she hadn't, except for an occasional sip of champagne at family celebrations.

Pulling the copy of *Grazia* out of her bag, she turned to the article about Bella, and with fierce concentration, attempted to decipher the words. The warmth of the wine flowing through her veins quickly relaxed her. This was good; she *could* read when she tried.

Temptresses!

Women who steal men from other women, who seek the challenge of taking a man away from his woman: what drives them? What motivates them? Such man-stealers are usually strikingly beautiful women who can take their pick; so why do they pick somebody else's man?

Bella Norman is the gorgeous model girlfriend of Euan Docherty, who's currently topping the charts with his first single. So what's the problem? Euan already has a girlfriend. And she's five months pregnant with his child.

So why would a girl like Bella go for a boy like Euan?

This was the thing that had got Jack so wound up. The pregnant girlfriend. She looked up from the magazine, took another sip of wine, and inadvertently caught the eye of the American. She looked away quickly. Rude bastard.

"Look, excuse me. Sorry. I must apologize."

Had he read her mind? Madalena waved a hand, mumbled, and picked up her magazine again.

Girls who steal men from other women are usually acting out deep complexes in their own personalities. The woman competes with her mother for the father she adores. Man-stealers are usually Daddy's girls, keen to show Daddy that they're better than Mummy: better looking, cleverer, superior in every way.

"No, really I'm sorry. Bad day. Very bad day. Not that that's an excuse to take it out on a total stranger. Unforgiveable. Since we're going to be travel companions, let's at least be civil. Not that you haven't been of course. My name's Bud." He thrust his hand towards her. "Let's start again. How d'you do?"

Madalena gave his hand the most perfunctory shake, nodded at him with a tight smile, and turned back to her magazine. Did he really expect her to be chummy now? Honestly, some people.

"What are you reading?" He was leaning across the divide between them.

Could she say mind your own business? She wanted to. What an irritating man. She looked at him coldly. He raised his hands in surrender.

"OK, sorry. No, I see, sorry to bother you, OK." And he settled back in his chair, apparently prepared to leave her alone, thank heavens. He called the stewardess and ordered a bottle of champagne.

Madalena continued her reading, starting on the commentary by a psychologist:

> *Stealing a man from another woman makes them feel they are superior to their mother in every way. This kind of behaviour needs to be viewed as a metaphor: the woman they are stealing from is a symbol of their own mother. She is essentially saying: "Look at me, Mum! I'm better than you! And Dad loves me the most! So there!" In that respect the man-stealers' behaviour is less about getting the man, and more about a triumphant display in relation to the woman. This is the female chest-beating equivalent to the alpha male, the way a woman shows herself as the queen of the female jungle.*

Goodness. That was a bit deep wasn't it? Though Bella was definitely a Daddy's girl, there was no doubt about that. She sipped some more wine; now she'd got used to the taste, it didn't seem quite so bitter. Yes, Bella was a Daddy's girl; but she wasn't as the article said, she really wasn't. But a Daddy's girl, yes there was no denying that. Did Bella have any idea at all just how lucky she was? How Madalena wished she'd been a Daddy's girl. An anybody's girl. She felt the tension behind her eyes, and she blinked, trying to hold back the tears that welled.

"Look, here's a proper sorry." Bud, with a contrite smile, was passing across to her a flute of pink champagne. His smile faded to concern as

Madalena looked up at him in surprise. "Oh no, you're upset, oh I'm sorry, what's the matter?"

Madalena looked down, putting a hand to her eyes, wiping away a tear, then leaned forward to take the champagne. "It's OK, nothing, I'm fine. Thank you for the champagne, that's very kind."

"I'm really so sorry, I certainly didn't mean to upset you that much, most unlike me, had a hideous time in Dubai."

"It wasn't you, don't worry, it's OK." Goodness, this champagne was lovely, sweeter tasting than the wine. She took a deep swig, looked at him; a thought struck her: "What was so hideous? What happened?"

"You don't want to know. I thought I was going to find out something, a family secret, but I got let down at the last minute. Put me in a dreadful mood. Disappointment's horrible isn't it?"

Madalena was feeling light-headed; she tried to concentrate on what he was saying. "A family secret? How mysterious."

Bud waved his hand dismissively. "Over, it's over, I'm never going to know now, I have to forget it." He leaned forward and held his glass towards hers. "Cheers. And sorry again."

Madalena clinked her glass against his. "Cheers."

"Here, let me give you a refill." He leaned over and topped up her almost empty glass, catching sight of the magazine on her table. "What are you reading?"

"*Grazia.*"

"Don't you just love all the gossip? Poor celebrities, they can't move any more without being splashed all over the rag mags."

Madalena smiled politely, and picked up her magazine again.

"Who are you reading about?"

Madalena had drunk a glass of wine and one and a half glasses of champagne, more alcohol than she had drunk in her entire adult life. She couldn't find the energy to blank Bud; he seemed desperate to make up for his earlier behaviour. "My daughter. She's in *Grazia.*"

"Oh my! Really? You have a daughter in *Grazia*? You must be famous, you look as though you could be."

Madalena laughed. "I'm not. But she's becoming famous."

"What for? Let me see. Show me. Can I have a look?"

Madalena passed the magazine across the barrier.

"Wow! What a beauty. Takes after her Mom."

The catering trolley stopped to serve their dinner. Madalena was hungry; she'd been drinking alcohol on an empty stomach she realized. No wonder it had gone to her head so quickly. She tucked into her chicken meal, and Bud ate his steak as he scanned the article. He glanced at Madalena, his eyebrows raised, his smile gone. "Jeez."

Madalena frowned, and took another swig of champagne. She put down her fork, not as hungry as she'd first thought. "Her father's very upset. That's why I'm going home. The press are besieging her, paparazzi everywhere. She's had some hate mail, we had to hire a bodyguard."

"Jeez. Some people feel strongly about things don't they?"

"I don't know why they blame *her*. He's the one with the pregnant girlfriend."

Bud leaned across to refill her glass. Madalena lifted it in front of her face, to watch the bubbles fizzing pink to the surface. It looked a bit fuzzy, she looked at Bud, and he looked a bit blurred too. Gosh he was good looking; she hadn't noticed that before, lovely eyes.

He lifted his glass in a toast. "Here … let's drink to Bella? Or … you … whatever your name is."

"Madalena." She felt light-headed and ready to laugh at anything. She pushed away her meal tray. The champagne seemed to be spinning cotton wool around her, muffling her conversation with Bud: his voice sounded a long way away.

"Here's to you then, Madalena. Great name. I guess you get called Mad."

Madalena giggled. "Nobody's allowed to call me Mad, my mother said. It's Madalena."

"Here's to Mad and Bud, then."

They touched glasses and said together, "Mad and Bud" then dissolved into laughter.

"I must stop, I feel a bit weird."

"After two glasses of champagne?"

"Three. And I had some wine. I don't normally drink alcohol."

"Never?"

"Never. Can I have the magazine back now? I need to read the rest of it." Bud passed the magazine back.

"I was reading what the psychologist said." Madalena leafed through to the right page.

"That she's a Daddy's girl?"

Madalena felt confused and fuddled. "Bella's … a … Daddy's girl? Mmm …. What else does it say?"

"Let's have a bottle of mineral water." Bud said. "I think you need to stop drinking for a while. You haven't eaten much, maybe eat a little more? Some bread?" He picked up her champagne flute and placed it on his own tray table, and called the stewardess to bring some water.

"Aww … I'd like to drink some more. I'm enjoying myself."

"You need some water first."

"Tell me some more, go on. Hang on, let me get this right. Bella's a Daddy's girl … she's more beautiful and clever than me. So what does all that mean?" Her words were beginning to slur.

"Read the rest of it, and see." Bud turned to the stewardess who had brought a large bottle of water. He poured a glass and passed it to Madalena, who was staring at the magazine article.

"My eyes have gone a bit funny, it looks blurry." Madalena squinted at the magazine, then squeezed her eyes shut and opened them again. "It's no good, I can't see it properly. You read it to me." She gave the magazine back to Bud.

"You want me to read it out to you?"

"Yes, go on, the bit after it says about the Daddy's girl."

"OK. You sure? Drink some more of that water. Here goes. *Being the queen of the female jungle has its upsides … you attract the best mate: the alpha male, the man who is willing and able to devote resources to his woman and their children. But take care, alpha queen … you may find yourself very unpopular with other women, even hated if you are too blatant in your competitive behaviour. You won't be liked, and for good reason … a recent study showed that women who try to steal someone else's mate tend to be disagreeable, untrusting, immodest, harsh-minded, mean, unreliable, adulterous, and highly focused on sex. History is awash with mythical figures who embody such women: the sirens, the Lorelei, the Jezebel. These women and the damage they do are as old as time itself.*"

"*I am not.* I'm not any of those things. How could they say that? It's not true." Mad was vaguely aware that the shrill tone of her voice was attracting glances.

"The article's referring to Bella, why are you taking it personally? Have some more water."

"Bella's not like that either, neither of us are. We know what we want, that's all."

"You and Bella are the same?"

"No. I never had a Daddy, never … never …"

"Everyone has a Dad at some point, however briefly."

Madalena sank back into her seat, her body sagging, and put her head back, closing her eyes. She felt a tear coursing slowly down her cheek.

Bud leaned across and laid his hand on her arm. "You OK?"

"My Dad, if you can call him that, was a sailor, in the port for one night only. He doesn't even know I exist." Madalena folded her arms on her lap, rested her head down, and cried.

Bud leaned forward and patted her shoulder. The stewardess stopped, and looked enquiringly at Bud, who shook his head.

Eventually, as her tears subsided, he asked if she'd like a tea or coffee? She sat up and reached for her bag, for a tissue. "Black coffee please …. I'll just go and tidy up." She edged out of her seat and went to the toilet. Staring in the mirror, she tried to focus. What the hell are you doing? she asked her reflection; talking to a total stranger like this? Who is he? You know nothing about him. Jack would have a fit if he could see you now.

Returning, immaculate once more, and calmer, she drank her coffee. "I'm sorry, I don't know what came over me … the champagne went to my head. You're so kind, thank you." She still felt slightly giddy, but the coffee worked quickly, and she became steadier. "How about you, Bud? Why are you going to England?"

Bud was a divorce lawyer, working on a complex and high profile international case. He lived in New York, had been on holiday in Dubai, and was now going to London to see his client, the wife in the case. "I'm known for winning big settlements for women. Especially trophy wives being traded in for a younger model."

Madalena was impressed. "You must know loads of famous people."

"And they behave just as badly as anyone else in a divorce, believe me. Worse, in fact. There's usually so much money at stake, and they fight tooth and nail to keep it. You've never seen such bad behaviour. But then, I've never seen worse behaviour in a divorce than I saw in my own parents. So nothing shocks me. My Dad was a divorce lawyer; he defended himself in his own divorce from my mother. Nightmare."

"What happened?"

"He was a complete and utter bastard."

"Why? What did he do?" Madalena could feel her heart beating faster.

"Blackmailed her basically. Knew some secret from her past, said he'd tell us about it if she didn't agree to his stingy terms."

"The secret you thought you'd find out in Dubai?"

Bud puffed out his cheeks, and shrugged his shoulders. "They're both dead. I thought I'd found someone who knew it. I was wrong. I'll never know now."

"That's sad."

"Yes, well, the lesson is, don't get divorced. Better still, don't get married."

"Not something I'll ever have to worry about. I've been with my partner for twenty years, but he's against getting married."

"D'you mind?"

Madalena shrugged. "He's funny about it. He's been married before, you see. Plus, his mother can't stand me, thinks I'm not good enough for him. Maybe he thinks things'll change between us."

"It puts you in a difficult legal position."

Madalena was feeling light headed and free. Perhaps she could tell Bud; after all he was a *lawyer*.

"Everything's in his name. I've been worried about it recently. It's not just Bella who's received hate mail."

"What d'you mean?"

"I got a letter, a few days after Bella first got in the papers. Not exactly a letter, a short note, quite threatening, actually now I come to think of the words."

"A posted letter or an email?"

"A posted letter. Written by a child by the looks of it."

"What did it say?" Bud was leaning forward, listening closely.

"It said: Tell Jack who Bella's father is." Madalena sat back, pressing her hand across her mouth. Saying those words out loud shook her. Someone had really sent her that letter.

Bud raised his eyebrows. "Jack's not Bella's father?"

"Of course he is! Jack *is* her father."

"Sounds like somebody's not so sure." Bud was looking into her eyes.

She tried to hold his gaze, but her eyes slid away, and she blinked rapidly. "Of course she's Jack's daughter. Of course."

"Someone seems to think there may be some doubt."

The stewardess interrupted them, took away their food trays and empty glasses, and they paused to stow away their tables.

Madalena realized that Bud was deadly serious. Gone was his humour and drama. She felt sick. She didn't know what it was to confide in anyone, or to tell anyone truths about what she thought and felt. Now, she found that confession hadn't unburdened her; it had simply made her aware of the trouble she was in.

Bud leaned across to continue their conversation. "D'you have the letter?"

Madalena shook her head.

"Where is it?"

"I burned it." Madalena bit her lip.

"What? Are you mad?"

They both started to laugh. Madalena felt light headed. How comforting, to have a friend, like having a brother, she imagined. Kind and concerned, but also funny and affectionate. She wondered if he had a boyfriend. Not really the sort of question she could ask.

"Why destroy it? It's evidence … how else can you discover who sent it? You checked the postmark first, right? You know where it was posted at least?"

"No I didn't. I burned the letter and the envelope."

"Why didn't you tell Jack?"

"I thought it was better to forget the whole thing."

"D'you have any idea at all who might have sent it?"

"Not a clue."

"No enemies?"

"No."

"You've got at least one, even if you can't think who. Someone who wants to hurt you, has a grudge against you. I've seen this sort of thing before; what lies behind poison pen letters is quite … well, quite poison."

"What d'you mean?" Madalena felt breathless.

"Someone's out to hurt you. Surely you can see that?"

Madalena stared at him, mute with fear. Bud leaned forward and patted her shoulder. "Just think about who might want to hurt you, that's all."

"Thank you, yes, I will." A thought struck her. "What will I do then, though?"

Bud raised his hand, shook his head. "One step at a time, think about who it could be. I'll help you."

"I don't …"

"I mean as a friend, that's all, OK?"

Madalena's eyes filled. "You're so kind. I've been worried sick."

"I can't bear the way men treat women sometimes. I saw it up close with my own parents. Horrible."

The cabin lights dimmed, the passengers were busy pulling out their beds and bedding and settling down for a few hours' sleep. Madalena rang the bell for the stewardess, standing aside so that she could make her bed up for her.

"Good night, Mad. Sleep well." Bud smiled at her, then settled down, disappearing below the lower half of the screen.

"Good night, Bud." Slipping off her shoes, Madalena lay down and pulled the cover over her. Lying on her back made her feel a little dizzy, as though the plane was spinning around her. Sitting up again, she tried to settle on her side, which was a bit more comfortable. She stared into the dark. Who could have written the letter? Her mind wandered, half dream-like, to glimpses of people she knew, presenting her with a vivid image of Thomas, looking at her, smiling, spilling laughter into her eyes. She turned, restless. Remembering. She nestled her head into the pillow.

CHAPTER SEVEN

Violent sunlight pierced Madalena's eyelids. She raised a shaky hand to cover her eyes. Vague noises assaulted her ears: the stewardess raising the window blind, and the clink of glasses of iced orange juice being placed on trays. Why was it all so loud? There was a sound beneath it all, throbbing and thumping; was that the sound of her own heartbeat? In her head?

She licked her lips, several times. Sitting up slowly, every movement jolting her head, she carefully uncovered her eyes and opened them slightly. The flood of light made her squeeze them shut again quickly.

A low laugh came from close by, and a voice: "Good morning."

In the course of her everyday life, Madalena had three straightforward categories to describe how she felt. There was Good—how she felt most of the time. There was Not So Good, which was how she felt in response to any obstruction to what she wanted, such as her (rare) inability to persuade Jack of something, or the failure of shops to stock the items she wanted. And finally there was Terrible, for anything to do with Jack's mother and Jack's refusal to marry her; and that was also how she'd felt (or possibly worse) since she got that damn letter.

She found now that all these categories failed her.

Absolutely Terrible presented itself as a new category, or if she'd been inclined to bad language, which she wasn't, Truly Bloody Awful would have been a more accurate description of how she felt physically.

Madalena never swore, not even to herself. Jack hated bad language, especially in women: he'd have a heart attack if he heard the way Bella and her friends spoke.

She wondered if she was dying, or had caught some terrible virus from the stale air of a night flight. Should she ask for a doctor?

"A little hungover, maybe?" Bud leaned over the divide between their seats, and handed her a glass of water, which she took and sipped gratefully.

She learned that sudden movements had a terrible impact on her head. Of course, the wine. Was this how her mother felt most mornings? No wonder she needed a drink again so early, if she did. For the first time in her life, she almost felt sympathy for her mother.

Absolutely terrible was a good general description of how she felt at the dawning splinters of memory of her discussion with Bud last night. What on earth had got into her, to say so much, to a stranger? Fear, that's what. She was scared stiff, scared of losing everything. She tried to remember what they'd discussed. She remembered the magazine article, the horrible suggestions about Bella. And then, oh no, the letter. *She had told Bud about the letter.* She tried to think ... had she told him anything else? Yes, about her missing father. The second time in her life she'd got drunk, the second time she had revealed too much about herself. No wonder she'd learned not to drink alcohol. Never again, Madalena, never again.

Giving Bud a weak smile, she waved a "can't talk at the moment" gesture, and leaned out to take a second glass of water from the tray of a passing stewardess.

Sipping the water, she tried to remember more about the conversation.

There was something else she was feeling, alongside the absolutely terrible that she couldn't identify, that was outside her experience. It wasn't good, exactly, but a variation. How would she describe it? Hopeful? Something was missing? Her worry, her anxiety about the letter ... it hadn't gone away, but telling Bud about it did give her new hope. He said he would help her, and he was a lawyer, so maybe he could.

"Take these, they'll help your head."

She took the two tablets he handed her, gave a grateful nod, and swallowed them. "Thanks. Sorry about last night."

"No worries. It was nice, I enjoyed talking to you. Helped me forget my own disappointment."

Madalena rose slowly to her feet and reached for her sponge bag. She needed to wash, clean her teeth, brush her hair. She leaned against the back of the seat in front of her, to steady herself. The effort of being vertical had created a dizzy spell; motes of light rushed past her eyes, and her head, resettling itself on her shoulders, seemed to weigh a ton.

Walking slowly, holding on to the seat backs, she made her way to the toilet.

Looking at herself in the mirror, she saw, in the dullness of her eyes and the unhealthy tinge to her skin, her resemblance to her mother.

Once back in her seat she felt a little better, physically at least, as Bud's headache pills did their work; and she felt fresher for her wash.

"How you doing?"

She gave a vague smile in Bud's direction, and busied herself tidying her bed and space, calling for the stewardess to help her fold her bed up. Remembering last night's conversation, she felt terrible, but in an unfamiliar way: probably something to do with telling someone such personal things, she thought. As though an ancient stone had shifted, releasing a violent hiss of steam. She wished she could revert to the sense of safety she normally felt in the depths of her own privacy, even though she felt lighter for having expressed her fears.

The distractions of the breakfast service kept her busily detached from Bud. She was starving hungry, opting for the full English breakfast rather than her usual light meal of fruit and yoghurt. She began to feel a little better, physically at least.

Bud was undeterred by her repertoire of disdainful expressions, her small discouraging gestures, and rejecting shrugs. "Talk to me?"

Madalena stared at him. Why was he so cheerful? (His words churned up the anxiety that sat, waiting for her, like a frightened new-born creature, in the pit of her stomach.) She shrugged her shoulders and sighed.

"There's no point trying to avoid it, this won't go away you know."

Madalena nodded slowly, and looked him directly in the eyes. "I said too much to you last night. I feel a bit ..." She pressed her lips together and shook her head.

"Embarrassed? You can trust me, I won't tell a soul."

Embarrassed, yes, that was it; a bit like the terrible feeling she had around Jack's mother. Or maybe worse: ashamed. Feeling as though she'd done something bad and everybody was staring at her, disgusted.

"I couldn't sleep for thinking about your question. Who could have sent the letter?"

"Why not just tell Jack and let him sort it out?" Bud was watching her intently. "I've just realized something about your amazing eyes: you almost never blink. It makes you look like a doll."

Madalena widened her eyes and pulled a face. "Everyone says that. You don't know Jack. Anyone who knows him would know why I couldn't possibly tell him."

"Surely he wouldn't want you hurt or threatened? Maybe he'd understand: Bella's in the papers—it's brought your family to the attention of all sorts of weirdos, people trying to get money possibly: maybe the letter writer is going to try to blackmail you. If you keep this a secret from Jack, they could succeed."

Madalena's sense of unease was rising. "I can't. You don't understand Jack, what he's like."

"If I was him, I'd just want to find the bastard and wring his neck."

Madalena smiled at him, touched by his chivalry. "Jack wants, above all else, complete and total loyalty from his family and staff. I saw what he did a few years ago, when he thought his son was disloyal to him."

Madalena told Bud the story of Jack's son, John, who had, on leaving school, gone to work in his father's firm. This arrangement had worked well for a couple of years: John learned about the business, he had a flair for the sales side of things; like his father he was street smart and engaging. Jack was even planning to add "& Son" to the company name, and thinking how to manage John's experience so that he could eventually take over the business. Then, something happened. Madalena was not entirely clear on the details of it. But it was to do with a contract that John was working on: Jack wasn't happy about it in some way. John had his own views. There was a huge falling out, over an allegation of cash, in brown paper bags, being used to oil the wheels. All Madalena knew was that for a few days, Jack came home fuming about John.

"If it's one thing I can't stand it's disloyalty. Stupidity, even laziness, I can put up with, for a short while anyway. But disloyalty, I can't tolerate it. After all I've done for him. After all I've taught him. Think of it. The nerve. To go against me like this. Who does he think he is? He's a nothing without me, a nobody. Does he think he could have built this empire like I did? Aged fifteen and fatherless? Does he? Does he really think so? I don't think so."

Madalena, frightened, had put her arms around him. "Maybe there's been a misunderstanding. John wouldn't want to upset you, I know he wouldn't."

Jack had shaken her off. "How would you know that? And another thing while we're on the subject, I don't like the way he looks at you. I've seen him. You must have noticed. Don't tell me you haven't. The disloyalty. The sheer fucking disloyalty, that's what I can't stand, after all I've done for him. I'm not having it Madalena, I am not fucking putting up with it, the little bastard. I'll have him over this, I'm telling you."

Madalena, scared, was silent. Jack almost never swore. She had never seen him so angry. People didn't generally cross Jack. If they did, he fired them. Most people in his firm had witnessed a summary dismissal, or heard about one. People learned quickly around Jack, as Madalena had. But John was his son, so it was altogether different; he wasn't really going to fire him, surely? But in the end, he did.

"You can fuck off out of here and don't show your face anywhere near me, do you understand? I can't stand disloyalty from anyone let alone from my own son. Son! Huh! I don't even consider you my son, I want nothing more to do with you."

Jack's ex-wife, Pat, had begged Jack to forgive him, and had even spoken to Madalena, for the first time in her life, asking her to try and influence Jack, but Madalena decided to keep out of it. John was distraught: he phoned and wrote to his father, apologizing. Jack was implacable. Jack's daughter Linda visited, pleaded her brother's case. None of it made any difference.

"I don't have a son," he said.

"So you see, if I did anything that might even hint at any disloyalty …" Madalena made a throat cutting gesture.

"Jeez. Hard-hearted bastard. He sounds worse than my Dad, which I would have thought impossible."

"If he can do that to his own son."

"I'm convinced. You can't tell him, I see that. I know what men like Jack are capable of, only too well. I saw what my father did to my mother. What are you doing with a guy like that? Oh, forget I asked, I know the deal."

"I know you're right, Bud, I have to find out who sent that letter."

"Yes. And what will you do then?"

Madalena hesitated. She hadn't thought about this. What would she do? "Stop them I suppose. Do something to stop them; I don't know really …"

"Whoever it is, they're in a complete stew. You'd have to hope you could soothe them, calm them down a bit, stop them doing something else."

"What else? What could they do?" Madalena could feel a knot of tension across the back of her neck.

"Write another letter? Go and see Jack? Whoever it is, they think they know something, and they want to hurt you. Who believes they know something that could hurt you?"

Madalena raised her shoulders, circled them slightly in an attempt to ease the tension. She shook her head.

"What about Pat? You wouldn't help her with the John and Jack thing … tell me about her? Does she know anything that could hurt you?"

Madalena gazed passed Bud, a small frown between her eyes. "I've never really thought much about it. She doesn't like me, obviously: Jack was married to her when I met him, and I was with somebody else too. Jack left her, so he could be with me. She wouldn't let her children see me for some years. She named me in the divorce actually."

"Understandable. The only legal way to hit back at the woman who steals your man." Bud looked at her, his eyebrows raised. "Where's that magazine?"

Madalena gave a short laugh. "I don't buy that man-stealer stuff. Jack made his own choice. Pat's always been nice enough to Bella. She sends her a birthday card every year, from her, John, and Linda. The kids all get on OK, though obviously we don't see John any more."

"Would she have any reason to question Bella's paternity?"

Madalena pursed her lips. She was doing it again: talking to a stranger, about personal secrets. Look what fear was doing to her. "I wouldn't have thought so, no. Nobody has any reason to, really, but you never know with gossip do you?"

"What gossip?"

"Pat never re-married, she has a big circle of friends, middle-aged women: I expect they gossip all the time. Bella's in the papers: who knows what sort of things people think or say?"

"What about the guy you were with when you met Jack? What happened to him?"

"Oh …." Madalena gave a vague wave of her hand. "Nothing important, an on and off thing."

"Who was he?"

Madalena squirmed slightly under Bud's direct questions. "Thomas. We weren't that big a thing, just casual, he was involved with someone else anyway."

"Could he have written the letter?"

Madalena laughed. "Hardly."

Bud looked at her enquiringly.

"He's dead." She felt a slight pressure, behind her eyes, at the thought of Thomas.

"His girlfriend then?"

"Oh, all these questions. You're like a detective." Madalena leaned back in her chair and closed her eyes.

"Worse, I'm a lawyer; I can't help myself."

"She married Thomas in the end, then moved to London after his death. I've never seen her since."

"Could it be her?"

"It was twenty years ago. She probably wouldn't even remember my name."

"D'you remember hers?"

"Of course I do. Honor Sinclair."

"Then I think you'll find she remembers yours too. May be she thinks that Thomas is Bella's father?"

These dreadful questions. Madalena felt hot with embarrassment. "People can think what they like. But they'd be wrong."

"Might Pat have come to the same conclusion?"

"Oh I don't know. Stop pestering me. I have to sort out my things. Drop it, let's just drop it."

A stewardess bustled by, collecting breakfast trays and offering final drinks before landing. Madalena, relieved to be free of Bud's questions, began to collect her things. She glanced again at the cover of *Grazia*. The trouble this was causing, she thought. Who was looking at pictures of Bella and wondering? What was it they were seeing? She opened the magazine and examined the close up photo of Bella's face. Could anyone imagine she might resemble Thomas? Most people saw Bella as a younger version of her mother, almost identical. She hardly looked like Jack at all.

The loudspeaker crackled into life with its routine instructions. Seat-belts on, seat backs up straight, tables stowed away, bags tucked under seats. Obediently, she carried out her tasks, and settled back for landing.

Madalena and Bud disembarked together and walked to passport control.

"Where are you off now, Bud?"

"Central London, meeting my client. Early dinner with my cousin later, then the overnight plane back to New York. How about you?"

"Our chauffeur's meeting me, taking me to our London place, for a show-down with Bella. I'm not looking forward to that."

Through passport control, they headed through to the baggage carousel. Bud, travelling light, had no luggage to collect.

"Here." Bud handed her a card. "This is how you can contact me. Stay in touch?"

Madalena took the card and smiled at him. "Thanks, yes, I'd like to."

"Just call me, or text, OK? You can rely on me."

Madalena looked down, swallowed a lump in her throat, and nodded her head. "Thank you, that's so kind."

"I don't like to see what men do to their wives sometimes. It makes me ashamed to be a man. One day I'll tell you about my parents' divorce … what a fuck-up that was." He placed a comforting hand on Madalena's shoulder. "I can help you, don't worry."

They parted at the baggage console, with a brief hug. Watching Bud walk away, Madalena shivered as she felt a rush of fear envelop her at the thought of her return to her normal life.

CHAPTER EIGHT

Madalena gazed out of the car window, up at the sky, the grey clouds a perfect echo of how she felt. The family were on their way to their monthly Sunday lunch with Jack's mother. She was feeling even more terrible than usual, as it would be the first visit since the publicity surrounding Bella.

Jack was clearly feeling the same. "Bella, don't you wind up your Grandma, d'you hear me? She's shocked by your behaviour, so just apologize and get it over with. I can't face a long discussion."

Bella, sitting next to Jack in the front of the car, puffed out her cheeks. "Oh for God's sake."

"I don't want her upset, you just eat humble pie. You know how much she adores you. She's an old lady, with traditional standards. Frankly it wouldn't hurt you to think about your own standards."

Bella turned around to exchange a look with her mother. Madalena raised her eyes heavenwards and shook her head slightly. Jack was right, if Bella simply smiled, apologized, and looked contrite, it could be over quickly. If she was feeling argumentative, the tension between Jack and Bella could drag on for days, with Madalena stuck in-between them.

"Just tell her the truth: you're not seeing Euan any more," Jack glanced across at his daughter. "It was all a terrible mistake, you wish it'd never happened, and you're sorry for all the embarrassment."

Bella muttered.

"What was that? What did you say?" He turned to glance at his daughter and Madalena could see, from the set of his jaw, that he was clenching his teeth. The knot in her gut tightened.

Bella gave a shrug that exuded contempt for her father and all he believed in. "Nothing."

"Yes, well you keep it that way, young lady. If you're expecting to keep your allowance and your trips to London, saying nothing is the way to do it."

Bella turned to gaze fixedly out of the window, her shoulders set at an angle that perfectly conveyed her desire to put two fingers up to her father. Madalena leaned forward and patted her shoulder in sympathy. Jack was a marvellous father to Bella, as long as she didn't challenge him. Now she thought about it, she could say the same about him as a husband.

As they pulled into the drive of Mother's pretty bungalow, set in the heart of one of Cardiff's most salubrious suburbs, Madalena couldn't help thinking of the shabby pensioners' flat that her own mother lived in. She remembered the day that Mother moved in here, and Jack's pride at her joy and his success, the same day he had started to call her Mother, instead of Mam. Madalena had never worked out whether Jack or Mam had instigated this affectation, but whenever she heard it, she had to suppress a smirk. And Jack was rightly proud, Madalena agreed on that: he had, against all odds, built a business empire from almost nothing when he left school, aged fifteen, a few months after the death of his father. In an act that seemed reckless at the time, he had invested his father's meagre savings in four second-hand slot machines that he sited in local pubs. Weekly, he set off on his bicycle to collect the takings, paying a rental sum to the landlords for occupying their premises. By the time he was twenty-two years old, he had fifty machines in a twenty-mile area, a small office, a van, a part-time secretary, a wife, and two young children. He provided his family, including his mother, with a comfortable and secure living. In the last ten years, his business had diversified, successfully, into the provision of casino equipment and supplies to international markets, and Jack had become seriously wealthy. He didn't take his success for granted, frequently exclaiming:

> "Who'd have thought it, Madalena? You and me, both poor kids from terraced houses; and here we are in a palace."

Mother opened the door instantly.

Bella laughed. "How long does she wait behind that door when we're coming? She's always there immediately."

"Hours probably, waiting for her favourite grandchild." Jack pinched his daughter's cheek, and she batted his hand away irritably.

Mother stood at the door in one of her "good" dresses: a green and white floral tailored shift. For a woman close to eighty she was still smart. Madalena admired her for that: she had never given up the effort to look her best. Madalena and Bella exchanged a secret smile about Mother's make-up: a smudge of sparkly green eye shadow inexpertly applied, and heavy dark red lipstick, applied outside the line of her lips. She'd been a sun worshipper all her life, so she used a thick dark face powder to even out the sunspots, wiped generously across her nose and chin. The combination of the vivid colours of her eyes and mouth against her darkened skin created an effect that was a little like a circus clown. When Bella was a child, she'd said to Madalena: "Gran wears funny make-up. I think she wants to be the same colours as you, Mummy."

Mother clasped Bella to her and hugged her tight, then held her away from her and inspected her. "Let me look at my beautiful girl. Look at you. You're a bad girl you know, in those papers like that, you'll give your old Gran a heart attack. But my word they're all saying how lovely you are, and they're right. You know what my neighbour said when she saw them? 'Ooh dear, she's in some trouble, but she's the image of you Mrs Norman, I can see where she gets her looks from.' And d'you know that close-up of your face reminded me of an old picture of me when I was about your age, the spit of you, the absolute spit."

Madalena's spirits rose at the prospect of any evidence of Bella's resemblance to Mother. Jack gave his mother a perfunctory hug, and moved past her into the house. Madalena was struck, as she always was, at the contrast between his tall, masculine presence, and the pink and lace décor, the cushions, candles, and floral chintz that his mother adored. She insisted on hosting these family lunches at home, despite Jack's repeated suggestions that they all go to a restaurant.

Mother gave a vague nod in the direction of Madalena.

When Jack had left his wife for Madalena, his appalled mother had commented on Madalena's impact on her adored only child: "She's got him completely mesmerized," a phrase that, in the twenty years that Jack and Madalena had lived together, became the closest they had to a private joke between them.

73

Madalena believed that if Mam (as Madalena continued to think of her) had witnessed her and Jack's first meeting, she would have understood Madalena's impact on her son.

Jack had done what most men did when faced with Madalena: he stared at her, for too long, transfixed. She smiled slightly, and gazed back at him, impassive.

"You've got the most amazing green eyes. I bet everyone says that."

Madalena smiled a little more, showing her pearly white teeth.

Jack continued to stare at her face. "Don't you ever blink?"

"Rarely," Madalena replied, and closed her eyes in a long, slow blink, like an old-fashioned china doll being turned upside down.

Mother followed Bella into the house, still talking.

"You're the image of me and you've got your father's brains, I don't know what went wrong with your A levels, it's still a mystery to me. Still, with your beauty I don't suppose it matters."

Madalena was practising her yoga breathing, slowing and deepening her breathing and repeating to herself: "It's a small price ... it's a small price ...."

Leading them out into the garden at the back of the house where she had set out drinks, Mother turned to Bella. "You sit there, next to your Dad, and tell me all about it. You be sure to tell me you've done what's right, Bella, come on, what did you say, how did it all end?"

Taking the only seat left to her, set a little further from the family, Madalena sipped her orange juice, took a deep breath, and allowed herself to fall into a relaxed reverie. Looking up at the sky, she could see some patches of blue; and a few rays of sunshine trying to push through the cloud cover. She breathed deeply and slowly: if it wasn't for her yoga breathing she'd never get through these visits without screaming.

In one of her more savage fantasies, Madalena dreamed of Bella pleasing Mother by marrying some nice, white, evidently British boy. She imagined Mother's pride at the elaborate wedding (featured in *Grazia*, maybe?; she considered various possible outfits she'd wear), and Mother's relief that Madalena, while clearly a blot on the family's reputation, at least didn't come with an entire set of relatives in various shades of brown ... just her embarrassing white trash mother.

She envisioned Bella's breathtaking beauty, the gown (probably Vera Wang, custom-made) and a handsome young man, faceless and nameless, immaculately dressed, by Bella's side. Then how thrilled the whole family would be, some months later, when Bella declared herself pregnant, and Mother's utter delight to find she was going to be a great-grandma. The day of the birth, right on schedule and after a blooming pregnancy (Bella wins a contract to model for Harrods' own maternity fashion line), Bella gives birth, quickly and easily to a startling daughter, 7 lb 2 oz and perfect.

The next scene was the one that Madalena imagined in full technicolour detail, and in slow motion.

Jack gives the news to his mother who is ecstatic and asks for an early visit to meet her new great-granddaughter. Madalena carries the baby, swaddled in a white shawl. The whole family goes into Mother's house, Mother a picture of expectant joy.

"Here you are, Mother," says Madalena, handing over the baby bundle. "Here is your new great-granddaughter."

Madalena doesn't take her eyes off Mother's face, just watches as her smile fades and the blood drains from her face, and she looks up at Jack, Bella, and Madalena.

"Oh! What …! How? But …?!" as she looked down at the beautiful black face of her great-granddaughter.

And Madalena looks at Mother and says:

"Isn't she amazing? It happens sometimes."

Which was a silly daydream really, as her own fantasy was quite the opposite: that she would look at the little girl and see that her hair was neither black nor curly, and that her skin was milky white.

"Madalena?" Jack was calling her. "Lunchtime."

Mother had laid the dining room table formally, with her best china and napkins. She had assembled a traditional Sunday lunch from the prepared food counter of Marks & Spencer: a ready roasted chicken, roast potatoes, and swede and carrot mash.

"How did I live my entire life without Marks and a microwave? The work it used to be, the hours it took, to prepare a Sunday lunch. This took me half an hour, that's all, you wouldn't believe it would you?"

Madalena tuned out Mother's voice and felt her customary relief that the days when her own mother was occasionally invited were over. Mother had only ever invited Jessie because of Bella, who, as a little girl adored and indulged by both her Grandmas, wanted them to be friends. As if that could ever have been possible. Like her son, Mother had adapted with enthusiasm to her new station in life, now the cosseted mother of a successful and wealthy businessman: she had succeeded in eradicating all memory and evidence of her humble beginnings.

Whenever she was in this room, Madalena recalled the incident, seven years ago, which had led to Jessie's banishment from Mother's house, and from Jack's protective mantle. Jessie ("Jezebel more like" Mother said) usually managed not to get *too* drunk at the family lunches, which she attended every few months. But one day she'd been unable to control herself and became visibly intoxicated. Then Bella asked her a question, a question that Madalena had been trained, since she was young, not to ask.

"Sophie and Lucy were asking me at school, Nan, and I didn't know the answer and Mum said she wasn't sure either. How dark-skinned was my grandfather? Because Mum's not that dark is she?"

An electric silence had followed Bella's question. Madalena had stared, from one mother to another, sitting opposite each other, looking, she realized, remarkably similar, with their matching lipsticked red mouths, and their deep liver-spotted cleavages on proud display in their bright frocks. Mother's mouth was a large crimson O, while Jessie's stretched back, horse like, over her ill-fitting false teeth, in silent, shoulder shaking mirth. As she had looked from one to the other, a stray thought wafted through her mind: these old ladies are locked in some weird lipstick war.

The silence was broken by Jessie's hysterical cackling; and Bella, looking around saying "What? What's the matter?" as they all stared at Jessie, doubled over, tears streaming down her face, trying to speak. Madalena did not dare look at Jack.

"Oh Bella, my darling girl," she gasped. "If you only knew. Black, brown, he could have been green. It was dark and it was quick, that's all I know, more than that I cannot say."

The price of it had been terrible. Jessie lived in one of Jack's investment houses, rent free, and received a small allowance to supplement her pension. She was summarily exiled from Jack's kingdom, and thrown to the mercy and the vagaries of the social services department, a miniscule state pension and a small council flat. Jack was categoric: on no account whatever was Madalena to give her any money or provide her with anything at all, and she and Bella were forbidden from seeing her. Thinking of it now, it reminded Madalena of her conversation with Bud, and the story about Jack's estrangement from his son. They were the same, weren't they? It had never occurred to her before. Since meeting Bud on the plane last week, she'd found herself seeing things a little differently. Sometimes, she thought about how she would describe something to Bud, and thinking about it like that made her see it from another angle. She even imagined what he would say back to her, how he might say something that she wouldn't have thought about. If he knew about the story of Madalena's mother alongside the story of John and Jack, Madalena thought he would say: what a very unforgiving man Jack is, even to his own family. She spent a lot of time in imaginary conversations with Bud.

With a slight shake of her head, she pulled her attention back to the meal. Mother was serving dessert: apple crumble with custard. They all yum yummed to Mother's delight. Despite the family scandal, she was in good humour, to see her two most adored people enjoying their dessert.

"You two go and sit down, while I clear up. I know Madalena will help me. Then I'll find that photo, Bella. You won't believe how like me you are."

This was the closest Mother ever came to speaking to Madalena, who dutifully went into the kitchen to start washing up. Their ritual was the same every month. No word was spoken. Mother handed Madalena rubber gloves and an apron, which she put on and stood at the kitchen sink up to her elbows in soapy water, washing dishes, while Mother bustled around the kitchen putting things away and humming under her breath. Madalena had a sudden image of Bud, laughing: "Mad, you're like Cinderella and the wicked stepmother."

She had to control a laugh at the thought.

Mother soon left Madalena in the kitchen, and went to join Jack and Bella. Bella had gone to the bathroom and Madalena strained her ears to hear what Mother and Jack were talking about.

"I don't think you should have let Bella do that hair advertisement. What were you thinking of?"

"I wasn't happy, but she's set her heart on this modelling thing. I can't refuse her; she was so excited and Madalena seemed to think it was fine. She talks to her mother about those things, not to me."

"You shouldn't be letting that woman make important decisions like that. I'm not sure you should trust her judgement when it comes to Bella."

Madalena swallowed hard. The woman was a witch, and she was confident that Bud would completely agree with her.

"Let's see." Mother was in her element, surrounded by photo albums and boxes of photos.

"Jack, you look in that album, see if you can find it … Bella you look through that box."

Madalena watched the three of them, inspecting photos. She looked at Bella. Did she look like her grandmother, as Mother was always so

77

keen to claim? Come to that, did she look like Jack? Most people who saw Madalena and Bella together said: well anyone can tell that you two are mother and daughter; you're like peas in a pod. There was, it was true, a remarkable resemblance. Madalena's hair was curlier, her skin a little darker. And the sprinkle of freckles across the bridge of her nose was hers alone. But in all other respects, the green eyes, the wide sensuous mouth, the high cheekbones, and the delicate jaw, they were almost identical.

"Do we have any of me when I was about Bella's age?"

Jack's question jolted Madalena from her reverie, and all three women stared, amazed, at Jack. The after-lunch rituals, of television soaps, or the frequent trips down the memory lane of the family photographs, usually bored him rigid; he often muttered about emails and disappeared, with his Blackberry, for a cigar in the garden. On a Sunday. Madalena wouldn't dream of challenging him, but she knew he was just escaping from the cloying atmosphere of his mother's adoration. She only wished she could join him, but she seemed to be required as a witness to the old lady's worship of Bella.

Mother flipped through the spines of the photo albums, and picked one out to hand to him.

"There, son, you might find some in there. I've got some somewhere of your Dad when he was Bella's age, when we'd got married, our wedding photos."

Jack took the album and started to idly flick through it.

Madalena watched him closely. What was he doing? And why? He glanced up, caught her watching him, and looked away, then back to the photos. Without saying a word, he handed it back to his mother.

"Anything there you liked son?"

"Nah …."

Mother handed him two more albums. "Try these … there are lots of when you were younger, around the time you married Pat." She took a sideways look at Madalena. "I love those photos of you, you look so young and carefree then. You weren't that much older than Bella."

Jack browsed through the albums, glancing back and forth between Bella and pictures of himself.

Holding her breath, Madalena looked at a photo album without really seeing it, and surreptitiously watched Jack.

"Found it." Mother was flushed with victory. "Look at this one, of me, see what I mean? Look, Bella, look at the likeness, the spit, don't you think Jack?"

Jack took the frail and faded photo. Madalena tried not to crane her neck to see it. Bella leaned across to look at it.

"Goodness, even I can see the likeness, Gran's right. Look Mum," and she passed it across to Madalena, apparently impervious to Mother's frown and the tightening of her mouth. Looking at the picture, there was no doubt that Mother had been a strikingly pretty young girl, with her fair colouring and light eyes. But like Bella? Madalena could see no resemblance.

"Yes she is isn't she?" said Madalena, making eye contact with nobody.

"There is something," said Jack thoughtfully. "Yes, something about the set of the eyes, you're right. It's funny isn't it, because now I come to think of it, no one has ever said that Bella looked like me. She looks so much like her mother I suppose."

Madalena looked at him and smiled brightly.

"It's Linda that's the image of you," said Mother. (And John, but Madalena knew not to mention his name.)

"How is Linda?" asked Mother.

And the conversation turned to family news, to Madalena's intense relief.

That night, Madalena lay awake staring into the dark. Jack lay beside her, one arm still flung across her breasts, left over from their brief coupling. Jack could rarely sleep without sex, he saw it as his own version of a sleeping pill. He snored gently.

She had to find a way to talk to Bud, and tell him how worried she was about Jack. She and Bud had texted a couple of times, and she'd called him briefly once from the home phone. But she had to be careful. Jack received itemized bills for her mobile phone and the house landline. He would recognize a new number, especially if it was repeatedly called. She was not sure how often Jack actually checked the bills, but a sudden increase in cost would definitely alert him.

Bud had said, "Mad, get yourself a computer, we could Skype."

At the time, she didn't have a clue what he was talking about, but since he'd said it, she was hearing that word everywhere. Bella said she talked to Euan on Skype (not in Jack's hearing obviously), and she had shown her mother, on her computer, how you called someone—and actually saw a film of them on the screen at the same time. If she could only talk to Bud like that. Maybe Bella might help her? Then a thought hit her: yes, she knew how to do it. She knew exactly what to do.

CHAPTER NINE

"What Honor? Whatever's the matter?" Eliot looked from Honor to the TV screen and back again. Turning her white face to Eliot, Honor pointed to the onscreen morning news. A woman in her thirties, estranged from her husband, had suffocated her two small children, then hanged herself.

"The woman, from Newcastle," intoned the newsreader "had been under psychiatric care for some time."

Honor leaned against the kitchen counter, and put her hand to her mouth. "Oh thank God, thank God."

"What Honor, what?" Eliot put an arm around her shoulders.

"For a dreadful moment I thought that .... Oh it doesn't matter Eliot, never mind, I'm fine now, don't worry." Shaking away Eliot's arm, she sat down at the kitchen table, where the children had paused, mid-breakfast.

"How could anyone do that? To their own children?" Eden looked to his father for answers. Eliot gave a despairing gesture.

"What about the father?" Celestine asked Honor. "What'll he do? He might commit suicide now."

Honor knew that was a real risk for the poor man. *A humane society might even endorse such a choice.*

"It's a terrible thing to do," Eliot said, "and yet I dare say this woman would claim to have loved her children above all else."

"She hated her husband more though," Honor said. "She wanted him to suffer more than she wanted to protect her own children. What worse revenge is there? Some say suicide is the ultimate revenge, but to murder your children first … she's ruined his life forever now."

Something in the discussion penetrated Thea's happy eight-year-old world. "What? What happened? What are you all talking about?"

Celestine zealously explained. Thea's face crumpled, and she climbed, weeping, onto her mother's lap.

"No, sweetie, you must understand, it's extremely rare, it's not normal, the poor woman was disturbed, she was ill in her mind." Honor stroked her daughter's soft hair and kissed the top of her head, rocking her as if she were still a baby.

"Why did they let her have her children with her then? Why didn't they stay with their Dad?" Eden, unmoved by Thea's tears, felt no need to drop the subject.

"Someone would have had to make the judgement about whether the children were safe with her." Eliot stood up and began clearing the table. "Someone like Mum. A very hard judgement to make, I should think. Come on kids, time to sort out for school."

"What would you do if you had to see someone like that?" Eden turned to his mother. "Would you let them stay with their kids?"

"I don't know. It's hard to predict how people will behave. Come on, you're going to be late for school at this rate."

Honor took Thea upstairs and helped her dry her tears and clean her teeth.

Driving to work, Honor tried to discard the heaviness that had settled on her from the breakfast conversation. She thought of the professionals who would have been involved in making the decisions about this woman and her children. In some of these cases, it comes completely out of the blue. A terrible dilemma, the worst: is this person safe to be around their own children? How quickly she had imagined that the news story was about Tisi; maybe she wasn't as sure as she'd like to be of her emotional state. She scanned a mental picture of Tisi, looking for fragility. No, it wasn't there. Those strong thighs gave the game away; despite her vitriol and despair, she was grounded in her adoration of her father, and, therefore, in objective reality: she'd never do such a thing. Surely? *I'm glad I'm seeing her today though.*

She stopped at the newsagents. Standing at the till she scanned the goodies: chocolates, sweets, chewing gum. Garishly coloured weekly celebrity magazines screamed out the latest celebrity news: Look how thin she is! Look how fat she is! Look at the plastic surgery! A headline, on the current copy of *Grazia* caught her eye, TEMPTRESSES! illustrated by a photograph of Bella Norman. *Would you believe it? I can't escape from this girl.* She bought a copy and left to drive to her office.

Where the hell am I? She wasn't paying attention, and had taken a route that was unfamiliar to her. She looked about, at street signs, then looked at the clock. Heavens: she'd been driving for half an hour, and was completely out of her usual area. She was lost. Switching on her satnav, she found she had headed south-west, towards central London. She pulled over, to look closely at the map: she was in St John's Wood, one street away, she thought, from Madalena's London apartment, which she'd seen when she'd googled her. She had noted that the family had their Cardiff home, a London flat, and a villa in Spain, though she'd needed to search some other web sites to get more detail. Jack's company was registered to a St John's Wood address that she felt sure must be their residential address.

She felt completely disoriented: how had she got here? Strange. Still, now she was here, she may as well take a look.

Driving around to the next street, she saw a series of tall modern blocks of luxury flats, in steel and shaded glass. Newly built, there was still a show flat, selling, so the sign proclaimed, "the last few luxurious state of the art flats in this award winning block, with full concierge service, secure underground parking, communal gardens, swimming pool and luxury gym". *Madalena's done well for herself.* She parked across the street and looked up at the building. She'd guessed right, it was a residential address. Which one was theirs? Each apartment boasted a broad terrace or balcony, elegantly furnished. She ducked down as a door opened on one of them, and a blonde woman stepped out.

Honor, this is crazy, what are you doing? You're stalking Madalena. Start the car, and get to the office, or you'll be late for your first client.

Putting the car into gear, she pulled away, taking a last look at the building.

Barbara wore her slightly disapproving face as Honor rushed in, dashed to the loo, and just managed to be in her consulting room before her first client arrived.

She tried to clear her mind, and listen, but she felt flustered by the morning's detour. Giving herself a mental shake, she focussed: and soon succeeded in entering her client's world, and putting aside her own concerns. Her professional training never let her down. *Except with Tisi.*

83

Once her client had left, Honor looked at her schedule for the day. Tisi was coming after lunch.

Barbara bustled in. "Ann called in and asked if you were free for lunch today, at hers?"

"Perfect, yes, tell her I'll be across about one."

That couldn't be better timing. Maybe she could talk to Ann about Tisi, and see if she had any new perspectives. She wouldn't tell Ann about her journey to work though; she wasn't the patient after all.

Honor knocked on Ann's door, and entered to the sonorous tones of wind chimes. She breathed in the fragrance from warmed essential oils, and guessed.

"Geranium with a hint of rose?"

"Close. Melissa with rose," Ann smiled in welcome.

Her office had the look and feel of an Eastern bazaar. Red and purple drapery hung at the windows, and covered the sofa and armchairs, untidily. Honor had to restrain her impulse to straighten them.

"One day I'm going to come in here and find you wearing a gypsy scarf, with a crystal ball in front of you." Honor hugged her friend.

Ann laughed. "Ah well. I can usually tell what's going to happen without a crystal ball."

Honor laughed, nervously. Ann did have an uncanny knack for apparent mind-reading.

Cold cuts, salad, some cheese, and fruit were set out on the coffee table.

"Help yourself, Honor. How's things?"

"Good. You? Busy?"

"Too busy. Over-committed on that teaching. I'm enjoying it though. But combined with my private practice as well …." Ann shrugged.

"Which d'you prefer? If you had to give up one which'd it be?"

Ann piled her plate high with food. "The teaching's a novelty, but it's not as flexible as my private practice or as satisfying. What could be better than the impact we have on people's happiness? Teaching's vaguer, less direct."

"I found that. I didn't mind teaching, but I'm a practitioner through and through."

"As your reputation reflects. Honor, the miracle worker."

Honor selected some cheese and fruit, and sat back in her chair. "If only it really was that instant and dramatic. It's more like that for you, I expect, with your focus on right now instead of the past."

"Gestalt is quicker. Only go back if there's a block. Much more cut through."

Honor sighed. "Mine's such a long process. I'm often left wondering: was it something I did, or was it just the passage of time that led to the recovery? All things pass, after all; maybe I'm just along for the journey."

"You make me mindful to look deeper. I worry that I'm putting sticking plaster on deep wounds." Ann tucked into her lunch.

"When it works, it usually works once and for all, it's true."

Ann nodded. "I'm too impatient. I like a quick energy read: what's blocking spirit right now? That's my start point."

Sitting up straight, Honor put her plate on the table. She smoothed her hair, and pulled her skirt over her knees, brushing away an imaginary crumb.

"Yes, well, I know that can work sometimes, you've taught me that, I'm not saying it's nonsense or anything, but it has no scientific basis. I do experiment, you've encouraged me, but in the end, I'm a doctor, a scientist."

This exchange was an echo of their ongoing debate of their different philosophies, which had started some weeks after they had both moved in to the building. Ann, refusing to retreat from Honor's hauteur, had eventually persuaded her to go for a glass of wine after work. The glass of wine turned into dinner, a bottle of wine, and a lively argument.

"What exactly is the point", Ann had asked, "of all the government funded psychology projects to 'scientifically prove' things that any old wife could have told them at any time in history? Some things are just phenomenological, many things, most of the truly important things in life. We all know this."

Honor, silenced and mutinous, eventually retorted, loudly: "If you ask me, phenomenological is just a really long word for magical."

They had both burst out laughing and had been close friends ever since.

"You busy, Honor? You look a bit tired."

"My list's pretty full. And my two days at the hospital are routine. I haven't been sleeping well recently. I've been having a repetitive nightmare. A fly caught in the sticky web of a hairy black spider."

"And you're the fly?"

"I'm the fly and the spider."

"Gosh, Honor." Ann clapped her hands. "You've made the perfect trap, predator and prey."

"I know." Honor put her hand to her forehead. "Comprehensively trapped. How I'm destroying myself."

"Or one part of you destroying another part of you. Which part wins?"

"That's the nightmare. I never get to know. I just feel the terrible strain they're both under, their desperation." Honor closed her eyes and sighed.

"Oh yuck, poor you. What's that all about?"

"A strange new client stirring up some old memories I think."

"Have you talked it through with Bill yet?" Ann knew Bill professionally.

"Not yet, but I will. I'm seeing her again today. Tisi her name is."

"Unusual …"

"Tisiphone, from a Greek myth. Last time I saw her I set her your unmailed letter task. Interesting to see how it goes. Does it ever fail, in your experience?"

"Not as long as it's unmailed, no."

Honor felt her stomach lurch. "What happens if they mail it?" She tried to keep her tone casual.

"It's hard to predict. Don't set that task until you're really sure they can stop themselves from sending it."

Honor tried not to show her growing sense of panic.

Saying her goodbyes, she went back to her office to prepare for her meeting with Tisi.

Barbara came in for five minutes to check some arrangements. "Anything else you need?"

"You could do a little research for me, please? This is a home thing more than work …."

An almost imperceptible pursing of Barbara's upper lip, the corresponding slight fade to her smile, told Honor she was on dangerous territory. Barbara didn't like to cross the home/work boundary, except in emergencies.

"I wouldn't ask you, but it's the sort of thing you'll be so good at, it's a technology thing."

"Oh, OK …" Barbara relaxed slightly.

"I've been cataloguing all my photos at home." Honor knew this would impress her.

"Really? Have you? What software are you using?"

"That's what I wanted to ask you about. I was hoping you could check out the best packages for editing photos?"

"You should be OK with something fairly standard. I'll check with Bob tonight, he's well up on photography packages."

"Great, Barbara, thanks. Ask him about packages that do that blending thing?"

"Morphing. Why do you want that?" she was looking at Honor with suspicion. She could be a bit psychic, in spite of her obsessive-compulsive tendencies.

"Eden was asking me if he could do that on my computer, some design project at school." Honor was shocked at the ease with which this lie tripped off her tongue.

She could see that Barbara still had some misgivings, but the thought of the elaborate, colour-coded spreadsheet she could construct to compare and contrast all photo packages was just too seductive for her to turn down.

Waiting for Tisi, Honor flipped through *Grazia*. She paused at a page showing a disgraced footballer in a staged family photograph. The wife, her over made-up face tense, her eyes blank, trying to smile, standing next to her husband, his proprietary arm around her shoulder.

I know what she's feeling, she's hoping desperately that she can hold together the life and family she's put her heart and soul into building. She's standing by her man, because, at this point, she's got no idea what that's going to cost her on a daily basis. She doesn't know the lies she'll have to tell the world; or the big fat lie she'll have to keep telling herself: that her husband loves her. She doesn't know, yet, of the callous that will form, year-by-year, layer-by-layer, over her broken heart.

Just once, she'd love to hear such a woman say: "He's not the person I thought he was, and he doesn't love me as he said he did. I will never trust him again. So I'm out. I'm divorcing him." She imagined joining the resounding cheer around the country, as betrayed wives everywhere heard the words they'd wished they'd said, instead of consigning themselves to a marriage of un-love and un-trust. It was a joke now, infidelity. In the press on a daily basis, as gossip and minor scandal: it was so common you could almost believe it didn't hurt, the bottomless anguish behind each story totally invisible.

The article about Bella was a piece of sensationalized popular psychology about why women steal men that already belong to other women. None of it was news to Honor. The pictures of Bella were spectacular, and the resemblance was more evident in these: especially to Caroline, Thomas's sister.

Shaking her head, she pushed the magazine into her handbag. Some great pictures of Bella, anyway, to add to her collection.

Tisi arrived in Honor's consulting room, a flurry of bags and energy. She'd been shopping on the way, and was breathless from the rush to be on time. Her cheeks were flushed pink, her eyes bright, and her hair a little curlier again, like a cloud around her face.

"How are you, Tisi?"

"Fine, Doctor."

Honor gave up the effort to get Tisi to call her Honor. *What is it about her that makes it so hard for me to treat her as a client, something I can do so easily with everyone else?* Tisi evidently needed an authority figure, and Honor needed all the control over her she could find, from any source.

"That's good. You look well." Honor relaxed. It was going to be OK.

"I did the letter thing: that was great, it made me feel much better." Tisi was grinning.

A glow of professional pride and satisfaction settled itself around Honor, warming her. "Excellent. Tell me about that."

Tisi stretched back in her chair. She was wearing a slimline dress in an intricate geometric pattern of stripes and spots in shades of brown and green, and knee-length brown boots.

"I wrote the letter, it was easy, it just flowed out. I wrote it all down, just as you said, everything I thought and felt, what Jackie had made me feel, and what I'd like to do to her."

There was a strange light in her eyes as she spoke. Honor's smug glow was fading. Something wasn't right. "And did you go back to it again after a couple of days?"

"Yes, I did, and I edited it, and you were right, my feelings had changed, they'd become more intense, angrier."

Honor held her breath. "What did you do next Tisi …? You didn't …?"

"Oh no, Doctor, don't worry, I didn't send it. I promised you after all, I'd never have gone against you, I gave you my word."

Honor's shoulders sagged with relief.

"But I thought of something better to do, that I knew would make me feel great."

Honor thought of Thea when they were all watching a family film, and it was becoming clear that something really bad was going to happen. Thea would cover her face with both hands, and peek through her fingers, to try to avoid seeing something she didn't want to see. Honor firmly and deliberately placed both hands together in her lap.

She looked at Tisi square on, full eye contact, and smiled. "Tell me what you did?"

Tisi threw her head back and laughed with great gaiety and joy. Then she sat forward, leaning towards Honor with that strange scoop of her graceful neck, and hissed: "I ssspoke to her. I ssspoke to the sssilly cow."

Honor's hands had moved, of their own accord, towards her face. She placed them carefully along the arms of her chair and held on. A part of her that still cared hoped her knuckles were not turning white.

"You spoke to her …."

"Yesss!" Her peal of laughter could have shattered crystal. "Yesss! I rang her up, and I told her what I thought."

Registering the look of alarm on Honor's face, she elaborated: "Oh don't worry, I don't mean that I read her the letter or told her what was in the letter or anything. I didn't do anything that I promised you I wouldn't, honestly, don't worry about that." Her face was a caricature of wide-eyed babyish innocence.

Honor did her best to collect herself. "That's good Tisi, well done. So tell me about your conversation with Jackie?"

It turned out that Tisi had called Jackie, and told her that she wanted to speak to her about her affair with Don. Jackie had tried to apologize, explaining that she hadn't expected to find herself having an affair, and was surprised that it had happened, and was sorry for any hurt she had caused Tisi.

"I'm not calling you up to listen to that kind of rubbish," Tisi had said. "I'm ringing you up to say two things to you: firstly, you'd better tell your husband about your affair, because if you don't I'm going to; and, secondly, if you bump into me at the gym, the supermarket, or anywhere else, don't speak to me or otherwise behave as though you're my friend, because you're not: my friends don't fuck my husband."

Honor had to stop herself from cheering.

How absolutely brilliant, no wonder she's feeling so much better. Imagine being able to say that to the woman who your husband …. What would I like to do? To Madalena? I want to disturb her. Back then I turned the other cheek, rose above it, never spoke to her about it, ever so dignified I was. Very Christian. What I controlled myself from doing was to land a resounding smack on that smooth as silk cheek, really hard, a smack that would hurt my hand as much as her face.

Honor knew she had to control herself; and, harder, she was going to have to try to control Tisi. She needed to stop her from escalating matters.

"Does Don know about this?" It seemed reasonable to assume that Jackie would have told Don about Tisi's deranged (*though perfectly wonderful*) call.

Tisi's joy noticeably faded. "Yes, she told him."

Don was absolutely livid. He didn't know what she was trying to achieve. Neither Don nor Jackie wanted Jackie's husband to find out, and Don asked Tisi not to go and tell him.

Honor leaned forward and spoke sternly. "Tisi, one of my concerns here is the same as yours—to ensure that your children are protected. And the more people know, the more chance there is of them hearing …."

Tisi sank back in her chair, anxiety pinching her mouth. Tears rose in her eyes. "Yes … I hadn't thought …"

"It only takes one of them to overhear a conversation … or Jackie or her husband to escalate things further: can you see the danger?"

I'm crossing so many professional boundaries, I don't know where to begin to get back on the right track. All she could think of was how to ensure that Tisi didn't continue to indulge her understandable desire to hurt the people who were hurting her. *I want to protect her from the remorse she'll feel if she takes any action that could damage her children. No woman wants to feel that her children have suffered by her own hand.*

"Yes, you're right, of course …." Tisi, her shoulders drooping, wiped away a tear.

Honor, regretting her sternness, and appalled by her own lack of control, tried to assert her professionalism.

"Do you remember our last session, when we tracked back a bit, and talked about your early experiences? How about we think some more about that?"

"Yes, OK. Early memories again?" Tisi fell easily into her obedient child persona; the joyful glow of standing up for herself and saying what she meant had disappeared.

"I'm interested to know about your name. It's unique I should think."

Tisi perked up. "Oh yes, people are always interested in that. My mother loved the Roman and Greek myths. The Greeks were her favourites."

"She chose some unusual names even for the myths. Why not Penelope, or Helen?"

"Her special subject was the lesser-known goddesses; she used to make a joke: 'I like the secondary goddesses, they're like me, never getting quite enough love and attention.' She was a world expert; she travelled a lot, to speak at conferences."

"I can see that you feel very proud of her."

Tisi spoke softly and with great seriousness, seeming more real than Honor had previously experienced her.

"She achieved a lot in her work and she found that satisfying. But her personal life was bitterly unhappy."

Honor hesitated. It was important that she understood more about Tisi's first female role model. But she didn't want to stimulate Tisi's hissing rage; she didn't have the strength for it.

"You've mentioned before that she wasn't happy with your father. How did you experience her as a mother?"

"I think she was happy as a mother, she was dedicated, and made sacrifices for us." Tisi gave a bitter laugh. "I think she stayed with my Dad for our sakes, but honestly, she needn't have bothered."

"Maybe she loved him, despite everything; that's usually why women stay with bad husbands. Let's talk about this next time we meet, Tisi, shall we?"

"OK."

"Tisi … I need your commitment, that you won't take any actions, won't do anything untoward?"

"No, OK, I won't." She was leaning down, fumbling for something in her handbag; she didn't look up as she spoke.

I don't believe her. I don't trust her, and I don't believe her.

CHAPTER TEN

On her way home that evening Honor could feel the tension in her tummy, at the thought of what Tisi might do next. She felt nervous, and slightly excited, by the sheer thrill she was getting from Tisi's wrath.

Driving down her road, she saw a car parked in her usual space on the drive. A jaunty little sports car, bright red, with the hood down. Who on earth was that? More to the point, why were they in her car parking space? She tutted with irritation and pulled into the kerb, in front of the driveway.

Stepping out of her Mini, she glanced towards the house and gave a gasp, and quickly ducked back inside the car. It was Amanda. She'd completely forgotten, it was the girls' play date today. Through the window of the front sitting room, she could see Amanda standing right up close to Eliot, with one hand on his arm, leaning into him, laughing into his face and him laughing back. Just the two of them, alone together, not a child in sight.

She breathed deeply and leaned over the steering wheel. *Come on Honor, calm down, don't let your imagination run riot.* But her imagination had already re-wound itself ten years, to a time when she was obsessed with suspicion of Eliot. She'd been convinced he was having an affair: too many unexplained absences, less sex than usual, deleting all his text messages from his phone. She had confronted him a number of times: she was sure she was right. He totally denied her accusations, with great irritation.

"Are you mad? Of course not. You're paranoid, seeing signs where there are none. Get a grip."

But nothing could convince her. She had confided her worries to Jackie (actually *confided ... in Jackie ...*), even telling her how she secretly took Eliot's phone to look at his call history. It all got on top of her one day, at work, so, in her lunch hour she had called around to Jackie's for some soothing comfort, from her closest friend. Eliot's car was outside the house. *He must have dropped something round, or gone to collect something. Dammit, I wanted Jackie to myself.*

She got no reply at the front door; but knew immediately that on such a sunny day, Jackie would be in the back garden. The house, an ordinary suburban 1930s semi from the front, opened out at the back to a large garden, containing numerous mature apple and pear trees, with paved paths winding through them.

Walking around the side of the house, into the garden, Honor was at first struck, as she always was by the lush beauty of the fruit trees, and the way the sun patterned the lawn, as it pushed its way through the dark green leaves. She smiled with pleasure at the familiar sight. Then she noticed Jackie and Eliot in a passionate clinch on a blanket on the lawn. For some moments she didn't understand what she was seeing. The world slowed down around her as she stared, uncomprehendingly, at the scene in front of her. She felt there was a flashing neon sign in her brain: *cannot compute ... cannot compute.* Neither her husband or her best friend saw her, faced away from the house as they were, exchanging a lover's kiss, absorbed in each other, in themselves in each other. She had looked, turned her back on them, closed her eyes tight, shook her head, then turned and looked again. The world seemed to swim, in blurry slow motion. *That's right, that's what I'm seeing, that's right: my Eliot with my Jackie. Can that be real? Have I made a mistake?*

A choked involuntary sound escaped from her lips, startling two of the people she loved most in the world. The two people she thought loved her in return. They both turned startled. As she slid to the ground in a dead faint, she heard Eliot say, "Oh fuck ...!" and Jackie say, "Oh God, no."

Even now, the memory could make her feel giddy and unreal. Recalling it, her memory flipped into action, bringing that day, and those that followed, flooding back in full technicolour detail. In the aftermath, she had shut down, frozen, showing no anger. She did not speak a word to Eliot for twenty-four hours.

"Talk to me, Honor, please speak, tell me how you feel? Please say something."

Finally she turned her eyes, still darkened by shock, to his face and said, "I wish I was dead."

Jackie had come round to see her later on that first day, but Honor had refused to see her. So she phoned the next day, but Honor put the phone down as soon as she heard Jackie's voice. So Jackie had written, apologizing and appealing for a chance to meet to talk, "to explain and apologize". Honor wrote back, the briefest note:

> *Leave me alone. Never ever contact me or my family. You are dead to me, you were never my friend. Some things in life are simply unforgiveable.*

She had never seen or heard from Jackie since, but had been intensely relieved to hear that she and her family had moved away.

Lifting her head, she turned to look again at the house. The sitting room was empty.

No wonder Tisi's rage has satisfied me so profoundly. I thought I'd erased my pain completely. How wrong I was.

She reminded herself, firmly: this isn't the same: this is Amanda, who flirts with everyone, she can't help herself. But her thoughts of Tisi gave her a strange new energy and strength. She gave herself a sharp talking to: Honor, don't do do what you did before: don't freeze, don't faint, don't be mute; don't worry about everyone else's feelings, don't turn the other cheek, don't be dignified. March right in there and do what Tisi would do, go in that house and assert yourself. Don't be Honor; be Tisi.

Taking several deep breaths, she set her shoulders back, tensed her jaw, and stepped out of the car.

Breezing into the hall and calling a cheery "Helloooo ….", Honor headed straight to the back of the house to the kitchen, where she could hear Amanda, Eliot, and the children. Amanda was chivvying Charlotte to get her shoes on and Thea was dancing around her friend. Spotting her mother, she ran to her and flung her arms around her hips. "Mummy! Mummy! Look, Charlotte, my mummy's here too."

Honor sashayed across the kitchen to Eliot, snaked her arm around his neck and kissed him, lingeringly. "Hi darling," she said, looking at him intimately. He stared back at her, his bewilderment evident in his furrowed brow and open mouth.

"Hi, Amanda," she said, turning to look at her with a bright smile. "How are you?"

I can see how you are. You're a bit flustered. And why is that exactly? You look a bit guilty actually. You both do, now I come to think about it.

"I, uh, yes, fine thanks, must be going, come on Charlotte." Amanda's face was pink, and she hurried her daughter into her shoes.

"No rush ... though Eliot and I are looking forward to a nice evening together aren't we darling?" She looked at Eliot and ran her hand up his arm and along his shoulders, and hugged him again.

Eliot mumbled, embarrassed.

Amanda made a hurried exit, hardly looking at Eliot and pulling Charlotte away from her extended goodbye hugs with Thea.

"What the hell was all that about?" Eliot was staring at Honor, his hands held out, palms upward in a gesture of confusion.

"All what?"

"All that stuff in front of Amanda? That's not like you, even privately, leave alone in front of a friend. You really did embarrass the poor woman."

"Really? Did I? What's going on exactly, Eliot? I saw the two of you in the sitting room when I parked, looking mighty friendly I must say."

"Oh for heaven's sake. What on earth are you suggesting? Surely you can't think that .... Oh come on."

And the discussion had degenerated into a series of accusations and counter-accusations, leaving them both bad-tempered and irritable.

After an early dinner and getting Thea off to bed, Honor retired to her study, despite Eliot's complaints.

"Don't just walk away from me, Honor. We said we'd spend the evening together. What could be more important? We said we'd always make this our priority." Eliot was frowning.

"I need some time alone, I'm sorry."

"Time alone for what? What's going on?"

"Some stuff I need to think through for work, that's all."

Eliot's eyes narrowed. "This is not something I want to coerce you on, we've always kept to this, we said we would. Especially if we're arguing."

Honor felt her heart soften at this reminder. "I'm just so busy, Eliot."

"If you insist." He did not meet her eyes.

"Let's have a drink before bedtime, in the garden?"

"Sure. Whatever."

Honor retired to her study. *It's all very well Eliot getting irritated. He's a bit quick to forget how close we came to the end. What it took for me to forgive him.* She tried to banish the painful memories surfacing; and succeeded in keeping thoughts of Jackie at bay. But she recalled a conversation between her and Eliot in the anguished days following her discovery, that was so vivid it was hard to believe it was ten years ago.

"But it's you I love, Honor. It's you."

"You're saying those words to me now and maybe you believe them. But I don't. Not for a second. You couldn't do this if you loved me. I think you hate me. I feel hated."

All Honor had wanted was to leave; to be as far away from Eliot as possible. Then she had to come to terms with another painful realization. She had absolutely nowhere to go.

Brushing away a tear, she sat at her computer, and turned her attention to her emails. Remembering Tisi, she opened her browser, and typed Tisiphone into the search programme. Tisiphone was one of three sister goddesses, the Eummenides, impossibly beautiful creatures who guarded a glorious garden, reminding Honor of Tisi's ambition to paint a garden so peaceful that she could call it the Garden of Eden; what an extraordinary coincidence ... or was it? *After all, what expectations do we set for our children when we name them? Of what they will do, who they will be, what we want from them or for them? What mysterious energies are set in motion as we crystallize our hopes and dreams into a name?*

Or, in Tisi's case into three names, all with the same energy.

There was a gentle knock at the door and Celestine peered in.

"Can I talk to you, Mum?"

Honor quickly closed the screen and beckoned her in. They were good kids, always respectful of her working time. They had grown up with it, and knew no different: if Mum's in her study you must knock and be quiet, in case she's on the phone to someone.

"Shall we go downstairs?"

"No, I wanted to ask you something ..."

"Let's go to your room then."

Celestine's room, a typical teenage girl's boudoir, was draped in scarves and jewellery, the floor a carpet of clothes. Seeing the mess, Honor bit back her desire to deliver a short lecture of the "You don't know how lucky you are" variety. Her kids had everything; they barely knew what it was to want: all their needs were anticipated and delivered almost before they registered. Not like when Honor was a kid; she could still feel the ache of the perpetual disappointment of not being able to have the things she wanted. No wonder she spoilt herself and her children: trying to heal old wounds. *Though, let's face it, isn't that what we're all doing, one way or another?*

"What's up?"

Sitting on Celestine's unmade bed, Honor smoothed the duvet, and plumped up the pillows.

"Nothing really, no big deal, Mum, just wanted a bit of time."

Honor waited.

"I feel a bit fed up at school …"

Celestine picked up a brush and started tugging it through her hair.

"Here, Cel, let me do that for you."

She handed over the brush and Honor began gently pulling it through the tangles. She was reminded of Cel as a little girl, when Honor used to do that one hundred brushes per night thing, looking at her daughter in the mirror while they talked. Now, sitting on the bed, Celestine's back to Honor, they had no mirror. Maybe she would say more to Honor in the absence of eye contact, like a psychoanalyst outside the client's line of sight.

Honor was itching to ask a question. She decided to give it another ten seconds. She began counting in her mind.

They spoke simultaneously: "What's on your …", "D'you know what …"

Then that dance: "Oh sorry, you go …", "No it's OK, you …", "What were you going to say?"

"D'you know what the girls at school say about me?"

Honor's heart clenched. "What?"

"It's not so much what they say. They laugh at me."

Honor's arms moved in a reflex to hold her daughter close. She controlled herself, with difficulty. *That's the second time today that I've had to prevent my arms from doing what they want.*

"Which girls?"

"The cool gang."

Honor could see them, in her minds eye. Cel's age, but just that bit more physically mature, so they all looked at least eighteen years old. Girls in women's bodies, full of themselves and their new found power. Dangerous.

"And what's so funny about you?" Honor continued to brush her hair, and felt her daughter's shoulders droop, her head drop.

"Celes-tiny tits."

Such a cruel taunt to a young girl, from the dizzy delight of their newly acquired breasts. Eliot teased Honor sometimes, with a French phrase: *l'arrogance des femmes qui on de la poitrine,* that captured the unique quality of feminine arrogance, the confidence of a woman with full breasts. She knew of no known word or phrase that could quite express its opposite: the shrunken inadequacy of the flat-chested woman.

"Pathetic. I can beat that. Honor-no-tits they used to call me."

Honor felt her daughter quivering as she started to laugh, and turned round to face her mother.

"Really? You? These?" She gestured towards Honor's ample bosom.

"Yes, really, me, these. It happened when I was about seventeen, they just sprouted, practically overnight, a right pair of bazookas, nobody could quite believe it."

"So I've got another eighteen months to go then …"

"Could you try and ignore them until then? Knowing how vastly superior you'll be quite soon?"

"I was going to ask you if I could get some padded bras."

"Brilliant idea. Of course you can. That'll surprise them."

"Thanks, Mum."

Honor hugged her, then went back to her study, where she sat and stared at the blank screen, overwhelmed by the pain of peoples' sheer mindless, thoughtless cruelty. She felt hyper-sensitive about everything, as though some inner skin or barrier had been removed, uncovering every wound she had ever sustained. News items, the children's experiences, Tisi, Jackie …. She was over-identifying with everyone and everything.

I am a walking bruise, anything that touches me feels like agony.

Honor opened her browser again, searching on Madalena's apartment building. That place must have cost a fortune. In choosing Jack, Madalena had done better than she could ever have dreamed. *I bet she congratulates herself on choosing the right man; anyway, Jack certainly proved a better provider than Thomas would have been. Though who knows? I don't even know what Thomas would've looked like now. Maybe Bella looks even more like him than I can imagine.*

Scanning the details on the screen, she discovered that their flat had cost several million. Jack, the fruit machine king, who'd have thought it? She hadn't known him well, but he'd always seemed to Honor to be one of those straightforward men with simple needs: a hot dinner, a good shag, and he was happy. Not so simple clearly, pretty smart in fact. She googled Jack. He'd built quite an empire, it seemed, an international organization providing fruit machines and casino supplies all over the world. There was about to be a lavish party, the opening of a new casino that Jack's company had kitted out. The event was billed as one of the social events of the season, attended by top celebrities, to be featured in *Hello*. Honor made a mental note to look out for the magazine.

Honor clicked on her photo file and pulled up the file of photos of Bella. Retrieving the copy of *Grazia* from the bottom of her bag, she expertly scanned in the pictures of Bella, then looked at them in close-up.

You would have been so proud and happy, Thomas, to know you'd left a child in the world.

Later, sipping wine in the garden in the cool evening air, Honor tried to relax. Eliot was in a conciliatory mood, apologetic that she may have misinterpreted Amanda's flirtatious behaviour. He had a habit of blaming women for flirting with him. That had been his defence over Jackie.

Now, he waxed lyrical about the sheer wantonness of some women, the way they just *threw* themselves at him, and there was nothing he could do to prevent this or stop it, and if they went too far, well (theatrical shrug), what on earth was a man to do?

"I'm only human after all, men will be men. It's women, that's who you should be having a go at over things like this."

Honor fixed him with a stony stare. "I can't listen to another word of this self-justifying *bullshit*. You see, Eliot, it's like this. You can deny all you like, and feel hurt that I don't seem quite convinced. But you've conveniently forgotten something. All the lies you told me in the past. And not just the lies. You said I was paranoid. I knew what I knew, I felt what I felt, and you denied my reality and called me mad. And I felt mad, completely deranged. Until I found out that I wasn't crazy at all, not a bit of it: everything I'd thought, felt, and suspected was truer and worse than I could have imagined. So don't be too bloody surprised, Eliot, if I don't always fall for your stories and reasons, will you?"

"Honor, I …" Eliot held up his hand in a gesture to ward off her words. "You don't have to remind me, I know what I did."

"And do you remember the choices you gave me? [*I'm not ready to stop yet, I haven't finished.*] Either I'm a mad woman married to a loyal, true husband, or I'm sane and married to a cheat. What I want is to know I'm a sane woman married to a man who is loyal and true. And I can never have that simple thing. So if I don't know which way is up now, it's not really surprising is it? But there's one thing you should know, Eliot, that you should be crystal clear about. I won't stay a second time."

She stood up and walked past him, back into the house and off to bed.

CHAPTER ELEVEN

Parked across the road from Madalena's flat, Honor watched the early morning sunlight glimmering across the glass panels of the tall building. The sun shone on the broad terraces: a woman sat, drinking her coffee or tea, in the fresh morning air.

Which flat was Madalena's? Which floor was it on? She'd thought about going in, or approaching the front door, but the security guard at the gates put her off. She was also horrified at the prospect of being seen by Madalena or Jack; but she was safe enough here. The entrance to the underground car park was around the corner, out of sight, and she kept a broadsheet newspaper open on the passenger seat, ready to raise in front of her face in an instant, if the need arose.

Gazing up at the front of the building, a movement caught her attention, on the second floor, and a door opened onto a balcony. Honor leaned forward, picking up the binoculars she'd brought with her. She couldn't pretend that this trip had happened unconsciously: she was well prepared.

She saw a young woman, with long glossy black hair: Bella. Honor would have recognized her anywhere: her creamy skin, and the set of her shoulders, the way she carried herself: it was Thomas incarnate. Her paternity was in no doubt.

Bella leaned against the balcony rail and looked up to the sun, stretching languorously. Moving gracefully to one of the sun beds, she sat down, pulling her skirt up to get the sun on her legs.

Honor felt overwhelmed by a surge of maternal love, as though she was looking at one of her own daughters. And then she felt pity. The poor girl, no wonder she was behaving so badly, her mother was a dreadful role model. *If only I could have some influence on her, help her think about her life and her ambitions. Wouldn't Thomas have expected this of me?* He wouldn't want his only daughter, his only child, behaving in such a vacuous and superficial way. The girl would be clever if she took after her Dad: he'd had a brilliant mind.

She watched Bella move to the terrace railings and look down and around: she seemed to stare directly at Honor, who hurriedly put down the binoculars and picked up her newspaper. Bella went back into the apartment, and Honor started the engine of her car and drove off quickly, her face aflame. Feeling the familiar heat, she had a childhood memory aged four, of herself and Faith, her older sister, in their shared bedroom, telling each other stories before sleep.

"The little black imp was tiny, only this big," Faith held her thumb and index finger an inch apart. "So he couldn't get any clothes to fit him from the shops. His mummy made his shirts from the white skin underneath the eggshell from boiled eggs."

"Ooh … and was his Mummy tiny as well?"

"The whole family was. You tell one now, tell me a story about Madam."

"That Madam was a very naughty girl." Honor saw Faith's eyes light up.

"What did she do, what did she do?" Faith bounced on her bed.

"The girl up the road played a horrible trick on her. She said they were going to all meet the next day for a dress-up party. So Madam made a whole dress out of a newspaper to go to it."

"A newspaper?" Faith had stopped bouncing. "What was she going as?"

Honor's mind raced. Yes, what was she dressed as? She took a deep breath and stared her sister directly in the eye. "The newspaper lady. She was the newspaper lady, in a whole dress out of paper, the whole thing."

Faith breathed out and nodded slowly. "Yes, that's right, yes, the newspaper lady. But what was the trick?"

"The trick was, the mean trick from the mean girl, was that nobody was there, just Madam in her newspaper and the mean girl, giving that horrible nasty laugh she does."

"Oh no, that's horrible, the meanie. What did Madam do, go on tell me." Faith was leaning towards Honor, her eyes gleaming.

"She sat on her and did a poo!"

Honor and Faith shrieked with laughter; Faith jumped on Honor's bed and hugged her, giggling, repeating: "She poo-ed on her! That'll teach her to be mean!"

Honor leaned against the warmth of her big sister, and giggled with her.

The sisters, enthralled by each other's characters inspired one another to ever-more dramatic stories; but their blithe conspiracy was brought to a halt one evening when their baby-sitter, a prim and over-protected young aunt, tucked them in and offered them a story.

Faith jumped up and down with excitement. "Honor can tell a Madam story, you'll love them Auntie, they're so funny, Madam is so funny."

Honor, revelling in the spotlight, excelled herself in the elaborate detail of a new tale of Madam's retribution. So carried away was she, with her story, and with Faith's admiration, that she didn't notice the growing horror on her aunt's face, until sharp words cut across her glow of success: "You disgusting little girl! I'll tell your Daddy; you are dirty and disgraceful, you should be ashamed of yourself!" And she left the room, leaving Faith and Honor in wide-eyed silence.

Honor watched her father nervously for a few days to see any signs of his distaste, and, seeing none, she pushed the memory deep into her mind, forgotten, until several decades later, when discussing her blushing with her therapist, she had remembered the incident. Attempting to diffuse its power over her, she had told her father, and asked him if Auntie had ever told him about it.

He had absolutely rocked with laughter at the story, and wiping away tears of mirth said, "No, she never told me. Trust my sister," leaving Honor fervently wishing that Auntie *had* told him.

I could have been a different person. No shame, no blushing.

Arriving at her office, she settled down to her day's work, with only ten minutes to spare before Tisi arrived.

She strutted in, on time, full of beans, dressed from head to toe in scarlet, including a red snakeskin belt and snakeskin boots. Honor couldn't help herself: "Where did you get those amazing boots?" Tisi threw back her head (her neck really was amazingly long) and laughed. One of her suppliers had given them to her: they were a sample. He'd thought of Tisi immediately, saying that the boots were made for her.

Her hairstyle had changed a little again: she had a number of thin plaits scattered in her straight silky hair. How striking. Though the red didn't suit her: perhaps it was the reflection but her skin looked too pink, and even her eyes seemed to be picking up on the red tones.

"Would you like a drink, Tisi?"

"Ooh, lovely, yes please, some coffee?"

A shrill edge to Tisi's voice alarmed Honor, reminding her of Tisi's tendency to swing from tearful and apologetic to damaging and joyful. Leaving Tisi to settle down, Honor put her head around Barbara's door, and asked her to bring coffee for Tisi and green tea for her.

Returning to her office, she noticed a strange gleam in Tisi's eye. What was the matter with her today? There was something electrical about her, charged. Barbara brought in their drinks, and Honor took several deep breaths, to calm herself. Hoping for a gentle and positive start to their session, she told Tisi that she had googled her name. "That's a coincidence, Tisi, that your namesakes were guardians of a heavenly garden; and there you are trying to paint Paradise."

Tisi smiled. "I know. My mother always loved that idea too. Tisiphone's story is more complicated than that, but that was the bit of it my mother loved: how they calmed their anger and settled down in the garden."

"What was that about?"

"I can't remember all the details to be honest." Her demeanour switched rapidly, her body sagging in the chair, tears welling up. "You're going to be so angry with me, Doctor ...."

"What's happened?" Honor's heart beat faster.

"I didn't mean to, it wasn't something I planned, it just happened. On my way here this morning in fact. I shouldn't have done it, but it felt so fantastic once I had, it really did. What's going to happen next? What have I done?"

She dropped her head to her knees, folded her arms over her head, keening.

Honor allowed some time to pass, controlling her impulse to pull Tisi to her feet, shake her, and insist she report what had happened. Her mind was racing. What could possibly have happened on the way here? A phone call maybe? She said something she regretted? She cast her mind back to their last session, to check whether she had specifically told her something she must not do? There was nothing.

"Would you like a glass of water?" Honor wanted a reason to leave the room.

Sob, mumble, sob.

"Tissues are just beside you."

One of Tisi's arms snaked out to take a tissue. Honor had never noticed how remarkably long and slim her arms were.

"Water?"

A bob of her head and a grunt. Honor thankfully left the room. What was it that happened to her when she was in Tisi's presence? It was as though Tisi created some energetic force field that changed the way Honor thought and felt, casting a spell over her. Was she even aware of the impact she had?

Honor returned and handed the water to a calmer Tisi.

"I'm sorry." Tisi took the glass from Honor.

Honor found contrite Tisi irritating, but preferred that to the alarm she felt in the presence of ebullient Tisi. "Tell me what happened?"

Tisi gulped, and wiped her eyes. Her eye make-up had been cried away, leaving her eyes looking fiery red.

"I stopped to buy petrol. I bumped into Jackie's husband, Steven."

Swallowing hard, Honor nodded encouragingly for her to go on. *Acting would have been a better profession for me, I'd have been brilliant.*

"We only know each other vaguely, we've met socially a couple of times, that's all."

"What did you say?" Even Honor could only stand so much suspense.

"We both said hi, how are you …. I didn't mean to say anything, it was like being taken over, like an out of body experience." Fresh tears.

"What did you say?"

"He said Jackie was working very late these last weeks, he'd hardly seen her, was Don involved on the same project? He was just making small talk …. I heard myself from a long way away say, 'Steven, I think you'll find that Don and Jackie are deeply involved in a project all of their own, just the two of them.' Then I turned around and walked out. I got in the car and I could see him standing there like a statue, his mouth open, staring at me. I waved and drove off."

At the memory, Tisi was taken over by the sheer heady pleasure of just letting herself go, and saying what she wanted to say. Her spirits lifted, and she started to laugh.

Honor felt exactly the same. *Yes, how amazing, just say it like it is; stop pretending, stop playing the polite civilized game. I feel sorry for Steven though.*

"I don't know why I'm laughing," Tisi said. "I dread to think what'll happen now. What may already be happening. Has he rung Jackie, or Don? I'm not looking forward to going home: if Don knows he'll go crazy."

"What d'you know about Steven? Can you predict his reaction?"

"No … no idea really. He's a detective, he works irregular shifts. He seems a nice enough chap. Big guy, looks like a rugby player. They've got a couple of kids, a pretty teenager daughter who's going slightly off the rails I think. No wonder with her mother behaving as she does; what sort of example is she setting for her daughter?"

Exactly! You can't just go ahead and do what you want. We all have to think of our children, the impact on them of the actions we take.

Giving herself a mental shake, Honor turned her attention back to Tisi.

"My worry for you, as this becomes increasingly tense and public, is that your children will know; they will suffer. What if Steven challenges Don? Or leaves Jackie? Do you understand the consequences of the action you have taken Tisi?"

Honor, appalled that her professional skills had so comprehensively deserted her, watched Tisi lean forward, tears running down her cheeks. In some nasty trick of the light, her eyes and tears reflected her scarlet clothes, and for a horrible moment, she looked as though blood was streaming down her face. Honor shook her head to rid herself of the image.

"I don't know what comes over me sometimes," Tisi said. "I know what I want to do and what I don't want to do, I have it all worked out in my mind, then something happens and I just can't control myself, all my sensible thinking deserts me. It's scary, I just don't know what I might do next sometimes; I really don't."

"Perhaps there's some comfort in the fact that the worst is done. You've talked to Jackie, you've told Steven, what more can you do really? It's in the lap of the gods now. You have to see what actions they take. You're no longer in control; you can't protect your children now, you just have to hope that other people might." *What am I thinking of? To frighten her like this?*

Tisi wailed at this sharp reality check. "What can I do? What have I done?"

"I can tell you what you haven't done. You haven't listened to me. You pretend to, when you're here, then you leave and you simply follow your vengeful impulses. I'm beginning to wonder what use it is for us to have these conversations at all."

Gosh it was satisfying to say that. To say what she really thought and felt. What she was saying was true, Tisi had acted vengefully and had set forces in motion that she no longer had control over. Personally, Honor completely sympathized with her: she was feeling towards others as they had acted towards her, simple as that. *But she'll never forgive herself if she hurts her children. She'll regret it forever.*

"Oh no, oh my God, oh I'm so sorry. You think I'm terrible, you won't help me any more. What am I going to do?" She rested her head on her knees and gave way to unrestrained wailing. "I'm driving everyone mad, even you."

Honor was obliged to make fulsome apologies in order to calm Tisi down.

Once Tisi had left, Honor paced to and fro, jangled by the encounter, and distraught at her own appalling behaviour. She lay down on the couch and tried to meditate, to calm herself. *What came over her, to talk to Tisi like that? So unprofessionally, so harshly, actually.*

Barbara opened the door. "Oh! Sorry. Ann just popped in and asked if she could see you."

"Tell her I have to take a rain check, I've just had a tough session and I need to recover before my afternoon client."

"OK." Barbara closed the door with exaggerated care, only to reappear within moments.

"Honor …" her tone was urgent. "Ann said she must see you … even if it's only quick. It's about Tisi, she says, it's really important."

Honor sighed and sat up. What on earth could Ann have to say about Tisi?

"Tell her I'll be in in a minute. Could I have a glass of water please?"

She searched her bag for a Nurofen. Honor had an avid dislike of pharmaceuticals of any kind, and a corresponding faith in vitamin and mineral supplements. But desperate times called for desperate measures, and the only thing that would shift the threat of a migraine headache was a double dose of painkillers. Barbara brought in her water and she quickly took the tablets. She sat for a few moments of silence, then took a few deep breaths and made her way across the hall to Ann's office.

Ann stood up, her face pale, her eyes wide. "Are you OK, Honor?"

"Tisi is a nightmare. It's like trying to hold back an unstoppable force of nature. I honestly don't think I can help her any more."

"I saw her as she left. Does she always dress in vivid red?"

"She always dresses dramatically. What's the mystery?"

"Maybe you know, I don't know. Sit down, here, eat something: it'll make you feel better." She pushed a tray of sandwiches towards Honor.

"Thanks. What's the deal?"

"Her name comes from the Eumenides, keepers of the celestial gardens, right?" Ann was sitting on the edge of her seat, looking intently at Honor.

"Yes …"

"Do you know the other name for the Eumenides? The unspeakable name?"

"What? No ... what d'you mean?" Honor set her sandwich down, uneaten.

"Before they became the Eumenides, they were called something else, a name that nobody spoke, as it brought their rage down on anyone who said it."

"What rage? What name? You're talking in riddles." Honor's throat constricted.

"I'm going to write it down. I'm not saying it; it's the most terrible bad luck. Don't you say it either, at least not in my office, in my hearing."

Ann passed a pad to Honor, on which she had written: *the Erinyes*.

Honor looked at it, then looked at Ann. This was Ann at her most barmy, the idea that saying two words could bring down fire and brimstone. She shrugged, lifted her hands, palms upwards. "What does it mean?"

"Tisiphone, Alecto and Megaera were three sisters, the Furies, who haunted those who committed crimes within the family. They haunted them to insanity, to death and beyond. Tisiphone was the keeper of the hell of the underworld, the fiercest of the three. She had snakes for hair and blood red eyes."

Honor stared at Ann. "But ... the garden ... they were keepers of the garden. I read it. I looked it up."

"Only once their violent rage was appeased. Before that they were the ...." She gestured towards the page on which she had written their original name. "Never say that name. You *are* dealing with a primitive, destructive force of nature. She'll stop at nothing in the name of retribution."

Honor took a sharp breath and stood up. "Look Ann, I have to get back, I only had a minute, I'm as busy as hell."

"Let's go out for lunch tomorrow, we can talk about it then." Ann patted Honor's departing back.

What on earth did Ann think, that Tisi was some kind of modern reincarnation of a mythical Greek goddess? Someone should tell her: they were myths, they weren't real. What was she suggesting? That someone's name determined their character? Honestly, talk about magical thinking. If there was some hard scientific evidence that Tisi's character was anything to do with her namesake, maybe she'd consider it.

CHAPTER TWELVE

After dinner that evening, Honor excused herself to her study. She could see tension etched in the tight line of Eliot's mouth. "Look, Honor, we have to talk."

"Do we?" Honor sat back down, and looked coolly at her husband. "I'm listening."

Eliot cleared his throat and shifted in his seat. "I've been thinking about what you said, and you're right of course."

Honor gave a regal nod and a slight smile.

"But honestly, are you ever going to trust me again? Am I ever going to be forgiven? It's impossible for me, where my every slight action is interpreted as some kind of transgression. When are we ever going to put this behind us?"

"All I can say, Eliot, is it may be easy for you to put this behind us, but it's not so easy for me. Remember what you used to say to me in our early years about this? Do you remember?"

Eliot ran his hands through his hair and nodded.

"Go on then. Remind me."

Eliot took a deep breath. "I used to say that if I ever found you had been unfaithful to me, that would be it, it would be over."

"Yes, you did say that. And you had a clear and specific reason for saying that if you remember. That once someone had been unfaithful once, it would happen again, like a violent man who hits his wife: he won't be able to stop himself from doing it again. Remember that?"

Eliot, head bowed, gave the slightest nod. Then he looked up and said, "Yes, I said that."

"I had a kinder view. [*I'm bullying him, but I can't stop myself.*] That the guilt would motivate a person to redouble their efforts to stay true to the marriage vow: loyalty, forsaking all others, in sickness and poverty, through good times—easy—and bad. Who can claim to love otherwise? Love's as easy as pie without that pledge. If it was easy you wouldn't need to promise would you?"

Eliot was staring at her, intently. "You're right. And I agree with you now. Are you going to punish me with grand theoretical statements I made when I was young and inexperienced? It's not how I think now."

"Well no, you wouldn't would you? We can all say things that don't get tested. From where I'm sitting, you want me to bless you with the forgiveness that you wouldn't allow me."

Eliot rubbed his eyes and sighed heavily. "You have to though, Honor, don't you see? We can't be happy if you don't. If you won't trust me or believe me, what the hell am I supposed to do next? How can I show my remorse, and get your forgiveness? Not some partial forgiveness, conditional on me never speaking, looking or laughing in the presence of another woman? Real forgiveness: forgive and forget type forgiveness?"

He's right. If only my heart could do what my head knows. How can I expect him to live like this? But then he has made me *live like* this.

"I don't know Eliot. I just don't know."

Later, alone in her study, she thought about what Eliot had said, in the early days of their relationship, cocooned by the bliss of new love. He was expressing chivalrous outrage at Thomas's infidelity with Madalena. And what about you, Honor, he'd said; were you faithful to Thomas? Yes, she'd said, and was about to tell him the whole sorry saga of the love triangle, and its devastating consequences. But he'd interrupted her to tell her his views on infidelity. He knew he may appear to be a bit of a rebel he'd said, but at heart he was a good Catholic boy, with strong views on sin. Honor had stared at him wide-eyed, but said nothing, silently swallowing the secret she'd been about to confide. A secret she had kept forever. From everyone.

When she and Eliot had decided to keep it all together, despite her despair, and her desperation to leave, her mantra had been "Be a Good Wife". She had tried so hard. She had given him the third child he longed for, paid more attention to their marriage, and to him; and had tried not to bring it up, tried her best to forget. Until now she had pretty much succeeded.

With an audible sigh and a shake of her head, she turned her mind from Eliot to Thomas, and turned to her computer screen. *OK, here goes, I'm going to deliberately torture myself.* Using Barbara's recommended software, she created a montage: Madalena, Thomas, and Bella, forming them into a family group. They made an attractive family. Staring at the screen, Honor reached forward and stroked Thomas's face.

"I'm so sorry, Thomas," she whispered. "So very sorry. You'd have loved her, I know you would."

She saved the portrait.

She googled: Tisiphone.

Half an hour later, she'd confirmed everything that Ann had said, plus more.

Tisiphone, Megaera and Alecto, the Furies of Greek mythology, were the daughters of darkness: the three goddesses of revenge, their heads wreathed with serpents and their eyes dripped with blood.

Tisiphone was the cruel and furious guardian of the gates of Tartarus, the hellish component of the underworld, a dungeon of torment and suffering. All three sisters resided there and unleashed their punishments: Tisiphone punished crimes of murder, Alecto was known for her unceasing anger, and Megaera for her jealous torture of the unfaithful.

The Furies descended like a storm, driving their victims insane through persistent haunting, until death and beyond, their torture continuing until a verdict was pronounced by the right person, and their victims showed true remorse. Then the Furies calmed and transformed into the Eumenides, or the Kindly Ones, the guardians of a heavenly garden, where they received sacrifices and libations.

So there it was. There was the energy she had been infected by, every time she sat with Tisi, the legacy her mother left her with, giving her all three names. That's what can determine character: a mother's intention, her desires, her deepest dreams and imaginings for her child. But why would Tisi's mother leave her daughter with such a burden?

The thing is, would this knowledge break Tisi's spell on Honor? Because it had been a spell, her own feelings awakened by Tisi's experience; her own desire to punish, to drive someone mad.

Had she lost that feeling now, as she understood what had happened?

Honor did a mental scan of her mind and body.

No, she hadn't lost that feeling; it was more confused, she was less certain who needed to be punished, but somebody needed to be, that was for sure.

She hadn't lost that feeling. She hadn't lost it at all.

The next day, on her way to work, Honor did a detour to Madalena's flat, and sat outside looking up at their terrace, hoping to catch a glimpse of Bella. She wished she could help her, and save her from her mother, find a way to do this last thing for Thomas: rescue his daughter.

She waited, hopefully, for ten minutes, but there was no sign of life, and she left, disappointed.

After Honor's busy morning, Ann arrived promptly for lunch at a vegetarian restaurant around the corner. Neutral ground, as Ann said, away from the Tisi effect.

It was a tiny restaurant, in the front room of a house, seating no more than twenty people. The room was simply decorated, in natural wood and pale colours, the big front bay windows drenching the room with brilliant sunlight today. It was run by a gay couple, with a love of simple, organic food.

The two women settled in a corner booth, and ordered from the two choices on the menu: butternut squash risotto for Ann, and goat's cheese salad for Honor.

"Tisi frightened me yesterday. There's something sinister about her energy," Ann said.

"She's pretty out of control. I don't know what to do next. I googled her name last night; I found the myth. But honestly, Ann, what the hell does it mean? For Tisi?"

"What does Bill say?"

"I haven't talked to him actually. I kept meaning to, but ..." Honor didn't meet Ann's eyes. She had cancelled her last session with Bill.

"Why ever not? How on earth are you keeping your own system clear of her without help?"

"Frankly, I'm not. She's sucked me into something, I can't explain. I feel weird when I'm with her, not quite myself."

"What's going on with her?"

"She's in crisis mode. Her husband's been unfaithful, and she wants to make him suffer. She wants to torment his lover, and drive her mad. She's probably succeeding too: when she arrived yesterday, she'd just told her husband's lover's husband—follow that?—about their affair. I've tried to help her maintain control but she can't seem to stop herself."

And I could say exactly the same thing about myself.

"She's behaving exactly like her namesake in fact." Ann looked serious.

"Yes, I see that."

"What's her history? How did she get those names?"

"Her mother was a classics scholar, specializing in the minor mythical goddesses. She named her three daughters: Persephone, Ariadne and Tisiphone."

"Phew. Hades … spiders … revenge …. Snakes, spiders and witches. What was going on with her?"

"God knows …"

"What's the history then? There must be clues there?"

Honor shifted in her chair, uncomfortably aware of her dereliction of duty. "I haven't taken a detailed history yet …"

"Really? That's one of the first things you do surely?"

Honor was relieved at the arrival of their food, and the distraction it made to being held to account. "She's been in crisis you see, it's rather undermined our normal process. Every time I see her there's some new drama. I've tried to pull her back to history but it drives her into a strange and murderous rage. She rears up, her eyes glitter, she *undulates*. I get so frightened that I feel compelled to try to calm her down."

"Red-eyed … snakes for hair."

"It's making me feel sick talking about it." Honor put down her fork and pushed her plate away. She wasn't going to be able to eat.

"D'you know any of her history at all?"

"She believes her father killed her mother. She died young, of cancer of the uterus. Tisi believes her illness and death were brought on by the strain of living with him. She thinks they should have divorced, but her mother stayed for the sake of the kids."

"What did he do, exactly, that was so awful?"

"I'm not really sure. I need to find out."

"Going by the myth, if she believes her father killed her mother, she'll haunt him till he goes mad and dies, unless he shows remorse."

Honor was gazing into the distance, piecing together bits of information, and pulling on memories of her discussions with Tisi.

"What's that got to do with her husband's infidelity? Her rage with him? I can't work it out."

"Simple. A new injury reopens an old injury. We've all seen that many times, surely?"

A new injury opens an old injury. Of course. Injury layered upon injury, till you can't tell one from the other.

"So her reaction to Don's affair is pulling up all the old pain of her mother's misery and death … Yes, I see, of course."

"There's something else." Ann held Honor in intense eye contact. "This is not difficult really, Honor, is it? Psychologically, it's straightforward stuff: something bad happens, and reminds you of something similar from long ago. The echoing dynamics of the two things get mixed up. The question is, why did it prove so hard for you to see what was right under your nose? You're used to dealing with more complex and dramatic cases than Tisi. How did she succeed in throwing you so thoroughly off balance? How come she infected you with her mood, rather than you having a calming impact on her? How did that happen? That's the real question. What was going on for you that first day, when you met her, that made this so different?"

Honor cast her mind back to the first day she met Tisi. A bad day. The painful date. Seeing Tisi. Remembering Jackie. Going to the park, seeing Bella in the paper, realizing she was Thomas's daughter. All those things happening together, the hideous coincidence of it, flooding her senses with old pain.

"Yes, well, you're right, I wouldn't normally struggle to contain a client like Tisi. Your question gets to the heart of it. It was a day when several things happened to make me hypersensitive and upset. I was stirred up by a shadow of my own when I met Tisi, and disturbed again by something that happened after I met her. I couldn't think, or see straight. Something about Tisi got mixed up in some old misery of my own, it blinded me."

"So how can you untangle that? If you're going to help Tisi, you need to, you're enmeshed with her."

"Yes, I am, and I must do something before Tisi escalates things even further. I'm frightened by what she might do next. She hasn't satisfied herself yet, I can tell."

And I don't know what I'll do next either … because there's something in me that wants to do something worse too.

"Can I help you? Maybe I could help you work out the way to manage Tisi? Will you talk to Bill?"

Could I talk to Ann? Tell her everything? I need to talk to somebody.

Honor smiled brightly. "It's been such a relief to talk to you. It'd be great if you could help me now you know all about it. Perhaps you could supervise me on Tisi, save me going through it all with Bill?"

"Definitely, of course, I'll do anything I can to help."

"It's been good to talk about it, I'll be able to manage her better now I think. What I need to do is get a detailed history; show her how her current outrage is pulling up her old anger against her father. Shed some light on the dynamics for her, and calm her down that way, d'you think?"

"Definitely. Point out to her, a bit humorously, the energy of her mythic naming."

"Yes, well, one thing at a time," Honor said.

"Once we understand the details of her history, maybe get some clues from the myth, we could think about a creative intervention to heal her."

Sometimes I think Ann sounds a bit mad when she talks like that. Next thing she'll be suggesting an exorcism.

"I'm sure her history'll be revealing enough, from what I've heard so far anyway."

CHAPTER THIRTEEN

Honor lay in bed, halfway between sleep and wakefulness. Eliot snuggled against her and nuzzled the back of her neck.

Sleepily, she turned her thoughts to the day ahead. She was seeing Tisi, and there were a number of things she needed to do to prepare.

She opened her eyes, looked at the clock, and pulled away from Eliot.

"Don't go." He pulled her back towards him.

"I have to, it's an important day today."

"What about me? Aren't I important? You never have time for me any more."

Honor leaned back and kissed him, hugged him. "Tonight let's have dinner together, alright?"

Eliot was not so easily deterred. "Ten minutes stay, let's have a cuddle."

"We know where that'll go." Honor sat up, leaned down and kissed him. "I really don't have time. Tonight, promise."

He looked at her, serious. She couldn't meet his eyes.

Honor dressed quickly and made her way to her study, trying to stifle her irritation with Eliot. He required a level of attention that could only really be provided by a woman without distractions. A job for instance.

Or children. Sometimes she felt she was in the perfect trap. Your family needs your salary. Your husband demands attention and resents your career.

She loved her job, which was just as well, as she'd have to do it anyway. Sometimes she thought Eliot would be happier if she hated it and resented the sacrifices she had to make for it. They needed the money so Eliot could play, do what he wanted, be a freelance musician. If Honor didn't work, he'd have to be different. Grown up, maybe.

She wanted to prepare for the day with a meditation. She thought about what she was *not* going to do: the things she'd started to do each morning, which wound up her state of distress. She was *not* going to review all her photos of Thomas, the montages of him, Madalena, and Bella, and feel the churning in her gut as she looked at them all. (So, no, today she was not going to prepare herself to be stimulated by Tisi's turmoil.) And she wasn't going to make her regular morning detour past Madalena's flat in the hope of getting a glimpse of Thomas's daughter, that would stab her with a desire to get close to her, to do for Bella what Thomas would have wanted: help her get an education, and possibly even a career. No, today she wasn't going to do that either.

She settled in her chair, closed her eyes and deepened her breathing, visualizing how she usually managed herself when faced with a disturbed person; the breathing, the deepening of her voice, the slowing of her words, the smile, the calming presence.

Thoughts of Eliot's reproach intruded, but Honor gently put them aside. Today's session with Tisi was going to be different; Honor was going to quietly take her history, as she should have done weeks ago.

She must resist any drama. Face Tisi with calm: neutral and curious. She spoke inwardly to herself: let Tisi have her own feelings: don't take them on; don't allow your own feelings to echo hers. Use your energy. Contain her with the hypnotic quality of your voice.

On her drive to work she continued to repeat them, over and over, like a mantra. Stopping at some traffic lights, she glanced to her right, to see a woman and child in the next car staring at her and laughing: talking to herself, the first sign of madness. *If only they knew. I'm way past the first sign. Talking to myself is nothing.*

Taking a deep breath, she pulled her attention back to the world, and looked out at the grey drizzling rain, the pavements busy with mothers taking young children to schools and nurseries. Watching them, she remembered, with longing, the simplicity of it. The sheer, mindless, devoted simplicity: keep these kids warm and dry; make sure they eat some fruit and vegetables; get them to school; bring them home again, feed them, bath them, tuck them, warm, into bed. *How dedicated. How easy. How lovely.*

Arriving at the office, Honor had fifteen minutes before Tisi's arrival. She tidied up her desk, checked in with Barbara, and collected a cup of tea.

"How's it going with Tisi?" Barbara, sitting at her desk, looked up at Honor, standing next to her.

"Fine. Fine. Why d'you ask?" Honor felt heat rising in her face.

"You've cancelled your session with Bill twice now."

"You know how busy I've been. Must go and get ready now." Honor picked up her cup of tea and went to her office. Barbara's words followed her.

"I'll call him this morning to re-schedule."

God, Barbara was a busybody sometimes.

Was it her imagination, or did Tisi look different? *I'm fascinated, and always amazed by the changes in her.* Her hair was in a sleeker style, and she was wearing the same soft blue dress and grey shoes that she'd worn at her first meeting with Honor. *That bodes well, we can pretend it's the first session and get it right this time.*

Tisi's face was heavily made up, one side looked darker than the other, but her eyes, usually so expertly painted, were tired and pink. Lack of sleep? Tears? She seemed subdued.

"How are you, Tisi?"

Her shoulders lifted in a deep sigh, and her hands twisted together in her lap. "Not good. Things are about as bad as they can be really. But it's almost as though I feel relieved, the worst has happened and there's nothing else to worry about."

Honor breathed deeply to control the rising cord of anxiety that Tisi habitually pulled on. "What I'd like us to do today, Tisi, is to talk about something we should have discussed earlier, but that got derailed by the crises that were going on. I need to understand more of your personal and family history, so that I can help you to develop your understanding of how what is happening between you and Don is reminding you, perhaps, of earlier painful experiences."

Another big sigh. "Okay. But can I tell you first what's happened since I last saw you, so you know the whole story?"

"Alright, Tisi."

"Don's in hospital."

Face it with calm. Neutral and curious. Resist any drama.

"I see …"

"He's concussed."

Encouraging nod. Quizzical raised eyebrow. *Why am I smiling?*

"It was my fault. I went too far. You were right last time, I lost control of things, and I relied on other people to do the right thing. And they didn't, they just didn't. I was laughing at first. It seemed like perfect justice. Karma, you know. We were home, early evening, I'd put the kids to bed. I was upstairs, tidying round; just making sure they were going off to sleep. I heard the front doorbell ring, and Don going to answer it."

Honor's sense of alarm was rising. She cautioned herself: you be the one to infect her with your mood, don't let her feelings get inside you, guard yourself against that at all costs. She nodded encouragingly again.

"I heard a man's voice, then a shout. I went to the top of the stairs, and I could see them in the hall, Steven, about to hit Don. I screamed and almost fell down the stairs in my panic to get there. Steven let out such a punch, right in the middle of Don's face. It made a loud cracking noise, and Don staggered back, his nose an explosion of blood; he put his hands to his face, and lost his balance. He fell sidewards, his head smashing against the wall. I rushed to stop Steven hitting him again, screaming, 'No! Leave him alone!' I got to Steven just as he let out another punch, I tried to turn away but he caught me on the side of my face. Don was lying on the floor; he looked as though he was dead. I turned on Steven, rushed at him, pushing him, shouting at him: 'Get out. Get out.' He stepped back and sneered, 'That's the least that prick deserves,' then he left."

Oh dear God. "What did you do, Tisi?"

"Don wasn't moving, I thought he was dead. The children were on the stairs, crying. I sent them up to their room, saying don't worry, Daddy's going to be fine. Then I dialled 999."

Honor felt sick to her stomach. In fact she thought she might throw up, so she excused herself and went to the bathroom, leaning over the bowl, her stomach heaving. She sipped some water and returned to her office.

"Sorry, Tisi." Tisi didn't seem to have registered that Honor had actually left the room.

"The ambulance came straight away. I couldn't go with Don, I needed to calm the children, and find a sitter. The police questioned me. Steven's been arrested. It's all my fault isn't it? It's all because of me. Don could have died; I'd have killed him, just as I wanted to. Just because I didn't actually smash his head in with a hammer doesn't mean I wouldn't have killed him? You've been brilliant, Honor, I know you tried really hard to stop me; and I tried to stop myself, and I nearly did. I just made someone else do it for me, but it was me all along."

What a long speech. And finally she had called her Honor, not Doctor. All that drama, yet no sign of the spitting fury. Well, the worst had happened, no need for rage any more.

"You won't help yourself by thinking like this. Don isn't dead, he's injured. And you didn't cause that. Steven did. Or maybe Don and Jackie did, by betraying their partners. We'll talk more about this, what is and isn't your responsibility. I want to help you, and I know how to. Before we move on, tell me, how is Don? What are the doctors saying?"

"His nose is broken and he has concussion from bashing his head on the wall. They're keeping him in for observation, but they seem to think he'll recover alright."

"And you? Were you hurt?"

"Bruised." She turned her head slightly and pulled her hair aside. Even beneath the heavy makeup, the discolouration was evident.

"And the children?"

She wiped away a tear. "Traumatized."

"Are you able to be strong for them?"

"Of course."

"This is going to seem strange, but if I am to help you, and I know I can, I must ask you some detailed questions, and I need you to answer these sensibly, without getting upset if possible. I need you to provide me with the factual information I ask you for. Will that be possible d'you think?"

"Yes, I can do that. I'll keep calm."

Honor had arranged to spend an hour with Ann immediately after her session with Tisi. As Ann had pointed out: "I can help you contain her and your feelings, if I see you straight away."

Ann was wide-eyed as Honor related the latest events and their apparent impact on Tisi.

"Well, I guess when all the drama is actually, really, happening, it doesn't need melodrama does it? Things are bad enough already."

"She was the calmest and most sensible I've seen her. She even spoke rationally about her history, without getting upset. And there's quite a lot of material to unpack, I can tell you."

"Go on then. Tell me. What's the story?"

Honor related Tisi's story to Ann, glancing occasionally at her notebook as she spoke.

"Tisi's the third of three daughters, all born within five years. Their mother, Daphne, was an academic and scholar of the classics with a particular affinity with the secondary, minor Greek goddesses. When Daphne was pregnant with Tisiphone, she discovered that her husband, Daniel, was leading a double life, having a bigamous wife in the next town and two sons of a similar age to their two daughters, Persephone and Ariadne. Daphne was distraught. Daniel wanted to maintain both families. Daphne had to accept it: if she reported him to the police he'd go to jail and she couldn't support her family. She was absolutely furious that she was forced to be so compromised."

"What a story. She was hoping her daughter would avenge her fate."

"Tisi's early years were awful …. God, I shudder to think of the events surrounding her birth. Soon after that, Tisi's father started splitting his time between both families, and Tisi routinely witnessed dreadful rows and arguments. Her mother was trapped and powerless: she was savage towards her husband. And Tisi fell into the role of appeaser, attempting to calm her mother down when she flew into one of her rages."

"Poor girl … what a legacy. Did they divorce eventually?"

"Yes … though Daphne obstructed that for as long as she possibly could. She died subsequently, seven years ago …. Cancer of the uterus."

"Tragic. How's Tisi with her Dad now?"

"Blames him for the stress her mother lived under for so long. She and her sisters refuse to have any relationship with their stepmother or stepbrothers."

"Bitterness. Awful. It eats everyone …"

"He's tried to redeem himself. He keeps in contact, showers them with gifts, and has shown remorse. He must be exhausted: but he seems to keep alive the hope that one day all his children will get to know and love each other."

"It sounds as though they enjoy torturing him."

"I think Tisi does, the way she told me, as though it satisfied her. She almost got what she wanted with Don: to murder him and drive Jackie crazy; she got pretty close. No wonder she's calmed down."

"Will it be enough for her though? What does she want to have happen, with Steven and with Jackie? Presumably Steven's on an assault charge .... So Jackie could end up as a single mother. Perhaps Tisi will too. That has a certain symmetry, I can see that. I doubt if that'll seem quite fair to her though."

"There's a clue in the myth: she'll become one of the Kindly Ones when she has a verdict, from the right person, and remorse from the wrongdoer."

Ann was thoughtful. "It makes perfect sense doesn't it, the myth? Once someone is remorseful, you can have pity for them; and then you can be kind. It's enshrined in our legal system isn't it? If a criminal expresses remorse, it's a mitigating factor, it can result in a shorter sentence."

On her way home, despite her resolve of the morning, Honor took the familiar detour to see if she could get a glimpse of Bella. The flat looked abandoned, blinds drawn, terrace furniture folded away; so she turned around and made her way home.

Honor moved easily around the kitchen, preparing the family dinner, her own favourite, grilled fish and green vegetables, with some oven chips for the kids, in an attempt to head off their grumbling at such a boringly healthy meal. As it happened, as though they sensed her need for family normality, they were model children at dinner, eating their food without complaint, and keeping bickering to acceptable levels. In fact, they ended up in an interesting discussion about friendship, stimulated by a school lesson of Eden's, and Honor privately congratulated herself on how intelligent and well balanced they were. Even clearing up after dinner turned into a cooperative family effort, before the kids went about their evening activities.

Putting away the last dishes, Honor smiled at Eliot. "Aren't they great kids?"

"We're so lucky, Honor, aren't we?" Eliot put his arms around her and pulled her towards him. "Brilliant kids; with a lovely Mum."

"Oh thanks, darling, that's nice." Honor circled his waist with her arms and pressed her cheek against his.

"What about us, though, Honor? I don't know what I can do to put things right. Tell me how?" Eliot stepped back, to look at her.

Honor looked back at him. She knew he was right, that she couldn't punish him so roundly at any slight suspicion she might have. And she hadn't until now. *I'd got over it, I know I had, I thought I had; but now it's all surfaced again. If I could only get rid of the pictures in my head.* Turning, she gazed out of the window, at the lilac trees, starting to drop their flowers now.

She faced Eliot again. "I wish I knew, Eliot, I really do. I know this isn't fair on you."

Could she tell him, she wondered, about Tisi, and what that was arousing in her? Or was it about Madalena and Bella? She shook her head, confused about the mix of events that were disturbing her so deeply.

"What's hard to understand is that it's all such a long time ago," Eliot said. "It's ages since we've spoken of it, or been reminded. I barely remember it myself it's so far back."

"Easy for you to forget, Eliot." Honor gave a bitter laugh. "You'd want to wouldn't you? It may be long ago time-wise, but some days, for me, like Amanda's visit, it could have happened yesterday."

Eliot shrugged.

"Like some sort of memory download, the whole thing," Honor continued. "What I felt and thought, all there for me to re-experience all over again. It's torture."

"And it's torture for me to be reminded of how I made you suffer. I'm so sorry, Honor, I think you do know how sorry I am don't you?"

Honor's throat tightened and she took Eliot's hand. Yes, she did think he was really sorry. "I'm just not 100% confident that it won't happen again. As you've said, if a determined woman sets her cap at you, what are you to do? It's as though you feel no responsibility for what happens."

"I don't know how I can convince you. You won't be sure, Honor, till the day I die … is that how long I have to wait for complete forgiveness?"

"That's ridiculous, of course I see that. It must be horrible not to be trusted or believed."

And it must be really horrible. He was a good man, who'd made one mistake, that was all. Surely everyone deserved a second chance. Everyone. That's what she would want, a second chance, to show that she could be good.

She leaned across and kissed him. "Let's put it behind us … I'll try, I really will try, to forget. To forgive *and* forget."

Eliot's relief was palpable. "Come on, darling. Let's go to bed and make up properly."

Later, Honor was unable to sleep, restless and disturbed by thoughts of Bella. Quietly, keen not to wake Eliot who was snoring contentedly, she slipped out of bed and headed up to her study. She called up the pictures of Bella. She clicked on her best picture of Thomas and allowed it to fill the whole screen. Those amazing blue eyes. Bella hadn't inherited those anyway, but then she wouldn't have would she? She'd take after her mother.

She opened her browser and typed into Google: Bella Norman. Within seconds, a list of pages appeared on the screen: top hits—all the recent newspaper articles about her. Honor scanned through them rapidly: she didn't need to read those again. Here was a model agency, proclaiming their recent signing: Bella Norman. Honor opened the page, to find a profile and numerous photos of Bella in a range of poses, including some at the "glamour" end of the spectrum. Thomas would be appalled. In the written profile, under the heading favourite books, Bella pronounced: "I'm not really into books, but I love to read all the gossip and fashion mags." *Oh for God's sake*.

And under the heading, occupation: fashion and glamour model; presenter; personality. What was that supposed to mean? Occupation: personality? Personality was a psychological attribute, not something you did. She must do something about this girl, get in touch with her, befriend her. Yes, become her friend, a mentor; eventually almost a second mother to her. She wasn't being raised as Thomas would have wanted, that was clear.

Yes, that was it. She had to find a way to meet her.

CHAPTER FOURTEEN

Harmony reigned again at the breakfast table.

Jack had agreed, reluctantly, after some extra special persuasion by Madalena, that Bella could spend more time at the London apartment without her parents, and she was going there this morning.

There were some stringent conditions: (a) she must not make the long drive herself, the chauffeur was to take her there and back; (b) no more than three days at any one time; (c) no visitors to the apartment without Jack's express approval; (d) Bella must speak to her mother every morning and evening while she was in London; and (e) … Jack reserved the right to add further conditions as and when necessary.

Bella was her happy self once more.

"It's nice to see you without that glower, princess," Jack said.

Bella smiled at him sweetly. "Thanks Dad. I'm going up to London this morning."

"You don't waste any time, once you've got what you want. Just like your mother," Jack grumbled.

"Have you done your packing?" Madalena asked. "Maybe now you're going to spend more time in London, you should leave more of your own things there, so you don't have to keep packing and unpacking."

"I've packed some stuff. I'll do the rest after breakfast. It's hard to decide what to take and what to leave here, I like having my favourite clothes with me in both places."

"Buy duplicates, it's much easier. That's what I've done with my wardrobe basics. Also, heavier stuff, just buy a second set for London."

"Yeah, toiletries, and I need to get another hairdryer and straighteners."

"Go shopping this afternoon and get new ones and leave them there. What else? Your iPod? Phone charger?"

"No, those'll be OK to carry."

"It's electrical stuff that's usually heavy."

"Getting my laptop packed and unpacked is a real drag."

Madalena glanced in Jack's direction. He was browsing through the newspaper, apparently not paying attention. She raised her voice slightly.

"Well, can't do anything about that. A laptop's so *expensive*."

Jack looked up from his paper. "What's expensive?"

Madalena waited, silent.

"A laptop, Dad. Me and Mum are talking about what I can take to London and leave there so I don't need to keep packing and unpacking."

"Great plan, girls! Do what me and your Mum do … buy two of everything, one for here, one for there."

Madalena studiously avoided Bella's eye, and busied herself, wiping her perfectly clean side plate with her serviette with great concentration.

"That's what we're saying, Dad," said Bella with patronizing patience. "We're talking about things that are heavy too."

Jack looked across at Madalena, who was still wiping her plate. He looked back at Bella. "Like what?"

"It's a nuisance packing up my laptop and carting it back and forth, that's what we were saying. You could listen you know, Dad, you make me get up early for breakfast then you sit there reading your paper and not listening to a word I say."

Jack cleared his throat. "Well … I … sorry, yes. Well, let's get another laptop, we don't have to worry about cost. Have one here and one in London. Or get a desktop for London, those new iMacs are fantastic, get one of those, you could probably do with a new one anyway. What d'you think, Madalena?"

Madalena looked up. "What? Sorry I was busy …"

"We should get another laptop, don't you think? So Bella doesn't have to keep carting one back and forth to London?"

"If you think so, Jack. It seems a lot of money."

"Aah … but then you could Skype. Perfect. See? Your morning and evening calls can be on Skype. You can see each other. Most importantly, Bella, your Mum can see you."

"Mum can't use a computer."

"She can learn. Any idiot can use a computer. Sometimes I think your mother is a lot cleverer than she makes out to be; a lot cleverer …."

"It's not difficult, I'll show you after breakfast, Mum."

"I'll get the guy from my London office to come over late afternoon, bring a new one and set it up for you. I know I shouldn't boast, but this is one of those times where my problem-solving skills are at their best, don't you think? Solve the problem, make a decision, straight to action." Jack stood up, his chest puffed out.

It wouldn't have surprised Madalena if he'd thrown his head back, roared, and pounded his chest with his fists. "Brilliant, Jack, you're brilliant," she said, and wrapped her arms around his neck to kiss him.

Once Jack had left, Madalena went to change for the gym. She was going over the breakfast discussion, imagining telling Bud about it. She could hear his American drawl: "You look like the cat that just got the cream …." Yes, she thought, and without raising so much as a paw. If only she could be so effective in the marriage stakes. Her mother had said, many years ago: "Don't worry about it, Madalena, hang on in there till he's old; he'll want to secure you as his nursemaid then; or just wait till the old bitch is dead, it's probably her that's putting the kibosh on it for you, she thinks you're not good enough for her son, the emperor."

With Bella away, Jack made an impromptu decision to take Madalena out for dinner. Madalena was thrown into disarray: she preferred to have notice of outings, so that she could plan, in meticulous detail, including much trying on and experimentation, what she would wear.

She was also tired: Bella had given her a quick lesson on the laptop, specifically on how to Skype her in London, and then had left, with the chauffeur, for the life of a single girl in London, to her mother's envy.

She'd spent much of the afternoon trying to understand how the computer worked: she had a surprising aptitude for it, though it took her a long time to do anything, without keyboard skills. She texted Bud: I'll try and Skype you later tonight if I can.

Before she knew it, hours had passed, and Jack arrived home, announcing that he'd booked a table for eight o'clock.

Jack had a tendency to be romantic at dinner. A good meal out was part of sexual foreplay; Madalena knew that bedtime would be leisurely tonight, a deliberately loving and concentrated experience, the sort that she enjoyed the most. Although hassled by her lack of wardrobe planning time, she welcomed this: maybe she was wrong about Jack, she was seeing things that weren't there? Imagining things?

She selected a short black dress, and a soft sage silk jacket over the top. High-heeled black suede shoes on her long bare legs completed the outfit.

"You look fabulous," Jack said, as she came downstairs.

Madalena knew that Jack had never got used to her beauty. He would stand, transfixed, staring at her as if she was a painting or a statue. Sometimes she'd be driven to say, "Jack, stop looking at me like that." Today, she was reassured to see his appreciation of her.

At the restaurant, Jack continued in complimentary vein. "You're as lovely as the day I met you, maybe even more so. D'you remember that day?"

"Of course, how could I forget?"

"I've never seen anyone who can hold a candle to you, except perhaps our daughter. No wonder I left home for you, what man wouldn't? Every man in town wanted you."

Madalena smiled warmly. The romantic side of Jack was the part of him that she loved the most. She softened to his words, and the intimate ambience of the candlelit restaurant. Everything was going to be fine, surely?

Jack's next words startled her.

"Remember that chap you were going out with at the time? Thomas what's his name?"

He was watching her closely.

She gave a vague smile and a wave of her hand. "I wasn't exactly *with* him, it was a casual thing …"

"He was married wasn't he? What was his surname?"

"Oh … um … Dyer. No, he wasn't married, he had a regular girlfriend. We just flirted a bit, there was nothing to it."

"Honor, wasn't it, Honor Sinclair? I remember her, an attractive woman, sort of a Grace Kelly, ice princess. What became of her I wonder?"

"No idea. Shall we order, Jack? What'll you have?" Madalena studied the menu.

"She moved away, didn't she? After Thomas died?"

"I think so ... will you have a steak? You like the fillet steak here best don't you?"

"I expect she remarried ... wasn't she very clever? A doctor or something?"

"Dunno ... I'm just going to the bathroom. If they come for my order, I'll have soup and the chicken, please."

Madalena gazed at her frightened face in the bathroom mirror. She leaned in and whispered to her reflection: Jack knows. He suspects. She had to talk to Bud tonight, and get his help. What was in Jack's mind? What was he thinking?

"Did you order? I wonder how Bella's getting on in London?"

"No, not yet. You spoke to Bella?"

"We Skyped. It couldn't have been simpler. We could see each other, it's brilliant, that's such a clever way for us to keep track of her."

The waiter arrived to take their order, distracting Jack for a moment.

"How did Thomas die? Remind me? There was something strange, wasn't there?"

"I can't really remember, I don't think they ever knew really." Madalena was looking around the restaurant. "Look over there, Jack, isn't that the woman who used to work in the office? Donna someone?"

Jack turned around to look, then waved his hand dismissively. "No, it's not. Come on, Madalena, you must remember; you were really quite involved with him. Wasn't it suicide or something?"

"*Definitely* not. He would *not* have committed suicide. It was an accident, that's all."

"How could they be so sure?"

"The inquest said it was an open verdict. Poison. They just didn't know how it happened."

"How d'you accidentally poison yourself?"

"God knows."

"Did they think he was murdered?"

131

Madalena blinked. "What makes you say that?"

"Isn't that what an open verdict means? Suicide or murder?"

Madalena waved her hand. "Or accident. It was all speculation. Are you sure it's not her? She used to work on the reception desk?"

"Positive, no, definitely not. Seems a strange kind of accident. What sort of poison?"

The waiter arrived with Madalena's soup and Jack's prawn cocktail. "Dunno."

"Not even you? You were sleeping with him weren't you?"

"Not when he died, no. That was sometime after my time with him, it just wasn't that serious."

"You're underplaying this. My memory is that at one stage he actually left Honor for you."

"That was before they were married, and only for a short time ... I'd met you by then."

"It was before I'd left Pat though." Jack leaned back in his chair and stared up at the ceiling. "I was trying to remember the other day, what the sequence of events was."

Madalena pushed her soup away. She was beginning to feel nauseous. "You're exaggerating my relationship with him, it was just one of those teenage things, like Bella with Euan, they don't know what they want at their age."

"Not the same thing at all. With those two, there's already a child involved."

Madalena shivered and pulled her jacket around her shoulders. She cleared her throat. "Exactly Jack. You're right, it's completely different, that was a stupid comparison to make. We weren't in that position at all; by the time we conceived Bella, you'd left Pat and Thomas and Honor had got married."

Is he convinced by my confidence?, Madalena wondered.

"Yes, that's true, I'd forgotten about that." A thought struck him. "So when did you stop seeing Thomas then? When *exactly*?"

"Once I'd met you, Jack. From the moment I saw you, you were the only man for me, always have been and always will be."

There was now no question in her mind. Jack had also got a letter, similar to hers. She didn't know exactly what it said, but she was sure of the gist: it had planted a seed of doubt in Jack's mind and he was no longer confident that Bella was his daughter.

Madalena lay awake, listening to Jack's steady breathing. She stretched luxuriously, relaxed from the sensuous lovemaking that had ended their evening. Whatever doubt he had in his mind, it had not taken root sufficiently to affect his feelings for her yet. Her body tensed as she thought of the letter, the looming threat to her secure and easy life. She had to find out who it had come from, it was her only hope.

She looked at the clock. It was one in the morning, so about eight in the evening in New York.

She slid carefully and quietly out of bed, hesitating as Jack stirred, and moving again once he re-settled.

Madalena couldn't believe how easy it was to use a computer. Why had she allowed her family to convince her it was beyond her? She got through to Bud with extraordinary ease. The computer screen flickered, and then his face appeared. Gosh, it's brilliant to see him, thought Madalena; and he looks so handsome on the screen. They agreed: if Madalena needed to, she would cut off the call and they would speak another time. She would tell Jack that she was looking at clothes sites on the internet (something she was fully intending to do as soon as possible.)

Bud was, sitting in his New York loft apartment: he picked up his laptop and took her on a virtual tour. Madalena found herself looking for clues. Did he have a live-in partner? There were no obvious signs. The apartment was immaculate, modern, and hi-tech. The enormous bedroom was minimalist to the point of Spartan; it was hard to imagine one person living in it, let alone two. The centrepiece was a king-sized bed with pure white linen.

"You live alone?" she asked.

"Yep."

She steeled herself, licked her lips. Why did she feel so nervous? Especially considering all the personal questions he asked her. She couldn't see Bud on screen: he was holding the laptop so she could see the rooms, not him. That made it easier.

"Have you got a partner?"

There was a long pause. "What, like, a business partner?"

Madalena cleared her throat, hesitated. "I meant a boyfriend."

She heard Bud start to laugh, and the screen flickered as he turned it around so he could look at her. "Ah, I see. So you guessed then. Is it that obvious?"

Madalena wished she'd never asked. She felt embarrassed. "Well, no, I …"

"The way I dress gave me away?"

"No, not at all, it's not that. It's just, I, when I first met you, I thought …"

"Ah, I know … the gaydar as you girls call it … you could see I didn't fancy you."

Madalena wished she'd never started this conversation. "Sorry, Bud, I didn't mean to be personal."

"No worries. We're friends. Don't worry about it. And no, I don't have a boyfriend."

"Right, OK." She would never ask him anything personal again.

Bud set the laptop back at his desk. "So, tell me, how are you?" His beaming smile and drawling tones drew a smile from Madalena, that quickly faded.

"Really worried. I'm in trouble. I badly need your help."

"Did you do the list? Knowledge and motivation?"

"Well not exactly … we said Pat, didn't we? At least for motivation …. But there's something else I need to tell you."

"Hmm, I thought there might be."

"I think Jack received a letter from the same person who sent me mine."

This wiped the smile off Bud's face. "Wha–a–a t?"

Madalena quickly told him what had happened on the morning she received the letter, and her uncertainty about whether there had been one letter or two.

Then she told him about Jack's behaviour at Mother's, and their conversation at the restaurant this evening.

"Why d'you think he hasn't confronted you with it? Just come right out and showed you it?"

"I don't really know. When Bella got those nasty letters, he just said there were some crazy people out there, they'd say anything. Is that it d'you think? He just thinks they're mad? Or did he only say that to comfort Bella?"

"God knows. It sounds like something's got under his skin: looking at photos, asking you about exes …. He hasn't confronted you yet at least. You have to find out who did this. Any more ideas?"

"I did wonder, this evening, about Honor Sinclair. The on-off thing with me and Thomas and her. It wasn't completely casual, and they split up at one point because Thomas wanted to be with me."

"She's got motivation then …. Has she got knowledge though, Mad? This feels like the question you're avoiding to me."

Madalena hesitated. "The truth is, I don't know what she knows."

"What's that supposed to mean? What could she know?"

"I just mean she might think she knows something, but there's nothing to know."

"And she might think that Thomas is Bella's father?"

"There were a lot of cross-over times .... Thomas and I met secretly a few times, even after he and Honor were married, and I was with Jack. It was hard for us to keep away from each other. It was all quite innocent, but I don't know if she suspected, and if she did, she might draw the wrong conclusions."

"Mad, I'm going to ask you this again; are you absolutely certain that Jack is Bella's biological father?"

"Yes. Yes! I've told you before. It's other people, they might think differently, that's all. I can't help what other people think, can I?"

"OK, calm down. So, the list is: Pat: motivation; Honor: may think she has knowledge, and motivation. Would she hold a grudge all these years, was she that sort of person?"

"I don't know, I don't even know where she lives or anything. London, I think … she was a psychiatrist or something. I think she remarried, I don't know what her name would be."

"A psychiatrist, hmm, in my experience they're usually more fucked up than their patients. You'll have to do some research, see what you can find out, see if you can locate her. Now that you're a technology girl you shouldn't find it too much of a challenge. Meanwhile, how about you go and visit Pat?"

CHAPTER FIFTEEN

Two days had passed since Madalena and Jack's dinner date.

Madalena wasn't sure if she imagined it, but Jack seemed to be talking to her less and less. Not that he'd ever been a big talker, but he usually chatted over breakfast. Recently, apart from the odd remark to Bella, when she was there, he seemed engrossed in his newspaper. She'd tried to seduce him one morning, when Bella was in London, and he'd laughed, and made a joke, but not actually responded.

This morning, conscious that she was off to visit Pat, she wanted to pacify him, as though he knew what she was up to.

"Jack …."

He glanced up from the newspaper. Something was missing in his face. Interest? Care? What was it?

"Hmm?"

"The Skype thing on the computer's great. It was a brilliant idea." She smiled at him.

"Good." He turned back to the paper.

"What are you reading?"

The paper rustled. "The paper."

"I mean what story?"

He looked up. "Why on earth d'you want to know that?"

"I'm interested."

"It's the business section, it won't interest you."

Madalena retired to reconsider how she could get his approving attention. She thought of locking the door, and removing her clothes, but after the other morning it felt too risky, she wouldn't want to have the brush off twice in quick succession. That would be unique, and she didn't want anything to happen to worry her any further: she'd hardly slept for the last few nights. She hoped that she'd convinced him with her decisive statement of dates at dinner.

She was nervous about her meeting with Pat today. She'd Skyped Bud yesterday and suggested to him that she shouldn't go, that maybe Jack was reassured after their dinner. But Bud had been adamant: "Whoever's doing this won't go away, believe me. If you don't act now, they'll do something worse soon: don't risk it."

It had been Bud's idea for Madalena to turn up unannounced. "You'll have the advantage of surprise, catch her unawares. Watch her reactions: is she surprised to see you? Anxious? Nervous?"

"How ever would I know any of that?"

"Check if she's behaving differently, out of character in any way?"

"I rarely see her, and when I do, we barely speak. The last time I saw her was at Linda's baby's christening a few years ago. If it'd been up to her, I wouldn't even have been invited."

But Bud had convinced her. "You have to find out if she's the one making trouble for you. If you ask her she could refuse and what would you do then?"

"She's barely civil to me. I think she thinks I could have done more to repair the rift between Jack and John."

"There's your clue. How to pacify her."

"What clue?"

"Come on, Mad, think—you can offer to mediate between Jack and John."

"I can't possibly do that now, I don't want to do anything to upset Jack."

"You don't have to do it …. Just tell her that you will," Bud said.

Madalena was admiring. "You think of everything, don't you? Every last detail."

Bud laughed. "As if you don't. When you want something, you're always working out what people will think, feel, how to work it to your advantage. Look how you got your computer."

So here, she was, a bundle of nerves, parked outside Pat's house, behind what was presumably Pat's car, a dark green Golf, solid and reliable. The house was a modest 1930s suburban semi; Madalena could remember Pat buying it with her divorce settlement. The front of the house, half red brick, half white stucco, was neat and clean. The front door, a welcoming yellow, provided a bright splash of colour. Simple cream blinds hung at the front bay windows, to Madalena's surprise: had she thought about it, she would have expected Pat to choose flouncy lace nets. The small front garden was equally unexpected: all the houses on this road had small manicured lawns with flowers around the edges, but Pat's was a meadow of flowers, of every kind and colour. Madalena realized, from the many *House & Garden* magazines that she browsed through, that this was a garden that looked as though it happened naturally, but must have taken an extraordinary amount of planning and maintaining. The light breeze on this sunny day moved some of the taller flowers and the longer grasses, and several bright butterflies drifted above and around the garden. How lovely: the colours and movement. She realized how little she actually knew about Pat; she just assumed she would be a rather boring middle-aged matronly type. She certainly wouldn't have imagined her as an imaginative gardener, or an imaginative anything if it came to that. She had never given Pat much thought.

OK, here goes nothing, time to go in. Madalena took several deep breaths, and got out of the car. Walking up the garden path, she could smell the sweet scent from the flowers, and she breathed in appreciatively. She stood in front of the front door, and rang the bell.

Pat opened the front door. "Oh. You. What's happened? What's wrong?"

"Nothing, no, nothing, don't worry Pat." Madalena reached out a hand instinctively, to calm the older women's fears.

Pat recoiled slightly. "What d'you want?"

"I've come to ask you a favour, Pat."

"You want a favour from *me*?"

"Could I come in and explain to you?"

Pat was holding the door slightly ajar. Madalena could hear the TV in the background, the *Jeremy Kyle Show*, a woman jeering loudly. A smell of coffee wafted out.

"Please, Pat? It's to do with Bella, some pictures I'm looking for."

"Oh .... Alright, you can come in, but not for long, I have to leave for work soon."

Stepping inside, Madalena was surprised at how tastefully decorated and furnished it was. She'd never thought of Pat as stylish, but her house was light and modern, with some unusual artistic touches: a graceful sculpture in the hallway, of a mother and child; a glimpse

139

of some modern prints on the sitting room wall, as they passed the door. Pat led her into the kitchen, a large space, across the back of the house, with wide French windows leading to a curved sunlit patio, surrounded by deep beds of mature shrubs and spring flowers. The far wall was completely covered in a collection of framed family photos, mostly of Pat's two children at various life stages, and of her grandchildren. Madalena noticed several of Bella with her half-sister and brother. None of Jack though, as far as she could see.

"Your house is nice, Pat, really lovely. Your front garden is so pretty."

"Would you like tea or coffee?" The TV was loud.

"Coffee please, black, no sugar."

"I must watch this last moment," said Pat, turning towards the TV. "Jeremy's about to announce the DNA results to see if this boy's the father of her child."

Pat filled the kettle and switched it on, then started to tidy the breakfast counter, deftly moving dishes into the dishwasher and tidying a scatter of papers and childrens' drawings into a neat pile. Something caught Madalena's eye, some writing on a child's drawing. "How sweet, Pat, were they done by Linda's kids?"

Pat, eyes fixed to she screen, flapped a hand. "Yes just kids stuff."

"Can I see? They look so good?" Madalena reached out to pick one up, but her movement captured Pat's attention, and she snatched the drawings away from Madalena and pushed them underneath a pile of magazines. Madalena blinked, puzzled: there was something familiar about them, what was it?

Madalena looked at the screen, at two wretched looking youngsters, Wayne and Shelley, sitting in armchairs, a few feet apart. The girl, hair scraped back into a ragged ponytail, her face scarred with spots in various stages of evolution; and the boy, weedy and underfed, his face a mutinous scowl.

"I like this programme, I usually watch it when I'm running in the gym." Madalena smiled at Pat.

"Lucky you. I usually watch it as I'm leaving for work."

They both held their breath as Jeremy Kyle opened an envelope, gazed at it in silence, as the girl and boy, clinging to each other, barely more than children themselves, waited for his verdict. The audience held their collective breath.

"The DNA results show that Wayne … is … NOT … the father of Shelley's son."

The audience gasped. Shelley dissolved in tears. Wayne stood up, and turned on her: electronic bleeps stood in for his language. He stalked off the stage, outrage and grief etched into the lines of his body.

Pat leaned across, switched off the sounds of human misery; and made Madalena's coffee.

"These programmes fascinate me. Imagine not knowing who the father of your child is." She was watching Madalena's face.

"Dreadful. Impossible to imagine how that must feel." Madalena blinked repeatedly.

"That's that relationship over, that's for sure," Pat said, with some satisfaction. "Another single mother to add to the armies of them supported by the state."

Madalena felt a little breathless. She thought of her yoga teacher's advice: "Feel your feet firmly planted, draw your energy down, through your feet, feel your connection to the ground …. Breathe deeply, downwards …."

"What did you want, anyway? I have to go to work shortly."

Pat worked part-time, in the accounts department of a local medical supplies company. She was ready for work, smartly dressed in a black suit and white shirt. She was a stocky woman, in late middle age; her hair, dark with grey streaks, was well cut in a jaw length bob, and she wore subtle make-up that emphasized her good bone structure. When Madalena first met Jack, he complained that his wife had let herself go after she had the children. She clearly took good care of herself now. I wonder why she never remarried?, thought Madalena. She'd had a couple of boyfriends, Madalena knew that from Linda, but nothing serious; after all, said Linda, who could follow Dad?

"Do you like your job, Pat?" What was it like?, Madalena wondered, to have a job, to go out to work, to be paid to do something?

"It's OK. I have to earn my living, it's a job, it's fine. What d'you want anyway? Why are you here?"

"Oh yes. OK, well, it's about Bella. She might be having a profile piece in a magazine, and they say they might want to use pictures from when she was younger. I've got loads, plenty, but Bella was looking for a particular one, of her with Linda and John, when she was about five. She said it was taken in your garden, so I thought you might have a copy."

"How peculiar," Pat said. "Jack came round only a couple of days ago asking for pictures of Linda and John, especially any with Bella."

"What? Did he? When? Why?" Madalena took a gulp of her coffee, and closed her eyes for a moment.

"He didn't tell you?" Pat raised her eyebrows at Madalena. She was trying not to smile.

"No …. Why? What did he want them for?"

"He just said he didn't have many pictures of them when they were younger and he'd like some. I didn't really ask why. I gave him the ones I had. He was especially interested in the ones I had of them with your Bella. Now I think of it, he was asking me if I thought Bella looks like Linda. I said no, Bella's the image of her mother, that's what I see."

Madalena felt sick. She sipped her coffee. She tried to focus on the plan she and Bud had made, but she found it hard to put out of her mind the image of Jack, here, asking for the baby photos. He never went to Pat's house, not as far she knew anyway. A new thought struck her.

"Does Jack come by here often?"

Pat laughed. "Feeling uncertain are you? Not a good feeling is it? Welcome to the world of the normal woman, with worries and insecurities."

Madalena knew that small beads of perspiration would soon show on her upper lip. "Does he come here often?"

"That's my business. Mine and Jack's. If I were you, I'd be wondering why's he taking this interest in his children, looking for old photos. If you ask me, it's odd. Why d'you think he's doing that?"

Madalena shrugged and shook her head.

Pat continued: "I've often thought you could've been more helpful to me, with the row between Jack and John. You could have got Jack to be a bit more forgiving of his own son. If it had been for yourself or Bella you'd have pulled out all the stops wouldn't you?"

OK. Here was her chance. "You could be right. Perhaps I should think about that."

"What?" Pat put her cup down and stared at Madalena. "Would you? You would? You're not joking?"

Madalena swallowed. "Yes, why not? Time has passed, maybe Jack has softened." She knew that neither she nor Pat believed that was possible.

"Thank you. You could do something good, Madalena. Even if it is a bit hopeless. You never know."

"Jack doesn't really do forgiveness, Pat, as you know, and there's nothing anyone can do about that. Not me, not anyone. But I'll do my best. I'll speak to him."

Madalena tried again to focus her thoughts on Bud's plan. The strategy he called it, whatever that was supposed to mean. She'd asked him at the time: isn't that something in a war? He'd laughed, yes, it is, and here's the thing, this is a war, and you stand to lose a lot.

Pat had the motivation, she'd thought that before, but this visit convinced her of it; in fact she was beginning to wonder about the nature of that motivation. But did she have knowledge? Did she think she had knowledge of something? They'd thought of questions.

"Come on, Mad, let's work it out, what could you ask her?"

"I could just say, do you know anything about the past?"

Bud had thrown up his hands, theatrically. "We have to be subtler than that, girlfriend. We have to be smart. Think like a lawyer. We mustn't lead the witness."

Madalena didn't know what he was talking about half the time. But she remembered his questions now.

"Jack's thinking back to the old days; we all do as we get older don't we? I know I do. D'you think about old times?"

"Jack and I had a bit of a reminisce, actually, looking at the photos. We came across a couple of our wedding snaps."

Madalena was impressed: Bud had been spot on: Pat had responded to her question straight away.

"D'you still have friends from back then?"

"Oh yes, they've been my lifeline all these years; what would I have done without them? You may remember Sue and Janet: I've been best friends with them forever. And the bigger group, you'll remember that crowd, from the King's Head on a Friday night? Where you first met Jack?"

Yes, that was true, Friday nights, at the pub, and the regular crowd there. It was the place to go, before moving on to the nightclub. There was Pat, with Sue and Janet, and the others … who were they? She scanned her mental image …. Her heart caught: there was Thomas's older sister, Caroline, a central figure.

"Yes, I remember. Are you still in touch with them all?"

"Most of them. Quite a few of us ended up divorced, of course, traded in, as I was, for a younger prettier model. Sue's divorced and Dinah Bennett, and Caroline Dyer. We went on holiday together a couple of weeks ago. We call ourselves the Ditched Wives Club. It's new for them, they're still bitter; it didn't matter how much I said about the contented life you can have, living alone. We had quite a reminisce. Your ears must've been burning, or Bella's anyway, we were talking about her in the paper."

"What were you saying?"

"The apple never falls far from the tree …."

"What d'you mean?"

Pat pulled a face. "Just that she's just like you, Madalena, that's all."

"The story's exaggerated, the papers just make things up."

"Linda's appalled … she's thankful that her married name means that people won't realize Bella's her sister. It's embarrassing for her." Linda was married to a wealthy and prominent investment banker, a marriage that had elevated her into high status circles.

Madalena felt her heart sink even lower. "I'll ask Bella to call Linda and explain to her what happened."

"Look, I must go, I have to get to work. Jack's got most of the baby photos, you'll have to ask him for them."

"I can't really, he's not exactly supportive of Bella's modelling career, and he doesn't want me to encourage her. I hope you won't mention to him that I've been here?"

"Oh dear, Madalena, are you sure you want to have secrets from Jack? You don't want to put a foot wrong with him, you know what he's like, you wouldn't want him to have even the vaguest suspicion, would you?"

"Suspicion of what?" Madalena could feel her heart beating fast and hard. She blinked repeatedly.

"Of anything. Anything at all. It must be a terrible pressure for you, as you get older. You look a bit nervous. That's karma for you though isn't it?"

"Well, thanks anyway Pat. Maybe when Jack returns the photos to you, I could see if the one Bella wants is there?" She remembered Bud's insistence: stick to your story right through to the end, don't forget what you've said you're there for.

Madalena drove off, her heart cold and tight at the thought of Pat reminiscing with Thomas's sister. What might Thomas's sister know? What had Thomas told her, back then? What did she know or think she knew, and might she have told Pat?

Bud's plan had worked perfectly. She had one answer for him: Pat had the motivation; she did bear a grudge, and a complicated one, and, probably, the knowledge. But it wasn't just about Pat. There were new questions now: Caroline Dyer, Thomas's sister; might she have knowledge? Might Thomas have told her something back then, and then she hinted at something to Pat?

Madalena pulled over to the side of the road, unable to think straight. She felt cold and dizzy, as though a web of old malice was tightening around her.

CHAPTER SIXTEEN

Madalena sat at Bella's desk and opened the laptop. It flickered immediately into life and she clicked on the Skype programme, feeling the increasingly familiar thrill of sitting at a computer, doing things, being capable, feeling smart. She wished she had a pair of spectacles.

She clicked on the green phone icon next to Bud's name, held her breath, and crossed her fingers. One ring, click, the screen flickered and changed, and there he was. She breathed out and smiled, as his face appeared, smiling broadly at her.

"I was just about to call you, Mad, you'll never guess, I'm coming to London on business tomorrow. Let's have dinner the day after? It would be so great to see you."

Bud's simple request had revealed to both of them: Madalena's life was not really her own. "However did you end up with a life where you can't even have a *friend*?"

He was right. How *had* that happened? "What would I tell Jack?"

"The truth?"

"He doesn't know about you, I didn't tell him."

"Tell him then."

"He'd think it was weird ... he'd question me."

"You could tell him I'm gay?" Bud was leaning into the screen, looking at her, laughing.

145

Madalena winced at a fleeting mental image of Jack's comments in this regard. "It's too complicated. I don't want to do anything unusual right now. He's behaving strangely enough as it is."

"Say you're having dinner with a girlfriend?"

"I don't have any girlfriends, apart from Bella, and I can't say her, obviously."

"Your mother then?"

Madalena shuddered. "You must be joking, Jack'd have a fit. I'm not allowed to see her."

"*What?* Are you kidding me? Don't you ever wish you had a life of your own?"

Madalena could see her own small face in the corner of the computer screen. She watched her mouth tense and thin, as she suppressed a sigh. "What about lunch? I could say I'm going to the beauty salon, that would be predictable."

"Oh for God's sake. That husband of yours, I don't know how you stand it."

"He's not my husband. Let me know the restaurant and I'll sort it out, I'll be there." She had to see him. She couldn't wait to see him. She had come to rely on her Skype meetings with Bud, and when she wasn't on Skype to him, she was thinking about him, the way he talked to her, the things he said. "I have to talk to you, I went to see Pat."

Bud leaned forward, eyes wide. "How d'it go?"

"Jack went to see her last week."

His reaction provided no comfort at all, his face registering his shock: he raised his eyebrows, dropped his jaw, and covered his mouth with his hand. His concern mirrored back to her the extent of the trouble she was in.

"It's great that we're going to get to meet, Mad, I can't wait to see you."

Madalena felt exactly the same.

In the end it hadn't proved so difficult to arrange, practically at least. It was always harder in her head, trying to overcome the worrying feeling that Jack could read her mind.

"Any plans today?" Jack's standard question.

Madalena waved a hand dismissively. "Usual … gym this morning, then the beauty salon. I'll be back by about three. What time'll you be home?"

When they were in Cardiff, Jack was home, like clockwork, by six. But his London schedule was less predictable.

"I'll be home by seven; we need to leave at eight."

They were going to the opening night of a new casino, fully equipped by Jack's firm. Madalena had spent weeks finding the right outfit for the occasion: a black and white Chanel dress, with black sequined shoes and matching clutch bag. She was looking forward to it: the press would be there, she might even get her picture in the papers: it was even more important than usual that she looked absolutely her best.

She arrived at the restaurant, early, a little breathless from the effort of driving in an unfamiliar area, and then finding a car park space close by.

The Italian trattoria had been carefully chosen for its location: away from the West End, or the area around Madalena and Jack's flat to ensure that she didn't bump into anyone who knew her or Jack. Bud knew it, a small family-run restaurant tucked away in the East End of London, that he used frequently for discreet meetings with distressed clients.

She ordered a glass of water, and sipped it, composing herself.

Bud arrived in a flurry of loud greetings, kisses, and darlings; and that was just to the maitre d' and the waiters.

Madalena found herself shy of him, after the strange detached intimacy of the aeroplane, and their Skype calls. Bud clearly didn't share any such embarrassment, greeting her with an extravagant hug, and a kiss on both cheeks. Madalena hugged him back, conscious of the strength of his arms around her, and her hands on his shoulders. She didn't want to let go of him.

"Mad! You look fantastic!" He called the waiters to come and admire her. "Isn't she gorgeous?" She found herself surrounded by adoring Italians, the familiar light of fascination and desire in their eyes. They bombarded her with Italian compliments: *Che bella. Molto bella. Molto molto carina.*

"Amazing isn't she? Have you ever seen a more fabulous woman? Get me some champagne, your best bottle: let's celebrate."

Madalena held up her hand in a vain attempt to stop Bud. "I'm driving, I can't have a drink."

"One drink won't matter. It's great to see you, let's celebrate. I can drive you back anyway, or you can get a cab."

He completely steamrollers everyone, thought Madalena. A bit like Jack in a way.

Eventually, excitement over, champagne delivered, and food ordered, Madalena and Bud picked up their Skype conversation about the visit to Pat.

"The thing is, you visited Pat thinking you had one suspect, and came out of the discussion with one more."

"It's going to make it harder for me to find out isn't it?" Madalena sipped her champagne and felt the unfamiliar warmth seep into her blood.

"And Jack's doing some investigating too. Tell me some more about this Caroline woman."

"She was Thomas's older sister; they were very close."

"Would he have told her about you?"

"Maybe ... especially when he left Honor to be with me, I'm sure he'd have told her about that. Honor might've told her anyway, they were good friends, I don't know if they still are. Honor and Thomas used to go out socially with Caroline and her husband. D'you think I should go and see her?"

"Let's have a think. We've got Pat, who might have some motivation, a grudge, and a desire to hurt you in some way. And then Caroline and Honor, who may think they have some knowledge, but if they did, what's their motivation? Thomas is dead, it's not as though he could come along and claim fatherhood. Why would Caroline or Honor want to reveal that? Honor, okay, she has the motivation, you hurt her in the past, she can hurt you back now ... but Caroline? What does she have to gain?"

He was so clear, how he worked everything out, divided it into sections. A bit like Jack's (a) and (b) though a little more complicated. She was relieved to talk to him: he alarmed her with his worries and concerns, and then soothed her with his analysis.

"Nothing, that's true."

"Except maybe a niece, the legacy of her dead brother."

"Yes." Madalena was thinking hard, trying to remember all her facts.

"That can be really important to some people, after a death, knowing they left a child, children in the world," Bud said.

Madalena felt tears rise behind her eyes. She nodded. She could see that.

"It's a bit obscure," Bud continued. "What's going on in her life? She's just got divorced, she's, what, nearly fifty? Does she have children? A career? A job?"

"I don't know." Madalena had drunk half her glass of champagne, and was relaxing.

"Mad, you need to know. Where's your curiosity? Why didn't you ask Pat?"

"I was so scared when she said she'd been on holiday with Caroline, I couldn't think straight."

"Here's the thing: we don't know the impact on Caroline and the other suspects, of seeing Bella in the papers. What it's stirred up in them. Look, we've established motive: Pat is pissed off with you for stealing her husband, and not helping to get Jack reconciled with John. Caroline might feel she has a niece from her dead brother; Honor maybe still hates you for stealing her boyfriend."

"Oh." Madalena felt giddy, from the mixture of champagne and accumulated ill will towards her. "Surely people wouldn't go on feeling so mean all this time? It was all years ago, wouldn't they forget?"

"You don't know much about people, do you sweetheart? Maybe I'm cynical from my years as a divorce lawyer. I see people heading for their graves with old grievances intact: they've spent years polishing an old slight or humiliation, till it's a glittering diamond of crystallized rage and resentment. A diamond so hard and sharp that it can cut through glass."

"You're not making me feel better. Pat said something weird, something about karma." Madalena downed the rest of her champagne in one go, and a hovering waiter stepped forward to refill her glass.

Bud raised his eyebrows. "Tell me exactly what she said?"

"She said you wouldn't want to upset Jack, would you? But that's karma for you ... and something like, welcome to the world of women who feel insecure."

"She's saying you'll be paid back."

Madalena blinked twice in quick succession. "That sounds like a curse."

"Do as you would be done by, as the kids' story says."

"What kids' story?"

"*The Water Babies.* The two fairy sisters: Mrs Do-as-you-would-be-done-by, who's kind to everyone and they're lovely back. And her sister Mrs Be-done-by-as-you-did: she made sure that people got their come-uppance for doing bad things; by shaming them. You didn't read it?" Madalena shook her head. "It teaches children to treat others as they want to be treated themselves. The same idea as karma, really."

"Pat's saying that I should be punished?" Madalena took a gulp of champagne. Two waiters descended on their table, bringing their first course. Madalena stared at her insalata tricolore, the colours sharp and bright, green, red and cream. She didn't think she was going to be able to eat much.

"I'm starving," announced Bud. "That's jet lag for you." He took a mouthful of his arancini, closed his eyes, ate, swallowed, and turned to the smiling waiter. "Mmm, buono Mario, buono, my favourite dish." Mario beamed, nodded, and stepped backwards with a slight bow.

Bud turned back to Madalena. "Where were we? OK, yes, Pat … karma … I suppose it could've been just a throwaway remark, but it sounds a bit ominous. Come on, don't get upset. We still need to work out who's trying to hurt you. If only you'd kept that letter, there might have been clues."

"Unlikely. There were only six words." Madalena speared a slice of avocado with her fork.

"Yes, but the paper, the writing … it could have been helpful."

Madalena conjured a mental image of the simple sentence, then drew in a sharp breath, and put the half eaten morsel of avocado back on her plate. "Oh! The writing! At Pat's there were some children's drawings, with writing, it was so similar to the letter I think. It reminded me of something at the time, but I couldn't think what."

Bud put down his knife and fork. "Are you sure?"

Madalena shook her head. "Yes. No. I don't know. Maybe I'm remembering it wrong, just imagining it. It's starting to get on top of me a bit, I can't sleep properly. I'm petrified of what'll happen if Jack acts on this."

"Poor Mad." Bud patted her hand. Madalena's eyes filled with tears. "Oh, there, my darling, don't you cry. We'll work it out."

Madalena used her serviette to dab at her eyes, taking care not to smudge her mascara.

"Let's try and see if we have any more suspects, OK? What happened with your mother, tell me about that?"

Madalena told Bud the story of her mother's disgrace and subsequent banishment.

"What a story." Bud was half laughing, half shocked. "And you haven't seen her since? She doesn't try to contact you?"

"I haven't seen her for seven years. At the beginning she would phone me a lot, crying. Begging to see Bella and me. But then she completely stopped trying to make any contact at all. I tried to get Jack to change his mind, but there was no chance. He didn't want Bella ever to see her again. I drove him a bit mad going on about it, he got quite annoyed. He said he'd put a stop to it once and for all, whatever that meant. He lets me send her a birthday card and Christmas card, but that's it."

"He's hard, isn't he? I know the type only too well. He doesn't take any prisoners."

Madalena dabbed her eyes and reached for her champagne glass, pushing her plate away, hardly touched. "I know what you mean, but that's not really how I think of Jack. He takes care of me, and keeps me safe."

"Not being able to see your Mum though? You weren't a Daddy's girl; maybe you were a Mummy's girl?"

"Oh, I'm a Daddy's girl, for sure. Not a real Dad though, my fantasy Dad, the one I imagined. He gave me anything, everything I wanted, anything at all. He adored me; he thought I was the most beautiful girl in the world."

"Sounds like Jack. He's your dream Dad."

Madalena appeared not to hear him, lost in her own thoughts. "I had nothing. You can't imagine how much nothing I had. No Dad, no Mum to speak of, not really, she was drunk most of the time. No clothes, toys, treats; no nice food. A small cold room. The night noises from my mother's room. No, I wasn't a Mummy's girl. I wasn't anybody's girl."

"So you needed the imaginary Dad to take care of you. Like Jack did. You poor darling. Your mother sounds a horror."

Bud was stroking the back of Madalena's hand. She reached out and placed her other hand over his, feeling the warmth of his hand in both of hers.

"She wasn't up to much as a mother, but she was all I had. And I look back now and I think she loved me as much as she could. Not much, I admit, but it was all there was."

"What d'you think your Mum would say about all this, if she knew?"

Madalena had given up all attempts to spare her mascara. Tears ran freely down her face. "She'd say what she said when I found out I was pregnant: 'He's your soul mate.'"

"What? Who? Jack?"

"Thomas."

The waiter arrived to take their plates. Madalena attempted to compose herself. All this crying in public, whatever was the matter with her? Bud's eyebrows were almost in his hairline, his eyes nearly popping out. The waiter was taking every opportunity to hang around: did they still want the bread? Would they like more champagne? He would get Madam a fresh napkin. Would they like extra vegetables, the green beans in garlic were especially nice? All the while gazing at Madalena with the look of a yearning puppy. Bud lost patience with him, dropped his charm and sent him packing.

"How do you stand all these drooling men all the time? It's like going out with my mother, the only woman I knew as beautiful as you."

Madalena pulled a face. "I just ignore them. I expect your mother did too."

"She did, yes."

"What sort of mother was she?"

"Wonderful. I adored her. I *was* quite a Mummy's boy, her third and last child and the only son. She doted on me. I'll tell you another time. We have to talk about Thomas. I think there's something you're not telling me."

Madalena wiped her eyes and gave a helpless shrug.

"Why would your mother say that? At that point?"

"She assumed it was Thomas's baby, obviously."

"And why did she assume that?"

Another shrug.

"You have to level with me. Were you seeing Thomas at the time that Bella was conceived?"

Looking down at her lap, Madalena muttered something.

"I can't hear you."

Madalena took a deep breath and looked him in the eye. "Occasionally."

"Riiiiight …." Bud leaned back in his chair. "So … Thomas is Bella's father then?"

Madalena shrugged miserably.

"You don't know? Mad, is that it, you don't actually know?"

She nodded, her eyes filling with fresh tears.

"And your *mother* knows you don't know?"

Another nod. "I was never sure, and she knew that. I wanted the baby to be Thomas's; my mother was right, I loved him. I told him I was pregnant with his child. He was married to Honor. He didn't believe me."

Bud took her hand. "Thomas sounds as hard-hearted as Jack."

"Oh, he wasn't, not at all." Madalena dabbed her eyes again.

"Great, here's our main course, I'm still starving."

Madalena looked at the plate of pasta that had been set down in front of her. What had possessed her? Pasta? With that slimline dress to get into tonight?

"I know this is a long shot, but is it at all possible that your mother sent the letter?"

"No chance. She'd never do anything to hurt me."

"She's the only one who has knowledge, though, as far as we know. Maybe she wants to hurt Jack? Who else knew that you continued to see Thomas?"

Madalena pulled herself up straight. She felt relieved to have told Bud the truth. "My mother ... maybe Caroline, Thomas may have told her."

"Honor?"

"I doubt it; Thomas wouldn't have told her."

"Maybe, if Caroline knew, she told Honor, after Thomas's death?" Bud said, cutting into his fillet steak. Madalena grimaced and looked away from the bloody piece of meat.

"Why would she do that?"

"True ... hard to find a motive for that. Does the photo of Bella in the papers look like Thomas? Or like Jack? This steak is gorgeous. Aren't you going to eat?"

Madalena picked up her fork. "To me, she's never looked like either of them. The first few years, when she was little, I used to search for some resemblance, trying to work it out. I used to have this daydream that Thomas would come and sweep us up and magic us away to be a family, the three of us together. I kept the most detailed baby diary imaginable: handprints, footprints, her first lock of hair, a million pictures that I could give to Thomas so he could catch up on what he missed. There were times that I wished he was dead, so I could stop hoping, I couldn't bear it, sometimes, the disappointment. And when he did die it was pointless, I knew I had to knuckle down and make the best of it with Jack. There is something of Jack in Bella, though there's something about her jaw line that reminds me, still, of Thomas. Really, she just looks like a paler version of me, everyone says. I gave up trying to work out who she looked like and learned to live with not knowing."

"Weren't you happy with Jack?" Bud picked up several chips with his fingers. "Eat something, Mad, else you're going to end up with a hangover from the champagne."

He was right. She took a small forkful of pasta. "Jack's different to Thomas. Thomas knew who I was, it seemed to me. The only person who ever did."

Bud took Madalena's hand and stroked it gently. "So Jack doesn't?"

Madalena smiled at Bud and closed her eyes, slowly, then opened them again. "I think Jack knows who he wants me to be."

"What a strain: trying to be what someone else wants."

"It's not relaxing." She had never thought of it like this before. The things Bud said, the questions he asked her, made her think

153

about her life in ways that had never occurred to her before. She ate some more pasta. It was delicious actually, and made her hungry for more.

"D'you love him?"

"I'm so grateful to him, for the good life he's provided, for me and Bella. Is that love? It feels close to it sometimes. It's not like I felt about Thomas though."

"It must be horrible, not knowing who Bella's father is."

"I haven't really thought about it for years. It's not like Thomas could claim her, or be her father. Jack's a fantastic father to Bella. He worships her."

"And that's what's stopping him from acting on the letter, his protectiveness of Bella. The risk with Jack is whether his male pride will be greater than his protectiveness."

"I hope not."

"D'you think about Thomas still?"

Madalena's eyes filled. "Sometimes. My mother was right, I really did love him."

"The thing is, if he was still alive, maybe with middle-age spread, or bald, you'd maybe have got over him. But you still remember him as he was, forever young and beautiful. I bet he was handsome."

"Amazingly. Blue eyes and silky black hair, Irish. Yes, of course, I remember him as he was back then."

"What happened? How did he die?"

Those days, weeks, months, after Thomas's death, and her searing grief; she didn't want to remember. "An accident apparently. He was found dead at home, the inquest gave an open verdict."

"Suicide?"

"No, he wouldn't have done that. An accident. Poison apparently."

"Poison?"

"Yep. I was sad that I couldn't go to his funeral. I knew I couldn't. Honor would never have stood for it."

"Since when did you care about her feelings?"

"I didn't want Jack to get the wrong idea."

"Or the right one."

"I had to make sure I didn't lose both of them."

Bud leaned across the table and squeezed her shoulder. "Come on, let's get clear about what to do next. Who are our suspects? And what is their level of motivation and knowledge?"

Bud pushed his empty plate to one side, picked up his napkin and wiped his mouth. "That was delicious. Come on Mad, finish yours."

Taking a small leather-bound notebook and pen from his bag, he quickly sketched out a chart:

	High motivation	Medium motivation	Low motivation
High knowledge		Mad's Mum	
Medium knowledge			Caroline
Low knowledge	Honor; Pat		

"That's amazing. How did you do that? That's like magic." Madalena ate a little more of her pasta, then pushed aside the plate, half eaten.

Bud laughed and blew her a kiss. "Smart, huh? Now we can see how to prioritize: the people with the highest motivation and knowledge."

"And I've already seen Pat."

"I think you need to go and see your mother next."

"Jack'd have a fit."

"Obviously you can't tell him. She's the only one we know has knowledge. It's my guess that whoever wrote the letters is waiting for something to happen. If it doesn't, they may send a second letter."

Madalena blinked rapidly. "Oh God. You don't really think so do you?"

"It would be typical, I've seen it happen. If you want to cause trouble, you keep going until you succeed."

"Yes, well, if it was me I certainly would."

They sat back as the waiter came to take their plates and give them dessert menus. Madalena didn't look at hers. "Nothing for me thanks, just black coffee." She glanced at her watch. "I'll need to get going soon, Bud."

Bud was gazing out of the window. He turned back to the waiter. "Tiramisu please, with an extra spoon for the lady. And a cappuccino." He turned to Madalena. "Thing is, Jack's on the case already. He's got no reason to believe you got a letter though, has he?"

Madalena shrugged and shook her head. "I don't think so. What d'you think Jack's letter said?"

"Maybe: ask Madalena who Bella's father is? Like, a mirror of yours? They'd be trying to get you to talk about it, I imagine. Anyone who knows Jack would know how he'd react, wouldn't they? All of our suspects know him?"

"Honor doesn't, only the slightest acquaintance. After Thomas's death she left the area, so she knows nothing about me, or what Jack's like."

"She may know something now, from the papers. She knows you're still together, you had a baby. Did you do some research to find out where she is? Maybe she looked at Bella and thought she looked like Thomas."

"I don't know how to do the research."

"Get Bella to show you how Google works, you'll soon find her."

Coffee arrived, and Bud's tiramisu. Bud handed her the extra spoon. Madalena handed it back to the waiter. "It's OK, Bud, not for me thanks."

The waiter hesitated, looking at Bud, who said, "Just leave it on the table, she'll want some."

Madalena sighed inwardly, smiled outwardly, and picked up the spoon and scooped some of the creamy dessert. She looked at it, then she looked at Bud. What was she doing? This was Bud, she could do as she pleased. She smiled at him, without the inner sigh this time, and put the spoon down on the plate.

"It looks lovely, Bud, but none for me thanks."

Sitting back in her seat, she closed her eyes, and just for a moment she experienced the most profound feeling of relaxation in her gut, as though a tight elastic band, stretched to breaking point, had finally snapped.

Opening her eyes, looking at him, he was looking back at her and laughing. He put his hand over hers. "Whatever you want, Mad, whatever you want."

Was she imagining it, or was he looking at her rather tenderly? She smiled back. "Or whatever I don't want, in this case."

Bud called for the bill, and Madalena shivered at the prospect of saying goodbye to him.

"Let's say goodbye in here," Bud said. "Then you can leave alone, just in case anyone sees you." He stood up and pulled her to her feet.

"Thanks, Bud. It's been so good to see you. I'm scared to see my Mum. I'll Skype you as soon as I'm back."

He held her close to him, and whispered to her. "It's been great to see you too. Be strong." She could feel his heartbeat and her own, as she rested her head on his shoulder and linked her arms around his waist.

It was so hard to let go, and leave.

CHAPTER SEVENTEEN

Madalena was lightly dozing in the back of the limousine, Jack next to her, reading the paper. They were on their way to Cardiff, after the casino opening the previous evening.

Slipping in and out of sleep, she was thinking about the party, a lavish affair, full of minor celebrities. Waking, she looked at Jack appraisingly. "That was quite a do last night wasn't it?"

Jack glanced sideways at her. "Hmm."

"You must have felt great; you worked so hard on that project."

Jack lowered the newspaper and turned to Madalena. A slight, triumphant smile lit his face. "It did feel good, yes. I must say I felt really quite proud of myself. And there'll be more business where that came from, especially with all the publicity."

"Paparazzi everywhere; it's going to be in *Hello*, an exclusive. We might be in *Hello*."

"I'm sure *you* will be. You were the star of the show."

Madalena warmed in the glow of approval. At the moment, she found herself grateful, pathetically so, for any small word of praise. She saved them up to comfort herself in the long sleepless nights of dread, fearing the collapse of the life she loved.

"So you liked my outfit then? A good choice?"

"Spectacular. I was proud to be with you."

Madalena snuggled up to him. "A pity we were both so tired when we got home. I'll make it up to you tonight, we'll have an early night shall we?"

"Sure, why not?"

"You know, Jack, a few months ago, I'd have been thrilled to be in *Hello*. But after Bella's experience, weird letters, I'd almost prefer not to be."

"Yes, well, she made herself unpopular by stealing somebody else's boyfriend, that's why."

"There are some strange people out there, aren't there?"

She tried not to flinch as Jack turned his laser beam stare on her face, his eyes narrowed. "I think we can rest assured that we won't get that sort of trouble. It's different, Bella's publicity set something off in people, something we can't control."

Madalena nodded, feeling her heart beating louder, faster. "I'm sure it'll be fine. I'll just sleep a bit more, till we get home."

She settled back and closed her eyes. But she couldn't sleep. The tension in her gut had returned: her moment of release after yesterday's lunch with Bud almost forgotten. She felt more tension than ever after her evening with Jack; and the thought of tomorrow, when she was going to see her mother, something she was both longing for and dreading. She hadn't even worked out yet where she was going to tell Jack she was going.

The limousine was so comfortable. She could feel the softness of the pale grey kid leather of the seating against her skin, like silk. If things went wrong between her and Jack, would she be able to afford a car of any sort? Would he cast her adrift with nothing at all, as he'd done to her mother and his own son?

Later, driving alone to her mother's flat, Madalena sipped a bottle of water: her mouth was dry, and she felt a little sick. She had become so used to the general feeling of turmoil that dogged her days that she had a new category of feeling to describe it to herself: absolutely dreadful.

She was trying her best to remember her discussion with Bud: if there was a spy hole on the door, she would stand to one side, to maintain the element of surprise. "She's not going to just come out and tell you she sent you a poison pen letter," Bud had said. "You're going to have to ask her questions, watch her reactions. Especially her first reaction, when she sets eyes on you. Is she surprised? Has she been waiting, expecting you? You'll get a sense of it, Mad, watch, listen, ask questions, OK? You're going to need to figure it out."

Jessie lived in a small council flat on a drab estate on the outskirts of Newport. At the time of her exile, Madalena had succeeded in persuading Jack to buy her mother a nice little bungalow a few miles from their Cardiff mansion, but Jessie's disgrace had scuppered that plan.

Grey concrete blocks of flats rose high in the sky, the walls of the lower floors decorated with elaborate graffiti. A carpet of rubbish covered the ground: fast food wrappers, cigarette packets, torn newspapers. An air of profound neglect sat like mist over the whole estate. Madalena felt conspicuous in her smart car; even in her jeans and a sweater she looked completely out of place. There were not many people around, just a middle-aged black man, and a small group of hooded teenagers, who all stared at her unashamedly. She quickly locked the car and half ran to her mother's flat. Entering the building, holding her breath to block the smell of urine, she hurried two floors up the concrete stairwell, littered with debris that she didn't want to look at too closely.

It was early afternoon, a timing that she and Bud had discussed at length. "I'll go in the morning, when she won't be drunk."

"Why not surprise her when she's had a few? You want to find out if she wrote the letters. If she did, she's likely to assume you're there to tell her that the dream has come crashing down around you, and you're now free to see her."

She stood facing her mother's front door, the pale green paint curling in forlorn strips. No spy glass anyway. She swallowed hard, suddenly overwhelmed by the realization that she was about to see her mother; and overcome to feel how much she had missed her. Despite everything, all the obeying Jack, her mother's general neglect of her, all the failures of care, the lack of love, Madalena had sometimes longed for her mother. She felt her eyes fill; she swallowed again. She whispered to herself Bud's last words: "Be strong." Taking a deep breath, she lifted the knocker and rapped it firmly against the door. After a few seconds of silence, she heard footsteps, and her mother's rasping voice: "Who is it?"

Madalena hadn't reckoned with this, and neither had Bud. Their whole strategy was based on those first moments of shock and surprise when her mother set eyes on her daughter for the first time in seven years. She tried to think, what would Bud do at this point?

"Who's there?" her mother repeated.

Madalena was shaking; what should she do now? Her mother's voice was querulous, a little slurred; maybe she was frightened. Panicked, Madalena knocked on the door a second time.

159

"Oh for heaven's sake," she heard her mother muttering. Sounds of bolts and locks prepared Madalena. The door opened, and Jessie and Madalena faced each other.

There was a moment of shocked silence. The last time Madalena had seen her mother, that dreadful day at Mother's, she was glamorous (if a little tarty) and heavily made up. She had now clearly given up all efforts on the personal grooming front. Madalena couldn't ever remember seeing her mother without lipstick, leave alone, as now, without teeth.

Then her mother appeared to implode, her frail body shrinking in towards her solar plexus, her hands flying to her withered mouth, tears springing from her eyes, as she doubled over, then leaned, almost fell, towards Madalena, reaching one hand towards her.

Madalena instinctively stepped forward towards her mother. The two had never shared much physical affection, the occasional pat or quick peck on the cheek for birthdays and Christmas. Now, some primitive urge prevailed and they found themselves clinging to each other, crying. The smell of cheap wine and tobacco permeated the air around Jessie, who appeared to Madalena to have shrunk. She was a tiny, frail thing, like a broken bird. An old, greying nightdress hung loosely from her shoulders, with a heavy beige cardigan, unbuttoned over the top; carpet slippers, once furry and pink, encased her feet. Her grey hair, in uncombed wisps around her head, was so thin that her scalp showed; the matted tufts at the front were stained with nicotine. Her skin was yellowed paper, her eyes bloodshot and rheumy.

"Oh, Mum …."

"Madalena, I'm so happy to see you, come in, come in. Is everything all right, has something happened? Oh I don't care what's happened I'm so happy to see you."

Jessie led Madalena into the tiny flat, as grubby and neglected as its inhabitant.

The pall of cigarette smoke sat heavily in the small sitting room, the walls stained nicotine yellow. An old winged armchair, with a floral nylon stretch cover of indeterminate colour was set in front of a single bar electric fire, an old-fashioned TV loudly showing an advertisement for a floor cleaning product. A dirty occasional table next to the chair held a half empty bottle of white wine, an empty glass, an overflowing ashtray, a packet of cigarettes, and a lighter.

"Sit down, sit down." Jessie pointed Madalena to the armchair and pulled up a rickety upright chair opposite. "You look lovely, dear, are you all right? Is Bella all right? It was great to see her in the papers and the magazine you sent me, thank you for that."

Madalena could see that her mother was in the early stages of drink, still able to walk and talk rather than stumble and mumble, but she was unprepared for how terrible she felt to see her mother in this awful squalor.

"I'm fine, and Bella's well, as you've seen. But how are you? You're so thin, are you OK? You don't look as though you're eating properly."

"I'm OK, so pleased to see you, so pleased …" Her voice broke. "And you look lovely, dear, like a model." She wiped away tears with the back of her hand. "Is Jack all right?"

"He's fine. Shall I make you a coffee?"

"No, no, I'll do it, let me make one for you. Everything's OK then? Why are you here, after all these years?"

"It's so nice so see you, Mum." Madalena's voice broke, as she followed her mother into the tiny kitchenette. An opened packet of biscuits was on the worktop, and a half-used loaf of sliced white bread next to the toaster, but otherwise there was little sign of food. No dishes sat draining after a meal, or stacked in the sink. On the pretext of getting milk, Madalena opened the door of the small fridge. It contained an open carton of milk, four bottles of cheap white wine, a packet of butter, a half-used carton of cream cheese, and a withered tomato.

She imagined telling Bud about it, and his response: What on earth did you expect? And what had she expected? She simply hadn't really thought about it. Once all her efforts to get Jack to change his mind had failed, there was only one thing she could do: train herself not to think too much about her mother, something she had done with a degree of success. Apart from the occasional disturbing dream, or days when she looked in the mirror and seemed to see her mother looking back at her. And some nights, unable to sleep, her mind would turn to her, and she would find herself wondering how she would get to know if her mother died.

They took their coffee into the sitting room. Madalena knew she wasn't going to drink hers, the cup was stained and unwashed. She put it on the coffee table. Jessie picked up her cigarettes and offered one to Madalena, which she waved away.

"No, of course, sorry, you never did, did you? Never even tried one. Or alcohol. Whoever would have thought it, a daughter of mine, doesn't smoke, doesn't drink. Marvellous really. It was the gym wasn't it? Couldn't keep you out of the school gym when you were a kid, you were like a piece of elastic, the things you could do."

"The only thing I could do."

"And look at you. You still look like a gymnast, or a ballet dancer."

"I still spend half my time in the gym, that's why."

"I was proud of that, remember that time when they thought you'd go in for the Olympics?"

"Yes, well, it didn't work out though did it?"

An image flashed across Madalena's mind, an experience; her happiness, standing on the balance beam, perched precariously, way up high. She never lost her nerve, performing gymnastic feats that were challenging enough on the floor, leave alone on a four inch wide beam. Her teacher said she was the most graceful gymnast she had ever seen. Madalena could remember the wonderful feeling of relaxation and control in her body as she bent backwards, almost double and placed her hands on the narrow beam, not far from her feet, arching her head back, her body forming a narrow oval shape. When she performed, she could hardly hear the cheering of the spectators, so intently was she focussed on the joy in her own body.

She shook her head, turning her attention back to her mother, who was saying: "We were dead proud though, weren't we, you and me, when we thought that would come off, remember? Madalena Morris, Olympic gymnast, gold medallist! That would've been a different life for you wouldn't it? You wouldn't have met Jack, or had Bella. Bet you're glad now you missed the trials after all, aren't you?"

No, Madalena thought, not necessarily, no. It would've been a different life yes, very different. Possibly a life of my own.

"That's all history. Don't worry about it."

"I do think about it sometimes though, especially these last years. I should never have stopped you. You could've been famous. Rich. Well, you are rich anyway, or at least Jack is."

"You didn't stop me deliberately, you couldn't help it."

"You say that, but I think you never really forgave me, having to play nursemaid instead of going to the trials, that's why you turned your back on me all these years, isn't it? Haven't been to see me ... didn't help me."

Mum, Madalena thought, you were drunk, not sick. "I didn't turn my back on you. You did it to yourself. Jack would have taken care of you, all you had to do was keep your opinions to yourself."

"I have to say what I think."

"Well that's your choice, but you paid a high price, didn't you?"

Jessie took a sharp breath. "Does Jack know you're here? There'll be trouble if he knows you're here."

"What? No, he doesn't know I'm here, and he mustn't know."

Jessie hurriedly poured herself a glass of wine and took a gulp. "You must go, you can't be here, he'll stop my money if he knows. Quick, leave now, go on, you must go." She stood up and tried to pull Madalena to her feet.

"What are you talking about? What? Hang on. Sit down. What are you on about? He'll stop your *money*? What money?"

"My allowance, he'll stop it he says, if he ever finds out that you or Bella come here. I can't do without it, I can't manage, not on my pension I can't, I'd have to get a cleaning job. I'm not well enough for it any more, look at me, you can see I'm not." Clutching her wine glass, Jessie, sat down, weeping helplessly.

Madalena had a strange, underwater sensation, dream-like and slow. "You get an allowance? From Jack? Now? Still? Since the row?"

"He's a good man, your Jack, he's stuck by you all these years, taken care of you and your Bella, even though you don't know whether .... Well, he's a good man. You know where you are with a man like Jack."

She took a deep swig of wine, prompting fresh tears.

"He says? He says he'll stop it? How does he? *Does Jack come here?* How does he give you your allowance?"

Madalena knelt down in front of Jessie, her hands on her shoulders, looking hard into her mother's eyes.

"Not often, just to check that you or Bella haven't been, that's all. I tell him you haven't, I always tell the truth. He came about a week ago, asking me something about Bella. I won't tell him you've been today, don't you tell him now, I'll be in trouble, don't tell him will you?" She took a deep swig of wine, and wiped her eyes with her arm.

"I won't tell him, no. What did he ask you about Bella?"

"I can't remember very well, it was the evening ... how pretty she was, we were both saying, from the pictures in the magazine. He said, oh that's it I remember now, 'What d'you think Jessie? D'you think she looks like her old Dad?'"

Madalena smiled a tight grimace at her mother, and spoke slowly and deliberately. "And what did you say to that, Ma?"

Jessie smiled back, through her tears, at her daughter. "Oh, I'm far too clever for him. D'you know what I said? Go on, guess?"

Madalena hoped Jessie couldn't hear her heartbeat. "I can't guess. Go on, tell me what you said. Share the joke."

"I said, I said ..." Jessie was cackling. "I said, 'Oh, that one, she's been the spit of you since the day she was born, Jack.'" Her voice finished on a shriek of hysteria.

Madalena started to laugh, infected by her mother's mirth and her own relief. But there was something else she wanted to know. "How do you get your allowance?"

"In my post office account, every month, he pays it in, I rely on it, I couldn't manage without it, have you any idea how much the pension is? Nobody could manage on it."

"They certainly couldn't buy your quantity of wine with it, that's for sure. How much does he give you?"

"It's not much, it's nothing to you. Thirty pounds a week, that's all, not much to you, but it makes a big difference to me."

"This is our secret, neither of us will tell him. But I can't risk coming here again."

The mean old bastard, Madalena thought. He'd calculated just the amount that would be enough to keep control of her, but not so much that she could move house, or live in any comfort. He probably knew she would just drink it all. The calculating, controlling bastard.

Well, that had proved easy after all. No need at all for the carefully worked-out story about why she was there.

She'd got what she'd come for, plus a little bit more.

Madalena Skyped Bud as soon as she got home, and told him what had happened.

"It definitely wasn't her, Bud, I'm sure of that."

"No, I see, you're right." Bud smiled into the screen.

"You know what? I tell you all this, and I watch the expressions on your face as I tell you, and it helps me understand what I feel about it too."

"Hey, don't say that."

"Why not?"

"Because that's what your mother should have done for you: helped you understand your feelings. As my mother did for me."

That was the sort of comment that Bud sometimes made that she didn't quite understand, but that made her feel a little upset. She would remember it and file it away and then muse on it later to try to work out what he meant. But now she was curious.

"What was your mother like?" Watching his face on her screen, she saw his smile fade, and a shadow cross his face, and wished that they were together in person, so she could reach out and comfort him.

"She was brilliant. A devoted mother."

"Not like your Dad, then." A thought struck her. "Your Dad's a bit like Jack, isn't he?"

"He was, yes. My mother was the opposite in every way." Bud was no longer looking at the screen, but looking to his left, shaking his head. "How those two stayed together for as long as they did. Well,

164

it was a straight trade between them, older than the Bible, nothing mysterious about that. He was fascinated by her beauty, he treated her like some rare species of pet, not like a person, with a brain and a beating human heart. He lost interest as she got older and lost her looks. She was part Malaysian, part American. Sometimes I wonder if *you* have Malaysian blood, Mad, there's something about the tilt of your eyes that reminds me of her. I'll show you a photo one day."

"That's so sad, that she died."

Bud sighed and turned back to look at her. "I know. I'm an orphan. You are too in a way, aren't you?"

Madalena smiled at him. He was right. She'd always been an orphan: she didn't really have a mother to speak of, not in the way Bud meant. She'd had to look after Jessie most of the time. How sad, to lose a mother who loved you and took care of you. Madalena leaned into the screen, touching the picture of Bud's face, stroking his cheek, wishing he was here; or, better still, that she was there, with him.

"What happened to her?"

"Drink. Never recovered from my father divorcing her. She died, bitter and disappointed."

Madalena sat back, her hands to her face. "Oh how dreadful."

Bud shook his head, then shrugged his shoulders. "Old news. A long time ago."

Madalena wished she could reach into the screen, put her arms around him, comfort him, as he always comforted her. "Your parents are like Jack and I, I've just realized. That's true isn't it? That's why you've helped me."

"Yes. They are. And I'm helping you because we're friends. Enough of me though; I think your mother's fucking amazing."

"I'm not sure you'd be saying that if you'd seen her. What d'you think about Jack giving her an allowance all these years?"

"Huh. Thirty pieces of silver."

"What does that mean?"

"You know, Judas in the Bible."

"I haven't read it. What d'you mean?"

"I mean one way or another, both your mother and your partner are selling you out."

Another one of those Bud remarks, thought Madalena. "So why d'you think she's amazing?"

"How she answered Jack's question. He's busy though, old Jack, isn't he?"

"I try and surprise people when I visit them, but I turn up, and I get the surprise when I find out he's already been there. He's always one step ahead of me."

"Story of your life. Will he visit Honor, d'you think?"

Madalena laughed. "Not in a million years, she's way off his radar."

"Now that your mother's off our list of suspects, we should plan for your meeting with Honor next. Did you do the research, Mad?"

"Yes, I did. In fact I'm a bit of a whizz with Google now, I'm amazed at what you can find out. Honor's a psychiatrist, and her office or clinic or whatever it is, is about half an hour north of our London flat. I've got that address and the phone number anyway."

"Good girl."

"So what shall I do then? Just turn up?"

"It's a tricky one. We have to keep the advantage of surprise, so it's either just turn up … but, she's a therapist, she might not be willing or able to see you, so …"

"Why don't I make a therapy appointment with her?"

"Brainwave, brilliant!"

Mad preened with delight.

Bud laughed. "Feels good to be smart doesn't it?"

"Amazing. Strong and powerful."

"Go on, work it out. You make an appointment with her, and then what?"

"I'd have to make an appointment under a different name, wouldn't I, I can't be me … so, I think of a name, make the appointment, then I turn up, right?"

"Then she recognizes you."

"Will she?"

"Undoubtedly. Once seen, never forgotten."

"So I have to think about what to say, about why I'm there, why I've tricked her."

"Good girl. So you have a think about that, and we'll talk again in a couple of days' time to plan our strategy."

Madalena had never felt so important. Emboldened, she said: "There's something else I want to ask you, that I want help with."

"Go ahead. Your wish is my command."

Madalena laughed again. It suddenly struck her that since meeting Bud she'd never been so miserable, but never laughed so much either. She adored him.

"I want to work out how to get Jack to let me visit my mother regularly. She's old and alone, and probably dying. I'd like to help her if I can."

"How d'you normally get Jack to agree to things?"

"Sweet-talk him, spoil him, think of how I can make him think it was his idea, seduce him in certain ways. But on this matter none of that's ever worked. I don't know what to do."

"OK. Listen. I'm going to suggest a radically different strategy, something you may never have tried before."

"Go on then. Though believe me, I've tried everything, and I won't go into detail but I mean *everything*."

"Have you tried just asking him, straightforwardly, as one grown-up human being to another?"

Madalena sat back in her chair, her eyes wide. "*What?*"

"Told you it was radical."

"It'd never work."

"How d'you know?"

"You mean just come right out and say: Jack, can I go and visit my mother?, just like that?"

"Why not?"

"Maybe if I said that when we're in bed, after, you know ... he's very receptive then."

"No, listen to me. Not then. Just in the normal course of conversation, over dinner or something. Just straight, adult conversation."

"I have to get my head around this, I've never thought of it. My strategies with Jack have to be smarter than that you know. You're very clever and all that, and you've helped me a lot, but you just don't know Jack."

"Be bold. Give it a try. You've nothing to lose after all."

Jinny served dinner to Madalena and Jack: steak, chips, and mushrooms. They always ate in the dining room, using the good china and silver and crisp white table napkins. Jack insisted on it.

"It's nice, Jack, isn't it, just the two of us?" Madalena smiled at Jack across the table.

He smiled slightly in return. "Hmm. I miss seeing Bella though."

"Me too, sometimes."

"Did you Skype her this evening?" Jack never failed to check that Bella's freedom conditions were being complied with.

"I did, yes, she seemed fine."

Madalena and Bella's call had been short: Bella was about to go out. They sometimes stayed on a call together for an hour or more.

"Look what I'm wearing, Mum, what d'you think? D'you think Euan will like it?"

She did a twirl of her slim golden limbs in her miniscule white dress.

"Gorgeous, Bella. You should think about loosely curling your hair: have you seen some of the new hair fashions?"

Bella had the facial expression of someone who had just received a sharp smack. "What? Why?"

"I mean big curls, loosely, like ringlets. I thought I might try mine."

"I'd love to try that. For some reason I always thought you liked me to keep mine straight."

"Fashions change, don't they? And we've both got black curly hair, what's the point of pretending we haven't?"

Bella had faced her mother through the screen and stared at her curiously.

"I've never heard you say anything like that before, Mum. Are you OK? Has something happened?"

Many things, thought Madalena. Where would I start? "Nothing pretty girl, everything's fine. You go and enjoy yourself."

"What did she say? Where's she going? When's she back here?" Jack liked to have full details of their conversations, interrogating them with suspicion, keen to ensure that nothing was going on behind his back.

"She was off to a party with some friends. She'll be home for Sunday lunch."

"Oh, that's good. Get my women in one place, that's what I like."

It was the first time that Madalena didn't mind being referred to as a woman. In fact she rather liked it.

She cleared her throat. "Jack? There's something I'd like to talk to you about. Ask you."

Jack, alerted by an unfamiliar tone, paid full attention. "Go on."

"Now that Bella's here so little … I find myself a little lonely sometimes. I'd like some company …."

Jack cut across her. "Don't start all that again, Madalena; friends are nothing but trouble, we found that out years ago."

"I meant something else. I was wondering, with Bella out of the picture, if I could maybe make the occasional visit to my mother."

Jack sat back, steepled his fingers, and inspected her. "You want to visit your mother …?"

"I wonder how she is sometimes. She's getting older, I doubt that she's well. I don't know how long she's got."

"She never struck me as a particularly warm or loving mother to you."

"Well, no, she wasn't, but that's not really the point. She must be lonely too. And I'm the only family she has."

"I don't know what to say, Madalena. You know what I think about what she did to Bella."

"It was completely unforgiveable, I know, but this is about me, not Bella."

"D'you know what she said to me about you once, when she was drunk? I've never told you this before because I didn't want to hurt you, but before you start some kind of mission to rescue the unrescuable, you should know how she thinks of you."

"What did she say?" Now it was Madalena who was all attention.

"It was at that party, when we'd just got the land here and were full of plans for building our palace. You'd just made your entrance. I said to Jessie, you must be proud that your daughter's life turned out so different to yours. She looked at me in that way she has, out of the side of her eyes, almost flirtatious. 'Not that different, Jack,' she said. 'I used to turn a trick for a fiver, she turns a trick for a fancy mansion. It's just a question of price after all.' And she walked off without even giving me a chance to say anything. That's your mother. And you want to go and see her."

Madalena smothered a smile. There was a truth at the heart of that story. "What she said is upsetting, for you and for me. But she is my mother and I haven't seen her for many years. I don't know how long she has left. I'd like to see her Jack. I'm asking you to allow me to see my own mother."

Jack frowned, a perplexed furrow narrowing his brow. "It's not like you to talk to me like this. I don't know what's come over you. Let me think about it. I'll let you know my verdict."

"Thank you, Jack."

CHAPTER EIGHTEEN

J ack liked his usual routine, whether the family were in London or Cardiff. Bella's social life was busy and late, and it was getting increasingly difficult to rely on her to be at the table for breakfast at eight o'clock. This morning Madalena breathed an inner sigh of relief when Bella appeared, just on time and looking serene. She was trying to please her father: she wanted to persuade him to buy her a car for her use in London, having utterly failed to convince him that she could drive herself to and from Cardiff.

"Morning Dad ... Mum ...."

She sat down and poured herself a coffee from the fresh jug on the table. Jinny hurried in from the kitchen to take her breakfast order.

"Just some muesli please, and some fresh-squeezed orange juice." Bella wandered over to the door to the terrace. "What a gorgeous day. It's like summer out here."

She stepped onto the terrace and surveyed London, then sat on a sunbed and pulled up her skirt. "It's hot enough to sunbathe," she called to her parents.

Moments later, she came back in.

"Dad, come and have a look at this."

Jack looked up from his newspaper.

"What is it?"

"Come and have a look at this car, Dad, it would be perfect for me to run around in, come and see."

"You don't need a car in London. Use the limo, or black cabs, it couldn't be simpler."

"Oh, Da-a-ad. Come and see, it's so cute." She pulled Jack by the hand out to the terrace. "Oh! See? It's gone now. Why didn't you come when I said? It was gorgeous, a purple metallic Mini convertible. Can I have one, Dad? Please? Pretty please?"

Jack laughed and hugged her. "Oh, we'll see. When's your birthday? Coming soon, I think. Come to think of it, I noticed a purple convertible Mini outside the other day. It was very cute, just like you are in fact."

Madalena was relieved to see Jack in a good mood. She'd hardly slept last night, thinking about today and her meeting with Honor. She harboured a secret dread that Jack could read her mind, that he'd know what she was doing, and was watching, waiting, to catch her out. She'd felt like that a lot of the time since getting the letter.

She looked at her watch. *Hello* was out today, and she'd ordered six copies to be delivered. They hadn't arrived with Jack's papers and she'd told Jinny to call the newsagents to see what had happened. Some mix-up: they were on their way now.

Trying to relax, she sat back and looked around: she loved this flat. It was so different from their Cardiff mansion, being almost entirely open plan, an enormous room, with two walls of glass looking over London. The space was divided by strategically placed furniture indicating the uses of the various areas: the dining area, the seating area, and the study area. The industrial sized kitchen, all stainless steel and orange glass was a separate room, as were the four spacious bedroom suites. Everywhere was light, glass, white walls, cream rugs on pale wood floors, and large pieces of vividly coloured art, selected by their interior designer.

Madalena had a perpetually heightened awareness of the airy spaces in which she lived, the luxurious cars she travelled in, the immaculate clothes she wore. Was it all about to come to an abrupt and bloody end? If she couldn't find out who was threatening her? Even if she did find out, it guaranteed her nothing, as she was beginning to realize.

Jinny bustled in, her face lit with excitement. "They're here, the magazines are here."

Reverentially, she placed the pile of glossy magazines on the table in front of Madalena.

"Bella. Quick, come and have a look." Madalena handed a magazine to Bella, and started leafing through another copy.

Bella found the pictures first. "Look Mum. Here it is. Here you are. Oh, you look *fantastic.* Look Dad, look at Mum."

They all gathered round to admire the stunning full-length picture of Madalena.

"How come you're on your own? Why isn't Dad next to you?"

"I didn't know they were taking it …. It was just a moment when Dad wasn't next to me. Lots of people wanted to talk to him, everyone was admiring his work. It was a great evening for you, wasn't it Jack?" She turned towards Jack, to see him visibly inflating in response to the glowing admiration of his womenfolk.

"Well, it was a long job and a lot of work."

"And a great success, everyone said so. It was a pity you couldn't come with us, Bella, you'd have felt so proud of your Dad. I know I did."

Jack beamed. "Well, it's just a job, after all …"

"That's not what is says here Dad …" Bella read from the magazine. "*This world class, state of the art casino, kitted out by Jack Norman Enterprises, boasts cutting edge equipment unseen anywhere else in the world, even Las Vegas. Fully computerised systems, including computerised croupiers, create a gambling experience that surpasses anything else available.* Wow, go Dad."

"It was your Dad's moment. I was proud to be there as his partner." Oh God, if only I could say as his wife …. Madalena looked directly at Jack with her warmest smile.

He couldn't resist, and smiled back at her. "You were the best-looking woman there, Madalena, by a mile."

"As it says here, Mum. You look fantastic."

Once Jack had left for work, Madalena went for her morning workout. She quickly got into her rhythm on the treadmill, with the morning TV on, but she didn't pay attention; she was thinking about how she wanted to look for her meeting with Honor. She was, on the one hand, going to be a different person, Maddie Smith, desperate for an hour of therapy; on the other hand she was meeting her old rival, Honor. She recalled how she used to try to get Thomas to say that she was prettier than Honor. She never succeeded. "You're both gorgeous but in different ways. It's impossible to compare." That was the best she got.

She showered, washed her hair, and settled down at her dressing table for the routine battle with her hair. She picked up the straighteners, stopped, looked in the mirror, put them down again. Yes, why not?

she thought. Be a different person. She ran her fingers through her hair, and called Bella.

"Can you try and do that thing with the straighteners, you know, make a loose curl?"

Bella was enthralled, as was Madalena. It was a mission, taking more than an hour to tame Madalena's curls into relaxed tendrils. Bella smoothed some hair wax along each curl.

"Mum, you look amazing. I want to do mine like this."

Madalena gazed at herself in the mirror. She moved her head from side to side: her hair floating, like seaweed, around her head and shoulders. Why on earth hadn't she tried this before?

"Maybe I should I leave it to dry naturally? Yours would look good like this, Bella, you should try it."

"When I was a little girl you used to iron it straight."

"I ironed my own too. Who did I think I was fooling?"

"Chill out, Mum, it's just a hairstyle."

"It's so not, Bella, it's so not. You have no idea."

"I'm off for my shower."

Madalena felt envious as Bella left for a carefree day. How amazing to have so little to worry about.

Madalena chose a slim-fitting, knee-length dress in khaki green, with dark brown leather belt and matching strappy high-heeled sandals. She regarded herself in the mirror, turning this way and that.

Classy, a bit sexy.

"Hello, Maddie Smith."

Pulling up two streets away from Honor's offices, with twenty minutes to spare, Madalena felt tremulous. She took a swig from her water bottle and licked her lips, then checked her make-up in the mirror.

Sitting back in her seat, she took a deep breath, and recalled her Skype with Bud.

"What if she refuses to see you?"

"Why? Pat didn't. My mother didn't."

"She probably hates you."

"Ouch." Madalena felt as though she'd been punched.

"Though Pat does too, and she was willing to see you. You had something to ask her of course, that made her curious."

Madalena stared at his face on the screen. He was wearing his thoughtful face, unsmiling, his brow furrowed, looking to one side, calculating. His most handsome look, she thought. Such a good-looking man, fantastic eyes. He turned to look at her.

"You need something to tell her. Something she'd want to know. What could that be?"

Madalena shrugged.

"Did you think about it? What you could say to pacify her, in case she's the letter writer?"

"Yes, but I couldn't think of anything at first."

Bud was leaning into the screen. "And then?"

Madalena laughed. "And then I thought of you saying, come on, Mad. Think. There must be something."

Bud grinned. "And that worked?"

"It always does." I love flirting with Bud, Madalena thought.

"My magic touch. I can always get the women talking. Part of my job. Part of my charm, thanks to my Mom. So, what did you come up with?"

"Something Thomas told me, the last time I saw him."

"What?"

Madalena related to Bud her last conversation with Thomas, and what he had told her about Honor. She was gratified, as usual, by the amazement on his face.

"He told you *that*?"

"He did. I'm not going to tell her that though."

"Maybe she already knows."

"She doesn't. He said he could never tell her, she'd kill him if she knew."

"So how did you feel, him telling you that? Why on earth did he tell you anyway?"

"It was part of his reason for refusing to believe that Bella could be his. *I* could have killed him. I was terribly upset."

"You poor thing. Cruel guy; you go for these hard types, don't you?"

"Thomas wasn't hard."

"He sounds it to me. You have to tell Honor. Not just so she'll see you. Because it's something she should know, she needs to know."

"I wouldn't give her the satisfaction."

"Look Madalena, you know what Thomas told you about Honor. What you don't know is what Thomas told her, about you. That's what you're trying to find out. Does she have knowledge? We know she has the motivation."

Madalena's chin lifted, her mouth set in a mutinous line. "I don't want to ask her anything or tell her anything."

"You're going to have to do both. Take it easy to start with, don't reveal your hand too early, definitely not your trump card. How about saying you're thinking of the past and you're feeling remorseful?" Bud said.

"Remorseful for what?"

"For hurting her. For stealing her man. What else?"

"I don't think she sees it like that. It was years ago."

"If she wrote the letter, she's still got a serious grudge. You need to ask for forgiveness, redemption. And you need to tell her what Thomas told you: it might give her some closure on what happened."

"Closure. What does that really mean? I don't get it."

"A final understanding of something you need to know. So you can forget, move on."

"That doesn't really mean anything to me."

"It does to me." Bud frowned, his mouth dropped. "When my parents got divorced, my father knew some secret about my mother's early life. She didn't want it to be known to us. He used that to force her to agree to his miserly divorce terms."

Madalena leaned back, her hand over her mouth, her eyes wide. "What secret?"

"We never found out. So no closure for us. If there was someone out there who could tell us, I'd want them to tell me."

"Even if it was something really terrible?" As Madalena spoke she was thinking: what if she was a prostitute, for instance?

"I'm not sure anything could be worse than all the things my sisters and I have imagined over the years. The truth would be a blessing. Closure is a blessing. Anyway, enough of me, back to you, and Honor, and you asking for forgiveness."

"I can't do that, I just can't. I'm not going to ask her for anything."

"You have to ask her several things. Does she know anything, or think she knows anything about Bella? So don't get all proud about it."

Madalena shifted in her seat. In a weird way, she liked it when Bud spoke to her like this. Nobody ever spoke to her in quite the way he did. He wasn't telling her off, exactly, because he wasn't angry. But he wasn't trying to charm her either. He was just very direct and to the point.

"No, OK, sorry. But the fact of the matter is, if it wasn't for her, I could have ended up with Thomas. She put paid to that." She grimaced at him.

"I think you'll find that was Thomas's choice. Anyway, you'd have ended up a young widow." Bud's face was serious.

"Maybe he wouldn't have died. Things could've been completely different. Couldn't they?"

"Well, they weren't. And now they are what they are. So set your feelings aside, and keep clear and focussed on what you're trying to find out. Got it?"

"OK, sorry, yes, got it."

He was completely wonderful. She adored him.

She checked her watch. It was time. Inspecting her face in the mirror, she applied a final slick of lip-gloss. Starting the car engine, she drove around to Honor's offices, parking her car a block away. She gathered her handbag, switched off the engine, and got out of the car.

CHAPTER NINETEEN

Stopping at the newsagents to collect her paper, Honor bought the new copy of *Hello* and flicked through to the photo spread of the casino opening. She found a full-page picture of Madalena, looking even more spectacular now than as a young woman: that's what money and care can do, even better than youth. Groomed to perfection, a picture of femininity with just a hint of sensuality, Madalena gazed into the far distance.

Madalena Morris, long-term partner of Jack Norman, was the undisputed beauty of the occasion: trumping everyone by a mile, in a classic Chanel design.

Though she didn't really care now, about Madalena. It was Bella that she was interested in.

A busy morning, with three clients back to back, left Honor with little thought for her own worries. The moment her last client left, Barbara hurried in, bright-eyed and pink.

"Honor." She spoke in a low tone. "You have a surprise visitor."

"Really?" Honor stared at her. "Who?"

"An old friend from the past he said. Jack Norman. A very handsome man, I must say." Barbara beamed, her eyebrows raised.

"What? What!" Honor's face had drained of colour.

179

"Are you OK? What's the matter? You look terrible, are you going to faint?"

Honor had leaned forward, her head down on her knees. "It's OK," she mumbled. "I just need some time." After a few moments she sat back up. "He's not here now, surely?"

"He'll be here in a few minutes. He came by earlier and I told him to come back at lunch time."

"What did he say exactly?"

"He said, he was an old acquaintance of yours, and he needed to speak to you. When he told me his name, I remembered Bella; I said, oh, are you related to Bella Norman, who was in the papers recently? Honor was very interested."

"Oh dear God." Honor doubled over, dropping her head to her knees again.

"What? I realized he wasn't some crank or anything then, that he really did know you. He said, yes, I'm Bella's father. So I said, well, Mr Norman, you have a lovely daughter, I must say, and he smiled. He seemed very nice."

"I need a few minutes to myself. If he returns, don't bring him in until I tell you I'm ready."

"Did I do something wrong? He seemed genuine."

"You didn't say anything else? You didn't mention the photos?"

"No, no, I didn't say anything."

"Well, if he comes back, don't, OK? Don't mention Bella again to him."

"What is all this? What's going on?"

"I don't know why he's here, or what he wants, that's all. He's a ghost from the past: it's upsetting. Thanks heavens I have a free session after lunch at least." Honor picked up her daily schedule and studied it. "It's not on here. Who's Maddie Smith?"

"Oh dear, Honor, I'm sorry, I had to use that slot for a new client."

"Barbara … we agreed; why did you do that?"

"She was distressed and most insistent. She'd heard of you, she thought just one session would help. I couldn't resist."

Honor paced her office, attempting to compose herself. What could Jack possibly want? Why was he here? She hardly knew him. A glance in the mirror, at her pink face, and her blotched neck, sent her scurrying to the bathroom to splash water on her face before Jack arrived.

Standing at the front window, she saw a black limousine making its regal way up the street, drawing up outside, dwarfing the Mini.

A uniformed chauffeur got out and opened one of the back passenger doors. Jack alighted. Involuntarily, Honor stepped back and to one side so she couldn't be seen. A good move, as it happened, because Jack immediately looked up towards the building. He was immaculately dressed in a dark grey suit. Suited and booted as Eliot would say. Eliot could never look like this, not even for a wedding: he'd wear a suit, but he'd never achieve the sharp edges that Jack did, as though he'd been drawn with a fine architect's pen. Eliot had mildly blurred edges, even in a suit.

Jack paused, looked around, then stood, apparently inspecting her car.

Moments later, the bell rang, followed by the entrance buzzer and Jack's confident footsteps.

Barbara put her head around the door, and spoke in a stage whisper. "He's here."

"Offer him coffee, and bring one for me. Then show him in."

Jack came in, followed by Barbara carrying a tray of coffee. He strode forward, his hand outstretched. "Hello, Honor."

She shook his hand. "Hello, Jack." She indicated the easy chairs, and they sat down.

"Thanks for seeing me, you must be very surprised, I should think. I've come to ask a rather odd favour."

"I am surprised, yes." Honor slowed down her breathing to compose herself. "I saw your daughter in the papers recently."

Jack picked up his coffee cup, and took a careful sip. "So your assistant said."

"Lovely girl." Honor smiled.

"She's behaving rather badly at the moment, I'm afraid." Jack placed his cup back on its saucer.

"Normal youthful experimentation, I'd say." Honor picked up her coffee.

"You probably know better than anyone else what weirdos there are out there. It set off a lot of bad things, strange letters, a blog, poison pen letters. I had to get her a bodyguard for a while."

"Why would I know better than anyone else?" Honor set her cup back down on the tray, aware of a slight quiver in her hand.

Jack stared at her. "Because you're a psychiatrist?"

"Oh. Of course, yes. What can I help you with?"

"I have an odd favour to ask. It's to do with Thomas Dyer."

"Another name from the past."

"Caroline Dyer is a close friend of my ex-wife Pat, they were on holiday together recently."

181

Where was this going? What did he want? "Caroline and I were close years ago, but we lost touch," Honor said. "You still see Pat then?"

"From time to time. It's Caroline's fiftieth birthday in a couple of months, and Pat's arranging a party for her. She wants to make a photo album of Caroline over the years, as a surprise."

"Right …."

"And she wants to include photos of Thomas. So we thought of you, as a person who might still have lots of photos of him. I'm sorry to bother you: we hardly know each other. You knew Madalena better I think."

"I can't say I knew Madalena, not personally. We knew of each other of course."

"Do you have any pictures of Thomas?"

Was he kidding or what? A complicated story to get his hands on some pictures of Thomas: definitely not a coincidence that he would be looking for these now of all times. "Yes, I have a few. You didn't know Thomas, did you?"

"Hardly at all. Me and my mates used to envy him, because he had you. Classiest bird in town."

Honor felt her face go pink again, and she smiled with pleasure. "Really? Did you?"

"Oh yes. And look at you now, still good looking, and successful." Jack gestured around the room.

"Thank you." Honor's hands fluttered around her hair, and she wished she was not wearing her usual dull work suit. Close up, she could see the expensive detail of Jack's cashmere suit, the Savile Row double stitching.

"You've kept pretty well yourself. How's Madalena?"

"She's fine. Same as ever."

"What's she doing with her life at the moment?"

"Oh, taking care of me and Bella, that's a full-time job for any woman."

Could she seduce him? Wouldn't that be perfect karma, so symmetrical and right? Was he seducable?

"So you like to have a wife at home then, Jack?" She raised an eyebrow and smiled at him.

"We never married. She likes to be at home, she's not a career type of person."

"Still stunning, I imagine. And clever too, she knows how to keep you on your toes, doesn't she, not getting married?" Honor's smile broadened and she looked directly at Jack.

Jack laughed. "She'd like to get married; it's me that drags my feet, God knows why."

"Keeping your options open then?" *Stop it, Honor. What d'you think you're doing?*

Jack laughed again. "Well you never know do you? We're all getting to that funny age, aren't we? Mid-life crisis looming, it gets most of us in the end doesn't it?"

Too far, Honor, you're going too far.

"Do you want to see these pictures? I can get them up on my computer, and email them to you."

"That'd be great, thanks. You're smart with technology."

"How did we live without computers? It's hard to imagine."

"Madalena's only just started using one; until a few weeks ago she wouldn't have known what to do with it. I spend most of my life in front of a screen one way or another."

"Me too. Have your coffee, while I find the pictures, it'll take me a couple of minutes."

Honor went to her desk and clicked the link to her home computer. She made a new folder, and quickly and expertly dropped into it: Thomas at various ages and stages; Thomas and his mother; Thomas and Caroline. Jack was looking for the same thing she'd been looking for, she was sure. A resemblance. She was going to make sure he got what he wanted.

"Come and take a look at these. Is this the sort of thing you want?"

He came and peered over her shoulder, staring intently at the screen as she flicked through the photo folder. She felt hyper-conscious of his close physical presence, and the citrus smell of his after-shave.

"That's great, Honor, thank you."

"Here's a good one, look: Thomas with Caroline. She'll like that one, I should think. She probably has her own copy, but it'd be nice to put in an album. Attractive, isn't she?"

"She is, yes."

"She reminds me of someone, I'm not sure who."

"Does she?" Jack leaned closer into the screen, scrutinizing the picture of Caroline.

"They're a good-looking family."

"You and Madalena certainly found Thomas irresistible. It must have been hard for you when he died."

"Horrible. Devastating."

Jack put his hand on Honor's shoulder. "I didn't mean to remind you. It was all a bit of a mystery, wasn't it, his death?"

"Tragic. Total tragedy." Honor could feel his hand on her shoulder, and faintly, his breath on the back of her neck. She stood up abruptly and Jack took a step back, dropping his hand. She sat back down.

"It must've been hard for you."

"Yes." Honor's throat tightened.

"All the mystery and speculation must've made it worse."

"It did. If you don't mind, I'd rather not talk about it." She swallowed hard.

Jack had moved to the side of the desk. He was watching her closely. "No, of course, I do understand, I'm sorry to remind you. But Madalena and I were talking about it recently. Could I ask you one last thing? I know it was an open verdict, but you knew him better than anyone. Did you think it was suicide?"

Honor dropped her head, and put her hand to her forehead. She could feel herself trembling inside. "This is too upsetting. No, it wasn't suicide; it was a freak accident, as the inquest found. It happens."

"Not foul play?"

"Whatever makes you say such a thing? Everyone loved Thomas. Nobody would wish him harm, nobody."

"It must have been so sad for you. Good that you didn't have children, at least."

Honor jumped up to face him, her eyes shining with tears. "*No!* It wasn't. I'd have *loved* him to have a child, to leave a child behind in the world. More than anything, I'd have loved to have had his child."

Jack leaned back, hands up in a gesture of surrender. "Sorry. I just meant it would have been hard to be widowed so young with a child to raise alone, that's all. Don't cry, please, don't cry."

Honor took a tissue from the box on her desk and dabbed her eyes. "I'd've been happy to. It'd have seemed less of a loss if I'd had his child. Enough now, Jack, not another word about it. Which photos do you want?" Honor sat down again, took a deep breath and flicked through the photos again.

"If you could email all of them to me that would be great. Sorry, Honor, I didn't mean to upset you. Did he never have a child from another relationship?"

Honor stared intently at the screen. *Control yourself.* "Not to my knowledge. Tell me your email address and I'll mail them right away."

"Jack dot Norman at J. N. Enterprises, all one word, dot com."

Honor rapidly typed in the address and pressed send. "There you go. Let's finish our coffee. Then I must move on, I've a new client arriving in half an hour."

Jack was admiring. "Thanks so much. You were always smart weren't you? And look at you now, *Doctor* Sinclair. You remarried?"

"I did." *Is he trying to flirt with me?*

"Children?"

"Two daughters and a son."

"I hope your new husband makes you happier than Thomas did. He led you quite a dance didn't he?"

God, he's insensitive. Still, here's my chance to stir things up a bit.

"He did, yes, me and Madalena."

"You were the one he married though." Jack's eyes flickered from her face down to her chest.

"I suppose that was some kind of victory." *He's brazen.*

"What was the timing of all of that? I think by the time I came into Madalena's life, there'd been a lot of to-ing and fro-ing, but Thomas was pretty committed to you by then, wasn't he?"

Here goes nothing, Madalena. Payback time. "It's hard to remember. It did drag on. I don't know when it ended between Thomas and Madalena. Even when we were married I had suspicions that they continued seeing each other."

"Really? What, even after I was around?" Jack leaned forward, his eyes narrow, his brow furrowed.

That's wiped the smile off his face. "Oh I don't know. They couldn't keep away from each other. I was helpless against her."

"Thomas chose you in the end, you should remember that."

"It's not something I think much about any more, Jack, it's all a long time ago." *If only that was true. It could have been yesterday.*

"Don't you? I still do, sometimes; I wonder what really happened back then."

So do I. "Speaking professionally, Jack, I can tell you that it's really better not to let the past haunt you too much."

Honor was shocked at her own nerve as she heard herself say this.

"I'm sure you're right. If only it was as easy to do as to say." Jack stood up. "I've taken enough of your time. Thanks so much for the photos; I know Pat will be pleased. It's been good to see you, so well and successful. If there's ever anything I can do for you, let me know?"

Like what? Is this a coded message of some kind? "Please ask Pat to pass on my best wishes to Caroline. And you let me know if I can help in any way, maybe with Bella? I'd be happy to talk to her, informally you understand, I don't mean professionally, if you and Madalena thought it might help."

"*Would* you? That would be so helpful Honor. Things are tough for her, and not about to get easier. Maybe we could arrange to have dinner, the three of us, then I can leave you two alone to talk?"

"Yes, that would be fine." Honor could hardly believe her luck, that it could be so easy. "Shall we make a date now?" Honor went to her computer, opened her calendar, and it was all arranged for the following week.

Watching Jack leave from the window, giving a little wave and smile, Honor felt supremely pleased with herself; she'd got just what she'd wanted, a meeting with Bella.

Yes, that has a certain symmetry. Madalena stole from me, now I will steal from her. Turn the other cheek be damned. It's time for an eye for eye, no more and no less.

Then I can feel whole again. Maybe.

CHAPTER TWENTY

Honor had a quick lunch to give herself time for a walk. She followed her usual tracks around the park, and settled on the bench beneath the willow tree, where all her turmoil had started, with the picture of Bella in the newspaper. She felt disturbed by a strange excitement at the thought of meeting Bella. What she really wanted was to become a mother figure to her, to treat her as the daughter that she and Thomas had never had. But should have had. She pulled a tissue from her sleeve and wiped away a tear.

Back at her office, she tried to prepare for her new client, not feeling ready for a new person, a new drama. She stood up, and shook out her arms, then her legs. Lifting her shoulders high, she let them drop, and slowly circled her head from side to side. *Snap out of it Honor, clear yourself, be ready for whatever anguished soul you're about to confront.* Sitting down again, she put her head back, closed her eyes, and took several long deep breaths.

Barbara put her head around Honor's door. "Maddie Smith's arrived, a couple of minutes early."

Honor opened her eyes, and sighed heavily. "OK. Can I have a glass of water, please? Show her in."

Honor stood up arranging her face in its welcoming expression of warm empathy: soft eyes, and a slight smile.

Barbara came in, bringing the new client. "Maddie, this is Honor. Honor, Maddie."

"Hello, Honor." Madalena had not seen Honor for twenty years. At a glance, she took in her old rival. Why did she look so drab? She was a good-looking woman, doing absolutely nothing to play up her assets. She felt triumphant to see Honor's shock, and suppressed a smile.

"You. *You*. What do you want?" Honor had flushed crimson, her eyes and mouth wide with shock. What the hell was *she* doing here?

Barbara stepped back into the room. "What? What? Honor? Are you OK?"

"This is *not* Maddie Smith. What the hell are you playing at? Why are you here? Get out. Go on, get out." Honor stepped towards Madalena, making a shooing motion with her arms.

"No, please, I need to talk to you." Madalena took a step backwards holding up her hand up like a traffic policeman. She glanced around, at Barbara, trying to think, how can I get to stay here, what do I need to say? She tried to remember Bud's words. What had he said? "Try and be humble."

"How dare you trick me like this, how dare you? Barbara, show this woman out." Honor took another step towards Madalena, and raised her voice.

"Hang on, please, no, let me stay. I'm sorry for tricking you, I didn't think you'd see me otherwise. I'm so sorry." There, thought Madalena, that didn't hurt so much. She could hear Bud's voice: "Focus on the goal."

"Well, you're dead right there." Honor felt a little calmer in the face of Madalena's apology. Her face was hot and she put her hand up to her neck: the heat told her that it was livid red.

"Honor?" Barbara stepped forward, placing her hand on Honor's arm, giving her a slight squeeze of comfort. "Let me show Maddie back out to wait, so you can think about what you want to do."

"Yes, that's a good idea, please?" Madalena tried her best to look contrite, lowering her eyes and clasping her hands together. "I'm sorry for tricking you, I didn't mean to upset you, I just wanted to talk to you."

"OK Barbara, give me a minute."

Barbara shepherded Madalena out, scolding her roundly. "You sit down there and wait." Her voice was stern. "I'm sure I don't know what all this is about."

Five minutes later, Barbara returned. Honor was pacing, her face still pink.

"What d'you want me to do? Will you see her? She's Bella's mother, they're the spit of each other, I don't know why I didn't realize when she arrived. What's going on? Who are these people? She said she's not here to upset you. She said she's got something to tell you, and she wants to apologize. Surely you can't turn her away?" Barbara had been completely captivated by Madalena's appeal.

"Apologize? Is that what she said?" *Was that possible? Madalena feeling remorseful? Whatever would have provoked that? The woman was ruthless.*

"Yes. She didn't say for what."

"No, I bet she didn't. I'm sure she didn't. *Huh!* Apologize indeed. I bet." *Unlikely. She just didn't have it in her: no empathy, so no remorse. Why was she really here?*

"Will I show her in?" Barbara was frowning, her mouth thin and tense.

"OK. But stay close, I may ask her to leave quite quickly."

Madalena returned, and Honor indicated the easy chair opposite her.

"Thank you. I'm sorry to shock you, I didn't really know how to approach you, how to be sure you'd see me." Madalena was meek.

"For future reference, lies and deceit are not designed to get you the warmest welcome." Honor straightened up in her chair so that she could at least look Madalena levelly in the eye. She would have preferred it if she could sit up taller so that she could slightly look down on Madalena. For a fleeting instant, she considered getting another cushion to sit on.

"No. Sorry." Madalena looked penitent, warning herself not to overdo it.

Honor was glad that the pictures in *Hello* had prepared her for Madalena who was even more breathtaking in the flesh than in print. Though she had done something different to her hair. In the magazine photo, it had been drawn back, straight, close to her head and wound into a neat pleat. Now, it was, well it was a bit like Tisi's actually, loose long Medusa tendrils. *Two in one day, two women coiling snakelike tentacles around me, squeezing the breath from my body, choking me.*

"You're a psychiatrist? Like, a shrink?" Madalena smiled at Honor, looking straight into her eyes, remembering Bud's advice: try and make friends with her, try to get her on side. She'd had to practise, in the mirror, for days. It had made her realize how very rarely she looked anyone in the eye, or smiled, really fully smiled, other than at Bud.

Honor gave a faint smile in return, finding it hard to resist the beam of Madalena's full on charm offensive. "I'm a psychiatrist. I don't like the word shrink. I work with people who are troubled in their hearts, or mentally disturbed. How about you? What do you do?" *As if I don't know. Nothing. You do nothing. You're a parasite.*

"Nothing … I …" Madalena shifted in her seat, feeling her confidence evaporate.

"Nothing? You don't do anything? Surely you must do something?" Honor's equilibrium was returning. Her face was cooler now.

"Well, I'm a wife." I wish I was, Madalena thought. "Well, not a wife exactly, Jack and I never married."

"So you're a mistress. Still." Honor raised an eyebrow and slightly curled her lip.

"I—I—uh, I never really thought of it like that." I'm stammering, thought Madalena. I may as well be sixteen again with Honor and her posh mates laughing at me at school. "I think of myself as a wife and mother, like you, I guess. No career though. You must've worked hard. I remember you were always very clever. Thomas always used to say how bright you were."

At the mention of Thomas, and the vision of Madalena and Thomas talking about her, even in complimentary terms, Honor felt a cord of anger rising from her gut, up her body into her throat. She wanted to slap Madalena. She placed her hands on the arms of her chair, and clenched her teeth.

"I did work hard, I still do. I love my work." She was not going to let this woman throw her off track, upset her.

"That must be so nice. Your office is so attractive." Madalena looked around, sincerely appreciative of the elegant room. How amazing, she thought, to have a place like this, all of your own, where you could choose everything yourself. A study. Your own study, and your own work. She sighed.

"Did you never want to do something? Don't you get bored?" *Stop it now. Enough. You're just being plain mean.*

Madalena looked vague. "Bored? My partner's old-fashioned, he likes me to be at home. He didn't encourage me to have interests."

"No pressing ambition then." *I can't stop myself. I just can't, I'm enjoying the chance to get my own back in some small way.*

"I did think it'd be nice to be a personal trainer, maybe become a yoga instructor kind of thing … but Jack wasn't keen. I was good at gym at school, I almost made the Olympic team one year." Madalena sat up straighter as she remembered this. Yes, she almost was someone successful too; it wasn't her fault that she didn't quite make it.

"A miss is as good as a mile." *That's enough. Stop right now.* "Anyway, what can I do for you?"

Madalena took a breath, glanced past Honor and paused, inwardly reminding herself of the plan she and Bud had made.

"I guess I've thought a lot just lately about Thomas and what happened between you and me and you and him …."

"Really?" Honor was cool …"And?"

"I was thinking about old times …"

"You're not the only one. Jack came by this morning with a similar story."

Madalena's mouth fell open, her eyes widened. "Jack? Came here? He was here? Today? Are you kidding me?" Madalena could feel her heartbeat. She could hear it in fact. Probably Honor could too. She glanced down to see if her chest was visibly throbbing.

"No, I'm not. He sat there in that very chair, an hour ago." Honor smiled at Madalena and raised her eyebrows.

"Why?" Madalena felt faint. She licked her lips. Jack was here? She had a sensation of a net tightening around her.

"He said he wanted pictures of Thomas for Thomas's sister, to surprise her for her birthday. She's a friend of Jack's ex-wife apparently. It seemed a convoluted story, I didn't quite believe him somehow." *I almost feel sorry for her, she's clearly in shock. Almost, but not quite.*

"What did you say? What did you tell him?" Madalena sat forward, looking at Honor, breathing slowly, trying to calm herself.

"I gave him the pictures, well emailed them to him anyway, I had quite a few, of course. I gave him some of Thomas's mother and sister too."

Madalena put her hand to her head. He'd been here; Jack had been here, looking for pictures of Thomas. There could be only one reason. She swallowed, and ran her tongue across her top lip, and blinked rapidly.

"What did he say?" She tried to alter the tone of her voice and her posture, to look more relaxed and casual.

"He said what a goodlooking family they were. He asked a lot of questions about what happened back then, when Thomas and you and I … when all that ended. He seemed to be trying to work out some dates."

"Oh really?" She couldn't stop blinking. She must look as though she had a nervous tic. "I wonder why? What did you say?"

"I told him the truth—it was all very vague wasn't it? Who knows when you and Thomas stopped your sneaking around and cheating? That's one of life's great mysteries, like the Bermuda Triangle."

"What's the Bermuda Triangle?" Someone else who talked in riddles, she thought.

"Don't worry about it." *She was never very bright, I should feel sorry for her really.*

"What did you tell him about dates? It was such a long time ago, I can hardly remember." Surely she won't be able to remember? Madalena felt a little calmer, as she realized this. Half the time even she didn't know. It was a secret: Thomas would hardly have told her.

"The truth: I didn't know. What's on Jack's mind, exactly? Bella's all over the papers."

"What did he say about Bella?" Madalena's heart jumped at the mention of her daughter.

"He asked if I thought she looked like him." Honor smiled at Madalena, watching several varieties of anxiety and fear flash across her face.

"What did you say?" Madalena tried to say this in an offhand way, as if she didn't really care either way. But her mouth was dry, and her head was thumping.

"Funnily enough we were looking at pictures of Thomas and Caroline at the time. It suddenly struck me that Bella looks like Caroline—odd eh? It made me wonder." Honor was triumphant.

Madalena sprang to her feet. "*Did you say that to him?*"

"That's for me to know." *See, Madalena? How your chickens come home to roost?*

Madalena took a deep breath to steady herself. "I'd like to know too. Did you say that to him?"

Honor ignored her question. "Tell me about the timings of all that, as you remember it. So there we are, I'm married to Thomas, you're with Jack. When did you and Thomas finally stop seeing each other?" She stood up to face Madalena.

"That's for me to know. You tell me what you said to Jack." Madalena stepped towards Honor.

Let's cut to the chase here. "What do you know, about me and Thomas, Madalena? What did he tell you?"

"And what do you know, about me and Thomas?" Madalena had a fleeting image of Bud's face, talking, offering his patient guidance.

It was no good, she couldn't do it. She just couldn't do this the grown-up way.

"You tell me first." They had both started to move slowly, circling each other.

"No, you tell me *then* I'll tell you." Madalena thrust her head towards Honor in a movement reminiscent of Tisi's strange scoop, her hair moving snakelike around her head.

"You—tell—me," Honor emphasized each word with a prod to Madalena's shoulder.

"Don't—push—me," Madalena said, prodding her back.

Honor watched her own right arm moving, back and up, independently of her it seemed, in slow motion. She noticed the glint of her sapphire ring, as it arced past the overhead light. There was a moment of profound silence, before her arm swung round, and her open palm made sharp, echoing contact with Madalena's smooth cheek. Madalena yelped and sprang back, holding her hand to her face, her eyes wide with shock.

Honor, flushed, held her hand to her chest: the impact had made her palm sting. She felt charged with shock and excitement, as she stared at Madalena. She felt totally appalled at her own loss of control, and, at the same time, thrilled and liberated.

"I should have done that years ago, that felt fantastic." *What have I done? I'm completely losing my grip.*

Barbara hurried in to the room. "What on earth's going on? I told you Maddie, if you're going to upset Honor you'll have to leave."

"She hit me." Madalena was holding her hand to her cheek, hardly able to believe what had just happened. Honor couldn't go around hitting clients, surely? She was here as a client after all.

"*What* are you thinking of?" Barbara stepped in between the two women, each breathing heavily, eyes bright. "Honor, what's come over you?"

Honor stared at Barbara, finding it difficult to think straight. What had happened to her? An out of body experience, completely beyond her control. She held up her hands in a gesture of surrender.

"I don't know. I'm sorry Madalena. That was completely wrong of me. Sorry, Barbara, sorry." *I'm not really feeling sorry though. I don't regret it for a second, she deserved that. That slap has been sitting in me for more than twenty years, just waiting for its chance. I feel exhilarated, as though I've just got off a roller coaster ride.*

Barbara was looking at her, frowning. She turned to Madalena. "Maddie, I think you should leave now."

193

Honor put out her hand to Barbara. "No, it's OK, I'm sorry, I completely forgot myself for a moment, I'm fine now. Madalena and I have to talk about this."

"Are you sure?" Barbara looked from one to the other. "Shall I make you both a nice cup of tea?"

Honor looked at Madalena. "Yes, that would be good. Madalena? Stay, please and have some tea?"

Madalena was struggling to contain her desire to get up and leave. She knew she had to stay, to try to find any clues: had Honor written the letter? Her comment about Bella looking like Caroline had made Madalena suspicious: at the very least Honor had *thought* about a resemblance between Bella and Thomas. At the very least. "Yes, OK."

"Let's sit down. I'm terribly sorry. All this talk of Thomas is upsetting. I don't like to be reminded; you caused me such a lot of grief. I apologize for my behaviour though." *Even though I really enjoyed it. However much I apologize, I can't get over how great I feel, as though I've just paid a long overdue debt. It's just not good for you, is it, to hold on to anger and resentment like that?*

"He caused us both a lot of grief, didn't he?"

Honor bit her tongue. *Grief. You. How dare you.* She gave a tight smile and was saved by Barbara's entry with the tea tray.

"Here. Some chocolate biscuits as well. You both need to calm down, it seems to me." She set the tray on the coffee table and left the room.

"What did he tell you? About him and I?" Honor stared at Madalena.

"You tell me what he told you about me." Madalena held her gaze, unblinking. She was calculating: she wasn't going to tell her yet, what Thomas had told her.

"That time he and I split up, when you and he tried to make a go of it. What did he tell you about that?"

"He used to talk to me quite a lot about you, actually." Madalena was starting to enjoy herself. Did Honor think she could slap her and get away with it? She could do something worse than a slap. A slap was nothing.

Honor's face had gone red. She could feel the heat of it. *Is she telling the truth? Thomas and Madalena used to talk about me? Does that mean she knows what happened? I'll play her at her own game.*

"He used to tell me a lot about you, too. I expect you thought I knew nothing about your secret meetings, but I knew more than you imagined."

Madalena looked as though she'd been slapped again. "He *told* you when he was seeing me?"

"Were you with him the night before he died?" *I'm sure you were, I always thought so. Where else could he have been?*

"Wha-a-a-t? What are you talking about? What d'you mean?" Madalena was blinking rapidly.

Honor was cool. "Are you denying it?"

"That's what you thought, was it? That he was with me? So what did you do, poison him? I always wondered." She was admitting nothing. Nothing could be proved. One thing was clear: Honor had a huge grudge against her.

Honor was unruffled. "Of course not. I loved him, I'd never have harmed him. You were losing him though, weren't you? You knew it was over. So what did *you* do, then?"

The two women stared at each other malevolently, their eyes locked, each trying to stare the other one out.

Barbara popped her head around the door, breaking the spell. "Have you finished your tea? Would you like more?"

Both women shook their heads.

I don't think she knows anything. She's bluffing. Thomas was never one to talk much about his feelings. "Look, this is just silly. Thomas's death was an accident, we both know it wasn't suicide."

Madalena nodded, and smoothed down her skirt. "You're right of course. We both loved him after all."

Too far, Madalena, you keep going too far, and now I want to slap you again. Honor slipped her hands, palms down, underneath her thighs. "You were always scheming, always plotting to take him away from me. Just like your daughter's behaving now in fact. Thomas would've been ashamed of her. Just like he was ashamed of you, sneaking around all the time, never being public about your relationship."

"What d'you mean? Why would he? She's nothing to do with him." She was sticking with this story to the end. She looked at Honor, thinking, if you only knew what I could tell you, you'd be a little bit more polite.

"So you say ... striking resemblance if you ask me ... did he know about her?" Honor watched Madalena closely. *Is she lying?*

"She's nothing to do with him. You're such a stuck up cow, you always thought you were better than everyone else."

Clever change of subject there, Madalena. Quite smart actually. Gutter smart. "Well, one thing's for sure, I'm better than you. I always was, not that that's a stretch for anyone."

"Oh yeah? You're pretty low and scheming yourself, aren't you? Showing Jack photos. I bet it was you that sent the letters. How classy d'you think that is exactly?" Dammit, she shouldn't have said that. Too direct. Bud would have a heart attack.

"I don't know what you're talking about." Honor felt herself flush.

"I think you know exactly what I'm talking about." She's gone very red, thought Madalena. That's it, it's her, she did it for sure.

"I don't, as it happens. You know, Madalena, I used to feel sorry for you. You were such a plain and gawky kid. Then you showed us, didn't you? You grew into a swan and hypnotized all our boyfriends .... How did that feel? Fantastic, I should think."

"Absolutely brilliant was how it felt. You were complete bitches to me, you and all your posh friends."

Madalena had a quick memory: Honor and a couple of her friends, being picked up outside school by one of their mothers, a well-groomed woman, smiling at them all from her dark grey Mercedes, promising them tea and cookies when they got home. It wasn't so much what they did to her, as what they didn't do. Like the rest of the world, they barely looked at her or spoke to her. As though she was invisible. Sometimes she had doubted her own existence.

"I noticed how you always needed the girl to know: to rub her face in it a bit. And it was always the prettiest girls you competed with, wasn't it? It seemed more important for you to triumph over the girl, than to get the man." Honor leaned forward and looked Madalena square in the eyes. "I expect you thought it was worth it. Here you are, with Jack all these years. He hasn't married you though. Is he faithful to you, as far as you know?"

"Completely." Madalena sat up tall, and unblinking. Of this there was absolutely no doubt.

"How can you be so sure?" Honor had never met such confidence. *Imagine it. How amazing.* Although she herself had that certainty, just in the opposite direction.

"It's easy, you should try it, any woman could. I satisfy his every possible need."

"Goodness me. It's normally only a newborn baby who can reasonably expect that level of need satisfaction."

"He's a very lucky man. And he knows it. He appreciates me."

"Not enough to marry you though. Why d'you think that is?" *The pleasure of being nasty. I'm overdosing on it today.*

"I, well, I ..." Madalena felt worse than when Honor had slapped her.

"Shall I give you a clue? You may think that all your husband wants is his meals on time and sex on demand; but most men want more than that."

"Do they? What?" Madalena was genuinely amazed.

"Challenge, interest, conversation. A bit of friction even. Not things you offer Jack, eh?" *She doesn't have a clue. Jack may as well be married to a blow up doll.* "Why would he want challenge? He wants his life to be easy, we all do. You don't know what you're talking about."

"That may be what you want, but then that's one of many differences between us. I like things to be tough, I like obstacles to overcome, the sense of achievement from doing something that's hard. It strikes me your Jack likes that too."

"All I want is to be safe and protected, that's hard enough for me, a big enough achievement for one lifetime. While we're on this subject, is your husband faithful to you?"

Honor felt her colour rise, the heat in her face. "That's none of your business."

"I know your first husband wasn't. What about this one? I'll take it that he isn't either from your answer." Madalena scoffed. "So much for your clever talk. You can't even keep your husband at home. What kind of woman are you? Pathetic."

"OK, I've listened to enough of this nonsense now." Honor stood up. "Time to go. And don't contact me again."

Madalena stood up. "I'm going, don't worry. To think I was coming here to try to make peace with you, I must've been mad."

"Yes, indeed you must've been. As if I could forgive you. The pain you caused me and Thomas."

"Huh! If Thomas had stayed with me, he might still be alive now."

"Get out. Get out now."

Barbara opened the door, and looked from one woman to the other. "Maddie, off you go, you've caused enough trouble for one day. We won't be charging you a fee."

Through her fury, Honor registered how smart Barbara was. No fee, so no complaint. Clever.

"I'm going, don't worry. She's crazy. And she's a psychiatrist? Don't make me laugh." Madalena picked up her bag, and, with her head held high, left the building.

Honor just about managed to hold herself together in order to make the drive home, barely seeing her surroundings on the way. She had gone straight through a red light, narrowly averting a crash.

Letting herself into the house, Honor closed the door, and leaned back against it, her head drooping. She dropped her bag on the floor, and sat on the bottom step of the staircase, leaning forward, her head to her knees. Could she gather her energy sufficiently to get herself up to her study before any of the family caught up with her?

Too late.

"Hi darling. You're home. Oh … what's the matter?"

Honor broke into tears at the sound of Eliot's cheerful voice.

"What? Oh darling, what's happened?"

Eliot looped his arm around her, and tried to pull her towards him. Honor resisted, tensing herself in her doubled-up position, trying to release the stress of the day by wailing and rocking.

"Honor? Did something happen? D'you mind if the kids hear you? Their programme's going to finish any second."

Honor stood up, mumbling. "No …. I'll go upstairs … don't want to see the kids." She hurried upstairs, followed by Eliot.

Once in the bedroom, she threw herself face down on the bed and gave in to her tears. Eliot sat next to her, giving her little pats and stroking her back.

"Honor? Could you just tell me? Is there bad news? It's a long time since I've seen you cry like this. Honor?"

She shook her head into the pillow and mumbled. "No … nothing … don't worry. Bad day …"

Eliot relaxed, then tensed again. "I don't know what's worse, you in this state because something bad happened, or because nothing bad happened."

"Daaa—dd—yy," they could both hear Thea singing out her parental call. "Daa—dd—y, where are yo–ou?"

Sitting up, Honor pushed Eliot, and whispered. "Go and see her, don't let her in. I'll change and come down in a few minutes."

Seemingly encouraged by Honor's capacity to pull herself out of her despair to spare the children, Eliot gave her a last hug, stopped quickly when this induced a fresh bout of tears, patted her arm and left.

Honor, left alone, lay down again. What was happening to her? She didn't think of herself as a nasty person. She tried to be mature, grown up, honourable. How had she got so far away from herself? Why was she crying? Because Tisi had upset her? It wasn't about Tisi; it was about Madalena, and what she'd made Honor remember, about Thomas, his death; and the terrible things Madalena had said to her. And her face. What chance had Honor had against that unearthly face? She was crying for the past, a past that nothing could change, a past that broke her heart. And because Madalena had a heart of stone, with no thought or care for who she hurts. She had hurt Honor back then, over and over again, and she could just walk right back into her life and hurt her again.

That's why I'm crying. For the past. I'm crying for the past and the things I did, the decisions I made, the regrets I live with.

Could she confide in Eliot? She longed to unburden herself of Madalena, Bella, and Thomas. Could she get him to listen? No. She could hardly tell him the truth of it all at this late stage. She should have told him right at the start, but she was so ashamed, and it made her cautious: she was so eager to keep his good opinion. Then it became too late, a secret that she could never reveal.

Oh well ... with a deep sigh, Honor sat up, catching sight of herself in the mirror, her face puffy, her eyes red raw. *Look at me: I'm like Tisi!*

Going into the bathroom, she splashed cold water on her face, then went back into her bedroom and took off her daytime clothes. She had felt so drab in her black work suit, next to Madalena's understated elegance. And, now she thought of it, next to Tisi's dramatic scarlet, recently. Even next to Ann, with her Bohemian style of scarves and floaty skirts in bright turquoise and chocolate brown. Why did she spend her working days trying to look as if she was not really, actually, a person? Just a neutral presence to be used for other people's purposes?

She pulled on her jeans and a fine knit white sweater, threaded with coral satin ribbon. She felt the need to look and feel pretty, feminine, a person, a woman. Back to the bathroom for another cold splash, then to her dressing table for some clever make-up tricks to try to make herself look bright and happy for her children.

Eliot came in. "Are you OK? You look better."

"Thanks, I'm OK now, sorry. Bad day."

"Bad day? I would say so .... What happened?"

"One thing after another. If you don't mind, I won't go over it all, it's just going to upset me again if I have to re-live the whole thing."

"Could you give me the headlines quickly? Give me a sense of what's upset you?"

"Tisi's bothering me."

"She always upsets you. D'you feel you're helping her?"

"I don't know. Ann noticed her leaving my office the other day and was very uncomfortable about her. It's worried me even more."

"You poor thing, no wonder you're upset."

Honor hoped that she'd now said enough to convince Eliot of her distress. Good. She'd told him nothing about Bella and her suspicions, and she wasn't going to tell him about Jack or Madalena's visit. Her secrecy about all these events was indicating something, she knew. She rationalized it: why upset him?, why talk about it?, it was all ancient history.

"Was there something else, Honor?"

Honor jumped. "What d'you mean?"

"Did something else happen? I can see how upsetting today has been. Something else must have happened."

"No, nothing else, just an upsetting day, and I'm tired. I'm OK now. I'll get it sorted out. I have to work differently with Tisi, she's really out of control; there's something frightening about her."

"If you say so. I'm not entirely convinced. I'm worried. You've changed; you're so quick to get angry and upset with me. I can't get your attention, it's all work with you. Or something."

"It is all work, yes."

"Not something else?"

"Like what?"

Eliot's eyes, dark and opaque, were searching her face. "Oh, I don't know, Honor …. When I think of what we've been talking about, when I see how hard it is for you to forgive me. It makes me wonder if you'd try to get back at me. Maybe do the same …."

Honor suppressed a bitter thought: *yes, well, now you can see how it feels: the wondering, the worrying. But I love him though, I don't want him to feel unhappy, why would I? I want his happiness, his peace of mind.*

She put out her hand to him, looked into his eyes. "No, Eliot, no, nothing else, it's work. Let's stop talking about it, I want to go and say hi to the kids. Did they eat already?"

She was relieved to see him relax a little, and the tension in his eyes soften. *I really must pay more attention to him, and the kids.*

"Yes, they're all done, I've cooked for us though."

"Let's go and see the kids, then eat. I've got some work I need to do this evening before bed, just an hour or so, I'm so sorry, I really must."

Eliot followed her out of the room, grumbling mildly. "There's no keeping you out of that study. You're never out of there."

"Keeping ahead of my emails, it's relentless."

Honor dreaded facing Barbara the next day.

"Are you going to tell me what's been going on?"

Honor's heart sank. Barbara wasn't going to ignore recent events. "Look, I'm sorry about yesterday, you must think I'm crazy."

"Well," Barbara said. "Breaking up fights between adult women is not something I ever imagined doing in this job, I must say."

"No, I ... of course. I really must apologize to you, Barbara, it was unforgiveable and you handled it very well." Honor couldn't meet Barbara's eyes. "I'm so sorry. Needless to say, it'll never happen again."

"Why did it happen? Who are these people to you?"

"It's a long story. Ancient history. Madalena and I were rivals, a long time ago, so we bear each other an old grudge. Bella being in the papers sort of stirred all that up again."

"Hmm, well I can see it stirred something up for you. But for them? Why are they visiting?"

"It's a complicated story. I'll tell you one day. It's over now anyway. I'm sorry about yesterday, I feel very embarrassed, ashamed in fact." *Please Barbara. Give it up. Stop harassing me, I feel bad enough as it is.*

"You looked like you enjoyed it at the time."

Their eyes met. Recognizing a gleam of mischief in each other, they started to giggle. Within moments, they were helpless with mirth.

"Her face when you slapped her!"

"I haven't felt so satisfied in years."

"No, I could see."

"I had to control myself, I wanted to do it again."

"I saw a different side of you, not so cool yesterday."

"Aah well, we all have our dark side."

"I must make sure I don't upset you, I don't want to get a good slapping."

Barbara left, still laughing, and Honor stretched, smiling, thinking how fantastic it felt to have a damn good laugh and relieve the tension.

CHAPTER TWENTY ONE

The minute she could, Madalena went to her computer to Skype Bud. It would be early for him, but she had to talk to him. She could feel the fluttering of her heart, and was conscious of her shallow, rapid breathing. She tried to slow down, to calm herself. Clicking the green phone icon next to Bud's name on her Skype program, she held her breath. Be there Bud, please be there. I need to talk to you Bud. I need you.

To her relief, he answered straight away. She smiled to see his face, beaming at her on the screen. He's the loveliest person, she thought, and he's so good to me, so kind. Just as well he's gay. What a pity he's gay. She leaned forward stroking his image.

"What have you done to your hair? You look amazing. How'd it go?"

Madalena looked at the small picture of herself in the corner of her screen and shook her head, watching the tendrils of hair floating around her head.

"Awful. Disaster."

Bud's grin faded, and he leaned into the screen. "Are you OK? What happened?"

Tears rose in Madalena's eyes, and she bit her lip.

Bud was sitting in his running clothes, a large glass of orange juice in his hand, his dark hair slicked with sweat from his morning jog in Central Park.

I'd love to be there, with him, thought Madalena. Wouldn't that be fantastic? "Did you have a good run?"

"Great. I'm still hoping you'll come and visit me, Mad, come jogging with me, and let me show you New York."

At that moment, Madalena had never wanted anything so much in her life; she had to stop herself opening her browser and searching for flights.

"I can't think of anything nicer. Honor hit me."

Bud's eyebrow shot up to his hairline. He was so satisfying to talk to.

"She *hit* you? Are you kidding me? What, like physically, you mean?"

"Slapped my face. Hard. But that wasn't the worst of it by a long way."

"What could be worse?"

"Jack went to see Honor this morning."

Bud sat back in his chair, both hands clamped to his mouth. After a moment, he leaned into the screen. "NO!"

"Yep." How could she be enjoying this? She was actually enjoying his shock and horror. It saved her from feeling her own.

"To say what? Oh stop this, tell me everything."

Madalena sketched out the visit. "You see, Bud? Wherever I go, he's already been there first. Pat, my mother, Honor, Jack is always one step ahead."

"This is scary. Let's take stock of what he knows. Look, I can't do this, it's first thing in the morning, I'm wiped from my run, I haven't had breakfast yet. You do it, what has he found out from his investigations? Take me through it."

"OK. Well, let me see." Madalena, leaned back, looked upwards, and started checking off on her fingers.

"Let's go right back to the beginning .... a) Jack's mother claims that Bella is the image of her and Jack. b) Pat told Jack that Bella is the image of me and looks nothing like Jack or his other two kids; I don't know if she told him anything else, but she'd recently been on holiday with Thomas's sister, and no doubt she told him that. c) *My* mother told him that Bella had been the spitting image of *him* since the day she was born, and d) Honor gave him a load of photos of Thomas and his family in response to a pretty flimsy story about Pat wanting them for Caroline's fiftieth birthday party. Honor hinted that Bella looked like Thomas or Caroline, but wouldn't tell me whether she had said this to Jack. Jack also questioned her about dates of the cross-over of her, me, Thomas, and Jack."

"Good. Yes. Anything strike you as you set all that out?"

Madalena sat up straight. Something had struck her actually, something rather clever. "Both grandmothers claim Bella looks like Jack. We can discount their evidence, don't you agree? Both hopelessly prejudiced."

"My my …. You've spent too much time around me; you're starting to think like a lawyer. Give your whiskers a wash."

Even Madalena could see that she was looking supremely pleased with herself. She purred and wiped her imaginary whiskers with a pretend paw.

"Put yourself in his mind," Bud said. "What's he likely to do next? Will he go and see anyone else, d'you think?"

"I didn't think he'd go and see Honor, so what do I know?"

"If you were going to go and see someone else, who would you visit next? Remember the chart? Motivation and knowledge?"

"If I was going to go and see anyone else it'd be Caroline. But there's no point. I'm convinced it was Honor."

"D'you think Jack's as sure?"

"No idea."

"Might he think that Caroline could tell him something?"

"No idea. What am I going to do?" She frowned, as the full impact of what had happened came back to her.

"Did you tell her what Thomas told you? Did it calm her down?"

"I didn't tell her. How could I? She slapped me. Then she was nasty and bitchy. Why should I tell her?"

"It would be a good thing to do, Mad. You could do something good, that's why." Bud was looking at her seriously.

Madalena squirmed in her seat and shrugged at him. "Are you upset with me now?"

"I'm never upset with you, I love you whatever you do. I just think it would be good for her and you if you told her what Thomas told you."

I love you whatever you do. Bud had really said that, and it had given Madalena a strange sensation, as though she had been wrapped, gently, in a warm blanket. She felt completely safe. She nodded at him, and wiped away a tear.

"Let's think, Mad … we need a plan … a strategy."

Madalena sat up and took a breath. How very comforting, yes, a plan. "OK, yes … I'll go and see Caroline, right? Tell her I'm reminiscing about Thomas, ask her how she remembers him, get her talking about him. Huh! Find out if Jack's been to see her more like. Yes? Good plan?"

Sitting up straight, pulling her shoulders back, and pursing her lips, Madalena felt like a really good investigative journalist.

"Not sure …. What if he takes action earlier?"

"What d'you mean?"

"I think he's already got enough doubt to get a DNA test."

Madalena dropped her head into her hands. "No … he can't. No."

"He can do that without even asking you or telling you. For all you know, it could be happening right now as we're talking."

"Doesn't he need my permission?" Madalena stared at Bud, blinking rapidly.

"No."

"Really?" She pressed her lips together and put her hand to her forehead.

"You know what you need?"

"What?"

"A contingency plan."

"What the hell's that?"

"A plan for what you're going to do when the shit hits the fan."

"When Jack discovers that Thomas is Bella's father?"

Bud's eyebrows shot up to his hairline. "You sound sure."

"I'm not, I've told you, I don't know, I've never known."

"If you were a betting woman … where would you put your money?"

Madalena paused. She turned her gaze away from the screen, looked into the distance. "On Thomas. But only because that's what I always wanted to believe, not because I have any real proof."

"So let's track this: DNA tests show that Thomas is the father of Bella. What would happen next?"

Madalena didn't hesitate. "Jack would send me away."

"Where to?"

"He wouldn't care. It'd be over. He'd be without mercy."

"It wouldn't have to be like that. You're not in a great position, I grant you that, not being legally married and all. But I won a case which had some similarities to yours last week."

Madalena leaned into the screen. "What happened?"

"The guy didn't want anyone to know he'd been cuckolded all these years. So he bought his partner's silence, offered her a modest house and a small allowance to keep shtum about the whole thing."

"Were there children?"

"Two little kids. He got custody, she got visitation rights. You don't have to worry about that, Bella's an adult in her own right, she can make her own decisions."

"Could you sort it out for me? Be my lawyer?"

"You need a British lawyer. Don't worry, I know people, I'll find you someone good. I'll set up for you to meet someone in the next few days."

What a completely adorable man he was. "I don't have any money, Bud. I can't pay."

"Don't worry. I can call in a favour. I'll sort it out for you, it'll be fine."

Madalena bit her lip and swallowed hard to stop herself from crying, then turned her head slightly towards a sound from downstairs. She leaned into the screen and lowered her voice.

"Must go, I can hear someone downstairs, speak later, thanks. What would I do without you, Bud?"

He blew her a kiss, and disappeared. Madalena shivered. She hated saying goodbye to him.

Madalena hurried downstairs to the kitchen.

"Jack?"

Jack gawped at her. "What have you done to your hair?"

"I left it to fall naturally. What d'you think?"

"Very sexy."

"What are you doing, home at this time? Are you all right? Has something happened?"

"As it happens Madalena, it has, yes, it has. I've made a decision and I've come home to tell you about it."

Madalena felt sick. "What's so important that it couldn't wait till tonight?"

"I haven't slept the last couple of nights. I need to talk to you."

Jack had been restless for the last few nights, last night in particular. She'd tried to soothe him but was unable to interest him, which had alarmed her. She had woken in the early hours, and he was not in bed.

"OK." Madalena realized she was holding her breath. She slowly breathed out, watching Jack.

"You spoke to me about your mother, in a very direct way .... I have thought about that a lot, it was so different to how we usually speak .... I have a verdict for you on that matter anyway, you can see your mother once a month."

"Thank you." Madalena leaned against the worktop, faint with relief.

"There are conditions."

No surprise there. With Jack, everything was conditional: on doing exactly as he said. She smiled brightly and nodded.

"(a) Bella must never go with you; (b) I do not want to be mentioned or discussed between you and your mother. Obviously, I can check the first one, the second is more difficult, so I must trust you."

"Thank you. Of course I'll do as you say. I'm grateful. I know how angry you are with her."

"There is another, delicate matter, that we need to get straight. I've thought of speaking to you about this for some weeks. I've decided to speak, as you have done, in a direct manner."

Madalena swallowed. She pulled out a chair and sat at the table, her hands clasped in front of her. She brought to mind Bud's advice, on what to do if Jack challenged her. Give nothing away; imagine you're playing poker. I've never played poker, she'd replied, what do you mean? Imagine you have a number of cards in your hand, he'd said, and you don't want anyone to know whether you have a good hand or a bad hand. Just be a good actress basically, you'll be brilliant with that no blinking thing you do, like you're staring the whole world down. Hmm, she'd replied, good actress; well, that's not a stretch, I can definitely do that; I've been doing it for years. Now, it felt more difficult.

"Bella drew attention to herself, having her picture in the papers." Jack pulled out a chair and sat opposite her, a burning look, straight into her eyes.

Madalena, unable to bear the penetration of his stare, dropped her head, looking down. Could he see hear heart beating. Inwardly, she tried to slow her breathing. "Hmm."

"She was not the only person to get hate mail."

Madalena attempted to assemble a shocked expression. He was watching her closely. Before she could speak he continued: "I also got one … it said, ask Madalena who Bella's father is."

Madalena looked at him, unblinking.

"You're surprised?" Jack continued to scrutinize her face.

"Not entirely. I got one too, and I suspected you did."

"Why didn't you tell me?"

"Why didn't *you* tell *me*, Jack?"

"What did you think?"

"I thought that there was a troublemaker out there. Would you like a tea or coffee?"

"Yes, coffee please."

Madalena jumped up, relieved to be free of his piercing gaze. The fear that had sat in her gut these last weeks was spreading through her body. Her limbs were trembling, and her heart was thudding. An image, dreamlike, skittered across her mind: a small newborn creature, skinned and blind, curled in her solar plexus, vibrating with fear.

She busied herself, making their drinks, silently encouraging herself to say nothing: leave the talking to him.

"What did your letter say exactly?" Jack said.

Madalena kept her back to him. "It said: tell Jack who Bella's father is."

"Why not do that then? Why not tell me who Bella's father is?"

Madalena turned around from the kitchen work surface, and leaned back against it in an effort to control her shakiness. She held Jack's eyes with her steady, unblinking stare. "You are."

"You seem very certain." He was staring her out.

"I am."

"So why didn't you tell me about the letter?"

Madalena shrugged, and turned back to the worktop, carefully pouring boiling water into the cups, noticing the tremor in her hands.

"Maybe you had doubts."

"No." She was thankful she didn't need to turn around and face him.

"You know what it made me realize, Madalena? I had doubts. I tried to ignore them, but I found there had always been a little niggle there for me. So I wanted to know for sure. I went to see Honor Sinclair this morning. Nice woman."

Madalena took a deep breath and collected herself. Think, Madalena, think. She turned and placed Jack's coffee down in front of him and sat down with her own cup of tea. "I suspected Honor of writing the letter, so I went to see her too."

"Good Lord, Honor's much too classy and intelligent to pull a low stroke like that. The woman's a doctor. She's going to have a chat to Bella."

"You must be *joking*."

"Why?"

"Why on earth should Bella talk to her?"

"She's having a tough time, and it may get more difficult. It'd help her to have a skilled professional to talk to."

"As opposed to her own biological parents?"

"We have to get this straight. There's no easy way to say this. I want Bella to have a DNA test. I have the testing kit, it's just a couple of swabs from the inside of the mouth, then it's sent off for the results. Then we'll know. Then I can be sure."

"What are you suggesting? How dare you? I'll never agree, I won't have a swab done … I won't hear of it." Madalena's fear provoked her to anger. She was filled with righteous indignation. Her energy rose, strengthening her, as the moment she had dreaded for weeks had finally arrived.

"*You* don't need to provide a swab … I'm not questioning that you're her mother, I'm questioning whether I'm her father."

"How can you even think it? You only have to look at her … she's the image of you, everyone says so, even your own mother." Her eyes glittered with rage.

Jack frowned. "There are differing views …. I would like the reassurance of a DNA test, it's as simple as that."

"I won't hear of it … is that all you think of me? You think I'd pass off Thomas's daughter as yours? That's what you think of me?"

"Why do you suggest I think Thomas is her father?" Jack stared across the table at her, one eyebrow raised.

Madalena cleared her throat, looked down into her teacup. Damn it. She'd given herself away. Get a grip. Try something else. "Well, because … I, well I … that's why I went to see Honor …"

"In case she knew your secret? Maybe Thomas knew, told her?"

"No, of course not, but she bore a grudge against me. I won't hear of it, I refuse to give permission."

"I don't need your permission. But it'd help if I had your cooperation. I can do my own swab, but I'd like you to do Bella's. Tell her it's for the dentist or something. She doesn't need to know what it's for."

Madalena started to cry. Jack hated tears.

"Haven't I loved and taken care of you all these years? You and Bella? Haven't I been as devoted as any legal wife? And this is how you repay me?"

Jack was unmoved. "Your refusal is making me think that you have doubts. If you were sure, you would quite happily help me to get the certainty I need."

A part of Madalena's mind was desperately calculating the chances of getting a swab from Jack's daughter, Linda, and putting it forward as Bella's. It might be possible, she could arrange to meet her; how? Linda didn't like her very much. Find a way. Get Linda to fall asleep, maybe put something in her drink to knock her out? Take a swab from the inside of her cheek? The obstacles were insurmountable. The game was up, it was all over. Unless she mounted a challenge to Jack that he would not rise to, because of his love for Bella. It was highly unlikely, but worth a last shot.

"I want no part of it. I want nothing to do with it. Think how you're going to feel when those results show that you're her father, imagine that."

"If that happens, and with all my heart I hope that it does, I'd have gone down on bended knee and begged for forgiveness. But your reaction is telling me a different story. You obviously have doubts. I demand complete loyalty, as you well know. When it comes right down to it, it's the only evidence of real love. If you were sure of Bella's paternity, you'd be unconcerned … 'Go ahead,' you'd say. 'You'll see, you're going to be so embarrassed.' But you're not are you? You're simply not sure."

Madalena took a deep gulp of tea. "That's not true." Even to her, her words sounded hollow.

"Will you collect the swab from Bella, please?"

"No, I won't, you'll have to find some other way." Madalena stood up, head held high, and stalked out of the room. Glancing back, she saw Jack, mouth open in astonishment.

Madalena shivered and wrapped her arms around herself as she made her way to her bathroom for a soak in a hot bath. Why was this place always so damned cold? Turning around, she made her way back to the kitchen and marched past Jack, still standing there in shock, and turned up the thermostat on the central heating.

CHAPTER TWENTY TWO

Eliot was going to be out the evening of Honor's dinner with Bella: he had a work commitment with Will.

"It's not on the calendar, Honor, how was I supposed to know? What's so urgent all of a sudden?"

Something in Honor's chest tightened into a clenched fist. *Oh shit! What poisoned part of me is about to say what I'm going to say? Why can't I stop myself? Why don't I cancel the dinner with Bella, and put my family first?*

"It's a hospital meeting, a case conference; it's terribly important, about a suicidal patient. I simply have to be there."

There was a long silence. "I can't change my plans. Who's going to baby sit?"

Honor gave a short, high-pitched laugh. "Surely Celestine is old enough? I asked her, and, you'd never believe it, she was completely adamant, she said it offended her that we'd get a sitter when she's fifteen. I insisted it was for Thea, not for her, and she said she'd take care of her. It's an early meeting, I'm not going to be late: I should be home by nine o' clock. *[Shut up, Honor .... Stop wittering on ... SHUT UP.]* Who'd have believed how difficult it could be, to be out for a couple of hours in the evening? I thought, well, thank goodness I'm not having an affair, the practical arrangements alone would defeat me, leave alone the emotional turmoil. How do people cope, live with the tension? Is it ever worth it?" She cleared her throat.

"Is that supposed to be some dig at me? After all your fine talk about putting it behind us, trying to forget?"

Honor winced. Why had she said that? "Oh no, no, I didn't mean it like that, no, it was just what I thought at the time, that's all."

"And as a point of interest you might like to know that, no, it isn't ever worth it; but you can't really see that at the time."

"Really, I wasn't having a go … I'm sorry, really … I …"

"I'm feeling so tired of going over all this. You're never going to trust me again, are you?"

Honor was mute. He was right of course, she knew that. She couldn't go on punishing him forever, there had to be an end point. Forgive him or leave him was what it would come down to in the end.

"We need to talk, Honor, we can't go on like this, I don't want to and I'm sure you don't either. Tomorrow night, let's have dinner, just the two of us, and talk properly."

* * *

She could hardly wait to meet Bella and tears rose to her eyes at the thought of meeting Thomas's daughter. *I can be a surrogate parent, on behalf of her father. Through me, she can find out what her real father was like.*

She waited till Barbara left for the day, then quickly changed and re-did her make-up, with more emphasis on her eyes than usual. Brushing her hair, she looked at herself in the mirror, turning this way and that to see herself from all angles. She'd spent the preceding days thinking about what to wear, trying on a number of outfits from her wardrobe, reluctant to turn up to dinner looking like a therapist, for either Jack or Bella. Eventually she'd decided she didn't have anything suitable, so she'd gone shopping, seeking a dress that would finely balance femininity, sexiness, confidence, and … what?, motherliness? She had settled for a far too expensive emerald green dress, very simple, but a perfect fit.

She felt elegant and self-assured as she left her office to meet Jack and Bella.

Jack had selected an upmarket French restaurant, discreet and intimate. Honor hesitated before she entered, feeling her heartbeat speed up. *Anyone would think I'm on a hot date.* Opening the door, she was relieved to see the entrance to the restaurant on her left, and ahead of her a staircase down to the ladies cloakroom. *Yes, go and take a moment to collect myself*. Downstairs she looked in the mirror, smoothed down her hair, licked her lips. *You look fine Honor, just fine.* Back upstairs, Honor moved into the interior of the restaurant, and glanced around; it was early, few tables were occupied. The restaurant was furnished in dark mahogany, and dimly lit by soft wall lights and candles on the tables. She didn't see Jack until he approached her from the back of the restaurant, and she felt a flutter of nerves as he kissed her on both cheeks. Goodness, he was really a rather good-looking man. His tall, confident presence made her feel fragile, and in need of his manly protection, as they were shown to the privacy of a corner booth.

"Thank you for taking the time to come. Bella's badly in need of help, I'm afraid, more so than when I originally asked you to talk to her."

Honor put on her best patient and enquiring psychotherapist face, and asked Jack what had happened to further upset Bella. Jack became increasingly agitated as his story unfolded.

He had told Madalena that he wanted a DNA test. A prickle of triumph lifted Honor's spirits.

Madalena's reaction had convinced Jack that she herself had serious doubts about Bella's paternity. He had expected her to be upset, obviously, but co-operative; but she had in fact been completely against the test and had refused to help him by taking Bella's test swab under the pretence of a dental procedure.

"The bizarre thing is, if she'd played her cards right, and obviously if the DNA test shows that Bella is my daughter, Madalena would have got what she's wanted all these years. I would have married her, finally. My reluctance to marry her made me wonder if I'd always had a slight doubt in my own mind. Is that possible d'you think?"

Honor struggled to hide her delight in a mask of sympathy. "Entirely possible. Your subconscious mind could have been guiding your actions all these years without you even knowing it."

"I often used to ask myself: come on Jack, what are you waiting for? It's not as though you've ever wanted another woman. I could hardly understand my own hesitation. But as the weeks have gone by since I got that letter, it gnawed at me, and I do remember, at the beginning of our relationship, her fascination with Thomas. And I did often wonder if she might be still seeing him. Of course, once he was married to you, I thought that was all over for good. I wonder now though, I really do."

"I always wondered myself. If I were a betting woman, I'd say that their affair continued, intermittently, certainly during the six months or

215

so of my marriage to Thomas. Working out the timings, it's quite possible that Thomas could be the father of Bella." *Payback time, Madalena.*

Jack frowned and drew a quick breath. "Another few days, and I'll know, once and for all, and it will be a great relief."

"A few days? The tests have been done already?" Honor held her breath. How had they been done, if Madalena had refused to help?

"Yep, all done. Shame about Madalena's attitude, it made it very painful for Bella. But as I said to Bella, when I explained what was happening, come what may, I'll always consider her my daughter. Thomas is dead anyway, it's not like she can form a relationship with him. No, I said to her, this is not about you and me, Bella; it's between your Mum and me. I need to find out whether she was loyal. I didn't tell Bella that I already knew the answer to that: Madalena's doubts told me all I needed to know. I hope I am Bella's biological father, but it seems to me that, basically, Madalena doesn't know. So she was unfaithful to me with Thomas."

Honor took a deep inner breath, and exhaled slowly, and, she hoped, quietly. "How has Madalena reacted to all this?"

"Moved out."

"Moved out?" Honor could no longer contain herself, now completely abandoned by her inner psychotherapist. "How? When? Where?"

"I told her she had to go. Now that I know of her disloyalty, it's over, it has to be, there is no other way. Bella won't speak to her, she's furious, beside herself, actually, that's why she needs your help, Honor."

Victory. "So Madalena is left with nothing then. No daughter, no home, no husband." Honor tried to hide the note of satisfaction in her voice.

"Not no home, in fact. If it had been up to me, she could have gone to live with her mother, a pair well met if ever there was. It turned out that Madalena had seen the writing on the wall when she got her letter, and had been exploring all her options. Nowhere near as stupid as she seems, that one, she had taken legal advice, the lot."

"Really?" Honor was disconcerted.

"Really. So I'm giving her a house, nothing flashy, a small terrace of the kind she grew up in, in fact. One of my buy-to-lets. I paid the tenants a wodge of money to get out straight away, and she's living there. I'm making her a modest allowance for the next five years, after which she's on her own."

"Why did you do that? You aren't married, she's not entitled to anything. After the way she behaved, she deserves nothing. *Nothing.*"

Jack searched Honor's face, his eyebrows raised. "Still bearing quite a grudge there, Honor?"

"No, no, not at all." Honor spoke quickly. "Just, well, it seems you have been a devoted partner and father, I wish she'd treated you better. You seem like a good man."

"Yes, well, thank you, I've certainly done my best, and it's not nice to feel you've been made a fool of. But at least I know where I am now."

"It was kind of you, anyway, to resist the temptation to leave her with nothing. Even though she started with nothing when she met you."

"It wasn't kindness. It was coercion, or bribery, depending which way you look at it. If I hadn't agreed to the house and the allowance, the whole sordid story would be played out in court, for all to see what a complete fool I'd been taken for all these years. Obviously I couldn't have that."

"No. I see."

"See what I mean about cleverer than she appears?"

"Indeed I do."

"See what you can do for Bella then. She's terribly upset."

"Leave it to me. It'll be my pleasure to help her as much as I can. Help her get on the right track."

A commotion at the door of the restaurant heralded Bella's arrival. Waiters stopped in their tracks, staring at Bella as she made her way through the restaurant.

Even Honor felt the pull of the girl's beauty as she approached the table. Dark silky curls bounced on her golden shoulders, bare apart from the spaghetti strap of her cream mini dress, her long legs made even longer by impossibly high-heeled gold sandals.

"Hey, Dad."

"You look delightful, off out after dinner?"

"Yeah." Bella looked towards Honor, turning the full light of her extraordinary eyes on her.

Honor met her eyes, and smiled slightly.

"This is Honor Sinclair, Bella. I'm going to leave you two ladies alone, to get to know each other and have dinner. Honor, I've dealt with the bill, so you don't need to worry about that. See you in the morning, Bella."

Kissing Honor on the cheek, he was gone.

Bella took her seat, and shuffled about in her handbag, taking out her mobile phone and laying it on the table.

"I may get a call, sorry." She looked at Honor, straight-faced.

"No worries, as you wish. Would you like a drink?"

"Champagne please."

Honor, a little taken aback, called the waiter and asked for two glasses of champagne. *Yes, why not? It's a kind of celebration, for me at least.*

Within moments, the drinks were in front of them. Honor lifted her glass to Bella.

"Cheers, Bella. Here's to … what? What should we drink to?"

Bella's sweet features darkened into a sullen frown. "Cheers. Fuck knows what to; everything's a right fucking mess if you ask me. I can't think of anything to celebrate."

Honor stifled a wince at Bella's language. *Looks like an angel, speaks like a navvy. I thought I would warm to her instantly, but I find myself turning away. What's happening? She is Thomas's daughter isn't she? The child I should have had?*

"To a new friendship, anyway?"

"To be honest, I don't know why my Dad wants me to talk to you. My mother doesn't want me to."

"I think your Dad thinks it might be nice for you to have someone to talk to during this difficult time."

"He said you're clever, a psychotherapist, and could help me make some decisions. My mother, on the other hand, said you're crazy and I shouldn't believe a word you say."

Just as well I was feeling no sympathy for Madalena, because it would have dissolved by now.

"Shall we order our food? Then we can talk; you could tell me how the situation with your family seems to you, how it's affecting you."

"Easy question. It's a screw-up."

"Let's order our food."

Bella glanced at the menu and put it aside. Honor gestured to one of the several waiters hovering close.

"I'll just have a steak, well done, and some chips. And another glass of champagne."

Honor ordered sea bass and a salad, and some mineral water. "So, it's a screw-up. What feels hardest about it?"

Bella gazed at Honor, and her eyes slowly filled. Honor felt not a shred of sympathy. Nothing. No feeling of any kind. Indifference. Actually, being brutally honest, a slight distaste.

"Pissed-off with both my parents. I want things back to how they used to be."

"Most pissed-off with whom?"

Bella chewed at her bottom lip. "My mother. She's ruined everything. Everything. I could fucking kill her, frankly."

Why don't I feel pleased? Because I don't care. I don't care about Bella. She's not who I thought she was, or how I thought she'd be. I knew she would be coarse and silly, but surely there would be some trace of Thomas in her? Could he really have been so comprehensively wiped out?

"And what about your Dad?" Honor's question was mechanical.

A tear rolled slowly down Bella's smooth cheek. "I feel sorry for him. But pissed-off that he couldn't keep it all together. That I even had to *know.* Why couldn't they keep it to themselves? Why did they need to involve me?"

"How do you feel about the possibility that you might have a different Dad?"

Bella gave her a cold stare, and a sulky shrug.

Surely, something of Thomas would show in her? Surely? How can I extricate myself now? "Tell me what else is going on in your life, the things that make you happy?"

Bella's sullen face brightened. "Euan, my boyfriend. He's gorgeous, so handsome. Everyone's after him, but he's mine and I'm not letting anyone take him away from me. My agent, well, he says I'm going to be famous, like, really mega famous. Like, a chat show host, like fucking Oprah! A model first, obviously, upmarket glamour stuff, nude, but quite tasteful. Then, in a few years, he says I could write my first autobiography. Not actually like, write it myself; that would be a fucking marvel! But someone writing it for me, I would tell them my adventures and my, philo ... my thoughts. A multi-millionaire before I'm thirty he says. Gonna get me and Euan a *Hello* spread of us on a Caribbean holiday soon. Can't wait ..."

Only half listening to Bella's profane chatter, Honor's mind drifted. Her surroundings seemed to recede and fade as she was filled with an apocalyptic realization. This girl was not Thomas's daughter, not her own longed-for daughter. She couldn't possibly be, this silly, vacuous girl: she was her mother's daughter. If she was Thomas's girl, Honor knew that there would have been some clue, a trace of Thomas; at the very least she herself would have felt a biological frisson, that would have told her, with certainty, that Bella was who Honor had believed she was through these last mad, obsessed weeks.

What on earth had come over her, had taken her over?
She had made a truly sickening mistake.

She allowed Bella to talk herself out. Honor picked at her salad, finding it difficult to swallow.

"Well, Bella," she said, with a bright smile. "It sounds as though you have many good things that you are happy with in your life."

"And, I've got my Dad. He'll always look after me. I don't care what DNA tests show, I know that he's my Dad, and he said that too. I'll always take care of you, Bella, he said, you'll never want for anything, I'll see to that. So I've got my Dad, and my mother hasn't now, so it serves her right. And I've got Euan, I'll be alright that's for sure."

"You certainly will, my dear, and I can quite see you don't need any help from me, you're going to be absolutely fine."

"It's been nice to talk to you though, I do feel better already, it's clever the way you do that."

"I'm going to be off, I must get home to my family. I wish you the best of luck."

Honor picked up her bag and walked out of the restaurant without a backward glance.

She hurried to her car and put the key in her lock. As she looked down, she was struck by the brilliance of her emerald green dress against the pearlescent purple of her little car in the evening sunlight. She was almost blinded by the contrast and squinted her eyes against the fluorescent glow. She looked down at the elegant angle of her feet in the black suede shoes. She wiggled her toes, and felt the hardness of the pavement beneath her. *Yes, here I am, feet on the ground, back to earth.* Raising her eyes to the sky, she lifted her hand in a salute of thanks.

Stopping at some traffic lights, she looked to her left where a bush of small vivid red flowers tumbled over a grey stone wall. Captivated by the contrasting colours, she felt she could see every leaf, every petal, up close and detailed.

I can see the world again, the real world out there. I've been blinded by what lies beneath it all, the thing I've been refusing to see, to know, to remember. Under all the layers of betrayal, I realize it, my own, my self-betrayal.

She could think of Tisi too, as her client, with her suffering disentangled from Honor's own. She knew exactly what she needed to do to help Tisi; it was as clear to her as the red flowers on that wall.

CHAPTER TWENTY THREE

Madalena opened her eyes, and did the same thing she'd done every day for the last two weeks: she wondered at the speed at which her life had so dramatically changed. When the end came, it was no surprise; she had known exactly what Jack's reaction would be. He had executed her banishment with ruthless efficiency, giving her twenty-four hours to pack her clothes and personal possessions in Cardiff. Jinny would pack her London things and send them on. Madalena had felt as though she had a weight on her chest.

"Where will I go, Jack?"

"Up to you."

That was when she told him what Bud's solicitor friend had said. She wished she'd taken a picture of the look on his face. So he'd sent her to a hotel for a few days, while he sorted out this house for her.

She looked around the room, the front bedroom of the terraced house that had been part of Jack's property portfolio, rented out, one year at a time, to young professionals.

Stretching her limbs across the small double bed, she luxuriated in the space, and the privacy. No Jack. The sheer liberation of it provoked her almost to laughter each morning, as she began to get used to the gut relief and lightness she felt. Pat's words, about the contentment of life alone, came back to her, along with the pang of envy she'd felt at the time. Who'd have thought that she'd end up like Pat?

She leaned over to her bedside table and picked up her book, one of several that Bud had sent her as a house warming present: *The Water Babies*. A child's book, in child sized print. She was actually finding it easy to read; and enjoying it; and thinking about it a lot, especially Mrs Doasyouwouldbedoneby, particularly after her conversation with Bud yesterday.

"Have you thought any more about telling Honor what Thomas said?"

Madalena sighed. She was hoping he'd let this drop. "I can't, she told me not to contact her."

"So are you saying, you would tell her, but she won't see you?"

"Not necessarily. I don't know if I want to tell her anyway."

"You could do something good, Madalena. Reverse the pattern. Be Mrs Doasyouwouldbedoneby. Do what you know to be right."

Madalena stared at him. "Reverse what pattern?"

"Betrayal. You were betrayed. Honor was betrayed."

"I wasn't betrayed."

"By everyone. Your father, your mother, Thomas, Jack in the end. Everyone betrayed you."

Madalena sagged over the desk, as the truth of his words hit her. "Is that true? I'm not sure."

"You know it is. Reverse it, change it. Do the right thing by Honor. Write to her. Tell her what you know. It would give her closure."

Madalena sighed. Was he right? Was it really as bad as he made it sound? And if so, was there a way to change things?

"I'll write it, but I'm not going to send it."

"OK, write it, and we'll talk about it again."

"Not everyone betrayed me, Bud. You didn't."

"No. Everyone else did though. Me, I love you just as you are, good and bad."

Madalena blew him a kiss. He reminded her of Thomas. Or of how Thomas used to make her feel, anyway.

The house was in quite good order, and Jack had settled a modest sum on her for any minor improvements and furniture she wanted. The first thing she'd done was replace all the curtains throughout the house, the heavy velvets and brocades, chosen by whom? Jack's foreman? Jack? They were gone now anyway; she'd driven them to the charity shop herself. Jack had let her keep a car, not her Mercedes of course, but the house-keeper's car. She'd never been to a charity shop before; she struggled with the heavy bags of curtains and was met by a kindly, bent-over old lady.

"Oh, you silly girl, you shouldn't be carrying those heavy things. Here, put them down, I'll get Stan to take a look." She yelled behind her. "Stan! Come and give a hand."

An old man emerged from a back room, and stopped dead at the sight of Madalena, his mouth dropping open.

"Close your mouth, Stan, you've seen a woman before in your life." Still scolding him, she sent him off to the back room with the heavy bags. Madalena looked around; there was an entire rack of designer evening dresses. She'd ended up staying for half an hour, and having quite a chat to the old lady, who tried to persuade her to buy one of the long frocks.

"Not something I need to be honest," Madalena said. "I might be able to add to your stock, though."

She had dressed all the windows with sheer white voiles to let in as much light as possible; and, in the bedrooms dark purple roller blinds shut out the light at night.

She had quickly grown to love the little house, in a small town, Penarth, on the sea, a few miles west of Cardiff. She was surprised to find that she rarely missed the mansion and the London flat. They had never really felt as though they were hers. They belonged to Jack, his architect, his interior designers, and project managers. This was her own little house, to do with as she wished; and what she wanted was the comfort of warmth. She kept the central heating on most of the time.

The house was tiny. The two downstairs rooms had been knocked through into one, and there was a small kitchenette, nicely fitted with white units and a black granite work surface.

Upstairs were two double bedrooms and a bathroom that had originally been the small bedroom, so it was, by normal standards, a nice size. Against Madalena's previous palatial standards it was tiny. In fact, her old bathroom was actually larger than her bedroom here.

Why had she cared so much? In the end she was able to give it all up in the blink of an eye. She fought to the end, but finally, she'd had it. She was up to here with Jack and his orders and his sex on demand, and his don't look at anyone and don't speak to anyone. She thought she had a life she loved, but it turned out to be only the life she needed. *This* was the life she loved.

She'd said as much to Bud, when she Skyped him to tell him what happened.

"You always used to say it was a small price to pay," he said.

"I was wrong. It was a much higher price than I realized."

"You know, I'm kinda keen to see who you're gonna be now you're not paying it."

Madalena had laughed to him, through the screen of her shiny new Apple laptop. She had laughed more in her conversations with Bud than in the whole of the rest of her life. And she didn't even care if it gave her lines around her eyes. "I'm curious about that too."

"You could do anything; after all, you spun yourself a life out of nothing, apart from your beauty."

Madalena looked at her face in the corner of the screen, unmade-up, naturally pretty. "I don't think of it like that Bud. It just happened, that's all."

"Whatever. You can realize your potential. Better late than never."

"Good. I'll start by finding out what potential means then."

"It's all the lives you could have led ... if you hadn't been fighting and struggling to make yourself safe."

"You wouldn't know this, but I can tell you: if you're not safe, the only life you want is one that is safe ... it's all you can think of. And I was protected; though it felt suffocating in the end."

"You were never really safe, though, were you? Jack could kick you out at any moment if you didn't behave. How safe is that? Don't you want to be loved even if you do bad things? That's real safety. That's Nirvana."

"And there's another word I don't know the meaning of."

Madalena glanced at the clock. Nine fifteen. She went downstairs quietly, made a cup of coffee and took it back to bed, where she switched on her TV to watch the *Jeremy Kyle Show*. Here was a family, Leroy and Kayleigh, waiting to find out whether Leroy was the biological father of Kayleigh's fourteen-year-old daughter. Madalena watched the sorry and familiar tale unfold with a wry smile. They had no idea what would happen next: the test, the question, seemed the only thing that was important.

"We have to know the truth. We can't move forward till we have closure." Kayleigh repeated this statement at every opportunity.

Madalena didn't agree with her. There was no closure. There was just what you knew; and she could never know who her father was. She knew who Bella's father was now anyway. She supposed that was a kind of closure, a relief to know and not have to keep that secret any more.

Madalena had emailed Bella several times, asking to see her, to explain what had happened: "To tell you my side, please, Bella?"

224

Bella's responses had been terse, until yesterday anyway, when she had replied, agreeing to see her.

Madalena jumped out of bed and into her running clothes. She was longing to see Bella; she knew she would come round eventually. All daughters did, after all, didn't they?

She set off on the five mile run to the park, around the park, and back, that she'd done every other day of her new life. A couple of the people in her street had already started saying Good Morning to her as she passed, and it didn't take her long to get back into the habit of responding with a wave and a Hi. She'd started to see the same people at the park, runners, like her, doing their circuits, intent on their training watches. They would exchange smiles, like members of a secret sect, with its codes and rules, its successes and failures.

Within forty-five minutes she was back home and in the shower, shampooing her hair and cooling off. She slipped into jeans and a T-shirt, ruffled her hair into curls, and went downstairs to her desk, in the back area of the double sitting room. Privately, and with some pride, she thought of this room as her study.

She had bought a wide glass desk, set against the wall, with a large black leather chair on wheels. Above the desk, a narrow shelf held Bud's moving-in gift to her, a selection of books:

Computers for Dummies
The Bible
The Oxford English Dictionary

Sitting at her desk, she put on her spectacles. The optician had said she didn't really need them, but she had insisted: anti-glare, she had said, so her eyes didn't get tired from the computer screen.

Opening her email programme, she sent a cheery mail to Bella, suggesting a couple of dates and times to meet. *Maybe you could come to my new place? I've a surprise for you here. I can't wait to see you, Bella. Lots of love, Mum xx.*

There was nothing from Bud, but they Skyped most days: he was trying to persuade her to visit him in New York. She'd gone so far as to look up the costs of flights, but it seemed unlikely that she'd ever be able to go.

Madalena tilted her head to one side and listened. She went to the foot of the stairs.

"Madalena? Are you there? Can I have some tea?"

"OK, yes, I'll bring it up now."

225

She went into the kitchen to prepare Jessie's morning tray. It had only been a week and she was already wondering: what had possessed her? Why did she do it? Yet she didn't think twice, she didn't hesitate; it seemed exactly the right thing to do, to go and get her mother from that grubby flat, and bring her home. Jessie, paralytic, had almost collapsed with pleasure and gratitude, and had become garrulous and maudlin on the car journey back.

"I knew you'd never leave me, not really leave me for ever and ever. You never did after all, not ever, even when you were little. Even before you were born." She started cackling and pushed Madalena's arm. "I tried my best to get you to leave me, hot baths, gin, the lot. None of it worked, you were determined to stick with me, come what may." And she had leaned forward, helpless with laughter, the tears on her cheeks an extravagant echo of the tear gleaming, unnoticed, on her daughter's face.

So here she was, waiting on her, monitoring her drinking, unable to travel. It was like having a baby, except that she was never going to grow up. She took the tray up to the bright little bedroom, with its cheerful yellow polka dot bedding that looked too youthful against Jessie's wrinkled face, its jaundiced hue giving away her long dependence on alcohol.

Madalena helped her mother sit up, arranging the pillows against her back. She was as frail as an autumn leaf; she felt as though she'd crumple if you hugged her. Not that Madalena ever had hugged her, Jessie didn't like physical contact.

Once her mother awoke, Madalena's day settled into a predictable routine: help Jessie dress and go downstairs, settle her in the sitting room; give her a second cup of tea, and discuss what she wanted for lunch. Then the interminable daily argument: she pretty much refused to eat anything until she had had one glass of wine at least. Lunch was a battle, trying to get Jessie to eat something, however small, then clearing up. Then arguing about the second glass of wine.

"Come on, give your old Mum a nice glass of wine," the old lady wheedled.

Madalena, at her computer, ignored her.

She typed into Google: "how to become a personal trainer UK", and pressed the search key.

"Just one, Madalena? Please? Have one with me … go on, have a nice glass of wine with your old Mum. Come and talk to me, tell me what you want to know, come on, I'll tell you anything, if you get me a glass of wine."

Madalena sighed heavily and went into the kitchen, opened the fridge and took out the wine bottle, already open from her mother's first drink. She took out a clean glass, and on a sudden whim, took out a second one. She took both glasses of wine back into the sitting room, and handed one to her mother. Then she walked down towards her desk, carrying her own glass with her.

"Talk to me, Madalena, stay with me. Tell me about Bella, come on."

Madalena paused, turned, took a step back towards her mother. "I think she's coming to see us next week. Isn't that great? I'm so excited."

Tears sprang to Jessie's eyes and she leaned forward. "Is she? She is? She's coming here. Oh, I'd love to see her. I'd love to see my girl. I'd give anything." She dropped her head into her shaky hands and gave a slight sob.

Madalena sipped her wine, and felt the warm thread spread across her body. Hmm, she had quite a taste for wine now; she sometimes had a glass at bedtime, while she was reading *The Water Babies*. Bud said he was going to teach her about wine. It's best to drink small amounts of best quality wine he said. Pity nobody had ever told Jessie that.

"You know what, Jessie? I know I should be miserable really, I dreaded this. But there are moments, sometimes, when I feel happier than I've ever felt in my life. So happy. Doing something on the computer, or just sitting talking to you, finding out about your life, asking you what you really feel about things. I feel so sorry that Bella's been hurt, but I'm sure she'll get over it eventually."

"What about Jack?" Jessie smirked at her daughter.

"I won't be seeing him. He wouldn't see me if I wanted him to; which I don't. Why do you ask?"

"He's still paying for you isn't he? Even now. You're not free of him yet, are you? He could come round any time demanding a return on his investment." Jessie started to laugh silently, her tiny body shaking with merriment.

Madalena stared at her mother. She was right; Jack was still paying for her. She could be sure of one thing, though, he wouldn't be coming round to collect what he'd paid for.

"It's completely over with Jack. The only man in my life now is Bud, he does make me laugh so much. And he makes me think. This must be what it's like to have a brother."

"Brother? There's not a man alive who wants to be your *brother*, you can be sure of that."

Ignoring her mother, Madalena continued her musing. "I can tell him anything; I have no secrets from him. That was the thing with Jack, you see, the secret I kept all those years, the not knowing. I couldn't speak freely about anything; I was always worried I might say something to give myself away. You can't be really happy if you're trying to keep a secret, I understand that now. Once you have a secret, it's hard to say what you really think about things, isn't it?"

"How would I know?" Jessie cackled. "I never kept one. Maybe I should have."

Madalena finished her wine, and smiled at her mother. Standing up, she moved towards her desk.

"I'll put the TV on for you, then I've got some stuff to do on my computer. I've got an important letter to write."

"You and your computer, that old machine. Stay with me, pour some more wine, come and watch TV with me. Don't leave me all alone."

Madalena stood, uncertain, between the two rooms. A glass of wine with her mother? Or do some more research on the internet? Or write that letter to Honor? She felt pulled both ways, each of them, her mother and her computer, calling out, tantalizing her.

CHAPTER TWENTY FOUR

Honor sat at her desk, in her study, looking at the full screen image of her favourite picture of Thomas. She stroked his cheek on the screen. *I have to say goodbye to you, Thomas. It's over. I made a terrible mistake. I'm so sorry.*

She turned, startled by a noise at the door. Click, click: Honor closed her email programme, and her photo of Thomas. Just in time. Eliot barged into her study, without knocking, his eyes darkened by rage, tension etched across his forehead and shoulders.

"Honor, we agreed. We said we'd have dinner. How could you?"

"Sorry, El … I …"

"You spend hours in here. What's going on? What on earth are you doing?" Eliot leaned forward to look at her screen.

"Sorry. I've been so busy, it's so hard to keep ahead of my paper work. I'm coming now, I'll come and cook us a nice meal."

"I already ate, with the children." Eliot was looking at the various papers scattered around her desk. Honor could feel her heart beating fast; she was uncertain what he might see. She stood up, and put her arms around him, pulling him towards her.

"Why didn't you call me? You could have called me, reminded me, would it have killed you?"

"There's no point. If you don't want to spend time with me, I don't want to nag, or impose on you."

"Oh, Eliot." Honor hugged him tighter, kissed his neck. "I'm so sorry. Let's go and open a bottle of wine and sit in the garden? Or shall I run us a bath?"

Eliot leaned back from her, unyielding. "I need you to talk to me, to pay attention; it's as though you're somewhere else all the time. You're so distracted, even the children have remarked."

"Have they?" Honor dropped her arms and stepped back. "What did they say?"

"See? You're more interested in what they say than what I say," Eliot grumbled.

"What did they say, though?"

"Mum's always working; Mum didn't listen to me. That sort of thing."

"Oh no. I'm so sorry, you're right, I've been so distracted. I'll go down now and spend some time with the children."

Honor hurried out of the room, downstairs, to her children, in the TV room, sitting herself down among them. "Hi, guys. How're you all doing?"

"Marmee." Thea jumped on her mother's lap, and showered her with kisses.

"Marmee? I have a new name now?"

"I've been reading *Little Women* to her," Celestine said, unsmiling. *Hmm, she's not quite so quick to forgive.*

"Ah ... and which sister d'you want to be?" Honor smiled at Thea.

"Amy, me and Cel both want to be Amy, don't we, Cel?"

Celestine thawed slightly, unable to withstand Thea's charm, and nodded.

"I wanted to be her, too. Those fantastic long blond ringlets." Honor smiled at Celestine.

Eden looked up from his computer game.

"Not that there's a great choice. One's dying, one's obviously a lezzer, and the other one's just a cissy Mummy's girl."

"Jo's not a lezzer, stupid, just a tomboy." Celestine's voice was thick with scorn.

"Whatever ... she's a lezzer," Eden said, impervious.

"What's a lezzer, Marmee?" Thea asked.

Honor and Celestine caught each other's eyes and started laughing.

"I can tell you that," Eden said. "It's a girl who likes girls, that's what a lezzer is."

"Come on," Honor lifted her little girl up. "Time for bed."

"But I like girls, so does that mean I'm a lezzer? And I like Meg, there's nothing bad about being a Mummy's girl, I like being my Mummy's girl."

"Course you do, sweetie, and I love that too."

Honor could hear Celestine and Eden laughing as she carried Thea to her room, and told her to get undressed and brush her teeth.

Crossing the landing, she saw Eliot coming down the stairs from her study. *What's he been doing up there all this time?*

"OK, Honor, I think I see what's been going on." His eyes, flint, glittered, a stark contrast to his face, white with the effort of control.

Honor's heart jumped. What had he seen?

"What? What do you mean?"

"Those *pictures* on your computer. I *saw* them. It's not work that's keeping you in your study is it? It's fucking *Thomas*."

"Look, Eliot, I can explain. I'll put Thea to bed and I'll be straight down."

Honor had never seen him so enraged, so shimmering with anger. *See, Eliot? See what it's like to feel jealous?* She was going to have to tell him everything, explain what had been happening.

Honor shivered slightly as she went into the garden an hour later, it had taken ages to settle Thea this evening. *Children just know, sometimes, when all is not well, some mysterious emotional contagion tells them.* The evening was cool, and getting dark. She paused to light the candles in the outdoor lanterns on the low wall at the side of the garden table, and looked towards the flowerbeds at the end of the garden. The candle flames highlighted the shapes of the rose bushes, and cast shadows across the lawn.

Eliot was pacing from one side of the small terrace to the other, gulping back wine in deep draughts. He refilled his glass as Honor took a seat, and poured her a glass.

"So, come on, tell me—what's going on?" He sat down opposite her, his mouth a tight narrow line.

"Nothing's going on, nothing. Stop looking at me like that, you're scaring me."

"I saw the pictures, the photos on your computer: I looked, I wanted to see what was going on. And now I know, now I see it." He ran his free hand through his curls, making them stand up like a black halo.

"What do you see, Eliot?"

With a swift movement, Eliot leaned forward, pushed his angry face close to hers, making her lean back, startled. "Thomas! Fucking Thomas fucking Dyer! You never got over him did you? How am I supposed to compete with a dead man? Go on, tell me that, if you can. Trust, well I know you can't trust me and that's my own fault, OK, I realize that. Lack of trust is one thing. Lack of love, though, that's different isn't it? He's been a shadow in our marriage from the start, you married me on the rebound, I always knew it. If he was alive I could fight him, but he's forever young and glamorous. I saw the photo on your screen, him at his most handsome. You never need to experience disappointment with the reality of him, not like with me, a mere mortal."

Honor, on the verge of telling him the whole story, about Bella and Madalena, held back. She knew what stopped her: the missing part of her story, the part that her meeting with Bella had revealed to her. The thing she had never told Eliot. Never told anyone, in fact.

* * *

Tisi turned up for her morning session, calm and self-assured, and Honor, though tired from last night's drama, felt fully in possession of her professional poise. *She's lost her power over me. Thank God for that.*

"You look rather tired, are you all right?" Tisi was frowning at Honor.

"Yes, I'm fine. How about you? How are you?"

Tisi sighed heavily, and looked evenly at Honor. "Don's much better, thankfully. He's out of hospital, back at home, but not back at work yet. His nose is a real mess."

"And the children?"

"They're quiet, a little scared of their Daddy, because of his face. And they don't like to see him in tears, as they have done a couple of times."

"Tears?"

"He hates it most that I got hurt. That I got hurt because of him, rushing to his defence. He's full of remorse. He's being very loving."

"That's encouraging. Why don't you tell me something of how you're feeling about it all? In the end, did you get what you wanted?"

Tisi sighed. "I wanted Don to die and Jackie to go mad. Maybe she will go mad, the police are thinking of charging Steven with assault."

"*Was* that what you wanted?" It was such a relief to be back on solid ground with her.

"Not for Don to die. For him to be sorry, to see how he betrayed me, to never do it again. Her, to go mad, well, I certainly wanted her always to wonder if I'd tell, if she'd be found out. I guess once I'd told Steven, the suspense was over: he knows. What drives a person mad is

232

the not knowing isn't it? The always wondering, what might happen? How could it have been? What might happen if? Those are the things that haunt you, aren't they? Not the knowing, however terrible the thing is that you know. If I'd really wanted to drive her mad, I'd have kept her never knowing *when* I might tell Steven."

"Not quite what you wanted then?"

Tisi shook her head.

"But it seems to have calmed you."

"What's happened seems worse actually, than what I thought I wanted."

"And how are you feeling about that?"

"Responsible … guilty … ashamed. But I have to confess, a degree of satisfaction."

"As you think about it now, who d'you think is responsible for these events?"

"Me for telling Steven? Steven for his reaction?" Tisi sat back in her chair and tilted her head back, stretched her arms upwards.

"Don and Jackie for relying on you and Steven to be more grown-up than they were?"

Tisi relaxed a little. She gave a slight nod. "The first event in the chain … Don and Jackie have an affair."

"Then?"

"They hoped their partners wouldn't find out. But I did."

"So he and Jackie are responsible for the infidelity …. And Don's responsible for you knowing," Honor said.

"Then I'm responsible for Steven knowing …."

"And Steven's responsible for?"

"Hitting Don, he could have killed him, that blow to his head only needed to be a little bit harder, I'm sure. See, if you behave badly, you have to rely on others to behave better; to be polite; not say anything; not challenge."

"Yes …" *She's a smart woman. She can piece all this together quickly.*

"Don must've been unhappy to have an affair. He said that: 'I have feelings, Tisi, I have passions.' Did he imagine that I didn't? That I would shrug and go, oh well, no worries, you're having an affair, let's all be civilized. Why on earth did he think I'd react differently to him?"

"And what made you think that Steven would react differently? You wanted to hurt Don, and so did Steven."

"I didn't think, that's the truth of it. I saw Steven, and out it came, on impulse. And it felt deeply satisfying for about half an hour, until I realized the possible consequences."

"Could you have imagined the consequences that played out?"

"Actually, I could, yes I could. Why wouldn't Steven, or anyone, feel as murderous as me when betrayed?"

"Indeed." *Why wouldn't anyone?*

"The question is, could they control themselves? I tried to … I could, just about. I could control my own violence anyway. I couldn't control what I said, though."

"That was hard for you …"

"So whose fault is it then? The person who does bad things, or the person who tells? The whistle blower. That was me wasn't it? I was the whistle blower."

"You were the whistle blower, that's right. You didn't do a bad thing in the first place. You were overwhelmed by the desire to punish someone else's wrongdoing. Now, talk to me about all that in relation to your parents. Apply some of this thinking to their situation."

Tisi turned and gazed out of the window. Honor felt she could almost hear the wheels turning in Tisi's head, connections being made, neurons being fired.

"Well. My mother was furious with my father, and felt trapped. She couldn't blow the whistle on him because if she did, he'd go to prison and she couldn't support her children alone; so she was trapped, humiliated, jealous, and powerless …"

"Quite a cocktail, Tisi, quite a cocktail …"

"And … she was pregnant with me …."

"So here are you, in the womb of a woman who felt …"

"A toxic cocktail of emotions … poison … poison …."

Honor held her breath. Poison indeed, but now said without the hissing emphasis. She nodded. "Go on, Tisi."

"I was poisoned in the womb … poisoned by her feelings."

"They were certainly transmitted to you, weren't they, in some way?"

"Passed across the placenta with my vitamins and nutrients, then enshrined in my name: Tisiphone, guardian of the gates of Tartarus. Avenger of wicked deeds."

"She wanted you to be powerful, to have the power she lacked … to not find yourself trapped, humiliated, jealous, and powerless. What d'you think she would be saying about the predicament you find yourself in? And what would she want you to do in relation to your father? I want you to think about that for our next session, Tisi: we'll explore that more."

Honor watched Tisi leave, her head held high. *Such grace and dignity. I have watched her go a bit crazy, and then regain her sanity, and more.*

Driving home, Honor could feel her heart racing. She breathed deeply in an attempt to calm herself. Her long talk into the night with Eliot, her attempts to convince him that she was not harbouring love for Thomas, had been fruitless: he was convinced that Thomas was his rival.

Eliot's car was in the drive. That was a good sign. Last night he had suggested that they have some time apart. "I need to think, Honor, get some space, think things over."

Her first reaction was shock, followed quickly by a sense of relief. Yes, a little bit of space, maybe not such a bad thing.

This morning, he'd said to her, calmly: "I may not be here when you come home. I'll maybe see if I can go and stay with Will for a week or so. So if there's anything more you want to say to me, now is the time."

She had pressed her lips together, mute. If only she could tell him. Tell someone.

She let herself in. The house was silent, still; no sound of life. Where were the children? Anxiety clutched her throat. She raised a hand to her mouth, unable to speak. Dropping her briefcase and coat on the floor, she sank slowly down on the bottom step of the stair, and leaned forward dropping her head down between her knees and breathing slowly.

Something bad has happened. I know it. I knew it would.

Standing, she steadied herself against the banister. Deep inside her, she could feel a quivering. She took another deep breath. *I'll try the kitchen first.*

The kitchen was eerily immaculate. Every surface was wiped, and polished. Had every machine, every appliance, been switched off? The absence of the background humming and whirring of machinery felt like a shroud of silence over this room.

Honor heard her own small voice, from a distance. "Eliot?"

Louder. "Eliot."

She opened the kitchen door and shouted to the house. "ELIOT."

The answering silence settled around her. She jumped, startled, at a noise at the front door. She spun around.

Eliot walked in. "Oh. Honor."

"Where are the children? Where are they?"

"I took them round to Stacey's for tea. I asked her if she'd have them over there for a couple of hours. I thought it'd be better if they weren't here when I leave."

Honor crumpled against the door, with relief, quickly followed by alarm. "You're leaving? Eliot?"

"It'll be good for us to have some thinking time. I need it. I love you, but I realize now, you never stopped loving Thomas. I knew it when we met, but I was confident you'd get over him: you seemed to love me."

"I can explain everything and I will, but I need a little longer. Something happened, at work, strange things, I can explain."

She'd never seen Eliot look so sad. Could she tell him everything, explain about Bella? She took a breath.

"I'm going to stay at Will's for a week or two. I've told the kids I'm going to be away for work; they didn't bat an eyelid."

"Oh." *All sorted out, no consultation, decision made.*

"Let's not talk during that time. I'll call to speak to the kids, and say hi, but let's get together after a couple of weeks, go out for dinner maybe, and discuss our future. If we have one. All I can say is that I don't want to spend the rest of my life with a wife who's in love with someone else. Even if he is dead. Now I come to think of it, especially if he's dead."

Honor wiped away a tear. "I can explain, Eliot, I'll explain everything to you, I promise, you'll see that you're wrong."

I went mad, Eliot, that's all. How could she make this story sound a better alternative than just a wife in love with a previous husband?

"I hope you're right." Eliot stepped towards her, held out his arms, and Honor leaned thankfully against him, as his arms enfolded her. She breathed his smell, moved her head against his chest, put her arms around his waist.

Eliot stepped back. "My case is in the car. I told Stacey you'd pick the kids up at seven, OK?"

Honor nodded, looking down, biting her lip.

She heard the front door open, and gently close.

CHAPTER TWENTY FIVE

Three days had passed without Eliot at home, and the household routines had adjusted to his absence. *It doesn't take long for a person to become dispensable.* She'd missed his warmth and humour; but not the emotional pressure of his demands on her attention. She felt freer in the evenings, able to do as she pleased.

Sitting at her computer, she was relaxed, rather than alert for any sign from Eliot that she should be with him, not at her work. She had a simple task to complete. She called up her various pictures, the montages she'd made of Thomas; Thomas with Bella; Thomas with Bella and Madalena. They couldn't move her now, it was over. She highlighted them all, and without hesitation, clicked the delete button. Deep inside her, she felt something settle back into place.

She wandered downstairs, looking into the children's rooms for her final nightly check. They were all fast asleep. She continued down to the kitchen, and stood, uncertain, not knowing what to do next. This was the lonely time. Nothing to do and nobody to do it with. She made herself a spinsterly cup of tea and took it to bed to watch the news. She fell asleep, and was awoken hours later by a noisy film on the TV, the tea stone cold on her bedside table.

Unable to go back to sleep, she turned her mind to the next day, a big day. She was going to see Tisi, and she felt clear and in control of how she would bring about closure for Tisi. She tuned herself in to Tisi, tried to feel her energetic presence; and fell asleep to dream of a snake-haired Gorgon in a peaceful garden.

* * *

She couldn't wait for Tisi to arrive, quite a contrast to the dread and anxiety she used to feel on Tisi days.

"You look perky. Even though you're seeing Tisi?" Barbara looked her up and down.

"Oh, I know how to help her now." Honor beamed at Barbara, and headed towards her office, where she went straight to her computer and scanned through her files, looking for the document she needed. Yes, here it was: guided visualization, the key to the unconscious mind. She printed off the sheets, and scanned them, reminding herself of the procedure, tailoring it, in her mind, to suit Tisi's precise situation. *Yes, this is going to work, I know it.*

Tisi arrived, serene and measured. "Hi, Honor."

"Tisi."

"I'm feeling better today."

"I can see. How are things?"

Don had made good progress, and Tisi's worries that Don would blame her proved unfounded. He had written her a letter: "Not one of our unmailed ones, Honor, he gave this one to me." He was full of sorrow for his actions, and took full responsibility for recent events; he was keen to reassure Tisi that he blamed her for nothing, and that his dearest hope was that the family could recover, and that Tisi could regain trust in him.

Honor wondered if there was any need to concern herself any further with Don.

"How do you feel about Don now then?"

"Terribly relieved that he didn't die. I know for certain that I didn't want him to die."

"Forgiven then?"

"Hmm. More or less, I think."

Still some residual reserve by the sound of it. I'll go ahead as planned, it won't hurt.

"Tisi, I want us to do something a little different today, a guided visualization. I'm going to teach you to relax, a form of breathing that will take you into a deep state of calm."

Tisi looked startled. "You're not going to hypnotize me?"

"Not hypnosis, no. Deep relaxation: almost a semi-dream state. Then I'm going to guide you to think about things slightly differently, so that your feelings will change by the end of it."

"It sounds a bit strange. I guess I can trust you, after all your efforts to help me. OK."

Honor instructed Tisi to remove her high-heeled shoes and place her feet flat on the ground, and relax her arms, put her head back against the back of the chair, and close her eyes. With practised ease, Honor slowed and lowered her voice, speaking in a rhythmic tone, talking Tisi through a deep breathing process, watching her body closely for the signs that would tell her that Tisi had achieved an altered state. She could see the tension in Tisi's body, her attempts to maintain control and fight the impulse to let down, to drop down into her deeper self. Persevering, Honor took Tisi through a sequence of tensing, then relaxing the muscles in each part of her body, starting with her feet and working upwards. If Tisi did not fully relax, the guided visualization wouldn't work.

Eventually, she could see the softness in Tisi, and her deep slow breathing. Honor matched her own breathing to Tisi's pace.

"I'll be silent for some minutes now, Tisi. So keep breathing as I've instructed you, and enjoy the peace and quiet. Next time I speak, I'll instruct you to use your imagination in a specific way. I may ask you questions, which you are not required to answer out loud, but to reflect on inside yourself."

In the ensuing silence, Honor watched Tisi: she looked like a child, her head back, and her face soft, like a little girl in the moments before sleep took over. She was flooded with tenderness for this poor woman: her hard work, her dedication to her family, her overwhelming love for her children, and her efforts to protect them from her own destructive impulses. It had all been so hard on her. Honor noticed, in Tisi's glossy chestnut hair, a few silver hairs peppering the hair at her temples. So much worry for a young mother.

Honor could see that Tisi had given in to the relaxation, and might even have fallen into a light sleep. All the better if she had, for Honor's purposes.

Once sufficient time had passed, Honor began to speak, slowly and quietly, in a slight sing-song tone.

"So, Tisi, imagine yourself in a garden. It may be a garden you know, or one you imagine or dream of, or maybe one you have painted. Look around you, at this garden, watch closely. Notice what the weather's like. Walk around the garden, looking and watching. Look down at your feet as you walk and see your shoes. What colour are they, what style?"

Honor paused, and watched Tisi, who was smiling. A small frown appeared on her face, quickly clearing to make way for another faint smile.

"Look around you, notice the flowers, trees, and shrubs, observe their density and colour. What are the sounds in the garden, what can you hear? What smells are there? What can you smell?"

Pausing again, Honor could see Tisi turn her head to one side, listening; her head dropped a little, then lifted again, her nose twitching faintly, her face softening.

"Pick a flower or a leaf. What does it feel like? Feel it between your fingers, appreciate the texture, and enjoy its colour. I'll be silent for a few minutes now for you to enjoy the experience of the garden that you have created."

In the silence that followed, Honor turned her head and gazed out at the shrubs that framed the window. She found it impossible to take someone through this activity without her own mind also turning towards the notions she was suggesting. Bringing her attention back to Tisi, she could see a single tear trickling from the inner corner of her eye, coursing down her cheek. *Good, we're getting there.*

"You're enjoying the garden, and you feel drawn to go deeper into it. You notice something's in your way; there's an obstacle that prevents you going any further. What's the obstacle that stops you? What is it like? How could you overcome it? Imagine that you can have a conversation with it. Talk to it now. Ask it what it wants, why it's stopping you. Listen carefully to its answer, and remember what it's telling you."

Honor paused again, and found her own mind turning to the same question. *What's in my way? And how could I overcome it?* Something fleeting, too fast to catch or hold, gave her a moment of insight that passed before she could grasp it. There was something, though. Quickly she pulled her energy back to the matter at hand.

"Now imagine that you can overcome the obstacle, you can go further into the garden .... Go and explore. What's the inside of the garden like? Notice the colours, the smells. Take a few minutes to walk around and have a good look at it. How does this garden feel to you?"

Honor watched Tisi's feet twitching slightly, sliding forward on the carpet. She was walking around the garden, looking around, a vision that would be just as real to her as if she really was there. Imagination is marvellous. The body reacts just the same way to an imagined event as to a real one. Such is the curse and the gift of the vivid imagination.

"You see a little glade to one side, and you go in to look around. There's someone here, but you can't quite see who it is. You move closer and look again. It's someone as familiar to you as your own reflection; at first you think it is you. Then you see that it's your mother, reaching her hand out to you and beckoning you closer. She enfolds you in a warm embrace, and you feel like a small child again as you nestle on her lap."

Tisi, weeping copiously, reached out her arm to take a tissue. Honor remembered an earlier session when Tisi's arms had seemed longer, thinner, snakier; none of that was evident now. *Where had that come from? Did I simply imagine it? I must have, people's arms don't get longer and shorter spontaneously, not in the real world.*

"Your mother gives you an important message, about what she wants you to do, how she wants you to behave at this difficult time in your life. Listen well to her advice, she'll tell you something important that you'll never forget."

Tisi leaned forward, doubled over, her shoulders heaving with a silent grief that seemed more real than her usual histrionics. Honor was moved to do something that she normally resisted. She leaned forward and placed a comforting hand on Tisi's shoulder.

"Stay with it now, stay with the conversation with your mother. Tell her your thoughts and feelings, and listen as she tells you hers. Take your time."

I wonder what my mother would be saying to me? I think she'd say, Honor, take good care of your husband and children and don't be distracted by anything else. Almost anything else is a figment of your imagination, and not to be trusted. She made a mental note, mouthed the words to herself: remember what she is saying, and think about it later.

Tisi had quieted, and was leaning back in the chair, her eyes still closed. Black runnels formed tracks on her cheeks, her eye make-up dissolving in the flood of hot salt tears.

"Are you ready to continue?"

Tisi gave the smallest nod.

"Say your goodbyes to your mother. It's time to leave this glade now and she cannot leave with you."

Tisi's arm lifted slightly, forming a circle of sorts, an embrace for her lost mother. There, closure, at last. Amazing really, how you can have closure with someone who's gone. The imagination is a wonderful thing; who knows how it happens? It's phenomenological; it can only be experienced.

241

Not that Honor had ever had real closure with Thomas exactly, not completely, despite all the tricks of her trade; it was as though she was not happy unless she was tormenting herself. *Maybe I don't want to be healed, I couldn't stand the peace.*

"You leave this part of the garden, taking with you your new understanding. You walk further into the garden. You notice someone ahead of you, waiting for you. It is Don. You need something from him and there is something he wants to say to you. Sit down next to him and take the time to tell him what you need. Listen carefully to his answer, and see what it is he wants to say to you. Let your responses come naturally to you, and express them simply and honestly. Imagine this conversation, take your time, and say and hear all that needs to be said and heard."

Tisi's lips were moving slightly. She pressed her lips together, tilted her head to one side, gave a slight smile, and a nod, then dropped her head. Tears flowed down her cheek, and she dabbed her eyes with a tissue. Honor waited until Tisi's tears subsided.

That looked promising. Honor hadn't known what to expect here. Tisi would be so relieved to return to the status quo that her hurt would be disguised by that relief for quite some time. She and Don would need to be careful as the years pass: final closure doesn't come easily on infidelity, unlike grief. People die, it's sad, you miss them, you grieve: simple, inevitable, human feelings. But betrayal is a deeper scar, true heartbreak: a toxic mix of grief and rage, often with a dollop of shame for good measure. One sharp knock and that wound will bleed again. *Hopefully, she can contain it for now, and hold it together for at least as long as the children need it. I could tell her the cost of that though: it's a high price to pay.*

"You continue to explore the garden, and you become aware of someone approaching you. It's the keeper of the garden, the person in charge. Who is this person? The keeper comes to greet you. You are told that happiness can be yours on one condition. What is that condition? What does the keeper tell you? Imagine the conversation between you. What are you being told? The keeper gives something to you, a gift. Receive it with gratitude."

Tisi looked calm and composed.

Honor instructed her to focus on the deep breathing that they had started the exercise with. "This journey's over, so shortly I'll help you leave the world of your imagination and return here, back to the world of real people. Take a moment to think of all you've learned in this time; commit those learnings to memory, you'll find that you'll never forget what you now know."

Honor sat back to give Tisi some time, then sat up straight, hit by the realization of the gift she herself would want, from the keeper of her garden. The ability to forget. To forgive, forget, and move forward. Not forget as in repress and bury. But really to forget, totally, so that minor coincidences could not awaken old memories with fresh pain.

"Walk back through the garden now, feeling light-hearted, surrounded by light. Feel your feet, touching the ground here, in this room, wriggle your toes, feel your feet in contact with the ground. When you feel ready, open your eyes."

Tisi wriggled her feet, took another tissue, wiped her eyes again, wiped her face. At last she opened her eyes wide, glanced at Honor, then looked quickly away. She looked down, mumbled.

"I can't hear you Tisi." Honor leaned forward.

Tisi looked up, directly at Honor. "Thank you. Thank you so much."

Honor smiled. It never ceased to amaze her how powerful this process was. Why didn't she use it more often? Because most people were accustomed to the talk, the analysis, the problem solving. They were wedded to it, seeing it as some kind of science that they could respect and trust. This, this flaky, dreamy stuff: well, surely that was all just so much new age hocus-pocus? That's what they think. *And that's what I think too, despite the evidence of my own experience.*

Honor passed Tisi a notepad and pen. "Write it all down, while it's fresh in your mind. Write down everything, as detailed as you can. Then we'll talk about it a little more at your next session. We won't talk about it a lot, we don't want to interfere with the impact. You can just tell me the things that taught you the most, OK?"

Tisi nodded and took the pad and pen. She started to write, and didn't stop for a full ten minutes. Then she tore the sheets from the pad, folded them and put them in her bag.

"Thank you again. Thanks a million. I'm new. Born again."

She stood up, picking up her bag, and stepped towards Honor.

Honor did the only thing that felt right and held out her arms. Tisi stepped into the circle and the two women exchanged a heartfelt hug.

Standing at the window, watching Tisi leave, Honor leaned her forehead against the cool glass. *I deal in heartbreak, mainly, that's the truth of it, the heartbreak of betrayal. Are there people who don't suffer from this? I don't see them, but I hope there are.*

For the sake of my children, I hope there are.

CHAPTER TWENTY SIX

H onor woke, stretched, and sleepily reached out a hand to Eliot. Not there. A week had passed and he was still not home. She'd missed him more than she could have possibly imagined, once the first few days of liberation had passed. Her lonesome evening cup of tea had turned into a large lonesome evening glass of wine. Two large glasses last night she remembered, as she felt the dull throbbing in her temples. With a heavy sigh, she sat up. That was another thing she missed, a hot cup of tea brought to her, with Eliot's cheerful smile. Who would have thought that starting the day with the comfort of a warm human body next to you could make such a difference to the way that you felt for the rest of the day? Yet she'd known this in theory for most of her professional life: after all, what were most of her clients seeking? Longing for, dreaming of? The simple return to that primitive embrace, a warm body holding yours. She knew it now, anyway; she really knew it, body and soul.

She sat up, checked the clock; she'd slept through the alarm, and she was going to be late. Hearing the sounds of the children waking, and of Celestine and Eden bickering over the bathroom, she closed her eyes and took a deep breath; they had become fractious and irritable during Eliot's absence. What a delicate eco-system a family was. One change and, in relatively short order, the whole system started to alter in several small subtle ways that added up to a noticeable shift.

Getting out of bed felt an enormous effort. She trudged to the window and pulled back the curtains. The grey day outside matched her mood. What had happened to summer? Though the garden seemed to be enjoying the rain at least. The rose bed in the garden was at its ethereal best, the blooms iridescent white against the morning mist.

"Marmee! Marmee!"

She hurried out of the room and into Thea's bedroom. "Look at the state of this room. For goodness sake just get yourself dressed."

Thea, at the best of times a crier, had become increasingly tearful and clingy as the days without her Daddy had added up. She sat down on her bed, dissolving under her mother's scolding. "I want Daddy. When's Daddy coming home?"

"Soon, another couple of days, he's busy. Come on, stop crying and get dressed, I'll go and get breakfast."

Thea wailed. "Hugs please, Marmee?"

"There's no time." Honor hurried out of the room and down the stairs, to the sounds of Thea's continued distress.

"Where's Daddy? I want to tell him Mummy's horrible when he's not here! Nobody loves me any more."

The dirty dinner dishes in the kitchen sink reminded Honor that she hadn't cleared up last night. She yelled up the stairs. "Get moving, kids, I need your help down here, and we're all going to be late at this rate."

Within ten minutes they were all in the kitchen, complaining and whining.

"Aw, Mum, we haven't got any cornflakes left." Eden had a face on him that Honor could have slapped.

"I haven't had time to shop, Eden, make yourself some toast."

"I wish Dad was here." Eden headed for the bread bin.

"Celestine, give me a hand with these dishes, please; just pile them in the sink anyway, I'll deal with them tonight. Thea, what do you want for breakfast?"

She looked at her little girl, slumped at the kitchen table, sucking her thumb, tears on her cheeks, a picture of abject misery. She felt her heart shift, something stony in her soften. "Oh, Thea." She stopped her clattering of dishes and went and sat next to her, lifted her stiff little body onto her lap, stroked her head.

But Thea was not ready to respond. "I want my nice Mummy back! And I want my Daddy!" Her crying intensified.

Honor looked up: Eden and Celestine had stopped what they were doing and were staring at their mother.

"Mum …?" Celestine stepped towards her. "Oh, don't Mum, don't. Please stop crying."

Eden and Celestine crowded around her. Thea had stopped crying, staring, shocked, at her mother.

The arms of her three children, patting her, attempting to soothe her was the undoing of Honor. She reached out to them all, gathered them to her, feeling their consternation, and warmth. Within seconds, even cool old Eden had joined in the sob fest, though he was the first to pull away, angrily wiping his face with his hands.

"I'm going to phone Dad. He has to come home, he has to." He headed for the phone in the hall, and Honor didn't stop him. He was right. Dad did have to come home.

"OK, girls, come on, let's get ourselves together. We're all going to be late, but never mind, just this once, it's not the end of the world. I'm sorry for being mean, I'm so sorry."

The two girls chorused. "It's OK, Mum, don't worry, you weren't mean, it's all right."

Celestine took control, giving Thea a hug and sending her off to her room to get her school bag.

"Everyone needs to cry sometimes, you know, Mum, it's good for you."

Honor smiled. "Yes, that's right."

"Are you OK, though? Because we're all worried about you and Dad. Last night, Eden said he thought you were going to get divorced. Are you?"

"Why ever would Eden say that?" Honor could hear the false amazement in the high pitch of her own voice. "No, of course not. Of course we're not."

"Dad's never been away this long for work. And you don't talk to him much on the phone." Celestine was watching her mother's face.

To Honor's relief, Eden walked in, and handed her the phone. "Dad wants to talk to you."

"Oh good, thank you. Now you two go and sort yourselves out for school, you've got five minutes."

"Hi, Eliot."

"What's going on, Honor?" She could hear the concern in his voice, and longed for him to be right there, with her.

"Can I call you back in five minutes? I just need to get the kids out for the bus."

She hurried the children through their final preparations and off out for the school bus, so that she could talk to Eliot with them out of the house, the only real chance of privacy.

"Hi, Honor …"

"Hi. What did Eden say when he called you?"

"We overslept and Mum was grumpy and then she started crying, and we all want you to come home, Dad."

"What else did he say?"

"He said we're all scared you're going to get divorced."

"Celestine told me that this morning, too. They're worried and upset, Eliot. I want you to come home too. Please come home, I can explain everything."

"You keep saying that, but you don't explain anything. We have to do something, we can't all go on being this upset. Shall I come round for dinner tonight?"

"Yes, please, Eliot. Come home, I'll explain."

Eliot was coming home. Thank God.

* * *

Honor arrived at the office fifteen minutes late for her first appointment, with one of her long-standing clients, who was five years into his therapy. Barbara's lips pursed, as only hers could, when she set eyes on Honor.

"I put him in your office, he's terribly upset that you're late. He said you were never late, he thought he must've said something to annoy you last time he was here."

"*Jesus*, can't a person have a life? Does anyone understand the strain of trying to be some kind of perfect *mother* to these grown up *babies*?"

Barbara looked stricken. "Shh! he'll hear you. Whatever has come over you? Are you all right?"

"Could you bring me a large glass of water and a couple of Nurofen, please?"

In the event, her client responded rather positively to Honor's uncharacteristic firmness and her failure to show any guilt for her shortcomings. *His poor mother. Is there a woman alive who could give this man sufficient fawning attention?* Still, a lesson learned. Speaking a little more bluntly had made both of them feel a bit better. Maybe she was just too soft with some of her clients.

Tisi positively bounced into the room, sparkling with energy.

"Tisi, you look marvellous." Honor smiled in welcome.

"And so do you. You always do, smart and a little remote, not quite of this world. But now I understand why."

"Do you?"

"Yes, because you're a magic witch, that's why. Of course you're remote, you're from a different place and you must hide your magical powers from us mere mortals."

They both laughed.

"So ... tell me about Don first, how is he? Then we can talk about your visualization."

"Don's fine. His nose is pretty much recovered, a little bent, but as I said to him, there's something rather appealing about that look, a bit of a street fighter, quite sexy. We're happy. It's over, behind us."

"Was Steven charged?"

"Policemen look after their own, don't they? No charges were brought. Good news though: he's being transferred to a new post in the north of England, that's enough punishment for anyone, I'd have thought. So they're moving, which is brilliant. We can leave it behind, and make a fresh start. Don says it was never worth it really, he just couldn't see that at the time. Why are you smiling?"

"Oh ...." Honor waved her hand dismissively. "He's not the first person I've heard say that, that's all. How are the children?"

"Well ... aren't children robust? It passes them by a bit .... They were upset at the time, but they don't seem to remember much of it. Though Pandora still makes jokes about Daddy's rainbow nose, as she called it. If only adults could forgive and forget so easily."

"Indeed, Tisi."

"So, shall I tell you about the visualization? How you worked your magic?"

Honor laughed. Tisi's return to herself, and her deep gratitude, were a typical response to a successful visualization session; but to see someone who had nearly gone crazy with grief and misery, so restored, never ceased to inspire her.

"OK, Tisi. And it is a kind of magic, working its miracles in a part of our brain that we can't normally access. Where language and reason don't exist. So, we don't want to interfere too much. You just tell me the three most important things you learned, OK?"

Tisi sat back, completely composed and relaxed. What a difference, like another person.

"There were four things actually, can I tell you four?"

"No. Choose the best three and tell me those."

"Don, then, he was probably the most important. He said he was sorry. He didn't actually say it. He conveyed it to me, let me put it that way. As though he was in my head, adjusting my feelings and thoughts. I know, without doubt, the depth of his remorse. Wonderful."

Perfect! Honor nodded and smiled.

"My Mum, oh well, that almost broke my heart." Tisi's eyes shone with tears. "Or maybe I should really say she mended my broken heart. She said I'd broken a chain of things: 'You've done what I wanted you to do; I can rest now. Thank you, my darling. It's over, your work for me is done and you can live your own life, you and your children, freely,' and then she hugged me."

A restrained tear trickled down Tisi's cheek. Honor could feel the pressure, behind her eyes, of her own tears, and her impulse to jump to interpretation. She reminded herself: *so important to resist the analysis.*

"And the third thing?"

"My father."

"Your father?"

"He was the keeper of the house."

"Aah."

"His gift to me was a vision, a picture that he put in my head, of the most heavenly garden imaginable."

Honor swallowed. She couldn't always get through these sessions without completely controlling her own tears. "How marvellous, Tisi, how truly wonderful."

"When I went home, I went to my easel and immediately painted it. I've brought it to show you."

From her capacious handbag, Tisi drew out a flat package, about twelve inches by eight. She removed the brown wrapping and held up an unframed canvas. Honor gasped, and held her breath, gazing at the numinous picture. However had Tisi captured that extraordinary quality of light? Honor felt an intense desire to enter the sacred space that Tisi had painted.

Honor peered at the corner of the painting to see Tisi's signature.

"Paradise" by

Tisiphone Alecto Megaera Clements.

"It's fantastic. You have truly painted Paradise. A garden to make anyone a Kindly One."

"Even the Furies. I'm going to paint another copy of this for my Dad, as a symbol of my forgiveness."

As Tisi turned to leave, Honor remembered something. "By the way, Tisi, what was the fourth thing?"

250

Tisi turned around. "Oh, that, yes, it was the obstacle. A hissing, spitting serpent stopped me approaching the house."

"Really?" Honor held her breath. "Oh … and what did you have to do to get past it, then?" She tried to sound casual.

Tisi smiled. "Apparently, he was fed up of me being so scared of him …. All he wanted was to be embraced."

Honor couldn't wait to get home to see Eliot, and as she bowled along through roads filled with sunlight, she felt like singing. She switched on her music system. She hadn't listened to music for weeks. An old Stevie Wonder song, *A Place in the Sun*, filled the air, and she began to sing along, her voice becoming louder and stronger, till she was singing, with all her heart, of what she wanted: some hope and peace for her own restless heart.

The song finished, and Honor hit the repeat button, to sing it again, one of her favourites, reminding her of one of the happiest days of her life, a picnic on the beach with Thomas; they stayed late into the evening, till it was deserted, and they made love to the swishing of the waves.

Pulling up in the drive, she got out of the car, and dashed up the steps to the front door and into the house.

Thea came running, flinging herself at her mother, all sins forgiven, her world of the present moment driving her actions, the morning long forgotten.

"Mummy! Daddy's home! He's here, come and see!"

She didn't need to go anywhere, he was right there behind Thea, his big smile and twinkling eyes, his arms pulling her forward for a bear hug, followed by Eden and Celestine, all piling around her, a big bundle of bodies and limbs, laughing and crying and hugging and kissing.

Here I am, here's my sunshine. How did I ever forget?

Later that evening, the kids happily in their beds, Eliot and Honor sat in the garden.

"Thank you, Eliot."

"For what?"

"For coming home. For your patience. For … everything."

"I love you, Honor, and I love our children, our family. I'm so glad to be home. But I need to understand what's happened?"

"I can explain now, because I understand what happened to me. In short, I've gone slightly mad, caught up in something from my past. I'll tell you the whole story, from the beginning, to the end, so you can see what happened."

"I'm listening." He poured them both a glass of wine.

Honor sipped from her glass, and took a deep breath. "Do you remember, Eliot, the first day I met Tisi?"

Eliot nodded.

"Several things happened that day, all criss-crossing each other, causing me a terrible upheaval in my soul, is the only thing I can say, the only way it seems to me. I was reminded of many things, old betrayals."

"You haven't said much about Tisi since those first couple of sessions. I asked you, I remember, but it wasn't something you seemed to want to talk about."

"She reminded me, you see. Of me. Of my old feelings when you …. Well, I didn't want to remind you either, I didn't want to make it more live than it already was."

Eliot leaned forward, holding her eyes with his. "Tell me now, remind me, come on."

"She was a woman betrayed by her husband, that was the first reminder. The second was the name of her husband's lover, Jackie …"

Eliot leaned back, sighed, pushed his hand through his hair, his curls springing up. "I see …"

"It made me remember my terrible rage, at the time, that I never expressed. With you, and with Jackie. With you for taking away my best friend. With her for taking away my husband, my lover. The loss of both of you at once."

"And we didn't sort it all out at the time? My remorse was not enough? Jackie's remorse was not enough?"

"Strange that it was easier to forgive you than it was to forgive her, don't you think?"

"Have you forgiven me?"

"Yes, I think I have. But her, well no, I never did forgive her, and I don't think I ever could. There's a code among women, different to the code between men and women I think. So I was reminded of her, of her dreadful betrayal of me, and of the damage she did to us, to my trust in you."

"What happened with Tisi?"

Honor told Eliot of the way in which Tisi's story had unfolded. "I was so caught up in it, I could hardly think straight. When she told me how much she wanted to haunt Jackie, to madness and beyond, I understood it so well, I lived it vicariously. She completely compromised me professionally, or should I say I compromised myself with my re-awakened rage against Jackie. Do you know what I learned, what I realized from all that? The energy it takes to bear a grudge … to bury it … the daily jaw-clenching effort of will to keep it down, buried, out of mind. But it grows in the dark, like fermenting dough, bubbling and doubling. And Tisi awakened that in me."

"And you couldn't tell me?"

"Something else happened on the same day. It was a special date, I should say, a sad anniversary that I stupidly never told you about, but one that I mourn each year. So I was already sad and recriminating myself. Then I met Tisi, and she told me of her desire to kill her husband. I had to go for a walk, try to clear my head. I went to the park, sat on a bench and picked up a newspaper left there. I saw a picture of a young girl, who was the daughter of Madalena, the woman who Thomas had left me for at one point. We competed for his love over some years, do you remember?"

"Yes, yes, now you mention it I do. Why was her daughter in the newspapers? And what's the anniversary?"

"Madalena's daughter, Bella is a model, in love with a pop star. I looked at her, and I was convinced that she was the daughter of Thomas; she looked so much like him. I became obsessed with the idea. I found old pictures of Thomas and compared them with Bella; she was so similar in subtle ways. And that reminded me then of Thomas's betrayal and of Madalena, another woman betraying the code between women. So many betrayals, I felt like a volcano, a thread of hot raging lava rising up through the core of me. I tried to control it, I tried so hard, but it consumed me, ate me up. I became obsessed, totally taken over."

"And what happened?"

Honor took a breath, and a sip of wine, slowed down her breathing, and thought carefully. "Madalena came to see me. It turned out that the publicity around Bella had brought out quite a few nutcases; they were getting nasty letters and even threats. Someone was suggesting that Bella was not the child of Madalena's partner Jack, and Madalena was trying to find out who might believe such a thing."

Eliot's eyes widened. "Surely she didn't think it was you?"

"Well, I did think that. It seemed her partner, Jack, was also doing some investigating and he came to see me too."

"And you never told me any of this … the Tisi thing, well I can understand that, but this new story …. I can't believe you couldn't tell me. Why ever not?"

"You were always sensitive about Thomas. I felt I couldn't mention him. And because it reminded me of some things that happened with me, Thomas, Madalena, things that almost destroyed me at the time, that I never told you about. Never told anyone about actually. I kept a deep secret, one I remembered each year, and tortured myself with. That's what Bella aroused in me, on a day when I was already primed, with old injuries already reopened."

"What happened?"

"I'll tell you, but I can't look at you and say it. I'm afraid of what you'll say, what you'll think of me, the verdict you'll pass when you hear what happened, what I did. I don't know if you'll forgive me; I can't forgive myself."

"I can't imagine what you could tell me that I wouldn't forgive you for. It's not like you've killed anyone. I'd probably even forgive you then."

Honor smiled at him, tears spilling onto her cheeks. Despite all they had been through, she knew he was good-hearted, and kind. Maybe he would forgive her, after all.

"I'll write you a letter, so you can read it, and I won't have to look at your face as you get to know it. I'll do it now: I'll go to my study and write it down for you to read tomorrow. Then we'll see what you think of me, when you know this."

A couple of hours later, Honor, sat at her desk, folded up several sheets of paper and placed them in an envelope, and wrote Eliot's name on the front, and left it on her desk. She would give him the letter in the morning before she left for work. Despite her fears, she felt cleansed, expurgated of her sins.

She went to their bedroom and undressed quietly in the dark, and slipped into bed beside Eliot, curling her body around the heat of his back. She folded her arms around him, placing a gentle kiss on the back of his neck. Stirring, he murmured and turned around towards her, pulling her into the warmth of his body.

How I will miss him, if he can't forgive me for not being the person he thought I was.

She slept, deeply, and dreamed the sweetest dream.

CHAPTER TWENTY SEVEN

Dear Eliot,

So, here's the question for you: when you know my worst secret, my deepest shame, will you still love me?

I couldn't get Bella Norman out of my mind. How would Thomas have felt if he'd known he had a daughter? Then a thought hit me that was so shattering that it left me breathless. Maybe he did know. Maybe he knew all along. Maybe she told him …. Maybe he visited her. As this thought took root, images flickered through my mind: Thomas and Madalena, with their illicit baby daughter, an idyllic picture of family love, the three of them, dazzling, like a photo spread in a gossip magazine.

These imaginings finally made me understand the source of my pain and vengeance. Not that Madalena had seduced Thomas away from me; but that she'd had his baby.

The baby that should have been mine.

Madalena stole my baby.

I never told you, Eliot. I never told anyone. How could I? I knew and Thomas knew. I couldn't bear the thought that Madalena might have known, though I don't now believe that she did.

Thomas wanted to go to her, you see. I could feel him pulling away from me, for months. I wanted to keep him, I couldn't bear to let him go. How could I make him stay? I hatched a plan. Fight fire with fire. I only partly realized then, what I now know for certain: I was no match for Madalena, with her total lack of morality or compassion: utterly and completely scheming and selfish.

It all happened with unexpected ease and speed. Within weeks, I was pregnant. I blamed it on a bout of tummy flu that led to the failure of my contraceptive pill. I look back and wonder what on earth I expected, from a man who never wanted children, and who no longer wanted me. If I'd known how it was all going to turn out, I'd never have done it.

But nothing prepared me for the granite set of his jaw and the icy hatred in his eyes. This was a Thomas that I had never seen before.

And he didn't believe me.

"You've done this on purpose."

I protested, too much I expect.

Then he said a lot of things. I turned my face away and held up my hands to protect myself, cringing, as his cold words cut through me.

He was leaving me. He and Madalena couldn't keep away from each other. This baby couldn't happen now: he didn't want a baby, never had, not now, not ever. He wouldn't stay with me and he wouldn't be trapped. It was an accident, never meant. He didn't love me any more; he was in love with Madalena.

"Get rid of it. I'll get the money together."

I felt he'd betrayed me at the time, though he'd always been quite honest with me about his feelings about children. Had I thought he was lying?

But in the end, it isn't other people's betrayals that damage you.

It was nothing at all to do with who had betrayed me: quite the reverse: what clever minds and hearts we have.

It wasn't Madalena's fault that I didn't have Thomas's baby. It wasn't even Thomas's fault. It was the failure of my own courage … it was me. It's so much easier to blame others though, isn't it?

The worst betrayal was the way I betrayed myself; how I went against my own instincts, my own conscience. My own betrayal of the precious thing I most wanted, Thomas's baby, my own baby.

How could I ever forgive myself for that? That's what haunts you most, as you get older. The babies that might have been. The babies you almost had.

So, you see, Eliot, in a way, I did kill someone, didn't I? However we dress these things up, rationalize them, find neutral euphemisms, I made a decision to end a life. So I hope you can forgive me, as you said. It's a test, isn't it, of your repeated assertion that you could forgive, overcome your Catholic beliefs on sin?

There were things I treasured. An instinct that the baby was a girl; the name I gave her in my heart: Bel, short for Beloved. And a date: the day she would have been born, that I commemorate every year; the date, this year, that I found the picture of Bella, in the newspaper. A date that hollows me out, empties me.

And Thomas, well, he drove me to the clinic; I sat next to him in the car, turned to him to speak, saw his stony profile, his clenched jaw, and turned away. I lowered my head and thought to myself what I wanted to say; hoping, perhaps, that he would read my mind: Please, Thomas, I beg you, please don't make me do this. Spare me this. Rescue me, tell me it will be OK? You do love me really, I know you do … you'd be a great Dad, I'm sure of it. Please, Thomas, change your mind, take me home. Please …. Oh, please, please …

I could feel a slight vibration inside me, the tremor, I imagined, of my putative child, as though she knew what the immediate future held for her.

He took me in, handed over the money, turned his back on me without a glance and left me there, alone with three other lonely girls, each of us imprisoned by our own misery, all praying, I expect, that we could protect our almost babies. I don't know how these things go these days, Eliot, but back then, there was no pity, no mercy. No soothing pre-medication injection, just the unaided walk to the operating table. I remember doubling over as though I could protect the little curl of life inside me. Ungentle hands unfolded me, briskly pushing my feet into cold metal stirrups, before the blessed smothering of the anaesthetist's mask.

I would die, Eliot, if either of our girls ever had to go through such a thing.

Thomas collected me the next day. He barely spoke, and his hard eyes would not meet mine; his clenched jaw never softened. He left me and went to Madalena.

Within weeks, it was over. Jack had promised her the world: he'd left his wife, and promised Madalena a secure home and a baby. She couldn't resist, it was all she'd ever wanted.

Thomas didn't want me initially, though I still wanted him desperately. Maybe I thought I could put things right, replace my baby. So I waited quietly, while he nursed his broken heart. I became a warm friend in the background, and a welcoming body when he needed it. Eventually he turned to me again, and we married. Then he died.

I met Bella, the other evening, when I told you I had a clinical conference. Her father asked me to; she's distressed because her father is insisting on a DNA test, and he hoped I could help her think rationally about it. She's not Thomas's daughter, I realized when I met her: she can't possibly be, she's nothing like him. I felt a terrible sadness and disappointment to realize this. It seems I wanted someone to have had Thomas's baby. I wanted to know his baby was somewhere in the world, that he hadn't just gone, leaving nothing behind. I hoped he'd left some legacy. If only so I could find that child and tell them: your father was a wonderful man: he would have been so happy and proud to know you.

And for myself, maybe I should apply the lessons of Tisi's myth: I need a verdict, and remorse.

Who can pass verdict on what I did? Thomas? Dead. Bel? Never lived.

I have passed verdict on myself. The badge of my shame and grief; the only secret I have ever kept in my life: how I broke my own heart. I have been my own judge, jury, and jailer all these years; my own Fury, haunting myself to madness. I thought it was Madalena that drove me mad, as though I remained the centre of her world. Before all this she would barely have remembered me, I'm sure. I drove myself mad.

So there it is, Eliot, my sorry tale: not just of what happened back then, but my failure to deal with it, letting it haunt me all these years. These last weeks, I have dreaded that my secret shame and grief would overwhelm me: my bad side, my shadow side, would be exposed. And maybe I would find that I am only loved if I am good. I work so hard to be good, I am furious with people who can't control themselves, who are selfish.

My hope is that, in telling you, the secret is over. I'm not sure why I feel you may be so unforgiving of me; your old Catholic views on sin I expect. Perhaps because I've been so unforgiving of myself. I've been trapped in my own shame and grief, at the loss of my child and the loss of my idea of myself as a person of courage and goodness.

I will hope for a dream now, a dream to finally put my lost child and my broken heart to rest.

Your loving wife,
Honor xxx

"Did you do the letter?" Bud's cheery onscreen face, smiling, eyebrows raised, looked out at her.

Madalena smiled back at him. Sometimes she felt like kissing the screen, she was so pleased to see him.

"I did an email."

Bud's eyes widened. "You sent it?"

"No, of course not. We agreed."

"D'you want me to look at it?"

"I'll read it out to you, OK? I'm not going to send it, even if you think it's good. She doesn't deserve it."

"Read it out to me."

With a few clicks, Madalena pulled the draft mail on to her screen, next to the video cam picture of Bud. She cleared her throat. "OK, here goes. Dear Honor, when I came to see you a few weeks ago, there was something I wanted to tell you, about Thomas. I think this is something you would want to know. The last time I saw Thomas, he told me about the baby you almost had. He said he'd never regretted anything so much in his entire life, and he would not be able to live with himself until he had put things right. He said when he took you to the hospital, he almost turned around and drove you home. He was very tearful. He wanted to make it up to you, to have a baby and be a really good Dad. He said he could never tell you, you'd be furious, but he'd show you how sorry he was, and how much he loved you and your child. I won't contact you again, as you asked, but I thought you would want to know this. Also, you may be interested to know that DNA results showed that Bella is not Thomas's daughter. So he died without leaving a child behind, which I think is sad, and I expect you think that too. Good luck for the future. Madalena. There. What do you think?"

Madalena turned her eyes from the onscreen letter back to Bud. He was looking at her softly.

"That's so good. Simple, direct. Can you imagine how she'll feel to receive that? To know that? Closure, at last, with someone she loved who died."

Madalena pulled a face. "Why would I want to make her happy? After she sent the poison pen letters?"

"You can't be sure of that."

"It was definitely her or Pat, I'm sure of that."

"You've got more evidence it was Pat, that child's writing you saw. Anyway, whoever did it, they did you a favour. Look at you now."

Madalena blinked. "They did, I didn't think of that, yes, I'm glad about the letters, whoever sent them."

"Send the mail then. Be Mrs Do-as-you-would-be-done-by. Go on, just click send, now."

Madalena's finger hovered over the mouse. The cursor, on screen, was on the send button. One click and it would go. She'd have done something good. She would be good.

"Done?"

Madalena shook her head at the screen.

"What's stopping you?"

"Dunno."

"If you send it, I'll tell you something that you don't know about me. That you might like to know."

Madalena raised her eyebrows at him. "OK, go on then."

"Send it first. Blind copy me in so I can see you've sent it, no tricks, OK?"

"It'd better be a good secret."

"Oh, don't worry it is."

Click, click, click. "OK, it's done."

She watched Bud's eyes move around his screen, hitting the receive button to get his mail. She put her hand on the screen, and stroked his hair. She loved him. She really loved him.

"OK, got it. See, that wasn't so difficult was it?"

Madalena laughed. "No, it wasn't, it really wasn't."

"Feels good, to be good, then?"

"Definitely. Feels great, actually. Now, the secret. What is it?"

Bud leaned into the screen, so his face was really close. He looked into her eyes. "Are you ready for this?"

"I am."

"I'm not gay."

"You're … what? *What?* But you told me … I …" Madalena stared at him, her mouth and eyes wide.

"You think back." Bud was laughing at her shock. "I told you nothing. You made some assumptions, asked a few oblique questions, then never mentioned it. So I thought I'd let you believe whatever suited you."

Madalena was scanning backwards in her mind. She'd thought that he … he'd showed no sign of …. She recalled her virtual tour of his New York apartment, her questions about a partner. His laughter, and slightly evasive answers. But whatever she remembered, she could not recall him actually telling her he was gay.

She sat back, her hand clapped over her mouth, looking at Bud, still laughing at her from the screen.

Then she started to laugh too, a deep belly laugh, until her laughter turned to tears, and she found that she couldn't stop crying.

CHAPTER TWENTY NINE

Honor awoke early the next morning. She stretched, feeling the deep relaxation in her body, rested at last. She turned over, remembering the simplicity of her longed-for dream: a smiling curl of life, waving, finally, goodbye. She wiped away a tear. Closure. Such a blessing.

Careful not to disturb Eliot, she slid out of bed, and went to her wardrobe to take out her work suit. A stray sunbeam had pushed its way in through the side of the blind, and shone on her clothes, hung in their neat, monotone rows. The sunlight glinted on the emerald green dress, bright against her black suit. On an impulse, she picked it out, slipped it on, took out the black suede shoes, and tiptoed out of the bedroom.

Going to her study, she collected the envelope for Eliot, and went back to the bedroom, where she stood it, prominently, on his night table.

There we are. All done. *Eliot can decide now, he can pass verdict on me. My remorse, well, that is beyond dispute: half a lifetime of it.*

Tiptoeing into her children's bedrooms, she dropped a kiss onto each sleepy face, and then went to the bathroom to wash, make up, and brush her hair.

She left the house quietly, keen not to be there when Eliot woke and read her letter. She couldn't watch his face as he read her story; she didn't want to see him look up at her.

The early sunshine bounced a scintillating rainbow of purple and violet off the bonnet of her car. She drove to a coffee shop near her offices, where she sat outside to enjoy a coffee and a croissant, feeling completely alive, all her senses tingling, and happier than she had felt for many years.

Letting herself into her offices, she sat in one of the easy chairs and surveyed her little kingdom, seeing it as if for the first time. In recent weeks, she'd barely noticed her surroundings; now, she gazed with wonder at the fresh vase of flowers in the grate. One of the white roses, past its full bloom, had dropped one large, pearlescent petal on to the floor. She felt drawn to its creamy glow against the blue-grey carpet. She sat for half an hour, looking at the wilting petal, lost to its mother flower.

Her reverie was broken by Barbara's voice. "Hello? Honor ....
Goodness what are you doing here so early? You don't even have a client until ten o'clock. I couldn't believe it when I saw your car outside. Look at you, all green, you look great. Going somewhere special? What? Whatever is the matter?"

"Nothing." Honor wiped her eyes. "I'm fine. I came in early, to think. But I'm fine, finer than I've been for a long time. Really fine."

"Well yes, I can see that; you look fantastic, that dress does wonders for your eyes. It's not like you to dress like that for work. What's been happening to you? You seem like your old self again, better actually ..."

"Maybe one day I'll tell you. It's all over now, though, and you've been marvellous, such a help to me; you must have thought I was going barmy ..."

"I admit I had my moments ...."

"I'm going to catch up on my mail, and sort myself out: I've probably neglected a number of things over recent weeks. Could you cancel my appointments today please, Barbara? I need some time for myself."

"I've never known you do that." Barbara watched her appraisingly. "All right, I'll get on to it straight away. I'll get you a drink, what would you like?"

"Green tea, please."

Barbara bustled out, returning a few minutes later with Honor's tea and a parcel.

"This just arrived for you. Were you expecting something?"

"No ...." Honor examined the large flat square package for clues.

She ripped away the brown paper, to reveal Tisi's painting of Paradise.

Looking over her shoulder, Barbara gasped. The two woman stood staring into the garden, hypnotized by the light, the colours, and the sense of perspective that Tisi had achieved. Barbara broke the silence. "How enchanting. I feel as though I'm actually inside that garden."

Honor noticed Tisi's signature in the corner.

Paradise

by Tisi Megaera Alecto Clements.

To Honor, with love and gratitude

Reverently, Honor placed it on the mantelpiece, moving aside the candles.

"Looking at that will be quite a cure for my clients, don't you think Barbara?"

"Completely. I've never seen anything quite so ... so *heavenly.*"

Honor sat at her computer, and opened her email programme. There was a message from Jack Norman, and another one from Madalena. She felt the heat rise in her face. What on earth did she have to say? She decided not to open it, she wanted nothing more to do with her, or her daughter.

She opened the email from Jack.

Dear Honor

I thought you might be interested to know that the DNA results showed that I am the biological father of Bella, which was a great relief to me and to Bella. Thanks, anyway, for the tip-off, as it was good to uncover Madalena's cheating and disloyalty. Thanks, also, for spending time with Bella, she said she felt a lot better after speaking to you. Let me know if you fancy lunch one day, I'm a single man now!

Love

Jack xx

Honor stared at the screen, and read the message over several times.

She started typing back.

Dear Jack

I have no idea what you mean. What are you suggesting?

No, that didn't sound right. She deleted it and started again.

Dear Jack

I'm pleased to hear such good news, and happy for you and Bella. Thank you for suggesting lunch, but ...

But what? She deleted it. Whatever could she say in response?

The mouse hovered over the mail from Madalena. She wasn't going to open it. Yes she was. No she wasn't. She moved the cursor to the delete button.

She jumped at the sound of her mobile phone. It was Eliot.

"Honor?"

Honor let out a long breath. "Eliot …"

"I've read your letter."

"Yes …"

"Come home, Honor. Come home to the family that loves you."

"All forgiven?"

"Nothing to forgive. Come home."

"I'm on my way right now."

Honor picked up her bag and keys, then put them down again and sat at her computer.

Dear Jack

I'm so glad to hear your good news, for your sake and Bella's. Thank you for your offer of lunch, but I won't take you up on it: I remain a happily married woman.

Good luck for the future

Honor

Her eye was caught by Madalena's name again. She had a vivid memory of the unmailed letter she had written to her, the day she had briefed Tisi to write such a letter to Jackie. She thanked her lucky stars she hadn't sent that, though it had been touch and go at the time: it had taken all her control not to print it and mail it.

Her curiosity got the better of her. She opened the email from Madalena and read it. She sat back in the chair, her hand over her mouth, her eyes wide. Then she leaned forward, read it again, and, covering her face with both hands, stifled several deep sobs. Weeping, she clicked the reply button, and typed,

Thank you, Madalena. Good luck in the future.

"Bye, Barbara, I'm off home," she called, catching a glimpse of Barbara's startled face around her office door, as she pulled the front door behind her.

In the car, she switched on the music system. An old favourite, by Enigma, caught her attention: an ethereal voice, chanting from another world: *The Eyes of Truth.*

That's right, that's it, that's what we must believe in. Karma. And no secrets.

She must get home, to her family. Her mother was right, everything else was just nonsense.

ABOUT THE AUTHOR

Voula Grand is a successful business psychologist and executive coach. *Honor's Shadow*, her debut novel, is a psychological drama about secrets, betrayal, and revenge; it is the first of a trilogy. Voula completed an MA in creative writing in 2006, and hopes to dedicate more of her time to fiction writing in future. She lives in Hertford with her husband Paul, and is mother and stepmother to five adult sons and daughters.